THE
REFINING
FIRE

VALLEY OF THE PEACEMAKER
BOOK THREE

THE REFINING FIRE

W. E. DAVIS

CROSSWAY BOOKS • WHEATON, ILLINOIS
A DIVISION OF GOOD NEWS PUBLISHERS

Library of Congress Cataloging-in-Publication Data

Davis, Wally, 1951-
   The refining fire / W. E. Davis.
      p.   cm. — (Valley of the peacemaker ; v. 3)
   ISBN 0-89107-936-X
   I. Title.   II. Series: Davis, Wally, 1951-   Valley of the peacemaker ; bk. 3.
   PS3554.A93785R4 1997
   813'.54—dc21   96-48569

05		04		03		02		01		00		99		98		97
15	14	13	12	11	10	9	8	7	6	5	4	3	2	1

To Bobby Cannon

CHAPTER

ONE

SHERIFF MATT PAGE stumbled through the moonless night, crossing Main Street, his eyes nearly shut—not just from the sleep still in them, but from the wind that forced his head down and his collar up. The air whistled past his red, icy ears so fiercely, he could barely hear his own dragging footsteps.

These pre-dawn security checks of all the businesses—demanded by the merchants' guild—were getting tiresome. Nothing ever happened in Bridgeport, at least not at 4 in the morning. Muttering to himself, he was heedless of the tall, black, fully enclosed, one-horse wagon bearing down upon him, the horse's hoofbeats and the wagon's rattling overcome by the wind and Matt's preoccupation. The driver, jarred by the bumpy ride and without the benefit of a lamp, not seeing the pedestrian until the last second, barked a warning as he straightened his legs against the footrest and pulled back hard on the reins.

Startled, Matt jerked his head around in time to see the flared nostrils of the dark horse as it began to squat on its rear legs and slide on the loose dirt. The lawman dove out of the way as the wagon rumbled to a stop, close enough for Matt to hear the groaning of the hubs. He glanced up from his resting place on the dirt street, still groggy but with his heart now pumping furiously.

It was one of those enclosed wagons traveling dentists and patent medicine salesmen use, and it backed up a foot or so as it came to rest. The side of it was discreetly painted with the name *Reverend Benson* and the simple declaration *Revival Meetings and Healings*. The driver, the Reverend Benson himself, judging by his appearance, stuck his head around the corner of the wagon and doffed his hat.

"Many apologies, friend," he said. "Almost didn't see you there."

Matt picked himself up and brushed the dirt off his clothes, waving the minister off. "No harm done," he said unconvincingly. He picked up his hat and knocked it against his leg. The less time he spent talking to one of these men, the better. He continued on across the road, and shortly the preacher shrugged, sat back down, gave his reins a flick, and proceeded up the street. From the safety and cover of a recessed doorway, Matt watched as the wagon bounced all the way through town, then breathed a sigh of relief.

"Keep on going," he mumbled aloud. "I've got enough trouble." He felt a slight twinge of guilt at his skepticism but managed to suppress it without difficulty. He began to make his way up the street when a commotion down an alley stopped him short. He drew back to the corner of the building and listened. He heard soft, deep slaps, followed by grunts, accompanied by the sound of leather shoes scraping on gravel. Then harsh words, too low to make out but clearly ominous.

Just as suddenly as the wagon had come upon him, running feet sounded their approach. Matt quickly judged the distance and jumped into the alleyway. His timing was correct, but his aim fell short, and he glanced off the leg of the ruffian, rolling over in the dirt. Only 4 in the morning and he'd already grounded himself twice.

Startled by the unexpected intruder, the fleeing man, whom Sheriff Page assumed to be a robber, chirped involuntarily but, despite being knocked sideways, did not lose stride. Undaunted by his failure to bring the suspect down, Matt rolled, sprang up in a single motion, and gave chase. His quarry had a head start and the benefit of darkness, but Matt was young and determined and wore gum-soled boots. In less than twenty strides he was so close that the man threw a worried glance over his shoulder and cut to the right, ducking down a side street and leaping a trough in an attempt to elude his pursuer.

Matt matched the man's movements and jumped over the trough easily, but the man he chased had the advantage of know-

ing where he was going before Matt did. Faking left, he wheeled
to the right again, gaining a step or two as Matt slipped trying to
make the sudden change of direction. No sooner had Matt picked
his pace back up than the fleeing suspect spun and squared off
against his pursuer, yanking a revolver from his waistband.

Matt would have no part of this. Unable to draw his Peacemaker quickly enough, he dropped his head, yowled, and dove
into the man's stomach, knocking his gun arm aside. Matt struck
him full bore, and they both went down in a grunting heap. The
lawman somersaulted away while the suspect, now emitting
shrieking gasps, strained to fill his deflated lungs. His gun all but
forgotten, the fugitive dropped it to the dirt and held both hands
to his midsection.

Matt eased his gun from its holster and waited for the man to
catch his wind, kicking the errant six-shooter out of reach. As
breath returned in spurts to the apparent outlaw and the color to
his face, he looked up at the young man sitting on his haunches a
few feet away, pistol at the ready.

"Don't shoot me, mister," the man pleaded between breaths.
"Here, you can have all I've got—" As he began to reach into his
pocket, Matt clicked back the hammer.

"Don't move another inch, friend," he told him, trying to disguise his own breathlessness. "You're under arrest."

"Huh? What th—?" The apprehended fugitive strained to see
on the dark side street. He noted the shining star pinned to Matt's
thick flannel shirt. "You're the law? I thought you was trying to
rob me."

"Rob you? You just beat and robbed a man back in the alley. I
heard the whole thing."

"You're mistaken, to be sure," the man protested. Wisely keeping both hands in view, he started to get up, then paused and
looked at Matt. The lawman nodded but kept the gun trained on
him. The man slowly sat up.

"Who are you?" Matt demanded.

"Russell Draper."

"New in town?"

"No, not really. I come and go, keep to myself. Been here a while."

"Have a job?"

"Not unless you call drinking and gambling a job."

"Not likely. No more 'n I call robbin' a job."

"That isn't what happened."

"So you say, but I know what I heard."

"I can't argue with what you think you heard, Sheriff, but it ain't what happened."

"Suppose we let the other man tell me that. Get up." Matt motioned with the gun.

Draper complied. "Don't worry, I ain't gonna try nothin'. I may be one sorry individual, but I like my hide the way it is. Perforations don't set too well with me, you know?"

Matt marched him to the jail and locked him up, then returned to the alley to seek out Draper's victim. There was no mistaking what he had heard—a beating, a man falling to the ground, Draper running away, probably after taking the other man's money. Why beat a man senseless, then run off without relieving him of his money?

But there was no one in the alley. Matt searched it thoroughly, just in case the man had crawled off into hiding, afraid Draper would return to finish the job. But there was nothing. The victim had apparently picked himself up and half-walked, half-dragged himself toward Main Street, where his tracks blended in with everyone else's. An hour before dawn, the street was deserted and silent once again.

Okay, so there would be no robbery or even a beating charge against Draper. Even if a crime had occurred, there had to be a victim for there to be an arrest. Matt decided to finish his rounds before returning to the jail and letting Draper go. A few hours in jail might just make the man think twice. That was the least Matt could do to pay him back for running from him.

When his rounds were finally completed, having taken longer than usual because he included a few out-of-the-way places he could only get to on horseback, he pulled Shadow, his spirited black Arabian, up in front of the jail. He dismounted, wrapping the reins around the hitching rail. A local mongrel who considered the porch his home growled at Matt as the lawman mounted the steps. Matt caught the dog lightly on the ribs with his boot—not hard enough to hurt, just to get his attention. Message received, the cur scurried away, keeping a wary eye on the human from a safe distance.

Matt shuffled into his office, made a production out of settling in, then let Draper loose with a warning. Matt could smell the stale odor of the whiskey Draper had consumed earlier and noticed the spoiled floor in the cell where he'd lost a good portion of it. Draper offered no apology as he sauntered out into the early light. Matt watched him go, then tossed his hat onto a peg and set about mopping the cell floor before turning to his more official tasks.

Outside, Bridgeport had begun to show signs of life. A few people were about, mostly shopkeepers, and a man paid by the city began to move slowly down Main Street, putting out the lamps that would be unnecessary soon. The sky was lightening as the sun drew nigh to cresting the mountains to the east—jagged, snow-covered peaks that stood black and purple with the sun behind them, only to burst into shades of blue and green as the sun continued its march across the sky. The snap in the air remained until high noon this time of year, then returned by 3 or 4 to remain until midday on the morrow, unless clouds warded off the little warmth that might otherwise seek out the town for a few hours each day.

But today was clear so far, and Matt anticipated taking his wife, Sarah, on a picnic lunch. Though the air was still a little chilly, perhaps she wouldn't mind if they could find a spot in the sun and she kept her coat on.

The sheriff stoked the fire in the small stove where embers from the night before still smoldered, placing a couple more hunks of wood inside and clanking the door shut. The lumber began to smoke, then burst into flame. He set a pot of water on top and stropped his razor on the leather strap hanging from a hook on the wall.

Removing his shirt with a shiver, Matt splashed water onto his face as soon as it was hot, then whipped up the soap and splotched it on his cheeks and chin. He stroked the razor across his face as he contorted it to tighten the skin, wincing every time he nicked himself. He rinsed off and put his shirt back on, admiring his mustache in the small mirror hanging from a nail on the wall behind the stove. He stroked the hairs into place with a toothpick.

Matt's appearance had changed over the last year and a half, since coming to California as a former Illinois farm boy seeking to make a home for himself in the West. His mustache had filled out, and he'd let it grow shaggy, over his mouth and down the sides

toward his chin. His ordeals had lined his face, taking off the naive
sheen and adding the much-deserved appearance of wisdom. He
wore his hat lower over his face and didn't make such an obvious
show of looking about as he had when everything was new. His
steel-eyed glance hadn't diminished, though, and his powers of
observation were much keener. Matt was the kind of man who
learned by his mistakes, and he'd learned plenty since coming to
California.

His choice of clothing hadn't changed much—flannel shirts and
blue jeans or gray wool trousers. But the sinewy muscles he'd
developed since coming here caused the attire to hang differently
on his lanky frame. Plus he had a new confidence about his person that was obvious to those who'd known him the longest—a
way of carrying himself of which he was unaware but that told
everyone who met him he was serious about his job.

Settling into his wooden chair with the leather-covered seat, he
grabbed the stack of letters and reports and began to read, his eyes
quickly growing weary with the effort. He'd been up two hours
already without any coffee, and he was ready to go back to bed.
If Sarah didn't arrive soon—

Footsteps on the boards and the doorknob's rattling saved him.
She came in with a smile and a tray, setting it down on the desk
and removing the blue checkered cloth from Matt's breakfast.

Hotcakes and coffee, with thick, fresh maple syrup and warm
cream and honey—all brought by an angel.

Heaven. Matt was in heaven.

How could he ever again long for the trail? Day-long rides on
a smelly, bumpy horse. Sleeping on the hard ground. Eating jerky
and cold beans and drinking coffee full of grounds and dirt.
Wearing the same long johns for days at a time. Shaving with icy
stream water and no soap.

And yet he did long for the open road, the adventure, seeing
something new every day, meeting new people and chasing thieves,
the excitement and satisfaction of the capture. He longed for it
every time he had to drag a drunk from an alley to a cell or settle
a dispute between a storekeeper and a cowboy with an unpaid tab.
Every time he settled behind his desk with a sheaf of papers, Matt
longed for the smell of his horse and the leather saddle and the feel

of his Winchester in the crook of his arm as he scoured the brush with a keen eye or read trail signs in pursuit of an outlaw.

He suddenly realized Sarah was speaking to him.

"Huh?" He looked up at her dumbly, his mouth full.

"I said, why didn't you wear your coat? You'll catch your death."

"Too bulky," he explained, waving a fork. "Restricts my movement."

"Dying will restrict your movement, too, Matt."

Matt grinned and swallowed. "I'm used to the cold. It don't bother me much."

Sarah wore a pale yellow checkered cotton dress with long sleeves and white, three-button cuffs edged with lace. The neck bore a circular collar that matched the cuffs, and the buttons were white bone. Fitting tightly at the bodice, the skirt billowed out from the hip to lightly brush the floor. Over this Sarah wore a white shawl she'd knitted herself, pulled tightly against the morning chill. She opened a satchel she'd brought that Matt hadn't noticed before and pulled out his coat, which she hung on a peg, and a clean pair of long johns.

"Here, put these on," she ordered. She grimaced but said no more.

Matt blushed but offered neither excuse nor apology.

"Later," he said. "When it warms up in here and it won't be such a shock to take my clothes off."

Sarah sat down to watch him eat and poured herself a cup of coffee from the pot she'd brought. Matt winked at her once but otherwise concentrated on his breakfast, and Sarah amused herself by looking at some of the new wanted posters he'd received in the previous day's post.

"You going to go out looking for any of these men?" Sarah asked, a slight hesitancy in her voice.

"Why should I?" Matt asked. "Any of them thought to be in this area?"

"No, I don't think so . . ."

"They only send me those in case I happen to accidentally see one of 'em. If I recognize any of these hombres, I'll hang the poster with the others." He pointed over his shoulder with his fork to a stack of posters an inch thick hanging from a nail on the wall behind him.

"Oh, my. So many." Sarah absentmindedly began fingering

through the posters, her head cocked slightly to one side as she considered the criminals' faces.

"Bounty hunters'll get most of 'em," Matt explained. "Probably already have. They send those things to all the sheriffs and marshals. Most of those posters were hangin' from that nail when I took over this job. Your pa put 'em up. I got just about enough now to paper an entire wall. That'd look pretty good, don't you think?"

"What? Pasting them up to cover that ugly wall over there?"

"No, sweetheart, I mean our parlor at home."

She glared at him playfully. "You do and you'll be living there alone," she cautioned.

"Ah, I'm just kiddin' around. Don't get your petticoat in a twirl."

"Oh, look here," she said, stopping at a poster near the back. "This one's almost two years old. It's one of the escapees from the prison breakout in '71. Was this one of the men you were chasing?"

"I don't know." Matt shrugged, not looking up from his desk. "What's his name?"

"Charlie Jones. He was serving life for murder, it says here."

"Yeah," Matt said. "He was one of 'em—the one who got away. Last seen headed to Death Valley, I heard. He's dead by now, no doubt. That's rough country. I don't know why your pa never took that one down . . . or any of the others for that matter." He reached over and yanked it and several others off the nail, letting them drift down to the floor. The posters slid underneath a small cabinet, nearly out of sight. "Most of those others can just as well come down too," he said.

"Well, I'll leave it to you to do," Sarah said, releasing the posters and letting them fall back against the wall and each other. They swung from side to side on the nail a few times before finally coming to rest. The last thing she wanted to do was get involved in a dispute between her husband and her father. She poured Matt another cup of hot coffee. "What do you have planned for today?"

"Well, I've got some paperwork to finish for the County Commission, then I thought I'd go see how Harvey and Mary are gettin' along with their move, then I thought you and me could—"

"I'm so sad to see them leave," Sarah said.

"Yeah, me too. But you know, we did without 'em in Bodie."

"Matt, that's a terrible thing to say."

"No, it ain't, it's true."

"It's still terrible. It sounds so . . . insensitive."

"I didn't mean it to be, Sarah. I was just sayin' we'll miss 'em, but we'll get by. So will they. You have other friends. I mean, Sarah, you grew up here. You have lots of friends."

"It's you I'm worried about. Harvey was about your best friend here. In Bodie you were okay, thanks to Uncle Billy and your pa."

"C'mon, Sarah, I'm a grown man. I don't need friends to hang around with like I was some kid growin' up. Besides, I've got a really good friend who goes everywhere with me."

"Who might that be?" Sarah inquired suspiciously.

"My horse, of course." Matt smiled at Sarah's scowling face, then said, "I mean you, silly. You're the only friend I need." He took her in his arms and planted an enthusiastic kiss on her lips. She moaned a little, then returned it. They might have stayed that way the whole day if the door hadn't opened.

"Page, it's high time you . . . Say, what's going on here?"

Matt and Sarah broke apart, both of them embarrassed, and gave the newcomer sheepish looks. It was John Taylor, Sarah's father and the elected sheriff of Mono County who was now on leave as he recovered from the complications of a bullet in his back. In the meantime, Matt was filling that crucial role.

"Oh, good mornin', Sheriff," Matt said, addressing him with the title that was currently rightfully his own. Whether on injury leave or not, to Matt, John Taylor would always be "Sheriff."

"Good morning." Taylor didn't correct him. "And good morning to you too, Sarah. Your ma never carried on with me this way when I was on duty."

"That's your loss, Daddy," Sarah said. Taylor's face soured, but he didn't respond.

"What can I do for you?" Matt asked, a little uncomfortable with Taylor's presence. The older lawman was very nearly recovered from his wounds, and even though he had talked about retiring ever since the upcoming election had been declared, Taylor had started coming to the jailhouse at least once a day. He claimed he just wanted to keep busy or to have someone to talk to. But Matt suspected his father-in-law was keeping an eye on him, double-checking his work to make sure he wasn't mishandling potentially dangerous situations.

"Saw Russ Draper leaving this morning," Taylor said. "What'd he do? Public nuisance? Drunk?"

"Both, but there's more. He beat a man, maybe robbed him."

"That explains why he was in jail all right, but not why he was walking out of it."

Matt sighed heavily. "No victim. By the time I got done chasin' and fightin' Draper, the man he beat was just a memory. Never even got a look at him."

"Made you chase him and then fought you? I trust you gave Draper something to remember you by."

"Like a black eye or a knot on the head? Is that what you mean?"

"More like both." Taylor's tone was matter-of-fact.

Matt shook his head. "Not my style. No need."

Taylor shook his head. "You do it the first time, there won't be no next time."

"Maybe. That's a chance I'll have to take."

Taylor shook his head again, unable to hide his disgust. But he said nothing as a flash of pain ran across his face, and his hand went to his back.

"Daddy, you all right?" Sarah asked.

"Back's a little stiff this morning," Taylor explained, resting on a chair by the wall. "Thought I'd take a walk and see if I could get the kinks out."

"This as far as you're gonna go?" Matt asked. Sarah nudged him in the ribs with an elbow.

"For now." Taylor reached over and picked up the stack of new wanted posters.

"Well, I'd love to stay and chat," Matt said, picking up his hat, "but I've got rounds to make. See you later. Sarah, can you meet me for lunch?"

"Sure, Matt. Where?"

"At home. I'll pick you up, and we'll go for a picnic."

Her face brightened.

"It's a mite cold for that, ain't it?" Taylor suggested, peeking over the top of the posters.

"That's why I didn't invite you," Matt said. "Your back would stiffen up awful bad." He turned to his wife. "See you later, Sarah," he said with finality as he stormed out the door.

CHAPTER

TWO

Matt mounted the steps and crossed the boardwalk, opening the door to Boone's Emporium. Gone was the tinkling of the bell, and Matt hesitated as he saw the inside of the place, taken aback by the sight. The Emporium was as empty as a Kansas prairie. Nothing had been left, not even the shelving. Only Harvey Boone stood there, planted in the center of the former store with his hands on his hips, giving the place one last look.

Matt did the same, and the two of them regarded the scene with a respect some might mistake for the kind reserved for a house of worship.

"Kinda eerie," Matt said finally.

"Yeah, now that you mention it," Harvey agreed.

"I figured you were packin' it up, but it took me by surprise just the same."

Harvey nodded. "Yeah, there are a lot of memories here." He pointed to a dark stain on the boards near where his cash register had been. "That's where that bandit you plugged bled out."

Matt nodded. "And over there is where Calamity Jane broke a bunch of stuff."

Harvey grinned. "I wonder whatever happened to her."

"I would imagine Wild Bill Hickok got tired of her and dropped her off in some town along the way . . . especially once he found out how much trouble she is."

Harvey laughed. "At least he took her off my hands. I just couldn't bring myself to let her go."

"Well, never mind now. She's gone," Matt said. "And from the looks of it, you will be too, pretty soon."

"Yep. Tomorrow or the next day. I'm done here, but we still have some work to do at the house. We're set to open in Bodie this weekend."

"Mary gonna open another restaurant?"

"Don't know yet. For now we're both going to work the store together. I figure it'll be busy enough to warrant the both of us, and that way we'll at least be together."

"Wish I could do that," Matt lamented. "Law enforcement just ain't woman's work, though. They ain't up to it."

"Not the fighting and riding and shooting," Harvey said. "But you haven't been doing much of that lately. Just a bunch of paper shuffling, to hear you tell it."

Matt grinned. "There's a thought. Maybe I could get Sarah to do all the paperwork for me—"

"So you can go out and ride the countryside, chasing outlaws and getting in fights? It would be hard to convince Sarah, even if the County Commission were to go along with it. No, Matt, I think you'd better leave things as they are."

"You're right, Harvey, as usual."

Harvey moved over to his friend. "We're going to miss you, Matt. Sarah too."

"Same here. What'll we do for a general store?"

"Oh, there'll still be one. I sold the building to Ah Quong Tai. He's going to move his store down here. That's why the rush to vacate."

"Quong Tai? Where's he from?"

"Most recently, right from here. Before that, San Francisco. Originally, China. You know Ah Quong Tai. Runs a little store at the edge of town. Deals mostly with the Indians and Chinese. White folk don't patronize him much, except in emergencies."

"Oh, him. So you sold out to a Chinaman?"

Harvey gave Matt a puzzled stare. "I never took you for a bigot, Matt."

"What? I'm not, at least most of the time. But I don't think too many of the good citizens of Bridgeport are gonna like a Chinaman runnin' their only general store. Especially Quong Tai. He don't strike most folks as being one hundred percent honest."

"They'll get used to it. They'll have to. Besides, if the prices aren't fair, they'll complain. Don't worry about it, Matt."

"What do you know about this fella?"

"Not much, except he paid cash."

"He likes to gamble, don't he?"

"Yeah, I suppose he does, now that you mention it. That's probably where he got the money. But a lot of folk like to gamble—even some of the good white men in town."

"Hmm." Matt was pensive, not because this was bad news or even cause for concern, but because there wasn't much else to say. He decided to change the subject. "Say, how 'bout you and Mary comin' over for supper before you go? Tomorrow night okay? Sarah'd love to have you. That way Mary won't have to go to no trouble, what with everything packed an' all."

"I'll ask her," Harvey assured him. "I'm sure she'll think it's a fine idea."

"Great. I'll tell Sarah."

They left the store, and Harvey locked the door behind him for the last time, looking at the key wistfully before pocketing it.

"Well, that about does it. I've got to get on home and help Mary box the dishes. See you later, Matt."

"See you, Harvey."

When Matt returned to the jailhouse Sarah was gone, but his father-in-law was still there, occupying Matt's chair. He made no move to get up when the new sheriff walked in, something that did not go unnoticed by Matt.

"So there you are," Taylor said, as though he'd been expecting Matt sooner.

"What do you mean, 'there you are'?" Matt stopped in his tracks and regarded Taylor with a serious gaze.

"Whoa, I didn't mean nuthin' by it," Taylor deferred, holding his hand up. "You're a mite touchy there, son."

Matt gritted his teeth and turned away from Taylor, making a show of removing his hat and hanging it on a peg. He said nothing but stepped over to the desk and waited for the other man to vacate the chair. Taylor didn't stir.

"Excuse me, sir, but I have some work to do," Matt finally said through clenched teeth.

"Go right ahead. I won't bother you."

You already are. "I need to sit at the desk."

"Oh . . . yes, of course. So you do." Taylor cleared his throat and stood up. "We'll, I guess I'd better mosey on back home. Irene'll be wondering what happened to me."

Matt didn't answer but thought, *Good idea. Go bother her for a while.* Taylor hemmed and hawed for a minute while Matt ignored him, then finally made his way to the door. Just as he reached for the knob, heavy steps sounded on the porch and Taylor instinctively drew back, narrowly avoiding being struck as the door burst inward.

"Sheriff!" a man called as he stumbled in.

"What?" said Matt and Taylor simultaneously.

The man looked from Taylor to Matt and back to Taylor, then spoke to the elder man. "There's a bear comin' down Main Street, Sheriff! And he looks plenty mean!"

"A bear?" Taylor growled. "Frank, are you sure?"

"Sure as I'm standin' here! Go look for yourself."

But Matt was already out the door, having snatched a Winchester he kept leaning against the doorpost so it could be put to use quickly. He squinted into the early-morning sun at the black shadow lumbering toward them, a hairy mass of thick flesh and fur, slowly walking upright down the center of the street.

Walking upright? Matt cocked his head to one side as Taylor came out onto the sidewalk, having retrieved his Sharp's carbine. Matt knew bears could walk upright, but they didn't do so for any great distance. This bear was doing nothing but walking upright, never once going down on all fours.

A cry rang out, and the few people who were out scurried for sanctuary. A mother grabbed her child and whisked him away; several men looked out cautiously from positions of safety.

Matt moved slowly off the porch and into the street, stepping around a puddle without looking at it except with his peripheral vision, keeping his eye trained on the bear. There was something odd about its walk, something very . . . unbear-like.

It was still a hundred yards off and just entering the town proper when it turned its head toward the sun, and the light caught him full-face. Matt relaxed as the profile proved the beast to be devoid of a snout.

"Do you know who it is?" Matt asked Taylor, still standing just outside the office door.

"Unless I miss my guess, it's the Wild Man from Bloody Canyon."

"Who?"

"The Wild Man from Bloody Canyon. No one knows his name. Maybe he don't even have one. He's just called the Wild Man."

"Does he walk up to folk and say, 'Good morning, I'm the Wild Man'?" Matt asked, not a little sarcastically.

"Course not," Taylor answered, finally moving stiffly into the street and over to Matt's side. "For the most part he don't talk to no one. Just grunts. That coat of his is a bear he killed—with just his hands, so they say."

"What's he doin' in town?"

Frank Pascoe, a local ne'er-do-well usually found hanging around town during the day, ventured out beside them in time to hear the question.

"Needs a new child to feed on probably," he said.

"That's nonsense, and you know it," Taylor scolded. "Now stop spreadin' that stuff and scarin' folk half to death."

The Wild Man was nearly abreast of them but did not acknowledge their stares, or those of anyone else. He kept his eyes straight ahead, his pace slow but unrelenting, just like that of the bear he so resembled from a distance, the fur of his heavy coat shining in the new sun. Fur wrapped his legs as well, and he wore a fur cap. No doubt about it, he looked like a bear. Only his whiskers, which had apparently never touched a razor, were of a different color— not gray, but brown with red and gray streaks. His age could not be determined, but Matt figured he had to be at least fifty.

He walked directly toward Harvey Boone's store and mounted the steps, grabbing the handle but finding the door locked. He leaned over and put his face to the glass, cupping a hand on the side of the sun to thwart the reflection, then moved away slowly, now scanning up and down the street.

"He's here for supplies," Matt said quietly, more to himself than to the two men with him.

"Probably. He comes in twice a year usually," Taylor said. "Spring and fall mostly. Stocks up on the staples."

"How does he pay?" Frank asked.

"He has money. Don't know where he gets it. Must have a stash somewhere. Maybe he scored big once way back when, been living off it all this time. Who knows?"

"Maybe he robbed a bank when he was young," Frank suggested. "Or dug up a big nugget."

"Or has a rich aunt," Matt said testily. "Who cares, Frank? If it matters so much, why don't you go ask him?"

"Not me! I'm not gonna get close enough for him to sink his claws into me!"

"What's he gonna do now?" Matt asked Taylor.

"What do you mean?" The sheriff gave his son-in-law a puzzled stare.

"Boone's store is closed, you know. Empty."

"It is?" Taylor squinted across the street at the bear-man as he moved slowly off the boardwalk, as if contemplating his next move. "Oh, yeah, that's right."

"We've had it now for sure," Frank said. "He'll go on a rampage, start breakin' into homes and snatchin' everyone's goods—and woe to anyone who tries to stop him."

"Shut up, Frank," Matt ordered, perturbed, as he took a step toward the Wild Man. "He'll do no such thing."

The cur ventured out from under the boardwalk, growling at the Wild Man, its ears pinned back. The Wild Man stopped, looked down slowly at the animal, then growled in return and stomped a foot, and the mongrel yelped and darted back into the darkness.

Matt stopped. "On second thought . . ." he said quietly.

"Leave him alone, Matt. He don't like to be bothered."

"Neither do you," Matt said. "I don't aim on botherin' him. He needs help, can't you see? With the store closed, where's he gonna get his supplies for the next six months?"

"For that matter, where are we?" Frank asked no one in particular.

"A Chinaman bought the building. He'll be movin' in soon enough," Matt explained. "But that don't help this man today."

"Well, you got me," Taylor said. He turned on his heel and strode back to the sheriff's office. "I, for one, am gettin' out of this cold. Makes my back stiffen up something fierce." He disappeared, followed quickly by Frank, whose back was fine except for a yellow streak that ran its length.

The Wild Man had watched the men in silence without letting on he was doing so. He had seen their weapons, their hesitation, the way the young one had been sizing him up. But he just stood there, looking up and down the street while the citizens of Bridgeport watched him from their hiding places, afraid his disappointment would turn into a tirade against the town.

Matt could wait no longer. He moved toward the Wild Man, able to smell the bearskin before he was close enough to see any detail in the fur. Realizing that coming up on the man's blind side wasn't a wise thing to do, he scuffed a foot to announce his approach. The Wild Man turned, his eyes suspicious.

"They've closed," Matt said, stating the obvious for no reason except to let the man know he understood his plight. "Can I help you with something?"

The man looked over Matt carefully, his gaze resting on Matt's star for a few seconds before continuing on. Finally his eyes locked on Matt's, as if to read his thoughts. He held them for a moment, then shook his head, turned away, and walked back the way he'd come, never looking at anything but the road ahead.

Matt stood and watched him leave. As the Wild Man crossed the bridge and disappeared over a rise without looking back, the people slowly moved out into the street, their stares remaining long after the Wild Man could no longer be seen.

"You coulda got killed," someone told the deputy.

"What did you say to him?" asked another.

"You stood him down," remarked Frank, bravely venturing out now that the danger had passed. "You stood the Wild Man down."

Matt said nothing, both amused and disgusted with the townsfolk. They called the peculiar visitor "the Wild Man," but there was nothing besides his attire to make Matt believe he was anything of the sort. A hermit maybe. A man who liked to be alone definitely. But the West was full of such individuals. No, there was something about the man's eyes, something that told Matt the Wild Man was approachable.

The thing was, why bother? The Wild Man obviously wanted to be left alone, and Matt had no reason to pursue his friendship anyway. Leave well enough alone, his mother always said. If a man goes to that much trouble to avoid people, who was Matthew Page to force himself on him? He shrugged and turned away from the small crowd of awed onlookers as they murmured among themselves, occasionally looking up to watch Matt as he walked away.

Matt pushed aside his papers and pressed his chin into his chest to stretch out his neck. He shrugged his shoulders and held them in place, then pulled them down and tilted his head back with a groan. He'd slept on hard ground in the cold after riding a horse all day more times than he could count, but he still never felt as worn out and stiff as he did after a few hours of paperwork. This part of the job was for old men like John Taylor who couldn't ride the hills anymore.

Matt pushed himself away from the desk, then walked around and stared out the window. Maybe this was Taylor's way of doing things, but it sure wasn't his. Maybe if he was sheriff—the real, elected sheriff—he could lessen the amount of record-keeping he'd have to do. Surely some of these reports weren't necessary. The County Commission could get their updates and proposals by mouth, couldn't they? He could just tell them what they wanted to know.

Or he could get someone to help. Not a deputy, but a . . . a clerk, that's what they called it. Like a law clerk, only for the sheriff.

His stomach growled, reminding him of his lunch plans.

He grabbed his hat and ran outside, locking the door behind him, then trotted down the street to their cabin on the edge of town—the opposite end from where the Taylors' house stood by the bridge with its white picket fence and red water pump, the one Matt was using to rinse the grime off his face when he saw Sarah for the first time.

He was smart enough to know that living next-door to the in-laws was not the wisest of decisions. And ever since he'd been named temporary sheriff, Matt had especially congratulated himself on his foresight for renting a small house on the opposite side of town. Oh, he loved Sarah's parents all right. Irene Taylor was a wonderful woman, and Sarah's father . . . well, he'd done a lot for Matt, giving him a job as a deputy when he could just as easily have turned him away or thrown him in jail as a vagrant.

But still, people have a way of changing as time passes, and John Taylor, Sarah's father or not, was getting on Matt's nerves these days. But Matt was keeping that to himself. The last thing he wanted was a family feud.

Sarah was waiting for him on the porch, her shawl wrapped tightly around her shoulders, her cheeks pink from the nip in the air that the sun had been unable to drive away.

"Are you sure you want to go?" Matt asked as he helped her into the wagon and set the basket of food on the seat beside her.

"We'll find a sunny spot," she said gamely. He rarely had time for her these days. She wasn't about to let this opportunity pass her by.

Matt smiled and flicked the reins, and the old horse flipped its tail at him and strained forward as the wagon creaked into motion.

"I heard about the Wild Man," Sarah said as they bounced up the road.

"Yeah? What'd you hear?"

"How you confronted him in the street and made him leave town without firing a shot or laying a hand on him."

Matt snorted and shook his head. "He left town 'cause he wanted to, that's all."

"Who is he?"

"Don't know. You've lived here all your life—haven't you ever seen him before?"

"Yes, once or twice. But Daddy never let me get close to him, and Daddy never bothered him either—just gave him a wide berth and let him come and go as he pleased."

"Why do they call him the Wild Man?"

"Because of the way he lives and dresses, I guess."

"Why's he do it?"

She just shook her head and snuggled closer to Matt.

"Bloody Canyon," Matt remarked, not wanting to let it go so quickly. "Where'd that name come from?"

"Don't know that either. Not for sure. I've heard several stories—don't know which of them's the truth, if any of them."

"Well . . . ?" Matt urged.

"Some say it was the scene of an Indian massacre of some early settlers. Others that a prospector murdered a man whose claim he intended to steal. Still others say . . . Wait a minute—Matt, didn't the Wild Man come to town to buy provisions?"

"Huh? Oh, yeah, yeah, he did. Why?"

"But Harvey closed the Emporium."

"Yep. The Wild Man got turned away. I offered to help, but he said no."

"He spoke to you?"

"No, I spoke to him. He just shook his head and walked away."

"What's he going to do?"

"What do you mean, what's he going to do? Go somewhere else, I suppose. Or come back another day. He knows a town like Bridgeport can't go long without a store. He'll figure someone else will be moving in soon to take over the trade. He'll be back."

"What if it's too late?"

"What do you mean?"

"What if he runs out of supplies before the new store opens?"

Matt shrugged, removed his hat, and adjusted his hair, then replaced the hat. "God will provide."

"Stop the wagon!"

Matt obeyed and looked Sarah in the eye, seeing a gleam there he hadn't noticed recently.

"What now?"

"Let's take some things to him. You know, just enough to tide him over until the store reopens under its new owner."

"You're not serious."

"Yes, I am. Bloody Canyon isn't that far by wagon. We can make it in a couple hours and be back by dark. Please, Matt?"

Matt sighed. How could he turn her down? "Okay, sweetheart, whatever you say. Sure you're not afraid of being massacred by the Indians? Or jumped by an old prospector—a grizzled old man with a shaggy beard, a mean glint in his eye, and only one arm?"

"That's your pa, and he's in Bodie." Sarah laughed. "No, I'm not afraid. Like you said, God will provide. In fact, we will be the way God provides for the Wild Man's needs. And He'll provide protection for us too."

Matt stared at her, incredulous. "You're really serious," he said. "Well, okay, that's what we'll do. At least let's break open that picnic basket. We can eat on the way."

Matt turned the wagon around and headed back for whatever supplies they could scrape up and afford to be without themselves for the next few days. As he shook the reins to prod the confused horse, Sarah handed him a fried chicken leg. Matt took it with a grateful smile and bit into it zestily.

CHAPTER

THREE

A MILE OR SO OUTSIDE TOWN stood a clump of aspens and firs—the former still naked, not having begun to bud, the firs full of green needles as always, providing a little protection for picnickers from town taking refuge from the elements. The road forked around the grove, the left leading to the Anderson spread, the right to Bloody Canyon. Matt urged the horse on, taking the right fork.

A curious curl of smoke rose from the midst of the grove; obviously a campfire. Matt said nothing to Sarah but wondered who would be setting up camp this close to town. Anderson's cowhands all had a bunkhouse to stay in, and Bridgeport's idle crowd spent their nights huddled around barroom stoves or stretched out on billiard tables. The hotels were filled with new arrivals and businessmen. So whom did that leave?

As they drew near, his question was answered. The angular shape of an enclosed wagon stood out from the shadowy tree limbs, and soon he could see the writing on the side, though he didn't need to read it to know who this was. Only one wagon like that was anywhere near Bridgeport this day.

Reverend Benson, revivalist and healer. So he hadn't kept going after all. Matt sighed silently and determined to return tomorrow—alone—to question the man regarding his intentions. It was his duty as sheriff to keep the peace. And that meant talking to strangers, regardless of the credentials they offered.

Besides, Matt knew full well that not all circuit preachers were honest men, and sometimes the crooked ones were difficult to spot. He didn't want a shyster coming to his town, especially one who came in the name of God. He'd have to keep a wary eye on the man until he could ascertain the truth.

He didn't comment on the preacher to Sarah, but she saw the wagon clearly through an opening in the sagebrush surrounding the grove.

"Oh, look, Matt," she said, her voice betraying a bit of excitement. "A minister. Maybe we're going to have a revival."

"Maybe," Matt said.

"Wouldn't a tent meeting be wonderful! They are so exciting. Lots of people coming around, all the singing, God's Word being preached."

"What's wrong with the minister and church we have already?" Matt asked. "We do all that every Sunday."

"I know," Sarah admitted. "But a revival is . . . well, different. It's the whole atmosphere that makes it a blessing. Reverend Stone is fine, certainly. I mean, he's a good man, and he preaches God's Word. But you've got to admit, he's . . . well, dull to listen to on occasion. You've fallen asleep plenty of times."

"That not Reverend Stone's fault. Those were days when I didn't get done sheriffin' until a couple hours before church because of the Saturday night crowd—you know that."

"Just the same, I'm looking forward to the revival. Anything to break the routine around this town."

"Hmm." Matt searched out of the corner of his eye for the preacher but couldn't see him. He was probably sitting beside his campfire, hidden by the wagon. No matter. Matt would see him tomorrow. He sucked his cheek sharply to goad the horse along and gave the reins a flip.

The buckboard rattled and bounced over the little-used road, so overgrown with vegetation that it was little more than two parallel footpaths.

"Slow down!" Sarah implored her husband. "You're rattling my teeth loose."

"This was your idea," Matt reminded her. "If we intend to return before nightfall, we can't go any slower. Do you want to be on this road when it's too dark to see?"

"No," she said quietly. "Just be careful. Do you know where we're going?"

"Harvey told me the Wild Man lived in a cave 'bout three miles up the canyon from the eagle rock. We passed that a couple miles back, best I can figure. We should be there pretty soon."

"Did Harvey have any supplies left from the Emporium to add to ours?"

"No, it was all shipped off to Bodie already. He and Mary sent a couple boxes of canned goods, though, and a sack of flour. Their own private stock, just like us."

Sarah nodded and stared at the canyon walls on either side of them. Not too narrow, with a wagon track centered between the steep cliffs. Sagebrush and scrub pine flanked the road, and grass grew high between the parallel wheel tracks. There was plenty of shadow here, and patches of dirty, untrodden snow still covered the ground in the places the sun never touched. She shivered involuntarily, more from the sense of foreboding that bolted up her spine than from the cold. She was well-insulated against the wintry temperatures, with her shawl around her and her woolen greatcoat over that with the hood up. This little shiver came from the inside.

"Maybe this wasn't such a good idea," she said softly.

"I could've told you that," Matt said. "Not that it would've done any good."

"God will protect us," she said softly, hoping to bolster her own confidence. "We're doing His work."

"Yeah, I suppose that's so," Matt agreed. "But we need to be careful not to do *His* work *our* way. The two don't always mix."

Sarah could only nod. He was right as rain.

They drove on, both of them searching the canyon for some sign of human occupation—litter, footprints, a path through the sagebrush and mesquite, the dark opening of a cave, a curl of smoke. . . .

Finally Matt spotted something.

"Over there," he said. "That might be it." Sarah looked in the direction Matt was pointing, seeing immediately what had caught his eye. But as the wagon slowly moved forward, they saw a different scene unfolding than what they had anticipated.

"No, guess not," Matt added.

The canyon had widened considerably here. A large patch of wild rye, the stalks six to eight feet high, waved in the breeze, their heads easily six inches long. Over the rye patch wafted a lazy blanket of gray haze, smoke from the cooking fires of a nearby Indian camp. A small group of Paiute women wandered through the rye, beating the grains from the heads and collecting the dark, sweet kernels in hand-woven winnowing baskets.

"Hard work," Sarah muttered sympathetically.

"You wouldn't know it by them," Matt said, nodding. Indeed, the Indian women were laughing and chattering in their native tongue, the Shoshone language, making a grand time of their labor.

The trail took Matt and Sarah past the camp, and they could see other women busy processing what the gatherers had already brought in—beating the husks from the grains with long poles and tossing them into the breeze on blankets, allowing the husks to be blown aside. Other women sat cross-legged at the grinding stones, pounding the grain into a fine powder to be mixed into dough and baked into sweet bread, a delightful aroma Matt and Sarah could already smell.

"Where are the men?" Sarah asked innocently. "Why aren't they helping?"

"They're off hunting, or gathering koochabee," Matt told her. "Some of them probably work on farms in the area. Besides, this is women's work." Matt grinned, keeping his eyes on the road ahead.

"I'm glad I'm not an Indian," Sarah muttered.

"Me too," Matt agreed quietly.

They rode another mile or two into the canyon when Matt abruptly reined the horse in, the wagon rocking to a rough halt.

"Do you see something?" Sarah asked. She peered down the canyon, shielding her eyes with her hand.

"Over there . . . by the trail." He pointed to guide her. Stuck in the dirt at the edge of the road was a stake overgrown by sagebrush and a sign barely readable due to weathered wood and fading paint—a rough, hand-painted sign ordering trespassers to keep out.

"Think this is it?" Sarah asked.

"What else would it be?"

"Maybe we should call out before going in."

Matt agreed and cupped a hand to the side of his mouth as he shouted, "Hey!" There was no answer.

"'Hey'?" Sarah asked. "What kind of greeting is that?"

"It's kinda hard to yell at someone when you don't know his name. I can't just yell, 'Hey, Wild Man,' can I?"

"What should we do?"

Matt gave the area a careful visual examination. "There's a footpath over there. I'll carry the stuff on in. He'll see my arms are full and know I'm not here to harm him."

"A rational man would, yes. But they say he's insane, otherwise why would he live this way?"

"He buys provisions, takes care of himself, and warns trespassers to stay away. Those aren't the actions of an insane man. Besides, he's wild because he doesn't live in a house, not because he's an animal. I've seen his eyes, Sarah. I'll be all right."

Matt jumped down, grabbed one of the two boxes they'd brought, and hiked up the path. Sarah held her coat tightly shut and stayed on the buckboard seat, her eyes darting warily around, searching for any sign of danger.

Halfway to the canyon wall Matt rounded a bend in the path and could see the man's encampment—a low cave with a crude shelter built of logs at the front of it, and nearby a small corral, currently empty. That was curious to Matt, since the man had walked into town.

Keeping one eye on the entrance to the cave, Matt inspected the corral, puzzled at what he saw. Horse droppings. Why had the Wild Man walked into town? Or maybe he had ridden most of the way, then left the horse tied up outside town. But why do that? It just didn't make sense.

"Hello!" Matt called out again. He stopped short of the log shelter and set the box down. "Anybody home?"

There was no answer, just an eerie silence. The breeze that is so prevalent in rock canyons made the only noise. Matt took a breath and picked up the box to set it under the shelter, then returned to the wagon for the second box.

"Did you see him?" Sarah asked expectantly, relieved to see her husband emerge unscathed.

"Nope. Must be off somewhere. I'll take the other box in too. You got any paper?"

"No, of course not."

"Well, I can find something to mark a message on the top of

the box, I guess." He hefted the second container out of the wagon and lugged it up the path, wondering how the Wild Man would have brought six months of supplies all by himself, without a wagon. He pulled a piece of charcoal from a nearby fire ring and scratched a greeting as best he could on the wood crate, then tossed the lump back into the pit and wiped his hands on his pants. He took one last look around, then strode back to the wagon. It seemed such a waste to come all this way and not see the Wild Man, but he reminded himself that their mission was to deliver supplies the man had been unable to get, and they'd accomplished that. Having him thank them was not their goal, and Matt felt a little ashamed for feeling slighted because they hadn't received the man's gratitude.

He mounted the buckboard and smiled wanly at Sarah, his eyebrows raised, then turned the wagon and headed home.

Moments earlier, from the mouth of another cave a short distance away, the Wild Man of Bloody Canyon had slowly lowered his rifle as he sat on a rock, thoughtfully chewing a piece of dried venison and watching with curious silence as one of his visitors carried a heavy box up the path and set it on his doorstep, then repeated the action. The hermit fingered the ancient Kentucky flintlock, then relaxed as the man returned to his wagon. He watched as the couple drove off the way they'd come.

The Wild Man waited until they were a couple miles away before coming out of hiding and making his way cautiously to the boxes, curious about the man with the sun glinting off the star on his chest and wondering what gifts he and his woman might have brought.

The trip back to Bridgeport was uneventful. Matt and Sarah talked about the Wild Man and where he might have been as they huddled close to each other to compensate for the cold and prayed together about nothing in particular and everything in general. It was a special occasion, and Matt wished he had more times like these to spend with Sarah. They were anxious to get home just the same, both of them ravenously hungry and in need of a cozy rest together next to the stove.

The preacher's campfire still wafted up through the center of the grove as they passed. They could hear the telltale clanging of pots and pans but could not see the man. Matt made no attempt to stop, and Sarah didn't ask why.

"We should see about his comforts," was all she said, not clarifying her meaning.

"There'll be time for that," Matt responded, "once he introduces himself to the town and makes his intentions known. Maybe he's just passing through and stopped here for the night. People do that, you know."

"He stopped rather early in the day, don't you think?"

"Maybe he's tired. Don't they usually advertise that they're coming? I haven't seen any posters or heard any rumors."

"No, neither have I," Sarah admitted. "But we can always hope."

"Yeah," Matt muttered, "we can always hope." But his meaning and Sarah's were not the same.

CHAPTER

FOUR

THE NEXT DAY, after morning rounds, shaving, and breakfast were complete, Matt excused himself from his office—where John Taylor was again hanging about—and took Shadow for a ride down to a small clump of aspens and firs outside town. He made no effort to be silent in his approach, wanting the preacher to be alerted to his arrival in order to avoid any charge of spying. If Benson was a true man of God, he'd happily greet the visitor.

"Good morning, friend!" came the welcome before Matt even saw him. The preacher stepped out from behind the wagon, shaving soap on half his face, his suspenders hanging down at his sides, a razor poised in his hand.

"Welcome to my home. As the Lord said, the foxes have holes, and the birds have nests, but I haven't a bed to lay my head." He laughed. "Just this old wagon. Let me finish shaving and I'll pour us some hot coffee."

"Please, by all means," Matt said. Taking the comment about coffee to be an invitation to alight, he climbed down from Shadow and picketed him to a wagon wheel. He moved over to the fire to warm himself and waited for the preacher.

Reverend Benson came over wiping his face with a towel. He was in his forties, about five-ten, medium build, with dark wavy hair graying at the temples and a large, thick mustache that extended nearly to his chin, around which he had carefully shaved off everything else. His eyes were narrow and dark, his eyebrows heavy. His smile seemed genuine enough. Matt thought he noticed a slight limp when he walked, but that could have just been early-morning kinks.

Benson tossed the towel over his shoulder after pulling his suspenders up, then poured coffee into the only cup Matt could see and offered it to the deputy.

"Sugar?" he asked.

"No thanks," Matt said. "There's too many times it's not available, so I learned to drink it black. Don't miss it that way."

"A man after my own heart. I'm Josiah W. Benson."

"*Reverend* Benson?"

"Yes, I suppose. I feel a bit awkward calling myself that. It seems rather pompous. Of course, I have to say it on the wagon—advertising and all. But when it's just you and I, well . . . But you can call me Reverend if that makes you more comfortable."

"Whatever suits you. Matt Page, Mono County Sheriff." He extended a hand, and the preacher grasped it firmly.

"I feel bad, drinking out of your only cup," Matt said.

"Don't worry about it. I have another. Excuse me."

The preacher reached into the back of the wagon and with much clanging produced his other cup, a blue enameled tin cup matching the one he'd offered to Matt. He poured himself a cup of brew.

"So, what brings you out here, Sheriff?" Benson asked with a smile.

"Not much. Saw you go through town yesterday." Matt tactfully didn't mention the near accident, though Benson was likely to make the connection since no one had been on the street except the man he almost ran over. But if it did register with Benson, his face didn't show it.

"I took a ride and noticed you camping out here. Thought I'd come over and say hello, find out what your plans are so I can take them into account . . . you know, make them part of my routine. Camp meetings have a tendency to disrupt a town, you know."

"Not in a bad way, Sheriff. People need the love of God spread around. Brings them peace and security in a troubled world."

Matt nodded. "Yes, I know. But it also brings a whole peck of folks together in one place, and with personalities being what they are, well . . . Besides, that also leaves their homes empty, and some vandals and thieves look forward to that. Makes the pickin's eas-

ier and more plentiful." Matt didn't have much of a problem with
vandals and thieves in Bridgeport, but the words had sounded convincing when he rehearsed his speech on the way out to the grove.

Reverend Benson's face took on a serious look, his eyes nar-
rowing. "So, what are you saying, Sheriff? Are you opposed to my
putting up my tent in your community and bringing the saving
grace of Jesus Christ to the lost people in this valley?"

Matt flushed but held his composure. "Course not." He took
a casual sip of coffee to give him time to think. The good reverend
had backed him into a corner on that one.

"Not at all. I just wanted to know in advance what your plans
are. You know, where you plan to pitch. Your tent, I mean. And
how long you figure on bein' here. Things like that."

Benson relaxed. "Well, I'll let you tell me where to pitch my tent
. . . just so long as it's not in the next county." He laughed and took
a drink. "Anywhere people can get to by walking. I'm not the kind
who think they need to be in the center of town. I noticed a nice
flat spot on the end opposite the bridge."

That was an understatement. There were miles of flat spots on
that side of town. In fact the whole valley was one big flat spot.

"Right on the outskirts is fine," Matt said.

"Good. Now . . . as to how long I'll be here, well, that's up to
God. I have no itinerary. I go when and where the Spirit leads,
though usually a week suffices. I like to empower the people to
carry on after I'm gone. Do you have a minister in town?"

"Yep. Reverend Stone. He's a very unassumin' man. Like you,
he's uncomfortable with the idea of being revered. He says only
God is to be treated like that. But we call him Reverend anyway.
Only seems right, him takin' all them years to go to school and all."

"I'm sure he's a good, righteous man," Benson said. "I'm anxious to meet him, make him a part of this ministry. He'll be the one
to carry on after I've gone ahead to the lost souls in the next valley. I'll also need some men to help erect my tent."

"I can't help you there," Matt said. "I'm not in the erectin'
business, and we have no layabouts in Bridgeport lookin' for work.
That is, we have layabouts. They just ain't lookin' for work, especially the kind you're offerin' . . . the kind for no pay. Maybe
Reverend Stone can aid you with that. I'm sure there are men in
the church who could give you a little time."

"Certainly." Benson rose, picked up the coffeepot from the rock next to the fire, and held it out toward Matt in a silent offer for a refill, his eyebrows raised questioningly.

"No thanks," Matt deferred, getting up and handing Benson his cup. "I appreciate your hospitality. I guess you'll be coming to town later?"

"I'd like to hold my inaugural meeting tomorrow evening," Benson declared.

Matt touched the brim of his hat and nodded once. "Ill see you then. You'll find Reverend Stone in the parsonage next to the church. Can't miss it. One block north of Main Street, center of town." Matt untied his horse and mounted. With a final nod to Benson he rode out of the grove and headed back to town.

As Matt strolled down Main Street, nodding at the men and smiling at the women, he considered the possibilities. *Matthew Page, Mono County Sheriff*. It had a certain ring to it. And that would get John Taylor out of his hair once and for all, at least in his official capacity. Matt didn't mind Taylor being his father-in-law. In fact, he owed him a great deal and thought the world of him. But Taylor was making things difficult coming around all the time, sitting in Matt's chair, going through his papers. Yes, Taylor was the elected county sheriff, but right now he was on leave after being shot, and Matt doubted he would be completely healed before his current term was up. He'd told Irene, his wife, who'd told Sarah, who in turn had told Matt, that he did not intend to run again for election. He was going to retire, hang up the star, leaving Matt uncontested for the position if he ran.

But that was when Taylor was confined to bed. Now that he was up and around—and bored, with nothing to do but get in Irene's way until she shooed him out of the house—he found it easy to gravitate to his old office at the jail and stick his nose into everything. "My body might be ailin', but my mind is just as sharp as ever," he told Sarah when she scolded him. "And this job is mostly brain-work."

But that small percentage of body-work couldn't be done without, Matt thought. And Taylor was slow in getting that ability back. The election itself was only a few weeks off, and whoever won would take office a month afterwards. Matt figured there was no way Taylor could be ready by then.

So Matt decided to run. He was the odds-on favorite, he figured, and greeting all the people he could each day wouldn't hurt
his chances. Of course, the election was county-wide, meaning
folks from Benton to Bodie to Coleville would be voting, not just
those in Bridgeport. But Matt figured he had the Bodie vote, what
with Uncle Billy and his pa there to stir things up. And there were
enough people there to just about carry it if he could drum up a
little support in Bridgeport. Those were the two population cen-
ters. The few votes he had in Coleville wouldn't help much.

So Bridgeport would get his full attention in the weeks to come,
and seeing that he was the working sheriff until voting, Matt figured he'd have to do something really wrong to lose the election,
and that didn't seem likely. Smiling and waving and maybe even a
little baby-kissing couldn't hurt.

The door was open to Harvey Boone's old Emporium, and
Matt stopped and peeked in. Boxes were stacked on the floor, and
some open ones were scattered about. Merchandise was being
arranged on shelves and tables, and the place was beginning to
look like a store again. A little Chinaman scurried about, his long
black queue flailing about from under his silk skull cap as he made
frantic preparations for his opening.

"How goes it, Mr. Tai?" Matt called in from outside.

The Chinaman stopped abruptly and turned toward the front door.

"Not open, not open," he said hurriedly. "Come back tomorrow." He waved Matt off.

Matt stepped inside. "I'm not a customer," he explained. "Not
right this moment anyway. I'm the sheriff. Just makin' my rounds."

Ah Quong Tai eyed him suspiciously, then saw the star on the left
breast of his shirt. "Ah, Mister Sheriff. I fine. Much work to do."

"You look like you could use some help."

"No help. I fine. Must work. Thank you for stop. Now go—I
busy."

"Okay, Mr. Tai." Matt smiled and tipped his hat. "See you
tomorrow. You'll no doubt have a lot of customers."

"No customers if Quong Tai not finish. Shoo, shoo." He
brushed Matt out as he would a bothersome fly and returned to
his work. Matt smiled and obliged the man and went back to his
campaign stroll.

A block away a man was pounding on a porch roof post with

a hammer, and Matt sauntered over to see what he was up to. He was trying to nail up a large poster, and Matt suspected it was for the revival. He was right.

"The Lord will be working tonight, Sheriff," the man said when he saw Matt reading the poster. He hammered home the last nail.

"So it seems," Matt answered. "You working for free, Tiny?"

"I'm working for the Lord," Tiny Reese answered. He was a large man, capable of manhandling just about any horse, but Matt had never known him to be particularly religious. Only what religion could be found at the bottom of a bottle. In fact, Tiny was a regular in the jail for picking fights after getting drunk. To his credit—and Matt's relief—Tiny had always gone without a struggle.

"Tiny, I never took you to be interested in God."

"Well, Sheriff," he said as an expectant smile crossed his lips, "the reverend explained to me that drinkin' and fightin' are things I can be healed of, and if I work hard enough for the Lord He'll do that for me."

"Well, it's true enough that He'll do for us what we can't do ourselves. I've told you that many times. So has Reverend Stone. But I never knew we had to work for it. How did Benson get you to sit still long enough to hear that message?"

Tiny grinned. "Reverend Stone told me about him, how he needed help. Said it would be good for me to help him, so I went to him and he explained things to me. I gotta go—I have to get all these posters up, then go back and help raise the tent." Tiny nodded, gathered up his posters, and made his way up the street.

Matt turned to the poster. "'Revival,'" he read out loud. "'Tent meetings begin Tuesday night.' That's tomorrow," Matt noted, then continued reading, "'Come and be healed. Rejoice in the Lord. Sing the great hymns of faith. No admission charge.'" He bent over to read the small print at the bottom. "'The plate will be passed. You may give as the Lord leads.'"

Matt rubbed his chin thoughtfully. "Oh well, circuit preachers gotta eat too."

He moved on as folks gathered around the poster and began to buzz.

The tent rose that afternoon—large, round, and as colorful as a circus tent. In fact, Matt wouldn't have been surprised if it used to be a circus tent. Inside, the dirt floor had been covered with fresh saw-dust—probably brought in from the lumber mill in exchange for heavenly rewards—and chairs were being set up. Matt knew Reverend Benson couldn't have stored all this in his little wagon and figured, since the chairs were of all shapes and sizes, some of them no more than planks on top of cut logs, Benson must have put out a request amongst the people.

He was sure of it when he saw Sarah lugging in their two dining chairs. He hurried over to her and relieved her of the burden, setting them in a row with the others.

"What're you doin'?" he asked.

"Reverend Stone said Reverend Benson needed chairs for the meetings."

"What are we gonna sit on at home?" Matt asked. "These are the only two chairs we've got!"

"Matthew, I never thought of you as being selfish!" she scolded.

"But who knows how long he'll—" Matt suddenly realized he was shouting and lowered his voice. "—how long he'll be here."

Sarah regarded him with a chastising glance. "I'm surprised at you, Matthew. We're doing this for God, not for Reverend Benson. What if two people couldn't come because we withheld our chairs . . . two people who would've been saved? Do you want that on your conscience for eternity?"

"Well, I—"

"You have to think of others, Matt."

"I don't think the lack of two chairs is going to keep someone out of heaven," Matt said. "The Holy Ghost ain't gonna be stifled because of two lousy chairs."

"No, maybe not. All the same, we must do our part. We were made for good works, Matt, just like we read the other night in the Bible. You read it to me, in fact. Have you forgotten?"

"Of course not. I just don't see how me standin' up to eat for a week constitutes good works. I always thought good works was feedin' the hungry or givin' clothes to Paiutes, things like that. Bringin' chairs to a revival . . . I don't know, that just doesn't sound like somethin' that's gonna send me to hell for not doin' it."

"Well, it's done," Sarah said. "I didn't think you'd mind. If you're really upset about it, I'll borrow a couple chairs from Ma. They've got four."

Matt glanced over toward another struggling woman. "Oh yeah? Think again."

Sarah looked over and saw her mother bringing in two chairs, followed by a chagrined John Taylor, his hand on his back, carrying nothing.

"Well, we'll figure something out," Sarah said. "Besides, this is just temporary. You're used to eating your supper sitting on a log or a rock by the fire with only the stars for a roof. Why should this bother you?"

Matt didn't have an answer for that. Still, there was something about Benson that disturbed him, and the idea that his two chairs were being used to help the preacher just didn't sit well with him. But he had no argument against it.

"Well . . . are they marked so we'll get them back?"

"Our name's on the bottom. Scratched it in with an awl," Sarah explained. "Not that I needed to. No one's going to take them."

"Hmm." Matt gazed up toward the front where a platform was being built—at least two feet high so everyone would be able to see Reverend Benson, with a ramp coming down to the center aisle, and no steps. *That's odd*, Matt thought, but he couldn't place why this too bothered him.

Then again, everything bothered him these days. Maybe he was being too critical, seeing everyone as a potential criminal. Maybe this job was getting to him. He shook himself out of his mood and turned back to Sarah, mustering a smile.

"How 'bout I take you out to dinner tonight before the meetin'?" he suggested.

"The Boones are coming over," she answered. "I've got stew on the stove and bread in the oven. See you at 5, no later." She puckered up and offered her face to him, and he gave her a self-conscious peck. The sheriff shouldn't be seen kissing his wife in public. That might make people think he's weak.

"See you later then, Sarah. Got some sheriffin' to do." What he really meant was, he had some election papers to fill out. He strode out of the tent and made his way back into town, heading straight for his office.

CHAPTER

FIVE

SUPPER WITH THE BOONES had been both happy and sad as the two families reminisced about old times and reluctantly said good-bye. The women cried, and the men rolled their eyes. Then the Boones left, and the Pages went to the revival.

Matt took his seat in the tent next to Sarah, uncomfortable in the necktie she'd made him put on. Feeling a little naked without his hat and gunbelt, he fidgeted and fretted.

"What if something happens?" he whispered.

"What could happen?" Sarah said. "Most everyone's here."

"The saloons are still full."

"They'll get along without you for an hour or two."

Matt sulked. It wasn't that he didn't want to hear the preacher; he just would rather have stood listening outside the tent, his hat on and his gun hanging from his hip, ready for action if the need arose. He felt trapped in the middle of all these people.

Soon a hush fell over the crowd as Jenny Miller, the organist from the church, made her way to the organ Reverend Benson had brought with him, an old pump job that had seen better days. She settled onto the bench and fiddled with the stops, then set her legs to pumping and began to air out the place with a rousing rendition of Charles Wesley's "Jesus, Lover of My Soul."

Jenny followed this with a tune Matt didn't recognize. Then the itinerant preacher came in through a flap at the front of the tent and mounted the platform. He looked out over the crowd as if sizing everyone up, a look of expectation on his handsome face. The air was still, the people silent as they waited for him to speak.

"Good evening, fair citizens of Bridgeport. I, Reverend Josiah W. Benson, welcome you to my humble tent. Tonight, and every night this week, we will worship the Lord our God in song, in prayer, and in teaching and will allow Him to work in us His healing power through the Holy Ghost. To begin our time together, shall we invoke our reverence for His majesty and grace with a few congregational hymns. Please turn in your songbooks to number 43, 'All Hail the Power of Jesus' Name.'"

There was a rustling of pages as the people did as instructed. Benson nodded to Jenny, she began to pump, and soon all voices were raised to the heavenly heights. Benson waved his arm and led the crowd in all four verses. Jenny was tiring already, used to her newer organ that didn't require so much work. But she didn't complain or slow down.

Two more songs followed before Reverend Benson set his hymnbook down and picked up the well-worn Bible that rested on his small lectern. Matt could see why he slept outside. What with the tent, the organ, the songbooks, and the podium, there would be little room left in Benson's wagon for him to stretch out. With a nod of his head toward her, he granted Jenny permission to take her seat in the congregation, then regarded his audience.

"Our text this evening comes from the book of Acts, chapter 2. It is a story with which you are all familiar, I'm sure. But it is nonetheless an important one, and worth the retelling over and over again, and a good Bible text to start off this revival because that is exactly what happened to the disciples there—they were revived and empowered. But first allow me to lead you in a word of prayer to our great heavenly Father."

He bowed his head and raised his arms, and the crowd bowed their heads as well, with the exception of a few men who hadn't spent much time in church and didn't understand the routine. However, a few female elbows thrust in their ribs did the trick, and all heads soon assumed a reverent posture.

"Our most gracious Lord and Father, we come to You today on bended knee, our hearts open and compliant, expecting Your grace and power to come down to us here in Bridgeport to touch us, speak to us, heal us, fill us, all in accordance with Your will and in the name of your Son, the Lord Jesus Christ, who gave His life on that cruel tree so long ago so all of us might live to serve You. We pray Your blessing on this humble servant, that his words might be Yours and that his actions might be Yours, so that all the credit will go to You, Lord Jehovah. With that we say, amen and amen."

There was a general rustling as everyone looked up, and Benson, keeping his arms raised, waited until everyone was ready. Then he lowered his arms slowly and was off and running.

And run he did, from one side of the stage to the other, as his arms flapped about to underscore and punctuate his preaching. He utilized the ramp to great effect, running and sliding down it to get within the congregation, only to turn and run back up with great clomping strides in a sort of cadence that echoed his delivery. His voice rose and fell with emotion as he ignored his intended text, telling instead the story of the sinfulness of man, starting with the original sin in the Garden of Eden by Adam and Eve, stressing the role played by the serpent, then describing what would happen to the enemy of human souls in the future. Benson waved his arms and deepened his voice as he read about the horrors to come upon Satan and all his hosts.

But he didn't stop there. He read from Scripture about what would happen to people who refuse to give themselves to God, who refuse to believe in Christ and accept His salvation. He turned to the back of his Bible and read, "'And whosoever was not found written in the book of life was cast into the lake of fire.'"

He paused, wiped the sweat from his brow, and took several deep breaths.

"But there is a way of escape, dear friends. Praise God, He has provided a way for our names to be written in the book of life. That way is through Jesus." Benson then recounted briefly the death of Christ and His magnificent resurrection, the encounters the risen Christ had with so many people, and His ascension into heaven, finally getting to the sermon itself in well over a half-hour. He slammed the Bible down on the lectern, crouched beside it, and pointed his finger while he spoke, then made his voice fade away and let silence grip the place before flipping the Bible back open and finding the appropriate passage.

As he did this, Matt hazarded a glance around. Ladies' eyes were wide, their mouths unconsciously hanging open; not a few men were clutching at their collars. If nothing else, Benson was one whale of a showman.

"My good people," Benson said quietly, "you have come here tonight to be revived, and the way to revival is through the power of the Holy Ghost. He is also the way to healing, the way to escape the things in your life that have control over you. He can get your lips off the bottle, your fingers out of other people's pockets. He can make you love your wives and honor your husbands. God can make things right, people. Your hearts, your lives, your marriages. He can make your crops grow and your cattle get fat. And the way to receive the Holy Ghost is to accept Christ as Savior, to let His death cover you with His blood and let His resurrection lift you to the heights, to the very gates of heaven itself.

"There are some people here who are not right with God. Before He will do any of those things for you, you must first get right with Him. 'How do I do that?' you ask. 'How do I get right with God?'" He paused, and a pin dropping onto the platform could have been heard as the people waited to hear how they could make their peace with God.

Benson took a breath and wiped his brow. People leaned forward, anxious to hear more. Benson had them in the palm of his hand, but he also had a week of meetings ahead of him.

"Tomorrow, dear friends," he said, "we will talk further. I fear you cannot receive it all in one sitting. You are exhausted, I can tell by looking at you. This is too much to bear in one night, too much guilt. That shall be the lesson for tomorrow. Return here, and bring someone with you who wasn't here tonight, someone who needs to get right with God. Mrs. Miller, a song please."

Just that quickly it was over, and the confused, frustrated congregation stood as Benson raised his arms. Jenny jumped up and attacked the organ, playing as though her life depended on it. After three verses Benson dismissed the meeting with prayer.

"There are baskets at the exits for your donations. All your gifts go to continue this work God has commissioned, and you'll be blessed for it. Good night."

He disappeared the same way he had come in, and the people began to file out, talking in hushed tones amongst themselves.

Matt could hear the telltale *chink* of coins dropping into the baskets as the tent emptied.

Sarah was quiet as Matt walked her home, after which he would tour the town one more time before retiring for the evening, but she could hardly suppress a smile.

"Wasn't that just a blessing?" she said as they finally went inside their little house.

"Hmm," was all he said. Matt undid his tie and pulled it off. He quickly buckled on his belt and hefted the gun, checking its chambers out of habit.

"I'll be home in an hour, Sarah. Do you think I could have a slice of your rhubarb pie when I get back?"

Sarah put her arms around him and rested her head on his chest. "Sure, honey. That's what I made it for."

He stroked her hair, then peeled her off. "Gotta go, Sarah. Stoke the fire, okay? I'll be cold."

"Wear a coat, silly."

Matt thought about a clever response but relented, pulling on his suede jacket with the fleece collar. He leaned over and kissed her forehead, then winked. "Try to think about me instead of that preacher while I'm gone, you hear?"

She slapped him playfully. "That's not it at all, Matt. I just think God's going to use him here, that's all."

"Yes, I suppose so," Matt said, "but in what way?" Without waiting for an answer he went out into the night.

Temporary Sheriff Matt Page took to the boardwalk, his horse already long since put away for the night in his stall at the livery. He entered the saloons in turn, giving them each a critical look to be sure things were quiet. Russ Draper sat quietly in the corner of one of them, nursing a half-empty bottle. He ignored the deputy, and Matt returned the favor. Matt continued up the street, rattling the doorknobs of the shops and peering at the vault door through the bank windows. All appeared to be peaceful.

Glancing down an alley, he noticed a light on in the rear of Quong Tai's General Store, formerly known as the Emporium. Checking first in the front, he saw that Quong Tai had finished his labors and was ready for his grand opening the next day. Everything appeared to be in order. Even the jars of penny candy had been filled. There'd be a line of children there tomorrow, that was for sure.

Matt stepped cautiously off the boardwalk and kept close to the building as he made his way into the alley toward the light. Quong Tai was probably just working late, attending to last-minute details, but sheriffs weren't paid to make assumptions. Matt didn't think burglars would have a light on, but he'd met some mighty stupid crooks since he first hung a badge on his shirt.

He heard talking coming from the room, the sound of chairs scooting against the boards, and glasses being poured full of what could only be rotgut. Matt peered around the edge of the window frame through the irregular, dirty glass and saw four or five men seated around a table. Quong Tai had his back to him, identifiable because of the silk skull cap and the long, black, braided queue hanging halfway down his back. To his left sat a white man Matt recognized but didn't know.

Two other men rounded out the party, one of them Sully Miller, the husband of Jenny Miller, the organ player. Matt grinned. Reverend Benson hadn't been entirely effective tonight. There was at least one man who hadn't been impressed.

The fourth man was a regular in the saloon circuit, a man just like Russell Draper—a ne'er-do-well without steady employment who was just good enough at cards to eat once a day and drink a little from time to time. He usually slept wherever he could—on a billiard table, in a hayloft, or, when he was of a mind to, in a hotel bed he had worked to earn. But that was rare.

The men were playing cards and drinking, but Matt couldn't tell who was winning. At cards, that is. They were all losers to the bottle. And because sooner or later they were all losers at cards too, it didn't matter who was currently ahead. One of them would win tonight; tomorrow it would be someone else.

Matt drew back from the window, listened a moment to make sure things were remaining on an even keel, then trudged back out onto Main Street to complete his rounds before going home to a slice of rhubarb pie, some Bible reading, and conversation with his beautiful Sarah beside the fire.

CHAPTER

SIX

THE NEXT DAY dawned like any other—the sun rising in the east. But unlike any other day, it had its own special beauty. Streaking windblown clouds criss-crossed the skies, flaming pastels bursting from God's palette. The burning sun finally crested the top of the immense Sierra Nevada mountains, drenching the snow-dusted peaks with blazing yellow pigment to replace the purples and pinks the passing clouds had sprinkled upon them.

At sunrise Matt was already up and making his rounds. He paused for a moment, awed and inspired by a God who created something just to make his children glad they'd accepted the challenge of one more day. Continuing his duties, he again found himself at the back of Quong Tai's store. Peering through the rear window, he saw that the table stood bare except for several bottles and dirty glasses, the chairs moved away from the table, evidently pushed back by the men when they left. The cards were gone, as were any chips they had used.

He planned to see Quong Tai later, to welcome him to the neighborhood and to remind him that as a good citizen a certain respect for the laws would be expected, though he would not question whether the gambling the Chinaman was engaging in was legal or not. There was no evidence the Chinaman was profiting from sponsoring the game like the owners of saloons and legal gaming tables did. For all Matt knew, it was just a friendly game among consenting men and therefore not subject to regulation.

Before the sun was high enough to warm the air more than a few degrees, Matt had completed his rounds and retired to his office. By the time the breakfast hour rolled around, Matt had disassembled his new Peacemaker, presented to him by the County Commission to replace the one taken by the Younger Brothers, and spread the pieces over a rag on his desk for cleaning. He wiped each piece with solvent and swabs until they sparkled, then rubbed a thin coat of oil on them and reassembled the gun, wiping it down, loading it with fresh ammo, and dropping it into his holster.

Even as he did so, Sarah came in with his tray. He quickly pushed everything aside, wiped his hands on a towel, and took a sniff of the morning's breakfast. The coffee Sarah brought was especially good and hot, and he savored every swallow. Even John Taylor's coming in and helping himself to a cup didn't bother Matt this morning.

"Guess what I've decided," Taylor said after making himself comfortable, this time not in Matt's chair, but only because Matt was already in it.

"I couldn't begin to," Matt answered.

"Well, I'll tell you then."

"Figured you would."

"I'm going to run for sheriff."

Matt took a sip of coffee and a bite of cinnamon roll and mumbled a noncommittal response.

"Well, ain't ya glad for me?"

"Why should I be?" Matt said. "You know darn well I'm runnin' for sheriff too."

"You are?" Taylor feigned surprise. "Well, let's keep it all in the family, I say. Don't matter who wins then."

Oh, it matters all right, Matt thought. Sarah read his face and gave him a questioning look, but Matt ignored her.

"Well, I wish you good luck," Matt said graciously, sounding very much like he was thinking, *Because you're gonna need it*.

"Why, thank you, Matt. You know, I have to tell you, you're the one who made it all possible."

"Huh?" Matt looked at him dumbly.

"It's because of you that I'm able-bodied enough to run for sheriff one more time. You bringing me back alive like you did."

Matt shrugged. "Please," he said with a wave, "I just did my job, that's all. Besides, you're my father-in-law. I certainly didn't take care of you so you could beat me out of a job." Matt grinned, but it was bittersweet.

"Daddy, you're embarrassing him," Sarah chided.

"You're right, sweetheart. Sorry, Matt."

Matt waved him off again. "You file your election papers yet?"

"Yesterday. Thought I'd call in some favors around the county so friends can campaign for me in places I can't get to."

"Well, you've got the edge on me there. Listen, if it's all the same . . . I'd rather not talk about this. I really don't want to hear your campaign strategy."

Taylor cleared his throat. "Sorry. I forgot for a second you were running against me."

I'll bet, Matt thought. *You're doing your dead-level best to discourage me, maybe even get me to drop out. Well, it ain't gonna work.*

Sarah, caught between the two most important men in her life, changed the subject. "Matt, you're coming to the revival tonight, aren't you? I mean, you don't have any work you need to do?"

Matt wanted to tell her there was something pressing to attend to, but he couldn't lie. "I'll be there."

"Daddy?"

Taylor cleared his throat. "Well, I . . . uh . . . you see . . ."

"There'll be lots of voters there," Sarah reminded him. "Exposure never hurts."

"Whose side are you on?" Matt asked.

"God's," she said diplomatically. "I'm just trying to get Daddy to the revival."

Matt grumbled, then pushed himself back from his desk, stuck his hat on his head, and ambled outside.

"I've got work to do."

He closed the door behind him and stood on the step long enough to look both directions and listen to the sounds emanating from the street and shops. All very routine sounding.

"At least Bodie had occasional moments of insanity to keep me out of the office," Matt lamented aloud as he stepped into the street.

"Bridgeport's just a pile of papers. No wonder an old man could handle the job." He kicked at the dirt and headed toward the saloons, halfway hoping a fight was brewing somewhere. Anything to take him away from the boredom and routine of paperwork.

Unfortunately, the saloons were more orderly and quiet than usual. "Too many men getting ready for the revival," commented one displeased bartender, Dave Hays. "Good thing it doesn't go on all the time."

"Well, I can't say I agree with you completely, Dave," Matt admitted. "Frankly, I wish you were all out of business. But the part about being glad the revival is only temporary . . . well, I have to go along with you on that."

"You're a regular attender at church, aren't you Depu—er, Sheriff?" the bartender asked.

"Yeah, as much as I can. But it's more than that, Dave. I'm a Christian, not just a churchgoer."

"Uh huh." Dave's expression was vacant, the bartender not understanding the distinction. "Seems like you'd be happy about the revival then."

"You'd think so," Matt said with a chuckle. "I guess it's just the lawman in me."

"How so?"

"I suspect everyone."

"You mean you think the preacher's shady? He ain't done nuthin' 'cept preach, so far as I've heard. And believe me, if he was sellin' home brew or dealin' stud, I'da heard about it."

Matt polished off the coffee he was drinking and set the mug down on the bar. "That's why I'm having such a struggle with myself, Dave. I don't know if you can understand this, but part of me is suspicious of him, and part of me wants great things to happen here because of him."

"That's a puzzle all right," Dave said, shaking his head. "But I think I understand it a little. I'm not a drinkin' man, you know. I've seen what the bottle does to a person. Yet here I am every day, pouring it for others. I feel kind of . . . guilty."

"Sell the place."

Dave shook his head again. He did a lot of that in this business. "Don't know what else I'd do. There's no work here, least not the kind I'm any good at. I'd try my hand at running a store of some kind—general merchandise, dry goods, stuff like that, but there's no real need. I was thinking about taking over for Harvey, but the Chinaman got to him first."

Matt was at a loss for words. "That's too bad. Well, at least think about what I said. I'm sure if you really want to get out, there's a way. I believe God will provide for you. I know He did for me."

"I've got two young'uns, Sheriff. I've got to work, and this is all I know."

Matt reached over the bar and clamped a hand on his friend's shoulder. "I'll be prayin' for you, Dave. Let me know if I can help."

Dave nodded, and a little smile creased his face. "Business is down because of the revival, but maybe that ain't so bad after all."

Matt winked and set a coin down on the counter. "Thanks for the coffee, Dave."

"Hey, pick that up," Dave ordered. "No lawman ever pays for his coffee in my place."

"That's part of your problem, Dave. You give away too much. Besides, I don't need charity. They pay me to be the sheriff. Buy the kids some candy." Matt smiled and hurried out before Dave could grab the coin and return it.

In the cool of the afternoon, when it was almost time for the revival, Matt decided to check in on Quong Tai, to see if the town had a general store again. He paused outside and peered through the window, half-expecting to see plucked ducks and other unidentifiable things hanging from the rafters like in Bodie's Chinese butcher shop; but it looked like any other general store he'd ever been in. Matt pushed open the door, ringing a little bell that Quong Tai had hung above it to replace the one Harvey took with him. It sounded tinny and sharp. Not at all pleasant.

At the front counter Quong Tai stood with his back to the door, busy with something. At the sound of the bell he wheeled around with a smile for the newly arriving customer.

"Please to help you," he offered. Then he saw the star on Matt's shirt, and the smile melted away. He put his hands together tightly in front of him. "Yes?" he said expectantly.

"Just wanted to drop in and say hello," the lawman told the merchant, "and to welcome you to your new store. We sort of met before, but . . . I'm Matt Page, Sheriff." He held out his hand.

Quong Tai bowed but pretended not to see the outstretched hand of the lawman. Matt shrugged and withdrew it, hanging his thumb on his gunbelt. "Good morning. Thank you," Quong Tai said, then turned and busied himself arranging a nearby shelf.

Matt couldn't tell if he meant his words as a greeting or a way of telling the sheriff to get out. He moseyed about the store, considering the differences between Quong's store and the way Harvey had set it up. Same stuff basically, just in different places. It would take the locals a few visits to get used to this, he figured, but no big deal. The prices seemed fair—a little more for this, a little less for that. He searched aimlessly through the stacks of pants and bolts of fabric and considered some colorful flannel shirts, read a few labels on tins of food, then drifted over to the counter and picked up a piece of penny candy, setting the money down on the smooth wood.

"Please to try this," Quong said, picking up a glass jar from the counter and unscrewing the top, then extending it to the sheriff. Matt looked at the pickled meat inside but shook his head.

"I'll stick with this," Matt said with a nod, sticking the candy in his mouth. "Thanks just the same." He turned to leave and doffed his hat to an incoming woman as he beamed at her, thinking, when she smiled in return, *That was another vote*. It never occurred to him that a law officer sucking on a candy stick presented a sight worth smiling at.

Quong Tai looked relieved that Matt was withdrawing. "Thank you for shopping at Quong Tai's," he told the departing lawman. "Please to help you," he said to the woman, giving her the same big smile he had almost given Matt Page.

The Chinaman waited until the door had closed, then scooted over to the window and watched the sheriff until he disappeared. Satisfied, he finally turned away from the window and again assumed a smile for his customer, though it was a nervous smile at best. Once the woman had made her selections and money had changed hands, she left Quong Tai alone in his store. He retreated to the rear room, busied himself noisily for a few moments, then came back out, his face visibly relaxed and his hands still. The smile was gone, replaced by drawn, closed lips that revealed nothing. He settled onto a stool by the counter where he was afforded a clear view of the street. Hoping for more customers, he sat watching, staring, waiting.

CHAPTER

SEVEN

S arah was waiting for Matt when he returned to his office.
"Hello, Matt." She smiled coyly.

"Hi, Sarah." He leaned over to give her an inviting kiss, but out
of the corner of his eye he saw his father-in-law lurking behind the
door, sitting on a chair by the window. Matt caught himself and
pecked his wife's forehead, leaving her with an unfulfilled pucker
and a puzzled look.

"Howdy, Matt," Taylor said cheerfully.

"Still here? You must be feelin' better."

"Yes, as a matter of fact I am. Much better, thank you."

Matt hadn't meant it as encouragement, just a statement of
fact, and it irritated him that Taylor took it the way he did. He
wanted to point that out but thought better of it and kept his
peace. Hanging his hat on a nail, he took his seat in his chair that
for once Taylor was not occupying. Sarah followed Matt and stood
next to him, stroking his hair.

"You know, I've been thinking . . ." Taylor said.

Since when? "What about?" Matt asked, disinterested.

"We need to reorganize law enforcement here in Mono County,
make it more effective."

"That supposed to mean somethin'?" Matt asked suspiciously.

"No, not at all. It just seems like the county's growing so fast,
we need to change with the times."

"I'm sure you have some ideas on how to do that."

"Yeah, I do. But I thought I'd get your opinion, seein' how you've worked pretty much all over the county at one time or another. You've gotten around, seen more than I have in recent days."

That was true enough, Matt knew. Maybe the old boy was finally beginning to realize that someone besides himself might have an idea or two. But why tell him? Matt was saving that for his campaign.

"Maybe I've gotten around," Matt admitted, "but I've been a little too busy to be thinking of ways to do your job. Until a few months ago I didn't need to think along those lines."

Taylor let it go at that, knowing Matt was cagey and wouldn't give anything away. There wasn't much reason to hang around.

"Well, I've got to be going."

"Don't let the door hit you on the—"

"Matt!" Sarah chided.

"Just lookin' out for his safety," he told Sarah unconvincingly.

"I get the hint," Taylor said, pushing himself slowly out of the chair, grimacing at the pain in his back.

"Need some help, sir?" Matt asked.

"No thanks. I'm fine."

"Daddy—"

"Don't 'Daddy' me, Sarah. I'll be fine. Just a little twinge. Doc says I'll be rid of that in no time. Be fit as a fiddle."

"Yes, but will you be fit as a sheriff?" Matt asked.

"Never you mind."

"I'm gonna bring it up during the campaign, you might as well know that," Matt admitted candidly.

"Matt!" Sarah scolded.

"Look, Sarah," Matt pointed out, speaking to her as though Taylor wasn't standing there, "he decided to run against me after he announced he would have to retire. Qualifications are what campaigns are all about."

"Don't you go makin' me into a cripple, Matt," Taylor ordered. "I ain't one, and you know it."

"No, but that don't make you fit to be sheriff. There's more to it than brains—"

"Lucky for you."

"You know, I wasn't going to make a big deal out of your physical limitations, but after a crack like that—"

"Daddy, Matt, you two stop this right now." Sarah stomped her foot, an action that in another situation would have caused both her husband and father to break out in laughter. Instead, both of them looked down at their shoes.

"Sorry, hon," Matt said finally, not really meaning it and making no attempt to apologize to Taylor.

Taylor just grunted, then adjusted his Montana hat and limped out of the office.

"I hate this," Sarah confided to her husband when her father was gone.

Matt only shrugged. "It's not my fault," he mumbled.

"You two used to be such good friends."

"Things have changed. He used to be my boss, but now he's laid up. I'm sheriff, but he's still tryin' to run things."

"He ran things for years, and he's still the elected sheriff."

"I know, I know. Everyone keeps remindin' me. Even the dog that hangs around outside barks at me like he don't know me. What your pa needs to realize is there can't be division like this. He should be supportin' me, not makin' my job more difficult. The County Commission made me sheriff while he's on leave; so he's just another civilian on the county dole. If he wants to run for another term, which is contrary to what he said, then he's gonna have to earn the win. I'm not gonna hand it to him. At first I was only runnin' because you and Harvey and a lot of other folk talked me into it . . . includin' your father, I might add. Now I think it's the right thing to do."

"Yes, Daddy encouraged you to think about running for sheriff. But that was when he was feeling bad and thought he was going to die."

"Die? Your father die? Didn't you notice, as soon as he saw me sportin' the sheriff's badge, he healed right up. The problem with him is, he never really liked me, he just couldn't help but hire me on, he couldn't think of a way to talk you out of marryin' me, and now he's afraid I'll take over and make him look bad. As long as I'm in town, he ain't gonna die, Sarah."

"Well, anyway, this bickering doesn't become you, Matt. It isn't

. . . Christian." She had Matt there, and he knew it. So he did what men usually do when women are right—he ignored the comment.

"I'm just upset at how he's been hangin' around here, tryin' to run things, like he don't trust me."

"He trusts you, Matt, it's just that he . . . he doesn't like thinking of himself as helpless."

"That ain't my problem."

"No, I suppose not . . ." She got up and looked out the window. "I'm worried about him, Matt."

"Why? He seems okay to me."

"He hasn't been himself since he got shot."

"Big surprise. A bullet in the back will do that to a man."

"Yes, but being dependent first on you, then on Ma, just to stay alive . . . that did something to him. He needs to feel like he's useful again. He's not ready to be put out to pasture."

"This sounds like somethin' your ma ought to be worryin' herself about, not you. You're my wife, Sarah, and you're supposed to be helpin' *me*. You left your father and mother to marry me, remember?"

"You're right, Matt," she admitted quietly. Sarah moved noiselessly to his side and bent over, putting her arms around him and giving him a slow kiss on his rough cheek. "Just be kind to Daddy, okay?"

Matt couldn't say no. "All right, Sarah, all right. Listen, I don't hate him. I just don't want him treatin' me like I don't know what I'm doin', that's all."

"I'll speak to Ma, see if she'll put a bug in his ear."

"Good luck."

Sarah spun quickly and sat in Matt's lap. "Now, let's hear your plans for the county for when you get elected," she asked with a bright smile.

Matt smiled back. "That's more like it. First off, we need more men. A resident deputy in each town of, say, more than 300 people—Coleville, Mono, Lundy. And Bodie's growin' by leaps and bounds; two men ain't enough. What we need is someone in charge to act as a police chief, with several officers under his command, enough to police the town day and night. With Bodie set to boom, if something ain't done soon, it's gonna be one hellacious place."

"How does Daddy feel about this?"

"I don't know. I haven't mentioned it to him. And I'd appreciate it if you'd—"

The door opened, and Taylor returned. Sarah jumped off Matt's lap in a reflex action, but doing so made her look guilty.

"Sorry, I forgot my—say, what's going on in here?" Taylor inquired. "Look, you two, I may not be the active sheriff, but I can tell you as a taxpayer that I don't cotton to no hanky-panky while you're on duty."

"Daddy, I was just talking to him."

"You don't have to answer him," Matt told her. "It's none of his business."

"Oh, excuse me," Taylor remarked. "I seem to recall that I'm the elected sheriff and you were my deputy, which makes what you do my business. My, we're getting uppity now that we're the *temporary* sheriff, aren't we?"

"You're the elected sheriff, that's true," Matt said. "But you're on leave because of your injury, which means you have no legal authority, in case you've forgotten. And what's more, I don't think I like your attempt to control what I do, seein' I'm gonna be runnin' against you in the election. With all due respect, sir, I believe you're tryin' to manipulate me to your advantage."

"Matt! Daddy!" Sarah scolded. "I thought we settled this earlier!"

"He's the one came back and started bossin' me around again," Matt said.

"That's it, Matt," Taylor said, stressing the point with his index finger. The action tweaked his back, and he quickly grabbed it with the other hand without breaking stride or missing a beat in his oration. "All bets are off. My best against your best. And may the best man get reelected."

"Can't happen," Matt asserted. "I ain't been elected the first time yet."

"So smug," Taylor muttered. He turned to Sarah. "I'm glad you married him, not me."

"Me too," Matt said. "I've eaten your cookin'."

"Insufferable." Taylor started to leave, muttering to himself, then stopped, turned, and flung the gauntlet. "Public debate, Matthew, one on one, a week from Sunday, at five o'clock. On the steps of the hotel so the whole town can listen."

"Fine," Matt said. "Bring a chair so you can rest your aging back."

"Yeah? Well, you best be ready to be whupped in public." Taylor stormed out of the office, slamming the door behind him. Matt and Sarah were silent for a moment before Matt remarked, "I feel much better now. How about you?"

Taylor sat in his parlor, puffing his pipe furiously, his brows trying their best to join in the center. He hadn't even taken off his hat. Irene Taylor, knowing better than to interrupt him when he was in a mood like this, busied herself in the kitchen with supper preparations. She even tried humming as a way of leading her husband out of his angry fog, but he wasn't listening to anything except his own thoughts.

An hour passed before his mood was broken by the opening of the front door. Sarah barely stuck her face into the front room.

"Don't shoot, Daddy, it's me."

"He send you over to spy?"

"Daddy!" Sarah came in and closed the door. "You know better than that. I know you two are feuding right now, but that doesn't mean you should bite *my* head off." She said it sweetly, and Taylor's face relaxed.

"I'm sorry, honey." He put down his pipe and tossed his hat toward the hat rack, missing it by four feet and causing a twinge of pain in his back. "Come here."

Sarah obeyed, and he gave her a fatherly peck on the cheek.

"That's better," Sarah told him. She sat on the arm of the chair. "You know, Daddy, Matt really isn't like you think he is. He's just under a lot of pressure right now, and he thinks you're looking over his shoulder all the time."

"I am."

"You shouldn't be."

The voice was Irene Taylor's, coming into the room as she wiped her hands.

"Aw, now you're gangin' up on me," Taylor complained.

"Give him some room, John," Irene suggested, braver now that she had reinforcements. "I'll bet you'd be surprised what he can do. Let your career speak for you in the election. Matt's new here; not too many folks know him real well. They've pretty much forgotten his heroics of last year."

"That's right," Sarah said.

"Whose side are you on?" Taylor asked his daughter.

"Matt's, of course. But I'm not against you. You're my daddy."

"You're burnin' your candle at both ends, little girl."

"No, she isn't," Irene defended. "She's just trying to stay kind of neutral, as much as that's possible. Stop making it hard for her by trying to divide her affections."

"Ideally," Sarah reflected, "you two would make a good team. You should listen to him sometime. He's not a kid. He has some good ideas."

"Like what?"

"Like how to set up a police force in Bodie, which it really needs."

"Police force?"

"Sure. A deputy sheriff in charge and a group of officers working twenty-four hours a day. Bodie's really growing, Daddy. Two men just aren't going to be enough in a few months. Maybe even in a few weeks."

Taylor was pensive. "Anything else?"

"Oh, sure. Lots," said Sarah proudly. "Lots."

Sarah had been quiet all during supper. That was okay with Matt; he didn't feel much like conversing. It was one thing to be in the middle of an election fight, but when your opponent was your wife's father . . . well, that made the whole thing doubly difficult. They both enjoyed the silence as they walked from their little house to the field filled with Reverend Benson's huge, colorful tent.

Matt and Sarah found their way to their seats through the murmuring crowd. Nodding greetings to several men, Matt quickly settled into his chair, still smarting over the afternoon's skirmish with his father-in-law. As he waited for the service to begin, he buried his face in his Bible, not wanting even to see John Taylor when he arrived.

Jenny Miller was again at the organ, playing favorite hymns to set the mood as the people filed in. They responded by confining their visiting to the out-of-doors, becoming reverent and silent as they passed through the flaps of the tent. Soon they were all in place, and the charismatic Josiah Benson mounted the platform. The congregation fell silent as he opened a songbook.

"Number 32," he said, and pages rustled in response. "Please rise."

After Jenny played a few bars of introduction, Benson's arm began to wave, and his booming baritone voice filled the tent. Soon the people of Bridgeport, who had left homes and saloons to listen to the traveling preacher, were worshiping God in song. When they had sung all the verses of four hymns, Benson closed his book and excused Jenny with a nod and a smile. He hooked his thumbs in the pockets of his brocade vest and stood at the edge of the platform, his smiling eyes scrutinizing the expectant faces of the faithful. Finally, after just about everyone had been made uneasy, he spoke, his voice quiet and subdued, a sharp contrast to the raucous shouting and theatrics of the first night.

Matt listened intently, but with a critical ear, as Benson laid out simply the reason Christ died on the cross and why, upon His ascension, He sent "the Comforter," as Christ called the Holy Spirit. He spoke of how all Christians are given the Spirit at the moment of their salvation and could be filled with the Spirit and His power whenever the need arose. Quite unlike his first sermon, Benson's second was far less theatrical and moving, but much more informative. In a surprisingly short time, he was finished, and the people were standing and singing the closing hymn, then filing out into the night.

Matt's mood had improved during the service, and as he and Sarah walked arm in arm from the tent he made a suggestion. "What say we go to the hotel for a slice of their pie?"

"My pie not good enough for you?"

"My word, Sarah!" Matt protested. "Of course your pie is as good. Better! But we don't have any pie at home, remember? I ate it all yesterday. Besides, I thought going to the hotel would be special."

Sarah smiled up at him. "I'm sorry, Matt. Yes, that would be nice. Thank you."

"That's better."

They turned and went back up the street, but before arriving at the hotel they noticed a small crowd gathering in front of the Bridgeport Pharmacy. Someone was standing on the boardwalk addressing them, and as they moved closer they recognized the tall frame and distinctive voice of John Taylor. He was delivering an impromptu campaign speech. Matt stopped at the edge of the crowd to listen.

"And furthermore, I propose a restructuring of my office to accommodate the recent changes in our population."

"What kind of restructuring, John?" the editor of the Bridgeport newspaper asked, his pad and pencil ready.

"Well, I can't tell you the details yet, because it would have to be approved by the County Commission. But I can tell you that part of it will involve Bodie, whose population is skyrocketing thanks to new strikes being recorded nearly every day. I will propose a deputy to be stationed there, in charge of a cadre of police officers who will handle everything in town and its immediate vicinity, giving twenty-four hour service."

This prompted murmuring and head-nodding from most of the crowd and note-taking by the newsman. Matt's eyes grew wide as he turned his head slowly to gaze in wonder at Sarah. She stared straight ahead, her face flushed, afraid to look at her husband. He eased his arm out of hers and backed away a couple of steps, then turned on his heel and walked away, leaving her standing alone on the street.

CHAPTER

EIGHT

THE CRY OF ALARM was so shrill, Matt's head jerked up fast enough to send a sliver of pain into the base of his skull. He'd slept in his office all night, and his neck was stiff. Nevertheless, he jumped up from his chair without grabbing his hat and ran outside to see who was being murdered, unconsciously rubbing the back of his neck with his left hand as he drew his Colt's revolver with his right. Alone when he went to sleep, he was still alone when awakened by the cry. His last argument with Taylor had kept his father-in-law away. Sarah also had not made an appearance.

Several citizens with horrified looks on their faces and with mouths agape stared up Main Street. Following their gaze, Matt saw several horsemen crossing the bridge. No, it was more than several. There were ten, twenty . . . upwards of fifty riders coming into town. Perhaps more, if there were stragglers.

And they weren't cowboys looking to whoop it up after branding the entire herd, or conventioneers in their Knights Templar regalia. They were Indian braves—Paiutes, though from the look of them not local Paiutes. Some of them wore the same type of clothing as the locals—white man's garb; but most did not, preferring their handmade trousers and blankets instead of wool pants and coats. They were obviously well-armed, though not aggressive in their posture. The only sounds were hoofbeats and the blowing of the tired horses.

For many Bridgeport residents, the Indian war of the previous decade was too recent for an arrival like this not to bring with it a deep sense of foreboding. As had happened when the Wild Man came to town, the citizens scurried away. Only this time Matt could hear doors slamming and locks being thrown. He could imagine guns being taken down and loaded.

As he watched the Indians make their way toward him, Matt remained in the center of the street, suddenly conscious of the heavy iron he held in his right hand. As discreetly as possible he slipped it back into its holster. Even if the Indians were looking for a fight, one revolver wouldn't be much use against fifty or sixty armed braves. Matt hailed the men as they approached. He kept his smile at the ready but did not put it on.

The Indian who rode in front came right up to Matt before he slid off his unsaddled pinto. He approached the lawman with respect in his walk and countenance. Short and thin, with a dark, wrinkled face, the Indian wore leather breeches and no shirt. A blanket was draped around his shoulders, tied at the throat by a leather thong passed through two ragged holes.

"Good morning," Matt said, assuming the man spoke English. It seemed a safe bet since he was the one who had approached him.

The Indian nodded. "We look for Poker Tom," he said unceremoniously, getting right to the point.

"Matt Page, Sheriff," Matt said, establishing his credentials and extending his hand. The Indian took it.

"White man call me Captain John," the Paiute said, obviously the leader of this band. Matt had heard of him. He was from Nevada; his father was Captain Truckee and had been a scout for John Fremont. The Indian leader wore a brown feather tipped with white in the band of his old bowler.

"Captain John, I haven't seen Poker Tom for a long time."

"He no return, many week now."

"Is that unusual?"

"Poker Tom like drink, it is true. But he always come home to wives. They miss him much. They say he no come back because he dead."

"If you don't mind, Captain," Matt said slowly, his face drawn, "why do you need so many men to look for one brave? Poker Tom is a man—he can look out for himself. Maybe he got drunker than usual."

"Maybe. But we know he come to trade with yellow man, buy cloth for wives to make new clothes."

"Who?"

"Chinee man."

"You must mean Quong Tai."

Captain John dipped his head once. "Chinee man sell to Paiute. And he have poker game in back when store close. Poker Tom play there before. We think maybe he play that night, then something happen."

Matt thought back to the other evening and the poker game in the back. He wondered if there could be something to Captain John's theory. "Well, I still don't think any harm's come to him, leastwise not so's you'd need so many braves to take care of it," he said to the Paiute. He thought for a second and added, "Pardon me for saying so, Captain, but could it be he decided to find a new wife? Maybe he met someone, and they went away together."

Captain John shook his head and motioned to a man near him, who slid down from his horse and brought a heavy sack to the Indian leader. Captain John set it on the ground, then opened it. Matt leaned over to take a closer look at a mass he couldn't immediately identify. His face blanched, and he inhaled sharply as he realized what he was seeing—a headless, limbless human torso, the flesh swollen and discolored from untold days in water.

"Where'd you find that?" the horrified lawman asked. "And how do you know it's Tom's?"

"Billy Shoes hunting rabbit yesterday, three miles upstream in canyon, find on bank of creek."

"What makes you think it's Tom's?" Matt asked again. In spite of an intense desire not to do so, he took another look at the body.

"Wives say so." That was obviously good enough for Captain John, but Matt couldn't see how even his wives could tell whose body this was, it was so decomposed.

Captain John read Matt's reluctance to accept the identification and pointed to an area on the chest. "Annie Tom get mad at Poker Tom when him get new wife." John managed a fleeting smile. "She jealous squaw, Annie Tom."

"Most women are," Matt agreed. *Especially under those circumstances.*

There was indeed a mark of some kind there, but to Matt it could have been where the torso had rested against a rock or received a wound from the river bottom. He wasn't convinced, not without something more positive. Of course, as far as he knew, no one from town was missing, so the body couldn't be explained that way. "Okay," Matt relented, "maybe it is Poker Tom. I still don't think it's a good idea for you and all your men to come to Bridgeport like this. If a crime has occurred—and I don't know that it has—maybe Tom fought a bear or something, I don't know . . . If there's been foul play, our laws will take care of the problem. I'll find the person responsible, and justice will be done."

Captain John motioned for the brave to cover the remains and shook his head. "Not good. We know white man's laws. They like little baby. All noise and no teeth."

"Even so, I can't let you storm through town. There's liable to be shootin' before you find the man responsible, and many people would die—some Indian, some white. People here are afraid of you when so many come, especially with vengeance on your minds. I'm afraid someone'll go off half-cocked out of fear, and that'll explode the whole mess."

Captain John was silent, weighing the white law officer's words. Matt had one more card to play.

"Tell you what, Captain John. You know Charlie Jack, don't you?"

"Yes. He friend of Nevada Paiute."

"He's my friend too. You can ask him about me. On my word as a friend of Charlie Jack, I'll ask around and see if I can find out what happened to Poker Tom, okay? It's not that we don't want you fellas in town, you understand, but the way you rode in makes everyone here a little nervous. You savvy?"

"Friend of Charlie Jack is friend of Captain John. I hear of you, Matt Page, the way you treat all men same. Your word is good to us. Okay, we go. You find killer of Poker Tom. We return two days. Camp upriver." He pointed toward the Walker River, indicating they'd go somewhere out of town. But not too far out, Matt surmised. They'd expect some results—and soon. This many Paiutes traveling this far . . . obviously they meant business.

Matt nodded. "We have a deal. I'll start working on it right now. Uh, is there anything I can get you fellas while you're waiting?"

"No, thank you, Sheriff. We have much." He turned to leave, and two braves jumped forward to reclaim the corpse. But Matt held them off with a raised hand, then explained to Captain John how they'd need the body so the coroner—a kind of medicine man—could examine it.

"He can tell us many things, maybe even who killed Poker Tom."

Captain John appeared concerned. "We must bury him our way, so his spirit not roam."

"I understand. As soon as the doc is done . . . how about giving him the same two days you're giving me? . . . then you can have him back. Fair enough?"

"Two days," Captain John reminded Matt. He pivoted his horse, and the others followed suit. In a few moments all that was left of the party was a cloud of dust and the memory of the muffled clamping of their unshod horses on the wooden bridge.

With their departure Bridgeport once again came to life, though slowly at first, just to be sure the Indians were gone. Matt wasted no time getting down to business, quickly yet reluctantly hauling his prize to Doc Keebles's place. By the time he came back outside, life in Bridgeport had returned to normal.

His next stop was Ah Quong Tai's store.

The store owner was busy with a customer when Matt entered, so the lawman walked casually over to the shelves of clothing and fingered through the shirts, trying to keep a discreet eye on Quong Tai. The Chinaman, suspicious of the sheriff, helped a woman pick just the right bolt of calico while his narrow eyes nervously flittered back and forth between her and Matt.

"Are you listening?" she asked him testily. "That's red. I distinctly asked for the blue."

"Huh?" Quong Tai looked down at the bolt he held, then up at the woman. "Many pardons. Quong Tai make mistake. I listen good, but not look when choose. Please to forgive." He bowed several times and replaced the red calico with the blue, from which he quickly measured three yards out for her.

"Check that again please," she said just as he prepared to cut the fabric. "I think it slipped a little when you measured—it's under three yards."

"No, not slip," Quong Tai insisted. He hazarded a glance at the lawman, but Matt had moved out of the Chinaman's sight, further frazzling the poor man's nerves.

"Well, if it didn't slip, you pulled it back. Measure it again."

"You not believe Quong Tai, maybe you go to other store." The storekeeper had apparently had enough.

"You know good and well, Mr. Tai, there is no other store. Now, are you going to remeasure it or not?"

Quong Tai rattled off a sentence or two in Chinese—or it could have been a couple words, neither Matt nor the woman could tell—as he yanked the material back and measured it once again, letting the woman put her nose down to it to verify the amount, then mark it herself with the scissors.

"There. That's the right amount."

Quong Tai mumbled something else that Matt didn't understand, though the words were familiar. The lawman had heard them many times in Mr. Song's opium den back in Bodie—while he was clearing it of addicts and ne'er-do-wells. Matt suppressed a grin. If only the woman knew what Quong Tai was saying. For that matter, if Matt knew, he'd probably run the Chinaman in on a public decency violation.

Finally satisfied she had gotten what she'd asked for, the woman paid for her paper-wrapped bundle and trudged out of the store, vowing to tell her friends to beware in case Quong Tai tried to cheat them as well. Quong Tai had almost forgotten the sheriff as he stood at the counter, mopping his forehead with a handkerchief while glaring at the retreating matron. He almost fell down when he heard Matt suddenly step around a shelf of kitchen implements just a few feet from the Chinaman. Quong Tai whipped his head around at the scuff of boots on the floor, and his long queue followed, slapping him in the face.

He's definitely disturbed about something, Matt thought, though with Chinamen it was hard to tell, the way they always moved in such sudden, unpredictable fashion and were always bowing and apologizing even when they hadn't done anything wrong. Maybe this one just wasn't used to lawmen.

"What you want?" Quong Tai asked abruptly, almost accusingly.

"Whoa, pal," Matt said softly. "Stand down from your high horse. I'm not here to do anything against you."

Quong Tai's shoulders drooped perceptibly, and his face relaxed. He lowered his head. "Sorry, Mister Sheriff," he said, his accent thick. "She make threat to me, I do nothing."

"Don't worry about Mrs. Grambs, Mr. Tai. She's all steam and no pistons."

Quong Tai regarded Matt blankly.

"All jabber and no action."

The Chinaman still didn't understand.

"She won't do anything. Her threats are empty."

"Oh." Quong Tai nodded, then began shaking his head without explaining what that meant. Matt didn't ask. Some things were better left unknown.

"What sheriff want? Need bullets? Can of peaches?"

"No thanks," Matt said. "What I want are answers. I need to ask you about someone."

"I know no one but Chinese . . . and customers."

"That's not true," Matt said. "You know several men, very well in fact. You entertained them the other night in a game of poker, in your back room."

"How you . . . No, no poker here." He shook his head some more.

"Well, Mr. Tai, I don't want to have an argument over that point, it'll just waste time. You were without a doubt running a poker game in your back room. I saw you through the window while I was doing my rounds."

"Poker legal—"

"Look, Mr. Tai, I don't care that you were playin' poker. I just want to ask you some questions. Have you had any other games? Say, a few weeks ago?" Quong Tai appeared about to begin shaking his head again, so Matt stopped him with a raised index finger. "The truth, Quong Tai. All I need to do is ask around."

"Yes, I have other games. So?"

"Did Poker Tom ever play?"

"Poker Tom? Who Poker Tom?"

"An Indian. Surely you'd remember him."

"Don't ask name."

"How many Indians play in your backroom poker games?" Matt was beginning to get testy, and he raised his voice.

"Many Indian play poker, come to my store to buy. They not go Boone's Emporium. I no remember one Indian. They all alike to me." He swept his hand backward in front of his face, then flipped it over his shoulder, brushing off the question. "Anyway, what so special about this Poker Tom?"

"He's disappeared."

"What sheriff mean, disappeared?"

"Never came home."

"Good!" Quong Tai spat, then shrugged. "Poker Tom Indian. Where he go, Quong Tai doesn't know. Why should I care?"

"He was supposed to come here and buy some calico from you for his wives," Matt told him.

"He never come. That all Quong Tai know. Now, you go please. Drive customer away." Quong Tai turned to busy himself with some task.

"Okay," Matt said. "But I'll be back. I don't believe you've been completely truthful with me." He turned and strode out of the store, never looking back. Quong Tai didn't watch him leave, though he did steal a glance out the window after he was sure the lawman was gone.

Frank Pascoe, standing silent and out of sight around a shelf while he eavesdropped on the lawman and the Chinaman, now hurried outside and raced up the street in the opposite direction.

CHAPTER

NINE

SARAH SNIFFED, then sipped the strong brewed tea her mother had made for her. She sat on the edge of an upholstered chair in the Taylor parlor, the chair her father generally considered his and his alone. But John Taylor was not home. He'd stormed off to find Matt after hearing that the acting sheriff was conducting a murder investigation without informing him. Frank had come through for him again. It paid to have folk who'd keep tabs on others and let you know what they're up to.

Irene Taylor took a place on the sofa, hoping to console her distraught daughter. Irene wasn't a pretty woman, not in the classic sense of the word. But she had nicely proportioned features—lovely, dark brown hair bordering on red; smiling hazel eyes with crow's feet at the outside corners; an ample figure, always attractive yet modestly concealed under simple clothing, most of which she made herself. Today she wore a cotton print house dress covered by a white full apron tied in back, with lace around the perimeter of the bodice. On her face she wore a deeply etched frown of concern for her daughter.

"Oh, Mama," Sarah moaned, "I've really done it this time. He'll never forgive me."

"Nonsense, Sarah. He'll understand you were defending him, that you're just proud of him."

"That doesn't excuse what I did, telling Daddy everything."

"No," Irene admitted, "it doesn't. But what's done is done, and you weren't being malicious, just a little . . . careless. He'll forgive you, I tell you."

Sarah sighed and took another sip of tea. "He didn't come home all night."

"He was upset, Sarah. He felt . . . betrayed. The Bible says a brother offended is harder to win than a fortified city. How else can I say it? You're his pride and joy, and you turned on him. I know you didn't do it on purpose, but sometimes our motives are of no consequence when we've wronged someone. Regardless of intention, what hurts hurts."

"I understand, Mama. But where did he go?" She burst into more tears, her mind overwrought with the possibilities.

"Now don't you fret about that. You know Matt better than that. He spent the night in his office, honey. I was looking out through the window when the Indians rode into town, and I saw him come out onto the street. It was obvious he'd been sleeping there."

"He won't trust me ever again."

"He loves you, Sarah. He's just under a lot of pressure right now. What's happened won't last forever."

Sarah was inconsolable despite her mother's efforts, so the elder woman took Sarah into her arms and tried to comfort her silently. After Sarah's grief had calmed some, Irene spoke. "Give him time, honey. He'll miss you. He'll be home soon, mark my words. After all, he's just down the street. But you need to be there when he comes back. Don't go trying to find him—he's busy, and he'll feel coerced. Let your reconciliation be his idea. He walked away, and he'll return when he's ready. Then you can ask his forgiveness."

Sarah looked up at her mother, her cheeks glistening with her sorrow. "I hope you're right."

"He's a Christian, Sarah, and a good man. He'll be back. He's just upset right now; he's trying to sort things out. On top of that, he has a lot of responsibilities around here." She leaned forward and lowered her voice, as though the walls had ears. "And your father hasn't been making it any easier, that much I know. Now scoot—don't sit around here feeling sorry for yourself. Go home, ask God to forgive you, then bake something and fix yourself up for the reunion. Shoo!" She pushed Sarah out the door much like she would a reluctant hound during a rainstorm, then watched through the curtain, biting her lower lip as her daughter hurried home.

A determined and angry John Taylor stomped up the boardwalk as fast as his legs—and back—would carry him, his jaw set because his teeth were clenched.

"Matt Page!" he called, but his son-in-law kept walking ahead of him, not even turning his head. Taylor sped up, wincing a little at the effort, then gained a few feet and shouted again, so loudly that a man ahead of Matt swung his head to see what was going on. Matt had no choice but to stop, though he still refused to turn and face Taylor.

"Deputy, what's the meaning of this?"

Matt's response was slow, his voice restrained, his face expressionless. "What's the meaning of what?"

"You know what. You startin' an important investigation without talkin' to me first. A murder!" Taylor immediately lowered his voice. "A murder. Why on earth do you think—"

"In case you forgot, *I* am the sheriff," Matt said calmly, refusing to let his anger rise to the surface. "By emergency order of the County Commission you have no official capacity. Why do we have to keep goin' over the same ground, Mr. Taylor?"

That stung the elder man. *Mr.* Taylor? That was an insult if he'd ever heard one.

"Look, *Deputy* Page, this sounds like a serious matter that could have long-lastin' ramifications for the citizens of Bridgeport."

"That sounds like a campaign speech."

"It's the truth, and you know it. Any time sixty armed Indians ride into town, it's important."

Matt shrugged. "I didn't have time to look you up. Besides, why didn't you come on out when the Indians showed up? Everyone in town knew they rode in."

"Never you mind where I was. The point is, once you found out what they wanted and they left, you had time to get word to me, to let me know what was going on."

"And who told you I was investigatin' a murder? It's just a disappearance."

"With a dismembered body?"

Matt's expression soured as he caught sight of Frank Pascoe lurking in the shadows of the alley across the street. Matt shot a glare at him, and the man immediately looked away and hurried off.

Matt sighed. "It never crossed my mind to tell you. I was focused on doin' my job, that's all. It wasn't intentional . . ." Matt's eyes narrowed. "But then again, you usin' my ideas that Sarah told you about in a campaign speech . . . that was pretty . . . well, I don't know what word to use, but I didn't like it. Ask Sarah how happy I was when I heard it."

"Don't you do nothin' to my little gir—"

"You're little girl is my wife, Sheriff, and it ain't none of your business what I do. That much I can tell you. It's not me she needs to be worried about, though—it's you. Usin' your daughter to advance your political ambitions . . . why, that's downright . . . underhanded, that's what it is."

"I didn't do nothin' of the kind. She came to me and volunteered the information. But just for the record, what makes you think you're the only one with ideas? For all you know, I had the same idea before she ever opened her mouth. Maybe you heard me say it in my fever when I had a bullet in my back."

"Well, I didn't. And as to you having that idea already, that'll be a little tough to prove."

"I feel no need to try. I've done nothin' wrong. But enough of that for now . . . Just what are you up to?"

Matt was tired of the argument. It wasn't improving their relationship, and it wasn't helping him find Poker Tom's killer—if indeed the body was Poker Tom's. Deciding to just let their differences be for the time being, he took a deep breath.

"I'm tryin' to find out what I can about Poker Tom. Captain John said they found his body in a river. He was last known to be at Quong Tai's store, maybe in a poker game in the back room. I saw a game goin' on there the other night. One of the players was Sully Miller. Thought I'd start with him, see if he was there the night Poker Tom disappeared."

"I'm comin' along."

"Suit yourself. I can't stop you. But I'd appreciate it if you'd stay out of my way."

"Yeah, as if I've never done this before."

"That ain't the point. It's on *my* shoulders right now. If the investigation goes to the dogs, I'll be the one to take the blame."

Taylor stifled a smile, wanting to make a wisecrack, but knowing that would just hurt his cause.

"Okay, Matt," he relented, "you do what you have to. But I'm gonna speak up if I need to. I haven't been a lawman for all these years so I could play second fiddle to you . . . or to anyone else for that matter."

Matt turned on his heel and walked away, neither inviting Taylor along nor doing anything to keep him from it. The elder lawman followed silently.

Any other time Matt would've welcomed Taylor's help, even turned the investigation over to him altogether if he could. He knew that youth and grit go only so far; experience and savvy get the tough jobs done. But having Taylor tag along today was like trying to eat cake while you're still choking on a piece of steak. Cake always tastes good, but the timing is wrong.

Their first stop was Pringle's butcher shop, where Sully Miller spent his days cutting meat for Sam Pringle. Matt didn't know much about the husband of the church organist, except that most of his religion was in his wife's name. The lawman stepped inside and scoured the shop, seeing the racks of various cuts of beef and lamb adorned with signs declaring it to be locally grown, along with the usual plucked fowl—chickens and geese—hanging behind the meat counter.

A special glass-fronted case full of ice, brought in from higher elevations each morning by an enterprising young lad, displayed the previous day's catch of local lake and brook trout. Sausages of pork and beef and blood made by Sully Miller himself decorated another part of the shop. And there he stood in the midst of his handiwork, wiping his hands on his bloody apron. Sully's smile faded when he saw Matt Page's hard-set face.

"What's this all about?" he asked the acting sheriff, eyeing Taylor over Matt's shoulder.

"I'd like to ask you a few questions."

"What about?"

"Maybe we could go in the back."

"Am I in trouble or something? What have I—"

"You haven't done anything that we know of," Taylor interrupted, drawing a cold stare from Matt. Undaunted, Taylor continued, "And we don't suspect that you're guilty of anything."

"Then why—"

"Please, Mr. Miller," Matt implored. "The back room? Just in case someone else walks in on this conversation." Matt's eyes flickered at Taylor for an instant.

"Okay, sure." Miller put down his cleaver and wiped his hands on his apron again, something he'd obviously done many times before, then led the lawmen into the small, dark room at the back of the shop. He raised the blind on a tiny window, allowing a square shaft of gray light to filter in through the dirty, flawed glass.

"Hardly ever do that." He grinned apologetically as the movement of the blind raised a silvery haze of dust that sparkled in the light from the window. "Now, what's the big secret?"

"Do you know Poker Tom, a Paiute?" Matt asked.

"Poker Tom." Miller repeated the name thoughtfully, as though the sound of it would spark some recognition. "Poker Tom. No, can't say that I do."

"He was the Indian playing poker with you at Quong Tai's place some weeks ago, don't know exactly how many." Matt wasn't sure Sully had been there that night but thought the gamble was worth a try.

Miller did his best to look blankly at Matt, but a flicker of concern twitched his brow.

"No . . ." he said slowly. "I don't believe I . . . Poker at Quong Tai's? I don't . . . What are you . . . Does Quong Tai have poker games?"

John Taylor cleared his throat.

"Listen, Sully, I don't know what Deputy Page is gettin' at exactly, but it's obvious you know more than you're lettin' on. You've always been a terrible liar. Matt here saw you the other night in Quong Tai's back room. You might as well just admit you sneak out now and again to engage in some card playin' without your wife knowin' about it. Then we can get on with this interrogation and hear what young Page has to say. We don't care if you play poker, and we're sure not going to tell your wife about it. At least I won't."

"Well, I . . . Is there somethin' wrong because of those games? Am I . . . are we . . . is someone in trouble?" He put the question to Matt.

"Not because of the games themselves exactly," Matt told him. "But because of what might have happened after a game . . . or maybe as a result of the game. Did you ever play with Poker Tom?"

Miller sighed, his shoulders drooped, and he leaned back against a stack of boxes.

"Yeah, I did. A couple times. The last was like you said, a couple months ago. Me and him and the Chinaman and two other men. We all got together at Quong Tai's store, just like you said. None of us were what you'd call regulars—except maybe Quong Tai, of course. I'd seen Poker Tom maybe twice in the last six months, the other two never before. Me, it was only my third game. It was small stakes. Nobody brought more than twenty, thirty dollars with him, 'cept the Chinaman. He always had more 'cause we were in his place. You know, his store."

"Who won that night?"

"The Indian mostly. I went away ten bucks to the good, them other fellows maybe broke even. The big loser was Quong Tai. He was near broke when I left, but he had brought twice as much money to the game as everyone else. Maybe three times."

"You left early?" Taylor asked, picking up the thread.

"Yes, sir. They complained, but I told them I had to go, that Jenny—my wife, you know—was expecting me. What's this all about?"

"Poker Tom hasn't been seen since that night," Matt explained. "Gone like a puff of smoke." He sucked on his upper lip to create the appropriate sound. "We think he may have been murdered."

Miller's eyes widened until white surrounded the pupils, then he repeated the word in a way that showed deep shock. "Murdered? I . . . I had nothing to do with that, I swear."

"No doubt," Taylor said. "No doubt. But what about those other men? Who were they?"

"One of them is . . . something Draper. Ron, Rob . . . I forget."

"Russell?" offered Taylor.

"Yeah, that's it," Miller said. "Russ Draper."

Taylor gave Matt a smug smile. "We almost had him in our

hands," he said almost to himself. "Now we'll have to go find him."

"Huh?" Miller asked.

"Never mind," Matt told him. "What about the other man?"

"Cowboy," Miller said. "Never saw him before, or since. Didn't catch his name. Didn't matter at the time. I remember something about the Anderson spread. Like he worked there or used to work there. Beyond that, I couldn't tell you a thing."

"What's he look like?"

"Medium height and build, kinda bowlegged. Sandy hair, no beard or mustache, though he looked to be starting one. A mustache, I mean. He needed a shave, but his skimpy mustache was longer than the rest of his whiskers. That's all I remember, really."

"Okay, Mr. Miller. Thanks for your help."

"I wish I could tell you more." Then he chuckled uneasily and added, "You're not gonna tell my wife, are you? You promised."

"She's a God-fearing woman," Matt said. "I wouldn't want to hurt her with this. Course, it'd be nice to have a promise from you that your sneakin' around days are over."

"You can't require that of a man," Taylor told his deputy.

"I can ask," Matt said. "No harm in that, eh, Sully?"

"No, heh heh, none at all," Miller responded. But he didn't make the promise.

Then again, neither did Matt.

"So, how well do you know this Russell Draper?" Matt asked as he and Taylor walked together down the dirt street toward one of the saloons.

"Well enough, I suppose. Been a guest of mine several times. Course, he never fought me. I made sure of that the first time I met him." Taylor took a cigar from his inside coat pocket, bit off the end and spit it out, then stuck the stogie in the corner of his mouth. "Drunk and disorderly, assault, even accused of petty larceny once, but Harvey Boone decided not to press charges." He stopped to scrape a match on the bottom of his shoe and light his stogie.

"Sounds like a fairly disreputable person," Matt noted. "How is he on tellin' the truth?"

"Don't know," Taylor said through a gray cloud of exhaled

smoke. "Never had no reason to believe him or not believe him before."

"Did he admit the theft?"

"Didn't get around to askin' him about it. As I was draggin' him away, Harvey called out and told me to let him go."

"Why?"

"Said he'd decided not to prosecute. Felt sorry for Draper. I argued, but Harvey wouldn't give in." Taylor drew on the cigar, then blew a series of smoke rings. "That's when I gave Draper something to think about. Never had any more problems from Draper after that . . . in that regard, at least."

They had arrived at their destination, and Matt didn't ask for any further explanation. In his mind Russell Draper was already proving to be of little or no value, though he'd still go through the motions with him. Draper certainly didn't seem like the murdering kind—at least the murdering and dismembering kind. Drinking, fighting, and stealing were a far cry from premeditated murder and mayhem. Draper was more the opportunistic sort. Matt wasn't sure his testimony, even if true, would be much good on the witness stand, regardless of what he had to say. How much credibility would he have with twelve Bridgeport men who knew what a rascal he was?

They mounted the steps and pushed through the batwings of the saloon. There weren't too many customers this early, most of the men inside having hung around from the night before. They sat in chairs around the stove in the middle of the room, drinking black coffee and trying to endure the effects of their alcohol consumption as they tried to focus their bleary eyes on the lawmen. Two men in the corner played a slow game of matchstick poker, just passing the hours while they honed their skills.

Matt glanced at Taylor, who nodded in the direction of a short man at the end of the bar, not five-five, with hollow cheeks and a red nose, his black unkempt hair sticking out below his hat on all sides. He had a several-day growth of whiskers, and his eyes were bloodshot. He cradled a half-empty glass of beer in his bony hands.

"Drunk again," Matt muttered.

"Surprised?" Taylor asked, the cigar wiggling in his mouth. Matt just shook his head.

Taylor puffed on his cigar. "Come on." He strode toward the

man, Matt following reluctantly several steps behind, more than happy to let Taylor handle this one. Draper stared into his glass, not even seeing the lawmen in the mirror behind the bar until they had flanked him. He shook his head to clear the cobwebs, then looked from Taylor to Page and back to Taylor again, anxiety obvious in his eyes.

"Sheriff Taylor, sir." His voice was thin and shaking, different than it had been the day before. "What'd I—I mean, good morning, sir. Something I can do for you?"

"Yeah, Russell, there is." Taylor put his arm on Draper's shoulder and leaned close to his face, so close their hat brims rubbed together. "Why don't you join us outside for a few questions? Dave?" Taylor addressed the bartender. "Keep his glass full. He'll be right back."

"Sure, Sheriff. You buyin'?" Dave Hays asked.

Taylor shot Dave a disgusted glare but slapped a dime on the counter, then escorted Draper outside by the crook of his arm.

Draper looked worried as he left the saloon, wondering if perhaps the events of the day before were coming back to haunt him. The lawmen took him around the corner and into the adjacent alley before stopping and explaining themselves.

"Poker Tom," Taylor said, watching Draper's face for a reaction. At first Draper appeared bewildered, and then, as his memory returned, his face took on an air of innocence.

"I ain't seen him."

"You saw him a couple months ago," Matt said while examining his fingernails.

"Yeah?"

"Yeah," parroted Taylor. "At a poker game at Quong Tai's. There was you, Tom, the Chinaman, Sully Miller, and a cowboy. Your memory comin' back?"

Draper stared back and forth between the lawmen. Taylor raised one eyebrow while lowering the other. Matt ignored the drunk, adjusting his hat and gazing up the alley.

"Uh, let me think . . . Yeah, now that you mention it, I do seem to recall something—"

"Not good enough," Taylor told him. "Look, Draper, we believe Poker Tom met an untimely death that night, and since you were one of the last men to see him alive, we figured—"

"Hey, I didn't kill him!" Draper protested, alarm spreading across his face as he recoiled from Taylor's implication. "Quong Tai done it."

"How do you know that?" Matt asked sharply, jerking his head around.

"Well . . . I don't actually know it. I wasn't there or anything. Quong Tai told me he did it."

Matt was incredulous. "He told you?"

"Yeah, you know, bragging like."

"Why didn't you tell someone?" Taylor asked. "Like me, for instance."

"To tell you the truth, I didn't believe him. I figured it was just the Chinaman spoutin' off. What do I know about them people? Besides, who cares? An Injun and a Chink. What's the difference?" He shrugged, and Matt looked away, shaking his head and working to keep his anger in check.

"Exactly what did he tell you?" Taylor asked.

"He said he killed Tom and got rid of the body."

"How?"

"I don't remember exactly. Buried him, that's my guess."

"Don't guess, Draper," Taylor instructed. "Try to remember exactly what he said."

Draper squeezed his eyes shut. "'Poker Tom cheat,'" he said slowly, trying his best to sound Chinese. "'So I . . .'" Draper ran his thumbnail backwards across his throat. "'He no more cheat.' That's what the Chink said—that wasn't me talkin'. That or somethin' close to it."

"Mr. Draper." Matt looked the man square in the eye. "Were you inebriated when Quong Tai told you that?"

Draper suddenly had a blank look on his face. "I don't remember. I was drunk at the time," he confessed reluctantly. "So was Quong Tai."

"Great." Matt threw up his hands. "Listen, Mr. Draper, what can you tell me about the cowboy who was there?"

"Not much. He wore a Montana hat with no band, and the heels of his boots was wore down somethin' fierce."

"What about his face?"

"Don't remember that."

"You remember his clothes but not his face?"

"Believe it or not," Draper said in a challenging voice, leaning toward Matt, "I used to work in a fine haberdashery back in St. Louie 'fore I come out west. I notice them things."

"Thanks," Matt said dryly, then turned and walked out of the alley.

Taylor watched him, peeved, then said to Draper, "That's good enough for me, Russ. Here, take this, get a decent meal, and clean yourself up. I want you sober, you understand that?"

"Sure, Sheriff, no problem."

Taylor left Draper in the alley and caught up to Matt, who was leaning against a post nearby, arms folded, his face still puckered in disgust.

"Well, that's it," Taylor concluded.

"That's what?"

"Our witness against Quong Tai."

"Hardly," Matt said. "He didn't see anything. He's just repeating what Quong Tai said, if what Draper says is even true, which I doubt. I think we should find that cowboy."

"You go ahead," Taylor said, as if riding a horse was even an option for him. "I'm gonna stay here and put together a case against Quong Tai." He paused, and a wry grin curled the edges of his mustache. "Mind if I use your office?"

"Suit yourself," Matt said. "Just don't do anything until I get back. It's too soon. There ain't enough evidence, in my estimation." Matt snorted. "And I haven't completely ruled out Draper . . . or Sully Miller, for that matter. But let me hear what the cowboy has to say. Fact is, he might be the guilty party himself."

"Suit yourself," Taylor said. "I'll see you later . . . Sheriff." He turned and headed for the jail.

Matt didn't bother watching him leave but spun on his heel and made tracks for the livery stable.

CHAPTER

TEN

T HE ANDERSON SPREAD bordered Bridgeport on the town's southern edge, but it was all open range for a good ten miles before one arrived at the cluster of ranch buildings. The only access to the mountains closest to Bridgeport was a pass on the far side of the ranch, completely blocked by Anderson's property. Because he was a fair man, Emil Anderson had permitted the county to build a road through his property, bordered its entire length by four strands of barbed wire on both sides, and he allowed free passage to all travelers.

This was not completely magnanimous on his part, to be sure. He got a nice road to his home for free and half his range land fenced in at county expense. Plus he had a pipeline, as it were, to the town's butcher shops.

Since the road passed within a half-mile of his house and the main outbuildings of the ranch, travelers seldom passed by unnoticed. Their comings and goings were observed by ranch hands, if not by Anderson himself, which on at least one occasion led to the rescue of a tenderfoot whose horse was frightened by a snake and threw him, somewhere up in the foothills. When the horse wandered down with an empty saddle, Anderson organized a search party and had the injured man down before dark, keeping the fellow at his place until he'd recovered sufficiently to go home, all at no expense to the poor novice.

Travelers using the road weren't bothered as long as they stayed on the beaten path. If they strayed, someone would alert the foreman, who'd send a couple men out to give the trespassers some directions . . . and a friendly warning. Only once did that fail to solve the problem, and on that occasion the cowboys relied on their follow-up tactic—some persuasive hot lead launched over the scalawags' heads. As one might expect, they quickly complied.

Matt knew his arrival would be heralded before he was close enough to make out the face of any of the ranch hands milling about the barn or bunkhouse. His hope was that the card-playing cowboy—if he still worked for Anderson—was busy elsewhere so Matt could locate him before he was tipped off. The second-best scenario was that the cowboy either knew nothing or had nothing to fear, so the sudden arrival of a lawman wouldn't frighten him into bolting.

If, however, the cowboy did flee, that could only mean he was somehow involved in—

Matt checked himself. This was all speculation and not based on anything reasonable. It could be the cowboy wouldn't think twice about the sheriff coming to Anderson's spread. After all, there were numerous workers on the ranch, all of them capable of getting into trouble in town at any time. And for that matter, why should there be anything unusual about the county sheriff riding out to visit one of the area's richest citizens, especially just before an election? And if the cowboy did make a sudden departure, he might be running from something else. A good number of ranch hands in the West were outlaws on the dodge.

Matt loped Shadow the last quarter-mile, slowing down to a walk as he passed the barn and the main ranchhouse came into view. Men were milling about—toting burdens, repairing saddles, greasing the axle on a wagon. A few cowboys were hanging around a corral, watching another trying to break a mustang that wasn't being very cooperative. Though no one actually stopped what they were doing, they did slow down, and all eyes locked onto the new arrival, including, it seemed to Matt, the reluctant bronco. The men followed him as he rode up to the house, tied Shadow to the rail, and mounted the steps.

Before the lawman could knock on the door, Emil Anderson opened it and stepped out. After a squint-eyed look from their boss, the hands once again began tending to their duties and minding their own business.

"Deputy," Anderson greeted, unaware of Matt's new assignment. He held out a brown, weathered, callused hand, which Matt accepted, noticing the venerable man's strong grip. Anderson was known as the kind of rancher who wouldn't ask his men to do something he himself wouldn't do and hadn't already done sometime in his life.

He wasn't a tall man by some standards, clearly two to three inches shorter than Matt, but stocky and solidly built, with a strong nose that had been broken at least once and clear green eyes shaded by heavy gray brows. A scar from a mean horse's hoof ran down the left side of his face. Clean-shaven with a square jaw, Anderson's broad shoulders and powerful arms left no doubt that he could still, despite his age, take care of himself in a one-on-one fight. Perhaps even against two opponents. Yet his voice was friendly, his speech that of an educated man, his demeanor kind.

"Mr. Anderson," Matt returned. "Fine day. Your place is lookin' real nice."

"You must be running for sheriff," Anderson said matter-of-factly, turning his head to spit a brown stream into the dirt beside the steps. "Kind of a long ride just to tell me how nice my ranch looks."

Matt grinned. "Yeah, I am. But that ain't why I came."

"That's good. John Taylor and I are old friends. You'd be wasting your time. How is the old goat coming along anyway?"

"He's fine," Matt told him. "Healin' nicely. Still has some stiffness or he'd probably have come out with me. Fact is, I'm here on official business."

"What kind?"

"One of your men was in town a couple months back—"

"They're in town at least twice a month."

"Yes . . . Well, this is about a certain event."

"What'd he do?"

"Don't know that he actually did anything—"

"You're talking in circles, Deputy."

Matt sighed. "I'm tryin' to get to the point. He might be a witness, he might be the perpetrator, he might not know anythin'. I just need to question him, find out."

"Sounds fair, I suppose. What's the so-called 'event'?"

"A murder. Happened after a backroom card game your man played in."

"What took so long to get around to coming out here?"

"It was just discovered. The dead man is an Indian, and he wasn't missed for a while."

"Indian, huh? Well, I guess they have as much right to live as anyone. And you think my man might have done it?"

"No, not really. It's possible, I suppose. I've got my eye on another man so far. I'm trying to question everyone, though, until I focus my attention on someone in particular."

"Sounds like you're being cautious, Deputy, I'll give you that. Who are you looking for?"

"Don't know his name. I'm told he's maybe five-ten, sandy hair, no mustache to speak of though he's tryin'. Usually needs a shave, maybe twenty years old."

"You just described half my crew," Anderson said with a sweep of his arm. "Got anything else?"

"He was wearing a Montana hat with no band and boots with the heels wore down real bad."

"Bowlegged?"

"Ain't they all?"

Anderson laughed. "No, they ain't, not by a long shot. But your man sounds like Eddie Kincaid. He's been here about four months. Good man. Should be out on the range today, cutting out part of the herd for branding. Him and a couple of my long-timers. You'll find them about five miles due east in the shadow of the mountains."

The clouds were building, and Matt rode from sunlight to shadow and back again repeatedly as he crossed the prairie, not only because of his own movement but because of the clouds above him moving quickly in the high-altitude currents. But down where he rode there was no wind, and the sunlight was warm upon him. He left his coat strapped behind him on the saddle, his flannel shirt sufficient, and kept riding. The coat was too much trouble anyway, too bulky, and he didn't like the way it restricted his movement and covered his gun. He'd rather be a little chilly than dead because he couldn't get to his Peacemaker quickly enough.

But it didn't stay fair and sunny. The clouds thickened, the wind picked up, and the temperature dropped quickly, forcing him to put on the coat, but only when a few sprinkles began to drift down. It wouldn't do to let your shirt get soaked; that only led to getting sick.

Thunder growled in the distance, but Matt rode on, undaunted, the coat he'd donned all the protection he'd need for now. Life was too full of difficulties to let a coming rainstorm send him scurrying for cover. If he found Kincaid quickly enough, he could be back in town before it hit anyway. He still had a couple hours, he figured.

Matt heard the cattle before he saw them and smelled them before he heard them. They were close, and he urged Shadow on, keeping a sharp eye on the range ahead. He spotted a low cloud of dust ahead and to the right, next to an odd outcropping of rocks at the base of the mountain. Matt eased back on the reins, then turned Shadow toward it.

When he got within a hundred yards of the operation he could see the cowboys, three of them, skillfully maneuvering their ponies as they guided cattle into a barbed-wire pen they'd set up for the purpose. Half the "fence" was nothing more than a thick growth of sagebrush, but it was enough to keep the cattle from wandering off. A fire at the edge heated the branding irons. There was no chuck wagon, so Matt guessed the men rode back to the bunkhouse every night. For lunch they probably ate food prepared each morning and brought with them, after beginning the day with a hearty breakfast at the ranch. A mental picture of the men eating ham, fried potatoes, and hotcakes caused his stomach to gurgle, and Matt remembered he hadn't had anything to eat since the night before. That in turn brought Sarah to his mind and renewed afresh the mixed emotions he'd battled throughout the sleepless night and managed to suppress only when Captain John and his band rode into town and distracted him.

He missed Sarah, there was no question about that. But what she'd done still rankled him. Anger, confusion, and longing chased each other deep within him. The last thing he needed now was to be on the road again, chasing cowboys down just to ask them about a poker game two months back. He needed to be home, taking care of things there.

Two of the cowboys suddenly broke away from their duties and rode toward him, bringing his mind back to the business in front of him. One of them eased his gun from its holster and rested it casually on his lap. Matt kept both hands in view.

"You're trespassing," one of them declared, pulling his horse across Matt's path.

"No, I'm not," Matt responded firmly.

"How do you figure that?"

"I have Mr. Anderson's permission. I'm Matt Page, sheriff of this county, and I'm here on official business."

"You got proof?"

"Already showed Mr. Anderson."

"Well, you kin jes' show us too."

"All right, if your partner'll keep that revolver where it is, I'll show you."

"Nick . . ."

"It's jes' restin'," the other cowhand said, a hand-rolled cigarette hanging precariously from his sun-darkened lip.

Matt kept his eyes on Nick and slowly unbuttoned his coat with his left hand, pulling it back far enough to reveal his badge.

"So, what's your business?" the first man asked.

"I need to talk to Eddie Kincaid."

"That's me."

Matt eyed the man, who looked about six-foot tall even in the saddle, wearing a black flat-crowned hat with a concho band. He had a full mustache that covered his lying lips.

"No, it ain't," Matt challenged. He looked beyond them for the third cowboy but couldn't see him. "You don't look anything like him."

"Then I guess it's me," said Nick.

"Fellas, life's too short to waste any of it jawin' with you two. I got no beef with either of you—yet, and frankly I've got no beef with Kincaid, so I don't know why you're protectin' him. But I've got a dead man in town, and Kincaid might have some valuable information. Plus I got a burr under my saddle and a wife who . . . Well, never you mind what she did. Suffice it to say, I ain't in no mood for all this. Now you let me do what I came to do or risk goin' to jail. And, Nick—" He addressed the man with the drawn gun. "You put that hogleg away nice and easy or I'll see that you eat it."

With that, Matt flashed the gun he'd secretly drawn from under his coat with his opposite hand while talking and keeping his gun hand in view.

"Where'd that come from?" Nick asked.

"From the depths of my patience," Matt told him. "Patience that's just about runnin' out right about now." Still using his left hand, Matt cocked the gun. "Nice and easy now."

When Nick's gun was holstered, Matt squeezed his legs, and Shadow moved easily forward. Matt casually transferred the Colt's into his right hand as he came abreast of the men, keeping it ready but pointed away from them. He had no intention of shooting them and didn't want an unexpected jolt from his horse.

"Now that we're on friendly terms, let me ask you one more time—where's Kincaid?" The cowboys looked at each other, and the one not named Nick leaned over to spit in the dirt.

"You on the level 'bout jes' wantin' to jaw with him?"

Matt nodded and holstered his gun to confirm it. "Yeah. But time's a wastin', and the advantage you're givin' him is gonna make my job even harder. Why's he runnin'?"

"You'll have to ask him that, Sheriff. He jes' lit out fer the mountains, tol' us ta git rid of you. We didn't know you was law, and we don't know what he done. We jes' look out fer each other, that's all."

Matt didn't answer, too busy getting out his monocular. He scanned the foothills slowly, finally locating what he was after. He slammed the monocular shut with his palm, then dropped it into his coat pocket and put heels to Shadow's ribs, leaving the cowboys in his dust. Shadow flew over the open range, Matt leaning down over the animal's mane to reduce wind resistance, ignoring the sting of the hair as it beat his face. The rain was beginning to increase, and Matt silently berated the foul weather that wouldn't wait until he got home.

Shadow was fast, and in no time Matt could see the cowboy clearly and knew he was gaining on the fugitive. He hadn't been seen by Kincaid, he was sure of that—the cowboy was too busy making tracks. But Matt was close enough that the first time Kincaid looked back, he'd know he'd been given away. Matt considered a warning shot to persuade the man to stop but decided against it, thinking it would give Kincaid's friends the impression Matt had been lying to them. Even though Page was a lawman, the cowboys just might decide to ride in their companion's defense.

Sure enough, as Kincaid started up a rise, he hazarded a glance over his shoulder, spied his pursuer, and without a pause shook the reins and kicked his beast forward. Too far behind to shout, especially with the wind and rain making hearing difficult, Matt could only parrot Kincaid's actions. Swallowing an uncharacteristic curse that had sprung up into his throat without his thinking about it, Matt pressed his eyes shut momentarily, then began to pray out loud as he continued the chase. "God . . ."

That was all he got out because his quarry suddenly alighted with his horse still in motion, took cover behind a large piñon pine, and fired a hasty shot in Matt's direction.

"What the—" Matt shouted, pulling Shadow up so fast, the horse spun in a circle. The bullet had ricocheted off a rock twenty feet away, arriving just before the sound of Kincaid's revolver. Too far to be accurate, yet still too close for comfort. Matt rode Shadow behind some trees and dismounted. Taking his Winchester from the scabbard, he moved toward his opponent on foot. Utilizing available cover, he zig-zagged toward Kincaid as the cowboy flung five more errant rounds in Matt's direction. He paused to reload, and the sheriff used the opportunity to gain ground, diving for cover when Kincaid's hat appeared around the pine tree. Matt figured he was close enough to use the Winchester effectively and to be heard by Kincaid when he shouted, yet far enough to be missed by everything but a lucky shot from Kincaid's pistol.

Matt removed his hat, placing it on top of a boulder, then moved a few feet away and spread himself on the rock, working the lever to chamber a round and sighting in on the cowboy. Figuring the range to be fifty yards, Matt raised the front sight a half-inch, then moved it to the right a hair and gently squeezed the trigger. The rifle roared and kicked, and a split second later the bullet splintered the tree trunk Kincaid hid behind.

"Kincaid!" Matt yelled. "This is the sheriff!"

"Yeah, right!" Kincaid rejoined. "And I'm the Queen of Sheba!"

"I'm just here to talk!"

"You're *shootin'* at me!"

"No, I was shootin' back at you. You started that game, Kincaid, remember?"

"Well, what'd you expect? You was chasin' me."

"I wasn't chasin' you—I was just tryin' to catch up. You ran off before I could explain my purpose."

"Okay, tell you what. You come out in the open, with your hands empty and your badge showin', and then you can state your business."

Matt sighed. *Why is it so hard just to ask some cowpoke a few questions about a poker game?*

"I got a better idea. How about you holster'n that shootin' iron and throwin' up your hands and comin' down here? Then I'll state my purpose, and we can both be on our way. And if I like your answers, I'll forget that you've been tryin' to kill me."

There was silence as Kincaid thought it over.

"I like my idea better," he said presently.

Matt muttered out loud to himself, "Kinda thought you might." He levered in another round and addressed Kincaid. "Trouble is, your idea might get someone hurt or get you tossed into the graybar hotel." He raised the Winchester and took aim, his shot again slamming into the tree.

"That was another warnin'. Next time I won't miss." Truth was, Matt knew that even hitting the tree was as close as his skill would get him. He just hoped Kincaid didn't know that. "I'm startin' to get fed up with this game. And I'm gettin' wet. You come out now and we'll have our discussion, then you can be on your way. Delay me any longer, and all bets are off. I'll see you get a fair trial for tryin' to kill me, then a long prison sentence."

"I ain't goin' to jail for protectin' myself. I didn't know you was the law. Still don't for that matter."

"Then who'd you think I was?" Matt grumbled to himself. To Kincaid he shouted, "Okay, fine. You come out now, and I'll forget about your little . . . mistake. Fair enough?"

Silence.

Matt added, "I've got plenty of food. I can wait all day, though I'm not likely to be pleasant about doin' so."

More silence, and then Kincaid answered, "Okay, fair 'nough. Don't shoot—I'm comin' out!"

True to his word, Kincaid stood with his hands up and carefully began picking his way down the hill. Matt came out into the open as well, keeping his hands on his Winchester just in case. He waited for Kincaid to come to him.

"Okay," said Kincaid. "I see your badge. I guess you were tellin' the truth."

"I guess."

"I'm no lawbreaker, you understand. I just had to be sure."

Matt sighed. "You can lower your hands. I'm not jumpy."

Kincaid did so, though slowly and with his eyes keenly focused on Matt's, as though trying to read his intentions. Matt obliged him by staring back and making a show of slowly dropping the muzzle of the Winchester toward the dirt.

"All right then," Matt said. "Finally."

"So what do you want, Sheriff?"

"Just to ask you a few questions—"

"About what?" Kincaid's tone was suspicious as his eyes narrowed.

A guilty man if I ever saw one, Matt concluded, *but guilty of what?* "About a poker game, couple months back."

"I play a heckuva lot of poker, Sheriff."

"This game was in the back room of Quong Tai's store. An Indian was there too."

Recognition flickered across Kincaid's face, and he nodded. "Yeah, I remember that game. Only because of the Injun though. Normally I don't play with Injuns. Lost my folks to 'em, back when I was a kid. Attacked our wagon on the way out here. They was Comanche though. This here one was Paiute. I know the difference. It's like the Irish and the French that come out west. Long as they keep their mouths shut, you can't tell 'em apart. But they're different as night and day."

"Okay," Matt interrupted, trying to hurry Kincaid along. "So you remember. Do you know what happened to Poker Tom?"

"Tom? That the Injun? Not much of an Injun name. Naw, I don't know. What happened?"

"He disappeared a few hours after the game. We think he was killed. Everything points to someone at the game as the culprit."

"Not me. When I left, Tom was alive and kickin'—I should say alive and winnin'—and I rode straight back to the bunkhouse. Got in before midnight. The other hands can attest to that. I woke 'em all up comin' in. Is that what this is all about?"

Matt nodded, and Kincaid pushed his hat back on his head and scratched his scalp.

"Someone from the game killed the Injun, eh? I don't have any more use for 'em than the next man, but why waste time and bullets killin' 'em? Just dirties your gun and gets their kin all riled." He grinned.

Matt ignored the cowboy's attempt at humor. "Do you have any idea who might have done it?"

Kincaid shook his head but thought about it anyway. "A drunk, a reg'lar fella from town, and a Chinaman. None of 'em seem too much like the type to shoot a man."

"He wasn't shot." Though Matt couldn't be positive, since he didn't have the whole victim, that seemed a pretty safe bet. The torso had no bullet holes, and leg or arm wounds usually weren't fatal unless they hit an artery. Of course, it could also have been a head shot, but Matt doubted it. Not if the deed had been done in town, which seemed most likely since Matt didn't see how Tom could be lured into the countryside. And shooting guns in town would be too noisy. Someone would've reported it, and there hadn't been any reports in the past few months of shots without the source being located.

"Eh? Wasn't shot, you say? I jes' assumed . . . How then?"

"Knife probably."

"Oh, yeah? That's a different matter. If I was you, I'd be lookin' at the Chinaman."

"How come?"

"Them others didn't have the stuff for dispatchin' a man close-up and personal-like. Besides, the Chink carried a knife. Seen it a time or two during the game when his hand fell to it."

"Why'd he do that?"

"Thought he was being cheated, I guess. Who knows? Jes' goes to figger, seein' how everyone who loses at cards thinks they're bein' cheated, that they're such good card players they can't lose." He chuckled. "'Ceptin' me. Shoot, I cheat and still lose. Not that night, though, the way that Chinaman kep' reachin' down and fingerin' the hilt of that pig-sticker. Besides, I was too busy tryin' not to lose to spend any time tryin' to cheat a man what's watchin' me like a hawk. Not that it did any good."

He laughed, and Matt puzzled his face at the cowboy. "What's so funny, Kincaid?"

"I jes' thought, that's the other reason I hate Injuns. That Paiute won all my money."

Matt thanked Kincaid for his time and turned to go back to his horse, then stopped and turned to face the cowboy.

"Tell me something, Kincaid. Who'd you think I was? Why'd you run?"

Kincaid dropped his head and tried unsuccessfully to stifle a grin while he pawed the ground with the pointed toe of his high-heeled saddle boot.

"Someone's husband maybe?" Matt guessed.

"Let's jes' say what I done weren't illegal."

"Just immoral."

"By some folks standards, I guess."

"By God's?"

"That too, though I don't know why you'd want to bring Him in on this."

"Was it worth it?"

This prompted the biggest laugh of all from Kincaid. "Not after the scare you give me. In fact, now that I think back on it, it weren't worth it 'tall."

Matt nodded and mounted his horse.

"Thanks, Kincaid. See you in town sometime."

"See ya, Sheriff."

The cowboy watched Matt retreat across the range until the lawman was out of sight, just to make sure, then slowly climbed on his mare and rode back to his duties at the open-range cattle pen.

CHAPTER

ELEVEN

SPECTACULAR as the scenery was, Matt wearied of it. Not because it wasn't beautiful, but because seeing it meant he wasn't home. He'd about had his fill of the trail, especially trails that led nowhere and exposed him to the elements with nothing to show for his efforts but a rifle that needed cleaning and a tired, dirty horse that required extra care.

And he wasn't home yet.

Ahead of him lay mile upon mile of Mono County open range—sagebrush plains and scattered piñon pines, rivers and creeks. And beside one of the creeks, the camp of Captain John and his band, who were without question anxious for word from the white lawman about the progress of the investigation despite the agreed-upon two days having not yet passed. In a way Matt didn't feel like talking to the Indians, but since he was this close . . .

He rode toward where Captain John told him they'd be, hoping they'd remain patient and let him do his job. Deep inside, Matt felt Quong Tai was responsible, but so far he hadn't uncovered enough evidence to prove it. Even without absolute proof, if Matt could gain enough circumstantial evidence to rule out anyone else and point the finger of suspicion in Quong Tai's direction, he'd breathe a lot easier. Hopefully that would satisfy the Paiutes, and they'd let the white man's laws take care of it. Hopefully.

A crooked line of trees in the distance, stretching as far as he could see in two directions, marked the river. Off to the east he could see a faint plume of smoke, most likely the Paiute camp he sought. He turned Shadow toward the river to water the horse before he set off to find Captain John.

Arriving at a clear spot at the bank, Matt stepped down from Shadow and grabbed a handful of pine nuts from his saddlebag to munch on before letting Shadow find his own way to the water. Wiping his hands on his pants, he followed the horse to the narrow river's edge and crouched down, dipping his hand into the cold water to drink. He slurped the water from his cupped hand while his eyes haphazardly scanned the opposite bank. As he pressed the droplets from his mustache and shook them off his hand, his eyes lit on something, just out of the water and tangled in some wild foliage, something the size and shape of which made it look oddly out of place.

He stood slowly, trying to make it out, but he couldn't. Going to Shadow, he retrieved his glass and focused on the object, sucking in his breath as it materialized in the monocular.

"Come here, boy," Matt said softly to the horse as he collapsed the glass. Shadow twitched his tail but continued drinking until Matt called him again, more sternly. Reluctantly the black brought up his head and regarded his master, then made his way to him. Matt swung himself up into the saddle, gauged the depth of the river, and urged Shadow across.

The horse took to the icy water, shying at first step, but obeying the gentle heel nudges of his rider and wading into the river. He crossed easily, the water never even reaching his belly, and clambered up the far side, which was a little steeper, being on the outside of a bend and undercut by the flow of the river. Matt dismounted and removed his bedroll from the leather straps behind the cantle of his saddle, taking it with him as he picked his way carefully down to what he'd seen. He pushed away the undergrowth with hands enclosed in deerhide gloves, which he had pulled on in anticipation of what he was about to pick up.

The object was at his feet, and its nature was clear. He opened the blanket, gently picked the object up with a grimace, and set it on the brown wool blanket, then rolled it up inside, tucking the open edges in before the final few feet were rolled. He tied the length of rope back around the bedroll, barely able to make the knot due to the increased girth. Matt made his way back through the brush to Shadow, whose nostrils flared as Matt approached. He tried to shy away, but Matt had anticipated this and caught him by the bridle, then worked his way along the horse's side to the saddle, tying the bulging bedroll back in place.

Speaking quiet words of comfort to the animal, he mounted Shadow and guided him back across the river, turning east and following it toward the Paiute camp, keeping a wary eye on the river banks the whole way. His watchfulness, however, went unrewarded.

Not that he was sorry. What he had found had been enough for one day. Enough indeed.

His arrival at the Indian camp, as he had expected, had not gone unheralded. Long before he could see the hastily erected wickiups, his arrival had been announced by a whistle from the brush. Matt saw no Indians and could not hear them moving in the bushes round about, but he knew they were there, watching him closely. So he kept his body erect and his hands on the reins as he rode steadily toward the encampment at an easy pace. Though the Paiutes were not legendary warriors like the Sioux or Apache, when roused they could be a formidable foe, as was discovered during the Indian war a decade before. They were not to be trifled with!

Especially when the odds were sixty to one.

When he broke into the clearing they had chosen for their camp, they were waiting—dozens of braves standing at the ready in the center of a circle of stick-and-hide huts. There were women present also, not among the greeting party but outside the wickiups, tending to the routine chores of Indian life. Apparently the band had planned on a stay of some duration, not just intending to come to town, grab their quarry, and leave. Matt was encouraged by this. They'd come prepared for a delay and probably were not surprised the white man wanted his laws to take care of the situation. Yet, there was certainly a limit to their patience.

Captain John moved forward with a hand raised in greeting as Matt pulled back on the reins and returned the gesture. A brave reached out to hold Shadow's bridle, and Matt swung a leg over and eased himself down.

"You come alone," Captain John remarked.

Not quite knowing what he meant, Matt just nodded.

"You no bring Poker Tom's killer."

"It hasn't even been a full day," Matt noted. "You gave me two."

"Then why you come?"

"To let you know I'm still looking, and to tell you what I've found so far. I figure I owe you that. Besides, I was in the neighborhood." Seeing the Indian leader's confused look, Matt explained, "My search took me not too far from here, so I thought I'd stop in."

Captain John nodded. "You come, eat. We talk later. Then sleep. Sun go down soon, too late ride home."

Reluctantly Matt agreed, if only for his horse's sake. But the thought of his blanket and its contents prompted him to seek a delay.

"Let me take care of my horse first."

"We do."

"Thanks, Captain, but he's kind of finicky. I'll do it." Without waiting for an answer, Matt led the animal to where the Paiutes had their horses picketed. Captain John grunted a few words to a nearby girl, and she followed. Without a word she reached up to pet Shadow's nose, and the black tipped his head down to let her, then nuzzled the maiden, much to Matt's chagrin. Afraid to glance over his shoulder and have to answer for his fib about Shadow's being particular, Matt ignored what was happening and removed the saddle—leaving his bedroll attached—and set it on a rock, tossing the saddle blanket over it while the girl fed the animal and began to rub him down.

Matt slapped the dust from his hands, then, with his saddlebags draped over his shoulder, returned to the circle of Indians sitting around the fire.

Captain John handed him a basket filled with Paiute delicacies. Without hesitation Matt took it with a nod, then dropped his head and closed his eyes to give thanks. Captain John said something to his braves in their tongue, and they laughed. Matt raised his eyes when he was finished and looked at the Paiute leader.

"Thought you go to sleep," Captain John explained with a straight face. A few braves chuckled.

"I was thanking God for the food," Matt explained.

"Captain John give food, not your god."

"Yes, and I thank you for it. But my God, the Creator of all, is my provider. I thank Him for all things."

Captain John nodded and explained that to his braves, many of whom spoke no English at all. Some of them responded with nods or grunts. Though believing in many gods, the Indians understood the concept of human reliance upon a deity. Their own lives were dependent upon the often fickle generosity of the gods they worshiped.

"Charlie Jack tell us strange tale of your god," Captain John said. "How He come to earth to live like man and die for all wrong deeds men do."

"Sins," Matt said, stuffing a glob of grain cake into his mouth with his fingers. "We call them sins, and everyone is a sinner. No one deserves to go live with God. We all deserve to die and go . . . below, to a place we call hell—to burn there forever. Jesus—that's the name of our God when He came to earth as a man—He lived a perfect life and didn't deserve to die, but He let Himself be killed and in that way paid the penalty for us all."

"Your god dead?"

Matt grinned. "No, not at all. This is the really good part. Listen . . ." He swallowed his mouthful and leaned forward, getting the braves to do the same. "After three days in the grave He got up and walked out—alive again. That's why He's God. You see, no one except God has the power to bring Himself back to life."

Captain John was quiet but thoughtful as the braves murmured to one another. For a moment no one spoke to Matt, so he figured the conversation was over. He concentrated on his dinner, finding nothing in his basket he hadn't eaten before. The small amount of roasted meat he figured was squirrel, of which he wasn't overly fond, though he choked it down with a mouthful of acorn meal mush. Presently Captain John spoke again.

"Is it sin to kill man?"

"Well," Matt said slowly, choosing his words carefully, "it's a sin to spill innocent blood, to murder. It's not a sin to kill someone in self-defense."

"To kill a killer of men—is that sin?"

"Not if it's done within the law."

Captain John, obviously puzzled, wrinkled his brow.

"What I mean is," Matt explained, "vengeance is wrong. But if a man is brought before a court of law and is found guilty, then hangin' him isn't a sin."

"If a man murder and he judged guilty, killing all right."

"Yeah," Matt said slowly, wondering what he was getting into, "pretty much."

Captain John nodded, and that was the end of the discussion.

No mention was made of Poker Tom the rest of the evening as the braves sat around a roaring fire, exchanging tales and smoking. Matt saw several young girls—one of them the girl who had patted his horse—around the fringe of the ring of men, giggling and pointing at him, until a brave barked something to an old woman who in turn shooed the girls away with a scolding string of Shoshone commands.

When the sun was fully set and the entire sky black, Captain John abruptly stood, and the entire party followed suit. Everyone retired to their own wickiup and went to bed. Captain John motioned Matt into a wickiup, which Matt entered and found being readied for him by the woman who had run off the girls. When she presented the bed of skins and blankets to Matt with a smile, Matt thanked her hesitantly. She moved closer to him.

"You find man who kill my Tom?"

Annie Tom, thought Matt. "I'm tryin', ma'am. Are you Annie?"

"I number one wife," she said. "I miss Tom. He good to Annie. Only beat when Annie do wrong."

"Uh . . . yeah . . . I see." Matt shifted uncomfortably. "We will find his killer."

That seemed to satisfy her. She nodded and smiled, then quietly withdrew from the wickiup, leaving Matt alone. He removed his boots, heavy coat, and hat, stacking them next to his gunbelt. He settled down on the skins with his feet next to the hot coals in the center of the hut, covering himself with the blankets.

His last thoughts before sleep overtook him were of Sarah.

"I just couldn't bear sleeping in that house alone," Sarah said, looking deep into the fire.

"That's all right, dear, I understand." Irene Taylor didn't look up from her knitting.

"I don't," growled Sarah's father, puffing on his pipe. "Not that I mind you being here, you understand. But what's so bad about a house without Matt Page in it?"

"John . . ." scolded Irene, giving him one of those looks.

"It's cold and lonely," Sarah told him. "That's what."

"Where is he anyway?" Mrs. Taylor asked her husband.

"Went out to the Anderson spread to talk to some cowboy." He paused to puff. "That shouldn't keep him this long, though. No tellin' what he got himself into."

"Stop being so hard on him, Daddy," Sarah implored protectively. "He's trying to do the best job he can."

"That's what your father's afraid of," Irene said.

"I am not!" Taylor defended.

"Daddy, you'd like nothing better than for Matt to fail. Then you'd get reelected for sure."

"I ain't worried about the election, little girl—"

"Don't call me that anymore, Daddy. I'm not a little girl."

"No, you're not—you're a grown woman. I apologize. What I was sayin' was, I ain't worried about the election. I got that sewed up. What I *am* worried about is a problem with them Indians. If we don't get Quong Tai locked up soon, they're gonna do some real damage to this town, maybe even hurt a few people in the process. We can't have that, now can we?"

"Why don't you just lock him up if you think he's guilty?"

"I just don't have enough proof. I need something else to tie him to the crime. Then Mr. Draper's testimony will make sure he never sees the light of day. Maybe even get Tai hanged."

"You'd hang a man on the testimony of that drunk?" Sarah asked, turning her head to face her father.

"He may tip a few now and then, but that don't mean he didn't see what he saw and hear what he heard."

Taylor glanced at the mantel clock and decided he'd heard enough dissension for one day.

"My back is getting stiff. I need to get some sleep." He pushed himself out of the chair with a wince and put his pipe on the table. "You women don't do too much plottin' against me, now hear? I ain't been your husband and father all these years for nuthin'."

"Of course we won't," Irene said, putting her knitting down to get up and help him.

"Don't need no help," he said.

"How about a kiss then?"

He grumbled but let her peck him on the cheek. Once he ambled out of the room, Sarah and her mother remained quiet until they could hear the rhythmic growl of his snore.

"Matt would've kissed me," she said quietly to the fire.

"And your father would've kissed me," Irene said, "'cept you're sitting here with your man gone and he didn't want to pour kerosene on your fire."

"Oh, Mama, where is he?"

"Sarah, he's out doing his job, you know that. You know as well as I do that sometimes one thing leads to another, and by then it's too dark to ride home. He's got a lot of pressure on him, what with this killing and your father breathing down his neck. Don't look at me like that. What am I supposed to do? He's my husband, and if he wants to be sheriff again I'm all for it. I'm sorry he's running against Matt. I know that really makes it hard. I think the best thing for us both is to just stay out of it."

"Will he . . . will he forgive me?"

"Matt? Oh, my sakes, child . . . Sorry, it's hard not to call you that. Anyway, I guarantee, if he hasn't already forgiven you, a night sleeping on the trail or in some cold bunkhouse at the Anderson spread will freeze the anger right out of him."

"You're probably right, Mama."

"Of course I'm right."

Matt was awakened at dawn, just before the sun crested the mountains, as Annie Tom shook him gently. Groggy, he blinked and rubbed his eyes, recoiling with a gasp when he saw her wrinkled face and gap-toothed smile. Recalling his surroundings, he sat up, the warm wickiup and thick skins having given him a restful night's sleep—much better than sleeping sitting up in his hard office chair. Satisfied he was awake, Annie offered to help put his boots on, but Matt declined. She shrugged and turned away to let him struggle with the task by himself.

Matt shook his head. What a difference between waking up to

Annie and to the pretty face of his Sarah. He felt a twinge of guilt as he thanked God he hadn't been born a Paiute.

His boots finally on, Matt grabbed the rest of his gear, stepping outside the wickiup to find Shadow at the ready, his saddle cinched, surrounded by a party of five mounted Indians. Matt peered uncomfortably at the bedroll, still tied tightly to the cantle of his saddle. It didn't appear disturbed.

Captain John regarded the white man with no expression. "We ready," he said. Matt's lack of response told the Paiute leader an explanation was needed. "We go to town, help sheriff find man who sin. We tired of wait, of doing nothing."

"Uh . . . yeah, sure." Matt looked around to see where he could go to complete his wake-up chores, and Captain John patiently pointed to a treed area about twenty yards outside the camp. Matt tossed his coat over the saddle, hanging his gunbelt over the pommel, and sheepishly retreated behind a tree while everyone watched. He returned a few minutes later, wishing he had about a gallon of black coffee, but quickly put on his gear in silence and mounted his horse.

He knew better than to try and dissuade the Indians. At least there were only five of them going, not the whole band. That they would actually be able to help him come to the truth of the matter, the identifying of the killer, he doubted. But there was little he could do to stop them, a fact that reminded him of the stubbornness of John Taylor.

They started out at a walk, and Captain John soon dropped back to Matt, who was bringing up the rear.

"Why you not tell me?" the Indian asked, keeping his eyes straight ahead.

"What are you talking about?""

"Poker Tom's leg," Captain John said patiently. He pointed to Matt's fat, lumpy bedroll.

So they found it after all.

"Oh, that," Matt said, trying to act unconcerned. "I didn't want to get you all riled up again."

"We gave word. Two days. We not get . . . riled."

Matt puffed his cheeks out and exhaled. "You're right, Captain, you did give your word." There was little point saying any more. The Indian had him dead to rights, though Captain John was apparently going to let him off the hook.

"Where find?"

"Downriver a couple miles. Washed up on the bank."

"Take to doctor man?"

"The coroner? Yeah. He can tell us if it's Tom's."

"It Tom's," John concluded. With that he bounced once on his pony and picked up the pace, the other braves and Matt following suit.

CHAPTER

TWELVE

The ride into town was chilly but otherwise uneventful. When he thought about it, Matt felt a bit conspicuous traveling in the midst of armed Paiute braves. So he passed the time imagining himself to be one of them, then their captor, and finally their prisoner. It was all pointless exercise, but it kept his mind off the cold and damp and Poker Tom and Sarah and Sheriff Taylor—

"Where we go first?"

The voice was Captain John's as he dropped back again to talk to Matt. The smoke from a hundred chimneys could be seen hovering over the plain ahead, and the Indians knew Bridgeport was just a short ride away. They hadn't been on horseback more than an hour, if that.

"I need to drop this off," Matt told him, jerking a thumb over his shoulder at the bulky bedroll.

They came to the road and urged their horses up the bank and onto it, then picked up their pace. Taking a sharp left, they crossed the bridge, rode past the Taylor residence, and entered town. Their arrival did not go unnoticed by the townsfolk.

The Paiutes came to a halt, and Matt, ignoring the gawks of Bridgeport's early risers, rode on to Dr. Keebles's place. The doctor was up and came onto the porch to greet Matt as he untied his bedroll.

"Here you go, Doc," the lawman said, handing the whole bundle to him. "Got a present for you."

"What is it?"

"You'll know when you see it. The bedroll's mine, though I don't know what I'll do with it when you're done." He shook his head and turned, hoisting himself onto Shadow's back as Keebles stood on his porch, clutching the bundle and watching Matt with a vacant expression as the deputy rode up the street.

The Paiutes were not where he had left them.

Matt sat on Shadow in the middle of the street, turning in the saddle to look in all directions for some sign of the Indians, to no avail. Unable to locate them, he shook the reins and guided Shadow toward the most likely place they'd be—Ah Quong Tai's store.

Sure enough, their horses were around back in a tight group, being tended by a lone Paiute, who smiled at Matt like an old friend. Matt nodded in return, then rode back to the front of the store, tying his horse to the porch post. He went up the steps but hesitated before turning the knob, not knowing what he'd be walking into. He didn't hear anything, and it was too dark to see through the dirty glass—the Chinaman wasn't taking very good care of the place. The lawman sucked in a deep breath and opened the door cautiously.

All was quiet, and immediately upon entering, Matt saw the Indians milling around the counter where Quong Tai accepted payment from his customers, doing his tallies on a little wooden box with beads on several wires. Though the Indians appeared disinterested, if not bored, Quong Tai himself had a look of abject fear on his face, his eyes darting from side to side.

But he always looked like that, Matt realized, so that didn't prove anything. Anyone would be nervous with four Paiute braves hanging around. Even Harvey Boone would have been on his toes in a situation like this.

Quong Tai, noticing Matt's arrival, engaged the Indians in conversation. Or perhaps he was just continuing a conversation that had started before Matt walked in. The merchant said something to Captain John that sounded to Matt like a denial, then tried to entice the braves into leaving.

"Here . . ." Quong Tai held out an open jar of pickled meat to them. "You take. Then go."

Captain John and each of the braves sampled the meat. Most were stoic, but one—the youngest in appearance, no more than a teenager by Matt's estimation—made a face and spit it out on the floor. His long hair hanging from under his beat-up hat and the secondhand cloth pants and coat he wore did not disguise his youthful, unlined face.

Quong Tai angrily said something to him in Chinese, and the scene suddenly resembled storm clouds moving in on a strong wind.

The door opened behind Matt, and John Taylor walked in. Captain John looked at the young Indian disapprovingly, then glanced at the floor where his brave had spit the offensive meat. Something there caught the Paiute leader's eye.

"What's going on?" Taylor asked Matt.

Matt didn't answer but watched as Captain John bent down and ran his fingers over the smooth floor boards. He looked up at the lawmen and opened his mouth to speak just as the door opened again. Matt turned to see Sarah step hesitantly inside. Not wanting her to get caught in anything that might be dangerous, he gave Taylor a questioning look as he started to move toward his wife.

"Get her out of her," Taylor said, reading Matt's face. "I can take care of this."

"Thanks," Matt told him as he went over to her. At the same moment, Captain John's finger was tracing the outline of a stain on the floorboards.

"Blood," he said to Taylor. Matt didn't hear him since he was busy ushering Sarah outside.

"You think so?" Taylor asked, squatting down to look at it.

The Paiute shot Taylor a perturbed glance. "Captain John see dry blood before." He barked a couple of orders to his men, and two of them stepped around the counter to flank the puzzled Quong Tai.

"Lemme get a better look." Taylor stepped over to the tool section and grabbed a large pry bar, which he crammed into the crack between the boards. Then, having second thoughts, he said to Captain John, "I have a bad back. Maybe you'd better open it up."

Captain John motioned to the youngest brave, who stepped over and began to work the pry bar. Quong Tai protested, but Taylor shut him up, and the two Indians guarding him moved closer, their hands resting on the hilts of the knives in their belts.

The nails seemed to protest being forced from the joists by the youth wielding the pry bar, and the board likewise groaned and splintered as it came up slowly, the brave straining at the tool. Taylor stuck a broom handle underneath the board, keeping it raised without further effort from the Indian.

On his hands and knees, with Captain John and the young brave peering over the white man's shoulders, Taylor squinted at the wood, running his fingers along the exposed edge. What had been a much-scrubbed stain on top was a dark blotch on the edge of the floorboard—both edges, in fact. Lighting a match, Taylor peeked at the edges of both adjacent boards and found the same thing.

At the lawman's direction, the brave pried some more boards, and Taylor lit another match, lowering it into the space beneath the floor. He moved the flame around, made some thoughtful noises in his throat, then uttered an innocuous oath as the match burned his fingers. He let it drop and stuck his fingers in his mouth.

"Just as I thought," he said. "Dark spots on the earth where something leaked through the cracks."

"What leak?" Captain John asked.

"The blood, of course," Taylor announced.

Quong Tai's eyes widened, and his hands began to shake, but he quickly buried them in the folds of his silk garments. He continued to face Taylor while his eyes shot from side to side, keeping watch on the Indians beside him.

"Lemme borrow your knife," Taylor asked. He held out his hand, and Captain John complied, though somewhat reluctantly. The braves all tensed, and their hands moved perceptibly toward their weapons as Taylor took the knife, hilt first, from their leader. Taylor, oblivious to their apprehension, focused as he was on his task, knelt and cut a slice from the edge of the board. When he motioned for the Indian with the pry bar to put the board back down, a sigh was released by the Chinaman.

The Paiute withdrew the broom handle and eased the pry bar out, letting the board down, then stomped it back into place. Noticing the nail heads sticking up, Taylor grabbed a hammer from the rack—over the protestations of an insulted Quong Tai— and pounded the nails back in to save someone from getting hurt, then carelessly tossed the hammer back into the bin.

"Well . . ." Taylor said slowly, putting it all together in his mind.

"Chinaman kill Poker Tom, like we say."

"I, uh . . ." Taylor began to answer as the Indians guarding Quong Tai responded to Captain John's insinuated command and took hold of Quong Tai's arms. The merchant let loose a string of Chinese profanity, the import of which was clear without translation.

"Whoa, you're gettin' a little ahead of me," Taylor said to the braves, then told Captain John, "I've got to arrest him first. Then we can take him to jail to await his hearing."

Captain John held up a hand to his braves, who relaxed their grip but didn't let go.

"We make promise to young lawman. We let white man's laws satisfy Poker Tom's death." Taylor assumed that meant the Indians expected Quong Tai to be executed. Taylor shrugged. That seemed reasonable to him. He was sure Quong Tai was guilty, murder certainly was a capital offense, and he figured there'd be no problem getting a jury of white Bridgeport men to convict a relatively disliked Chinaman of murdering a little-known Paiute—especially when they considered the consequences of failing to do so. The entry of sixty armed braves into Bridgeport the day before was sure to be on everyone's mind for some time.

Taylor had no doubt that Judge Fales, after considering the evidence, would bind Quong Tai over for a trial by his peers, so to speak. Fales was a reasonable man.

"Quong Tai," Taylor said to the Chinaman, drawing himself to his full height and speaking loudly, "you're under arrest for the murder of Poker Tom the Paiute. Men, take him to jail."

Captain John repeated the command in Shoshone. With fear in his eyes, Quong Tai stared frantically at the two Paiutes holding him. But before he could wriggle away or go for a weapon—if indeed he even considered such foolishness, they squeezed his arms and hoisted him like a sack of grain, carrying him toward the door.

Matt ushered Sarah out of the store and around the corner of the building and looked deep into her face, his mouth open slightly as if to speak. They wrapped their arms around each other silently. When they finally broke their embrace, they both began talking at once.

"Sarah, what are you—"

"Oh, Matt, I'm so sor—"

"You first, Sarah."

"No, you go ahead, Matt."

"I, uh, was just gonna ask . . . ah, it don't matter. It's so good to see you. How long has it been? A month?" He gazed into her face, flushed from the cold as tears began to form in her eyes.

"Matt, I'm sorry. So very sorry. I didn't mean to hurt you. I know I was wrong to tell Daddy those things . . . I couldn't help . . . I'm just so proud of you, I couldn't contain myself."

"I know. You were defendin' me. I'm sorry I got upset. I should have known better. It's just that—" He looked away for a second, determined not to qualify his apology. "Will you forgive me for walkin' out on you?"

"It's me that needs to be forgiven, Matt. I'm sor—"

Matt placed a rough hand over her mouth to stop her, not taking it away until he'd leaned down and was ready to deliver a kiss.

A commotion out on the street finally broke them apart, and they peered around the corner of the building to see what was happening. Matt remembered the investigation when he saw John Taylor leading the small band of Paiutes up the street, and in their midst a petrified Quong Tai.

"What's happening, Matt?" Sarah asked.

"I don't know for sure, but it looks like Quong Tai's under arrest." He walked slowly toward the advancing group of men, keeping his focus on Taylor. Matt fell in beside the elected sheriff.

"What's goin' on?"

"What's it look like, Junior?" Taylor snapped, a sly grin beneath his shaggy mustache. "I arrested a murderer."

"Then he confessed," Matt concluded.

"Nope. Not yet anyway."

"You found conclusive evidence."

"Yep." Taylor wasn't going to give anything away without being pressed. He was enjoying this little victory over his adversary.

Matt glanced back at Quong Tai and Captain John. The Indian remained stoic, his face revealing nothing.

"So what is it? I have a right to know."

"I s'pose that's so. Anyway, it's no secret. There's evidence of blood on his floor. It's where he killed Poker Tom."

Matt's brow furrowed, and he slowed his pace, dropping back and letting the group pass him, then stopping altogether. Taylor didn't look back, figuring Matt was stunned at being outdone in the investigation. But that wasn't what brought Matt to a halt. Blood at the scene of the murder would be good evidence all right, but something about that bothered him. He stood in the middle of the street watching them as they continued on their way and finally disappeared into the jail.

Sarah caught up to her husband but said nothing as she lightly grasped his arm. Matt didn't acknowledge her as he chewed on his thoughts. He quickly deduced the problem with the blood Taylor had found and, more to the point, what he was going to do about it. A wry grin flickered across his face.

"Matt? What is it?"

"Nothing, Sarah. It's okay." He put his arm around her, and she pressed against him. He waited a moment, then gazed down at her. "So what's for lunch?"

"How about a bath?" she suggested. "Then we'll talk about it."

CHAPTER

THIRTEEN

TWO THOUSAND FEET HIGHER than Bridgeport, in the mountaintop valley where Bodie had been established, the snow that made travel so difficult throughout the winter had subsided, only patches remaining in shady spots where the sun's rays couldn't reach them. The streets were full of people, horses, and wagons. The sounds and smells of Bodie marked the scene: talking, shouting, the clomping of hoofs and the rattling of wagons, the ever-present pounding of the stamp mills, steam whistles, an occasional report from a far-off rifle, the slamming of lumber being stacked on a platform, the squeals of children chasing each other through Main Street's mud, the metallic squawks from a brass band in one of Bodie's better saloons; the aroma of fresh pies, sage, manure, and stagnant water.

Despite the number of people in Bodie and the daily influx of new arrivals—not to mention the current state of unemployment because there weren't enough new jobs to keep pace with the available workers—occasionally there were days when very little happened. This had been one of them, so far.

Harvey and Mary Boone's new store opened without fanfare, but word of mouth about the opening passed through Bodie quicker than a collection plate through a pew full of drunks, and soon Mary and Harvey were up to their eyeteeth in potential customers.

Deputy Jeff Bodine, a relatively new appointee to the position, had been one of them, and he sucked on a fresh stick of licorice as he sauntered down the boardwalk toward the Frisco Saloon. There'd been a report of a fight, but Jeff wasn't concerned. It was still the middle of the day, and he'd heard no shots. It would no doubt be over by the time he got there. Unlike his brother and fellow deputy Josh, Jeff Bodine wasn't of a mind to get into the middle of every battle between drunken miners or layabouts. Let them pummel each other. They'd regret it in the morning.

Jeff pushed through the Frisco's batwings, the licorice still hanging from his mouth, and surveyed the peaceful scene. Not wanting to be derelict in his duty, he began to question the patrons. But no one seemed to recall anything.

"Did you see the fight?" Jeff asked one well-dressed man in a bowler.

"Are you serious?" he replied. "There's fifty men in here. Of course no one saw anything." This prompted hooting and laughter from the sporting crowd, so Jeff just waved them off as if he were batting at a pesky fly and wandered on through the establishment.

Not even the two men standing at the far end of the bar trying to look inconspicuous while hiding behind dime beers—one with a bloodied, fat lip, the other sporting a newly shined eye—had noticed a disturbance of any kind.

Jeff shrugged it off and resumed his patrols, stopping to watch the passengers disembark from the newly arrived stage. He counted sixteen as the coach slowly divulged its contents; the folks stretching and shaking to get out the kinks from the arduous overland trip from Aurora. Sixteen people in a coach designed to hold twelve.

Two men had elbowed their way outside the crowded compartment, and one woman of the painted variety must have sat on the lap of some self-sacrificing volunteer, now standing on the boardwalk trying to get the blood circulating in his legs while he simultaneously smoothed the wrinkles in his trousers. Two other passengers had ridden outside the stage, one on top, the other on the rear baggage shelf, hanging on for dear life the whole time. He was easy to spot as he stood somewhat bent over, rubbing his arms, trail dust clinging to him like snow on high peaks in January.

These two men especially caught Jeff's eye, but he couldn't put his finger on why. Maybe it was their attire—trail duds with genuine cowboy boots. Or maybe it was the squint in their darting eyes. Perhaps it was the well-worn hoglegs weighting down the leather belts around their hips. Two more bad men come to Bodie to make a name for themselves. Jeff made sure they saw him looking at them, gave them a single nod, then turned away, filing the information away for later.

Sixteen more citizens for Bodie. Some good, some bad; some here to work, some not. An average group. When the stage took off again with much clattering and groaning, it was empty except for some mail and small cargo items.

A ruckus at the corner snagged Jeff's attention. A ring of men, several deep, had formed at the intersection of Main and Green Streets. They were shouting, cheering, and cajoling, and money was changing hands rapidly at the fringes. He could hear the growls and snarls of two animals locked in combat.

Jeff ventured up to the men and bent over to peek between their legs at the action. A large mongrel dog and a badger were lunging at one another, seeking to bite each other with a death grip. Both were bleeding, but it was obvious the dog was losing. Jeff saw several other dogs at the edge of the ring straining on their ropes, anxious for their chance. Their turn would come since ultimately the badger always lost. It was just a question of how many dogs it would go through first. An aging Paiute man stood on the opposite corner, counting the money he had been paid for bringing in the badger.

"Kinda cruel, ain't it?" said a deep voice behind Jeff.

Jeff turned to see a huge black man standing behind him.

"Yeah, I suppose," Jeff said with a shrug. "Then again, it's just animals."

"They have feelin's too."

Jeff studied Billy O'Hara's face. The man had been one of the first to call Bodie home. He now ran the Empire Boarding House.

"You're lookin' kinda peaked," Jeff said.

"How can you tell?" the black man said with a smile.

"It's your eyes. You look tired. You feelin' okay?"

"Ah'll be all right. It's been a tough winter."

Jeff nodded. "And you miss Matt Page, don't you?"

"Sure. Course Ah do. But Ah ain't sick over it. Ah've met lots a folk Ah miss."

"You should see a doctor."

"Don't you worry none, Ah'll be fine."

"Yeah. Well, Billy, I hate to run, but I gotta go."

"Sure. You be careful now."

Jeff nodded. "Always, Billy. Careful is my middle name."

Conscious of his mission, Jeff wandered reluctantly off, leaving Billy to watch the badger finish off the dog as bets were called in by the boisterous winners.

As Jeff strolled up the boardwalk, the merry sounds from the saloons on both sides of Main Street began to blend together in an undistinguishable mass of noise that sat on top of the thundering mill stamps like gravy on mashed potatoes. But suddenly an unusual roar erupted over and under the batwings of the Magnolia. He stopped and peeked in, expecting to see a fight but was surprised. A crowd—in fact, everyone in the place—had gathered around a crusty old stiff who stood at the bar with a blindfold tied around his hairy head. Curious, Jeff slipped inside.

A short drink was placed in the old-timer's outstretched hands by the bartender. The elderly man held it under his nose and took such a hard sniff, Jeff thought he was trying to snort the glass dry. Then he exhaled happily and poured all the contents of the glass into his mouth, swished it around in his cheeks, and swallowed. The crowd was quiet, and everyone leaned forward, anticipating his decision.

"Gin," he pronounced. "East Coast vermouth."

The men roared again, and those close by slapped him on the back as the bartender wiped out the glass and poured another drink.

Intrigued, Jeff pushed through the batwings.

"What's going on?" he asked a man at the fringe of the crowd.

"Ol' Noah," the man laughed, "he bet the bartender he could identify any drink blindfolded. If he's right, he doesn't have to pay for all the liquor he can drink tonight."

"And if he's wrong?"

"Don't know. He hasn't missed one yet."

The bartender gave the glass to Noah, who took his characteristic strong whiff, then set the glass down and pushed it back.

"What's this?" the bartender asked as the spectators murmured. "Too tough?"

Noah spat blindly onto the floor and wiped his sleeve across his nose. "Naw, Jakie, too easy. Don't even have to taste it. That's Mono Brewery Beer."

The bartender shook his head, and the crowd took a singular breath. "I don't know how you do it, Noah. That's right!" The loudest roar yet billowed across the room.

The barkeep held up a hand to quiet the crowd and put a finger to his lips to keep them that way.

"One more," he said to Noah. "If you get this one, I'll concede."

"Bring it on, Jake. I'm ready."

Jake slid a glass of clear liquid into Noah's waiting hand. His wrinkled, callused fingers closed confidently around it, and he moved it slowly, dramatically up to his nose. He took a whiff and twitched his mustache, but then the confident smile faded.

Noah inhaled a second time, deeply, and his shaggy eyebrows knit together. He took a drink, swished the liquid around in his mouth, and swallowed. Licking his lips, he took another drink, swished again and gulped, sniffed the drink, then downed the rest of it.

He slammed the glass down on the counter and pulled off the blindfold. "I don't understand it, Jake, but you got me this time. I just don't reco'nize it."

A cheer was raised for Jake, and there were a few groans for Noah and some conciliatory pats on the back.

The old geezer shook his head. "What was that stuff?" he asked, scratching his scalp.

The bartender looked around at the men, a sly grin quivering at the corners of his mouth. He waited until all eyes and ears were on him, then opened his mouth slowly to announce the identity of the mysterious drink.

"Water."

Noah stood up straight. "Water?"

Laughter and back-slapping swept through the room at the joke on old Noah as the men drifted back to their card games and conversations. Jake set several consolation drinks in front of his man of the hour.

Jeff shook his head, retreated out onto Main Street, and with his hands stuffed deeply into his pockets set off at a casual pace, whistling a little tune.

With any luck, the rest of his day would be this easy.

After a hearty dinner at the Quicksilver, Deputy Josh Bodine—not yet on duty—made his way to the Bodie Pharmacy. He'd been fighting a cold all winter and needed another bottle of medicine to quell it. He wore a heavy coat now but would take it off later, so it wouldn't be a hindrance to him if he had to fight anyone. He also wore a new Texas hat, one of the few in Bodie. No one else except a few of the local sheep ranch hands wore cowboy boots, but Josh did.

He also displayed something more rare in Bodie than a church building (of which the town had none). He had his prized holster rig strapped around his hips, the kind with a low-hanging, low-cut, stiff holster, leather loops full of spare bullets all the way around the belt, and a well-oiled Colt .44 pistol held in place by a small leather thong slipped over the hammer. The rig made Josh stand out like a recently hammered thumb since in Bodie the fashion was to drop a small revolver or derringer into a leather-lined coat pocket. But he didn't care. Actually, he enjoyed being different.

His hair had gone uncut since the first snow five months before, though he made every attempt to keep it clean, buying a dime bath at the American Hotel at least once a month. His face he shaved once a week, but only because he didn't need to shave more often than that and because he always cut himself while trying. Josh Bodine without spots of blood on his clean-shaven face was as uncommon as a preacher in a poker game.

Josh stood in the center of the Bodie Pharmacy and examined the room, trying to find what he needed. He spotted the shelf of patent medicines and walked over to it, passing the racks of seltzers and bromides.

He scanned the shelf, glancing briefly at the door as the bell tinkled and a short, stout, stuffy woman came in. Perry Davis Pain Killer, Hostetters Stomach Bitters, Hall Pulmonary Balsam, Jayne's Tonic Vermifuge . . . He picked up a bottle of Tarrant's Cod Liver Oil, making a sour face as he did so, remembering his childhood, and took it to the counter.

Plunking down a few coins, he watched as the clerk wrapped

his purchase in brown paper. He accepted the package, stuffing it in his rear pants pocket, thanked the clerk, nodded at the heavy-set woman, and stepped out into the sunshine. He crossed Main Street, stepping carefully over the drainage gully that ran down the middle of the road, and headed for the bakery.

His nose got there first and pulled the rest of him in. Josh's mouth watered as he lusted over the glass case of delectables, finally deciding on a sweet cream-filled eclair for which he declined a sack. As he stepped outside, he gently stuffed half the pastry into his mouth and turned up the boardwalk.

Pausing at the cigar store Indian standing sentry in front of the tobacco shop, Josh entered the pungent-smelling store and was greeted by the tobacconist, the same man who had sold him his first sack of chew and who had provided Matt Page, when he was deputy in Bodie, with a vital clue to the mystery of the powder magazine explosion.

"Mr. Gordon," Josh said with a nod, "an ounce of fixin's please. And some papers."

"You sure you want to pick this habit up?" Gordon asked him while dropping a handful of finely cut leaves on a small scale.

"Some kinda question from a man in the business of sellin' tobacco."

"Some men aren't cut out for cigarettes, Deputy. Maybe some ought to stay with pipes or even cigars, which wise men don't inhale. Or even an occasional chew. But it's up to you."

"Thanks," Josh said with a hint of sarcasm. He paid for his purchase and accepted the bag. "See you 'round."

"Good day, Deputy."

Despite not feeling a hundred percent, Josh was anxious to begin work. When not on duty, he had nothing to do and longed for physical activity, perhaps something involving fisticuffs or, better still, firearms. Anticipation curled the corners of his mouth and sharpened his already keen eyesight.

He paused in the alley to down a hefty swig of aperient and roll a cigarette, then with a hack and a spit continued on his way.

That night was unusually chilly. Mist from low clouds drifted in through the pass from Aurora just before dark, dropping the temperature five or ten degrees in only fifteen minutes. As always, Josh

had removed his coat. Jeff wore a thick flannel shirt and sus-
pendered pants but also had the sense to put on a jacket.

The brothers decided to have a final cup of coffee at the twenty-
four-hour Cosmopolitan Chop Stand before parting company for
the evening. Jeff wanted to go home and get some sleep, but Josh
suggested one more walk through the bad part of town first. So far
he'd been denied his desire for action. So just before midnight the
Bodine brothers strolled together down Bonanza Street.

"Maybe we can stir something up," he said hopefully.

Jeff snorted his opinion of that idea but stayed by his brother's
side nonetheless.

Twenty minutes later, as they passed Mrs. Hall's brothel, they
heard arguing from an upstairs room. They stopped to investigate
and saw two silhouettes on the window shade, shadows thrown
by a kerosene lamp on the far side of the room. Two people were
visible. A man was leaning toward a plump woman, shaking a fist
in her face while he shouted at her.

"You want to take care of it?" Josh offered.

"Not really," Jeff said.

"Me neither," Josh admitted.

"They haven't done anything yet."

"True enough. Shall we watch?"

"I suppose it's our public duty."

"I heartily concur."

Jeff cast a sideways glance at his brother, who was grinning
with anticipation like a kid in a candy store.

They stayed put as the argument heated up. Though unable to
make out the words, the actions of the shadows on the shade sup-
plied all the information they needed.

Josh took out the makings for a cigarette.

"Tell me what's goin' on," he said, looking down while he
poured some tobacco onto a paper.

"When did you take up smoking?" his brother asked.

"Just recently, for protection against the elements. It gets cold
at night, which you would know if you ever worked the overnight
shift." He flipped a squint-eyed glance at his brother. "Besides, I
don't inhale 'em. I just puff on 'em and cup my hands around 'em
now and then to keep warm. Plus it helps people see me, with the
glow and all."

"I thought you had your fill with the chewin' tobacco them two outlaws foisted on you."

"That was different." Josh didn't explain further. He began rolling the paper around the tobacco.

Jeff just shook his head and continued watching the window. "She's got her hands on her hips, and he's yelling . . . Now he's shaking a fist . . . She's waving her hand around . . . Now she's pointing at something . . . Whatever she meant, he apparently didn't like it—he just smacked her upside the head."

Josh looked up. "Shoot, I missed it." He put the unlit cigarette over his ear. "I'll be right back."

Jeff stood and watched as Josh went into the brothel. He could hear his brother tromp upstairs and kick open the door. The light went out, and there was a short commotion. Furniture was shoved and knocked over. Glass broke. Someone grunted. The woman screamed. At least Jeff hoped it was the woman. A minute later multiple footsteps sounded on the stairs inside, and Josh came back out, a handcuffed James McCarthy in tow with a swollen eye and Louise DuBarr, one of the local soiled doves, wrapped in a blanket with a red mark on her cheek.

Josh's cigarette was still behind his ear.

"Need any help?" Jeff asked, his hands in his pockets.

"Don't think so," said Josh as he dragged his catch off to the jail.

"Okay." Jeff watched them trudge down the street. "I'm goin' home. See you tomorrow."

Josh waved a hand as the darkness swallowed him.

CHAPTER

FOURTEEN

WOOD PIRATING was a serious problem in Bodie. A very precious commodity any time of the year, thanks to Bodie's location above the tree line, in winter wood became nearly as valuable as the gold the miners dug out of the mountain. At least gold was a local product; wood had to be hauled in from miles away, and in winter the heavy snows buried the roads and made bringing it in a difficult, sometimes impossible task. The price for a cord doubled or tripled after the snows hit. In order to have enough wood for heating and cooking for the whole winter at a reasonable price, people stockpiled during the summer and fall. Large stacks of cordwood sat in almost every yard, and the storehouses were full. Those without wood likely wouldn't live through the season; they would die in their beds as the freezing air leaked into their homes through the gaps between the siding boards. Having not properly prepared for winter, their only option was to steal from someone else's pile.

The citizens of Bodie had little compassion for those who did not plan ahead for what they all knew was coming, and they were particularly incensed when those who had not made provisions for themselves stole from those who had. Such thieves had to be stopped.

They couldn't rely on the Bodines to protect their woodpiles. The lawmen had enough to do with the likes of James McCarthy and Louise DuBarr streaming into town. And the folks couldn't watch every woodpile in town day and night, so they booby-trapped them. They packed black powder into the cracks and crevices of several pieces of firewood and placed them here and there throughout the stacks of cordwood, marked in some clever way so they would not accidentally put a piece of the explosive fuel in their own stoves. Then, to be fair, the *Bodie Gazette* published a notice to all would-be pirates, telling them about the doctored wood. Some people felt the notice was enough; they didn't need to actually pack in the black powder. The threat, it was hoped, would do the trick. After all, their goal was not to injure someone but to keep their wood supply intact. But others wanted to make sure, figuring anyone stupid enough to steal dangerous, tainted wood deserved to have his home blown to kingdom come.

While stealing was risky business for the desperate wood pirates, without sufficient firewood freezing was a sure thing. So despite the potential for harm from an explosion, and though winter was nearly over, wood continued to disappear during the night—sometimes a few sticks, sometimes a good part of a cord.

It was only a matter of time.

Billy O'Hara stood in the kitchen of the Empire Boarding House, a towel draped over his head, his face low over a pot of boiling water, inhaling the steam through his nose with great gulps of breath. The cold or whatever he'd contracted during the winter—his tenth Bodie winter—had clung to him as tenaciously as moss on a vertical rock face, and he was wearing down under its burden.

He'd run the boarding house for the Empire Company since the first shovel was sunk into the side of Bodie Bluff, giving the employees of the mining company—the only inhabitants of Bodie in those days—a place to call home. He'd fixed their meals, done their laundry, and nursed their illnesses, and now he was beginning to tire. Though the expansion of the town the previous summer had allowed him to stop preparing meals—except for his own—his joy had dissipated like smoke in the wind. It was still there, just less apparent.

And then came this seemingly perpetual malady that had snuck up on him when he wasn't looking the previous November and refused to leave, not unlike distant relatives who come "for the weekend" packing all their earthly possessions.

The doctor hadn't been able to pinpoint what was wrong and was treating it as a lingering influenza. Deep down Billy believed it to be more serious—he'd never coughed up blood with the flu before. But he didn't see much need to seek medical treatment elsewhere. Bodie was his home, the people he loved were there (and nowhere else), and, after all, he'd lived a good, long, and worthwhile life, a life he was satisfied with and about which he had nothing to be ashamed. If God's plan was to take him home now, that was fine with Billy. After all, as the Apostle Paul had written, "To live is Christ, and to die is gain."

As he sucked the steam into his murky lungs, though, he wished that whatever God was going to do, He'd hurry up and do it.

A scuffing of shoes on the well-worn floorboards reached his covered ears, and he turned and looked out from underneath the towel at Rosa Page, wife of Jacob Page, the father of Sheriff Matt Page. She stood silently in the doorway, her hands full of a large, steaming bowl, her face tinged by her compassion for the large black man.

"Miss Rosa," Billy said, slowly unwrapping the towel. He appeared disconcerted at being caught tending to his own needs.

"Brought you some chicken soup." She invited herself in and set it on the butcher block. Billy wiped his forehead with the towel.

"Thank you, Miss Rosa."

"Please, Billy, don't be so formal. I'm just plain old Rosa."

"Not to me," he told her.

She blushed, something that up until a few months earlier she hadn't done, not in recent memory at least. Brothel madams, as a rule, aren't easily embarrassed.

"Thank you, Billy. You're a dear." She ladled soup into a bowl and handed it to him. "Here, you take this. It'll make you feel better."

"Ah hope so. Ah'm gettin' a mite tired of this."

"Anything else I can get you?"

Billy forced a chuckle. "A new body."

"Thank the Lord, we'll both have a new body someday."

"Why, Miss Rosa, Ah declare, you been readin' the Bible, ain't ya?" He picked up a spoon and tested the steaming broth.

She nodded. "More so lately, what with everything happening."

"That's usually how God gets our attention. When things is movin' along normal-like, we have the tendency to think we don't need Him. This is good, Rosa. You make it?"

"Molly Carter."

"Oh, Miss Molly. How's she workin' out?"

"She's a good little cook."

"Ah can taste that, but that ain't what Ah meant. Ah'm speakin' 'bout her little diff'rence with you . . . you know, that incident with her and Flora Bascomb—"

"Ancient history," Rosa assured the old man. "As far as Molly's concerned, at least. Regarding Flora, well . . . she's a horse of a different color, and I'm not wasting any time worrying about her. I'm more than happy to be cordial to her, but it's up to her to accept it. She's the one with the . . . what's the Bible call it? . . . 'root of bitterness.'"

Billy slurped a spoonful of soup, sucking up two long noodles that left moist trails on his chin before they disappeared from sight with a pop. He ran the back of his hand across his face.

"That's true enough. But Ah'm glad you and Jesus come to terms. Ah trust they was His terms."

"Jacob and I got to reading God's holy book," Rosa explained, folding her arms in comfort as she leaned against the small counter. "And talking to Reverend Duncan. He set us on the right course, explained what it means to be a Christian so it made sense, not that holy, pious business you hear most of the time."

"Trouble with most folks here," Billy said, "is they think 'Christian' means they go to church on occasion and don't spend too much of their time in jail. They take food baskets to the poor, don't openly degrade the Chinese, and have a Bible somewhere in their house. They stop swearin' when women get within hearin' distance, don't murder folk, and don't get drunk more than is necessary. When they gossip it's for all the right reasons, and they are sure to mention when they do it that they ain't gossipin', just passin' on the information for the prayer chain. Some think that because they's white or was born in the United States, or because they ain't a Buddhist or some such thing, that makes them Christian." He coughed hard and deep, turning his face away and burying it in his towel.

Rosa's heart went out to him, but she knew there was nothing she could do to comfort him. She let her eyes find something behind her to concentrate on until he finished. When Billy was through talking, he apologized.

"Look, you eat all that soup," Rosa said. "I'll come see you later."

"Maybe tomorrow, Miss Rosa. Ah think Ah'll go to bed in a bit here."

"Anything else I can get you?"

"No. Thank you kindly, Miss Rosa. Ah'll be okay. Ah appreciate the soup, and Ah thank you for comin' over. Praise the Lord. You and Jacob keep prayin' for me."

"We will, Billy. You can count on that." She stepped over to him and put her arms on the shoulders of the big man. "We love you, Billy." Quickly she released him and left. When the front door had closed behind her, Billy lifted his head, wiping the tears from his cheek with his damp, cold towel.

The sporting crowd in Bodie, those idle members without jobs or wives to keep them busy, had thought up a new pastime. Not content with the usual horse racing and badger fights, they decided to create a contest of skill and daring. A man on horseback would ride down the street and attempt to pick up an object on the ground without slowing down his steed and without falling off, either of which meant immediate disqualification. To make it even more interesting and difficult, it was decided the object on the ground should be moving about, yet remain in one place.

So they dug a small hole and buried a rooster, leaving only his head sticking up.

Men took their turns, sometimes coming up with just handfuls of dirt and rocks, other times with a fistful of feathers. But so far the irate, flailing rooster had eluded them. The men hadn't figured on the rooster being quite so animated, but that just made the game more riveting. They also hadn't calculated on what would happen if someone managed to get a good grip on the rooster's head. They just assumed his body would follow it and pop out of the ground.

Molly Carter, hearing the whooping and hollering, peered out the window of the Quicksilver to see what was going on. Unable to make out the nature of the thrashing object in the street, curiosity drew her outside the restaurant.

She walked slowly onto the boardwalk, wiping her hands on a towel, and stopped when the racket made by the rooster became clear amidst the noise of the spectators. Horrified by this cruelty, she hurried to rescue the bird, heedless of the horse and rider bearing down on her. Someone shouted a warning, but it didn't register, and Molly bent over to help the rooster. The rider, at a full gallop with his head down, was nearly upon her when he finally looked up. Unable to stop his horse as he hung from one stirrup, his body nearly dragging the ground in preparation for his attempt to snatch the fowl, he did his best to clamber back into the saddle, but there wasn't time.

The approaching hoofbeats caused Molly to jerk her head around toward the oncoming horse, but she didn't fully perceive her danger. Transfixed and confused by the furiously galloping animal with the hanging rider, she just stared. At the last moment her fate became clear, and she opened her mouth to scream, but something suddenly circled her waist and she was wrenched back violently, spinning and falling. For a moment she was blinded, her eyes a blaze of colored light, her mind black and foggy.

Molly slowly came around and realized she was looking up at the sky, then at concerned faces as they formed a circular frame around the blue and white picture. She felt movement and looked over next to her. On the ground was one of the young deputies, Jeff Bodine. He regarded her with both fear and apology in his face.

"You okay, ma'am?"

Molly stared at him, then at her surroundings. Someone shouted to give her room, and the crowd drew back. She heard the rooster squawk. A man leading a horse joined the group.

"What was she doing?" he asked. "I coulda kilt her."

"Saving the durned rooster," said a man with disgust.

Molly remembered, then realized she was about to be run over by the horse when . . . when the deputy . . . He must have pulled her out of the way.

"Oh, my," Molly said, looking at Jeff. "You saved my life."

Jeff just shrugged and got up on his haunches. "Are you okay? Are you hurt? I didn't mean to yank you so hard."

"I think I'm okay." She took stock of herself, then with Jeff's help got up. She brushed herself off as her husband, summoned by an onlooker, rushed up to them.

"Molly! Molly, are you okay?" Joseph Carter asked breathlessly. "What were you thinking? Why did you—"

"Aw, don't be too hard on her," Jeff said, adjusting his hat. "She was just concerned for that old rooster." He pointed with his thumb, and Molly and Joseph looked, but there was nothing to be seen. Just a small hole in the ground. "Where'd it go?" Jeff wondered.

No one knew, but since there was nothing left to grab, the game was called off, all bets were returned, and the crowd slowly drifted away. In a short time the street was back to normal, the rescue of Molly Carter by the young deputy the topic around many barroom stoves.

After a brief time to collect herself, Molly told her husband she was fine, gave him a hug, and sent him back to work, then did the same herself. Jeff decided he was hungry and accompanied Molly to the Quicksilver.

"All this talk about chickens," he said, reading the menu. "Think I'll have some of Rosa's fried chicken, with a biscuit and some mashed taters."

"Certainly," Molly said, pouring him a mug of black coffee.

"It's on the house," Rosa yelled from the kitchen.

"You don't have to do that," Jeff said.

"It's the least I can do to thank you for saving my partner." Rosa smiled as she plucked the last feathers from the bird and plopped it onto the cutting board.

Several weeks had passed since the notice about the booby-trapped wood was printed in the paper—without incident. But the same morning that Molly was saved from being trampled, one Bodie citizen had awakened to find a good portion of his woodpile missing, including one of the loaded logs. Once word got out, anticipation and excitement gripped the town. Bets were even placed as to when it would go off and who the thief was.

They didn't have to wait long to find out. That night a midnight explosion woke the town. A few recalled the powder magazine disaster the previous year, but this blast wasn't nearly as big, so it had to be the wood pirate. Men all over Bodie jumped out of their beds and went out to see what was going on, standing outside their homes in various stages of dress and gazing about, trying to figure out where it had happened. By comparing impressions with one another, they were able to pinpoint the direction the sound had come from. The farther north they walked, the more they realized the explosion had originated at the edge of the valley outside the town proper. There were only a few cabins up there, and it didn't take long to find the one they wanted—only one of the little shacks was blown to bits.

There wasn't anything left except some twisted iron from the stove. But the strangest concoction of goods and artifacts was strewn over the patchy snow for fifty feet all around where the shack had stood. There were articles of clothing, broken tools, wheels from old ore cars, bent frying pans, a baby carriage with no wheels, shoes, empty cans . . . all of it looking as if it had been discarded by someone long ago.

"Look here," someone said, picking up a twisted steel pot. "I threw this out two months back."

"And that's our old baby carriage," said another.

"Uh oh," said a third. "Here he is!"

Everyone rushed over, expecting to see a deceased wood pirate. He was lying on his back, legs and arms outstretched, black with soot from head to toe. At first he didn't move, and the people just stood about and gazed at him, assuming he was dead. Some felt sorrow, others satisfaction. Most were indifferent. Then they heard a groan and a timid whimper for help.

"Hey, it's Noah!" someone shouted.

"Figures," said another.

Josh Bodine and a man wearing a nightshirt stepped forward to inspect the body and got a surprise. Noah wasn't hurt or burned at all; he just had the wind knocked out of him.

"He'll be all right," Josh said.

"His house is totally destroyed though," the man in the night-shirt observed.

"His shack you mean," commented an onlooker. "It weren't nuthin' but junk nailed together."

"Can't say we didn't warn him," clucked a woman. "We put the notice in the *Gazette*."

That they had. Unfortunately for Noah, they never stopped to think that not everyone in Bodie could read.

Josh dusted Noah off, made sure he was okay, then left him to his own designs while the good folk all wandered back to their cozy homes and beds or their saloons and bottles, relieved that the pirate had been exposed at last.

One citizen stayed, though, watching the dazed Noah wandering aimlessly through his belongings, trying to see what he could salvage. There wasn't much, and Noah soon gave up. The one-armed man called out to the old geezer, "Noah, why don't you come home with me? It's warm, and we can feed you."

Noah looked up at the man, squinting in the darkness to make out the face.

"I don't want to be a bother to ya," Noah said quietly with uncharacteristic humility.

"No bother 'tall. It's jes' till you can scratch together another place, okay?"

Noah ambled over, his lower lip beginning to quiver from the cold. "Thank you, Mr. Page. You sure that wife a yours won't mind?"

"Rosa? Naw, she'd ask you herself if she was here."

Noah considered the offer . . . for all of three seconds.

"Okay. I'll pay ya back someday though."

Jacob grinned. "Sure, Noah, sure. That's fine." The two bearded men left the scene of the disaster together, Noah taking with him only a small metal box he'd picked up from the debris.

He never returned for his other possessions.

CHAPTER

FIFTEEN

ASSEMBLING A JURY in Bridgeport was almost always an ordeal. People were reluctant to do their civic duty. Many times Matt had to physically lay hands on people and compel them to serve. A few months back, a trial was actually delayed for two days so four of the jurors could finish a card game. Obviously civic duty was not high on the list for most citizens of Bridgeport. The only reason the town had so many volunteer firemen was because volunteer firemen didn't have to serve on juries.

Matt was relieved that today's proceeding was just a preliminary hearing, so no jury would be required and testimony would be brief. He figured they'd be finished in a few hours, though with the number of Indians lurking about the building and the town, anything was likely to happen.

The time for the hearing arrived, and Judge Fales's court was filled to overflowing. The courtroom was on the second floor, above the Palace Saloon, which—not so coincidentally—Fales owned. Many times he would call a recess, and everyone would file downstairs, buy a drink, then go back up to continue whatever proceeding was in progress. The courtroom had an outside staircase, but most men found it "more convenient" to exit through the Palace.

One of the few brick buildings in Bridgeport, the structure was generally called "The Brick" by the locals. Today everyone was glad Fales had chosen that material for its construction, in case things got out of hand. Brick didn't burn.

The outside of the building was ringed with Paiutes—quiet and polite, but well-armed and stern of face. All the exits were covered, and their horses stood at the ready on Main Street. Captain John and two braves of his choosing would be allowed inside the courtroom to monitor and possibly, in Captain John's case, participate in the inquest.

The remainder of the Indians were assembled on the edge of town, this side of the bridge. They milled around, talking, cleaning their guns, or playing cards, and kept watch on the town and its people.

The townsfolk were tense. There was no doubt that if Ah Quong Tai was not held to answer for this crime, the Indians would not let the sun go down with the Chinaman alive. Captain John had said so within the hearing of several citizens. Whatever it took to extract revenge, the Paiutes aimed to do it. They weren't happy that Ah Quong Tai had not been immediately turned over to them. Only Captain John's respect for Matt Page had forestalled an execution.

Very few uninvolved parties would be allowed in the courtroom itself, Fales had stated that morning. County and city officials, witnesses, the lawyers, the designated Paiutes, and of course Ah Quong Tai and the lawmen were the only witnesses to what transpired within, with one exception—a journalist, a man of Fales's choosing whom he knew to be honest, or at least as honest as a member of the fourth estate could be.

Fales banged his gavel, no more than a household mallet. It served a dual purpose, occasionally coming down on the heads of rowdy saloon patrons downstairs.

"Let's commence this thing. Bring the prisoner in."

A hush fell over the crowd as Matt and John Taylor, each holding an arm, brought Ah Quong Tai into the courtroom. The crossing from the jail had been done under cover of darkness before the Indians were able to figure out where the hearing would be taking place. It was one of the few things Matt and Taylor had agreed upon recently. The three men had remained in the back room of the Palace waiting until Fales called for Quong Tai, then used the inside staircase.

Captain John and the other Paiutes in the courtroom cast long, hard looks at Quong Tai as he entered the courtroom between the lawmen. The accused did his best to ignore them but nonetheless shook visibly.

"Court's in session," declared Judge Thomas Fales, banging on his table with the gavel when Quong Tai and the lawmen were seated. "Sheriff, are the prosecution and defense ready?"

"Both attorneys are present, Your Honor," Matt said quickly, seeing John Taylor's mouth begin to open. The elder man glared at him but said nothing and kept his seat.

"Will you state their names please?"

"Pat Reddy and John McQuaid."

"Which is which?"

"This here's Pat, and that's John over yonder."

"I know that, Sheriff, but which is for the defense and which is the prosecutor?"

"Pat . . . uh, Mr. Reddy will be for the defense." Behind the flustered Page, John Taylor made no attempt to conceal his smirk.

"Thank you, Sheriff. Ah Quong Tai, please rise." The Chinaman did so hesitantly. "Ah Quong Tai, you stand accused of murder against the person of Poker Tom, a Paiute. How do you plead?"

"Not guilty," declared his attorney.

"I figured as much," the judge declared.

Already a legend in two states, Reddy was a large, one-armed Irishman and a former miner and outlaw who, some said, lost his arm when he caught a round during a holdup attempt twenty years earlier. That incident apparently set him on the straight and narrow, for he then attended law school and began his practice in Aurora, moving to Bodie a few years back. He had never lost a case, whether acting for the prosecution or defense, and many a case was decided simply by which side got to him first. He presented an imposing figure at well over six feet, was broad-shouldered and barrel-chested, and was always impeccably dressed. Few dared challenge a man of his stature. He had dark, auburn hair, and his mustache traveled down past his lip and exploded over his jowls, his chin remaining bare and his sideburns short. In capturing the attention of a crowd, no one was his equal. Matt hoped the Indians weren't aware of his perfect record or they'd go on the warpath before the trial ended.

"The defendant pleads not guilty," the judge repeated. "Mr. Tai, has your attorney explained the purpose of this hearing to you?"

"Yes." He dipped his head politely.

"To clarify to all in attendance, then, this is a hearing to determine if the defendant, Ah Quong Tai, should be held to answer to the charges, to determine if there is enough merit in the prosecution's allegations to warrant a full trial. Is that clear to all? Testimony will be brief and to the point, and I will render my decision at the end of the arguments. Understand?" Everyone nodded, and Fales looked at John McQuaid. "You're the prosecutor, Mr. McQuaid. You may make your opening statement. Remember, keep it short."

McQuaid stood up. "Thank you, Your Honor. The people will show that without provocation or excuse the defendant, Ah Quong Tai, murdered the Indian known as Poker Tom and hacked his body to pieces, pickling it, then tossing most of it into the river, all because of a small matter of fifty dollars won from the defendant by Poker Tom in a backroom poker game." He sat down.

Fales waited a moment, then said, "That's it? You're done already?" McQuaid nodded. "Well, praise be," said Fales. "Okay, Mr. Reddy, let's see you do that well."

Reddy stayed in his seat. "We will prove, Your Honor, that there is no merit to the prosecution's case." He rested his single arm across his ample stomach.

Fales was amazed. "This is a red-letter day in Mono County history, boys. Keep this up and we might be out of here before lunch. Mr. McQuaid, you may call your first witness."

"Thank you, Your Honor. I call the leader of Poker Tom's band, Captain John." Captain John got up hesitantly and walked to a chair at the end of Fales's table, looking lost and very out of his element. McQuaid whispered directions to him, and Fales produced a Bible, holding it out flat to the Indian. "Raise your right hand, and place your left hand on the Bible."

"What this?" Captain John asked, gazing at the imposing black book.

"This is how we swear you in," McQuaid told him. "To be sure you tell the truth."

The Indian regarded him with disdain. "No need put hand on

book. Captain John always tell truth. Putting hand on book no make man tell truth."

Matt put his hand over his mouth to cover a smile. That was exactly the way the Bible itself said it should be—don't swear by anything or anyone, whether in heaven or on earth; just always tell the truth.

All eyes were on the judge. How would he handle this development? Pat Reddy spoke first though.

"Your Honor, the defense will stipulate to the veracity of Captain John. We wouldn't want him to violate his principles."

Fales cleared his throat as he withdrew the Bible. "Very well, then. Captain John, you may sit down. Mr. McQuaid, the floor is yours."

"Thank you, Your Honor." He paused as he looked square at the Indian. "Captain John, we're here today to consider the matter of the disappearance and murder of Poker Tom, one of your band."

"Captain John know that," the Indian said, drawing a few giggles from the gallery. Fales banged his gavel and glared at the offenders, and the men quieted instantly.

McQuaid went on, "We need to establish a few facts first, so please bear with us. How long has Poker Tom been missing?"

"Long time. Plenty time to go to town and buy cloth for wives."

"He came to town to buy cloth for his wife?"

"Wives," Captain John corrected, holding up two fingers. "Poker Tom brave man."

Even Fales couldn't suppress a smile, and he let the crowd have their chuckle. McQuaid proceeded, apparently undaunted.

"And he never returned?"

"That true."

"Can you tell us what you found in the river the other day?"

"Poker Tom."

"Objection!" interrupted Pat Reddy, drawing a glare from the Indian.

"Why he object to Billy Shoes find Poker Tom?" the Indian asked the judge.

"He's a lawyer," the judge explained. "It's what he does best, next to collecting fees. Don't take it personal, Captain. This is just how we do business. We have many rules." The judge turned to Reddy. "The basis for your objection?"

"I have two, Your Honor. One, Captain John said Billy Shoes found the body, not him. He can't testify to it—it's hearsay. And two, we don't know it's Poker Tom's body. That hasn't been established."

"Those are good objections, Pat," Fales admitted. "So good I'm going to overrule them both. Captain John here isn't familiar with the minute details of our laws and rules, and I'm inclined just to let him tell his story so this doesn't take all week. Besides, if you took a good look outside on your way in, you noticed a whole slew of folk like Captain John who'd take exception to your objection, if you catch my drift. The court will note the circumstances, and you can refresh our memory in your argument when this is over. Okay with you, Pat?"

"Of course, Your Honor." Reddy again rested his arm over his stomach and smiled slyly.

"Keep going, Mr. McQuaid," Fales said.

The attorney nodded. "Captain John, what exactly did Billy Shoes find in the river?"

"He find body of man—no head, no legs, no arms. He take to camp, we look, Annie Tom say it Poker Tom."

"Annie Tom is Poker Tom's wife?"

Captain John nodded. "Number one wife. Sally Tom no look, she cry too much."

"Did *you* think it to be Poker Tom?"

"I think if Annie say it Poker Tom, it Poker Tom." He shrugged.

"How tall was Poker Tom?"

"Same as me."

"May the record reflect that Captain John is five-eight?" McQuaid asked Fales. "We measured him this morning."

"We'll stipulate," Reddy said. "I know McQuaid wouldn't fudge on something like that." The implication being, of course, that he might fudge on something else, an insinuation not lost on John McQuaid, who shot angry looks at his counterpart.

"No further questions," McQuaid said as he sat down at the counsel table.

Reddy thought for a minute, then waved off his turn. "No questions, Your Honor." He turned to Ah Quong Tai and whispered something to him, causing the Chinaman to nod his head.

"Okay, Captain John," said Fales, "you may step down." The Indian complied. "Call your next witness, McQuaid."

"The people call Acting Sheriff Matthew Page."

Matt stood and made his way to the witness chair, where he was sworn in by Fales. He had considered echoing Captain John's sentiment about always telling the truth, but wisely decided that wouldn't be received too well by the judge. He settled down in the chair.

McQuaid led him through the whole incident, from the time he was first approached by Captain John, through his questioning of Ah Quong Tai and the other men who had been at the poker game, his finding of the leg in the river, and on up to the confrontation in the store that ended with Quong Tai's arrest. Since Matt wasn't there at the time of the actual arrest, McQuaid didn't ask him about the bloodstains on the floorboards in the Chinaman's store, though he did refer the lawman to a curious jar of pickled meat.

McQuaid produced the bottle and set it on the counsel table for Pat Reddy to inspect, then brought it to Fales and set it before him. The judge leaned over and inspected the contents with a pinched face.

"I present this as people's exhibit number one," McQuaid said.

"No objections," Reddy said.

"So be it," Fales declared.

"Sheriff Page," McQuaid said to Matt, "have you seen this jar before?"

"Yes."

"Where was that?"

"In Quong Tai's store. He offered me some of the meat inside."

"Did you take it?"

"No. I've never been too big on pickled meat."

"You already related to this court your finding of a leg in the river, and you described the strange look it had to it. Looking now at the meat in this jar, do you notice anything about it you can describe in relation to that leg?"

"I object!" Reddy said.

"I thought you might," Fales commented. "Overruled. His opinion regarding the observation of his senses is being sought. That's okay by me. Answer the question, Sheriff."

"Well," Matt said slowly, "the meat in there and the meat on the leg look the same to me."

"How do you mean 'the same'?"

"Same color, same texture. And the leg was missing some of the . . . well, some of the pieces were gone."

"But wouldn't the river, the soaking of the water and the bouncing off rocks and logs, have damaged the leg, making it impossible to tell what you just described?"

"It would, I suppose," Matt speculated. "Except this leg never made it to the water. It was dropped onto the bank."

"How do you account for that?"

"Dark of night probably. The murderer thought he dumped all the pieces in; he didn't see the leg that didn't quite make it."

"The act of a man in a state of panic?"

"Careless, in a hurry . . . Beyond that I couldn't say."

"So the missing pieces of flesh from the leg . . . were not torn off in the river."

"No, sir, not in my estimation."

The import of McQuaid's questioning was not lost on the crowd, and there was a general disturbance that ran through the men as uncomfortable folks coughed and changed position.

"I object to this line of questioning, Your Honor," Pat Reddy said. "My colleague is obviously suggesting that the meat in that jar is the former Poker Tom, something there is not a shred of evidence to prove."

The room fell immediately silent as all eyes stared at the jar and its insidious contents in front of the judge. After a few strained moments, Fales cleared his throat

"That would appear to be the insinuation, but unfortunately we have no means to prove or disprove the theory. Do you have any more questions for this witness, Mr. McQuaid?"

"Yes, Your Honor, just one. Sheriff Page, what did you do with the jar, the leg, and the torso the Indians found?"

"I turned them over to the county physician, Dr. Keebles, for analysis."

"Thank you. Your witness, Pat."

Reddy nodded, thought for a second, then once again waved off his turn.

"You sure?" Fales asked.

"Yes, Your Honor, I'm sure."

"If you say so." Fales regarded McQuaid. "Still your turn."

"The prosecution calls Russell Draper."

CHAPTER

SIXTEEN

A hasty attempt to sober Russell Draper had obviously been made, the success of which was largely a matter of opinion. He wore clean clothes and had freshly greased hair, combed straight back and plastered to his head. His exposed skin was still red from the scrubbing, and so much black coffee had been poured down his gullet, he sloshed when he walked. His eyes couldn't be fixed, however, and were bloodshot and watery, betraying his condition to all.

He ambled unsteadily to the witness chair, most everyone in the room holding their breath in anticipation of a fall. But he made it in one piece and half-sat, half-fell into place, only to be asked to rise to be sworn in. With both hands pushing on the arms of the chair, he did so and raised his right hand while using his left on the Bible to prop himself up.

Once the wayward witness was sworn in and again seated, McQuaid began his questioning.

"Mr. Draper, did you have the occasion to participate in a recreational competition in the posterior chamber of Quong Tai's mercantile about two months ago?"

"Huh?" Draper's mouth hung open stupidly.

McQuaid exhaled. "Did you play poker at Quong Tai's with some other men a couple months ago?"

"Why didn't you say so? Yes, I did. I do that every now and then. Ain't no law against it."

"Was a Paiute man in attendance there also?"

"Only once. Poker Tom—that's who you're gettin' at, ain't it?"

"Yes, Mr. Draper, it is, but please restrict your answers to my questions, okay?"

"Sure. I ain't comfortable, that's all. Sitting in front of a jury makes me nervous."

"There's no jury here, Mr. Draper," McQuaid reminded him. "And it's not you who is the subject of this hearing."

"Oh." He visibly relaxed. "That's right."

The gallery laughed, and Fales banged his makeshift gavel on the table. "Mr. Draper, just answer the attorney's questions please. When we're done with you, you'll be free to go. I guarantee it."

"Unless he confesses during the course of his testimony," Pat Reddy pointed out with a smirk.

"Objection!" McQuaid shouted. "Counsel's trying to intimidate this witness."

"Sustained," Fales said, "though the witness is doing a pretty good job of it all by himself. Mr. Reddy, please confine your utterances to questions when it's your turn and appropriate objections when it is necessary."

Reddy smiled. "Certainly, Your Honor."

"Proceed, Mr. McQuaid."

"Thank you, Your Honor. Mr. Draper, on the night Poker Tom played with you and Quong Tai and the others, what was the outcome?"

"Poker Tom won the most. He was real lucky that night. Either that or he cheated."

"Was anyone upset?"

"Yeah, of course. We all were. How do you feel when you lose?"

"Were you upset enough to kill Poker Tom?"

"Heck, no! What're you sayin'?"

"I'm just asking the question, Mr. Draper. Was anyone else upset enough to kill him?"

"Objection," cried Reddy. "Calls for a conclusion."

"Normally I'd sustain you, Pat. But Mr. Draper isn't qualified for deep thought today. Mr. Draper, you may answer the question."

"What was it again?" he asked McQuaid.

"Was anyone there mad enough to kill Poker Tom?"

"Quong Tai was, definitely."

"How do you know this?"

"Well, you could kinda tell by the way his face got red and he spit when he talked. Oh yeah, and he threatened him, in a way."

"What did he say?"

"Objection," shouted Reddy. "Calls for hearsay."

"Speaks to what the witness heard," responded McQuaid, "not what he was told someone else heard. And the speaker is present in the courtroom and can answer to it himself."

"Overruled," Fales said. "You may answer the question," he told Draper.

"Your Honor," Draper protested, "tell that Reddy fellow to stop interruptin' me. Makes me forget what I was gonna say."

"Unfortunately, it's his job, Mr. Draper. He's a lawyer. Spend your life teaching a child manners, he gets a law degree, and manners are chucked right out the window." Fales got his laugh, then whacked his gavel. "Would you like to hear the question again, Mr. Draper?"

"No, I'm okay this time. Quong Tai said that was the last time Poker Tom would ever win that much money from him again."

"And you took that as a threat?" McQuaid prodded.

"If a man says that while getting on a horse, it means he ain't coming back. If a man's fingering a knife when he says it, it has a whole different meaning."

McQuaid continued without asking if Quong Tai was in fact fingering a knife, hoping the implication was sufficient. "Did you have any other conversations with Quong Tai regarding Poker Tom?"

"Well, not exactly a conversation."

"What do you mean?"

"He was the only one did any talkin'. That ain't what I call a conversation."

"All right then, what did he say?"

"A couple days later he told me he made sure Poker Tom wouldn't win any more poker games. He told me he killed Poker Tom."

A murmur rippled through the onlookers, and Fales rapped his mallet.

"Quiet down, men, quiet down or we'll never get through this. McQuaid?"

"That's all for now, Your Honor."

"Okay. Pat, it's your turn."

Reddy remained in his seat.

"Just one question, Your Honor. Mr. Draper, were you drunk when Quong Tai allegedly told you this?"

Draper looked to McQuaid and then to Sheriff Taylor for a hint, but neither man indicated what he should do.

"I'm a drinkin' man, Mr. Reddy. I usually have alcohol in me, that's true enough."

"The question was, were you drunk at that time?"

"Maybe. That don't mean I didn't hear what I heard. I'm drunk now and I'm doin' okay, ain't I?"

Amidst the laughs from the crowd, Reddy said, "No further questions, Your Honor."

"You may step down, Mr. Draper. Any more witnesses?" Fales asked McQuaid.

"Yes. Sheriff John Taylor."

Taylor stood, one hand on his back and the other on the arm of the chair, but walked tall and proud to the witness chair. When he was sworn in, McQuaid led him quickly through the activities of the previous day, emphasizing the finding of the bloodstain.

"And you gave the chunk of wood to Dr. Keebles, is that correct?"

"Yep."

"And did he report a finding to you?"

"Calls for hearsay," objected Reddy.

Fales waved him off. "Obviously Dr. Keebles could testify to it, since he's sitting right here. To save me some time I'm going to allow the sheriff to answer. That okay with you, Mr. Reddy?"

"Certainly, Your Honor. I withdraw the objection."

"Too late, you're overruled."

Taylor didn't wait for an invitation. "Keebles told me it's human blood."

Finished, McQuaid sat down. Reddy, after a whispered comment from Matt Page, declined to cross-examine Sheriff Taylor.

"All right then . . . Mr. McQuaid, any more witnesses?"

"Just one. The prosecution calls Doctor T.A. Keebles."

A well-dressed, heavy-set man with a distinguished gray beard stood and proceeded to the witness chair, where he was sworn in and took his place with great dignity. His gold watch chain glistened as much as the sweat on his forehead.

"You are Doctor Theodore Keebles, a licensed physician?"

The good doctor nodded. "Yes."

"And are you in private practice?"

"Yes, that is so."

"Are you also retained by Mono County?"

"Yes."

"For what purpose?"

"I am the county physician. Some locals refer to someone of my position as coroner. I do all autopsies and look into all evidence of a medical nature."

"Would body parts fall into that category?"

"Certainly."

"Did you have the chance—"

"Your Honor," interrupted Pat Reddy, "we'll stipulate that he examined all the evidence in this case. Let's just get on to what he found."

"I agree," Fales said. "McQuaid?"

"Thank you. Dr. Keebles, what are the results of your examination of the leg?"

"It is a human leg bone—left, to be precise—probably male. It was separated from its host with a fine-toothed saw and a sharp knife, very likely a skinning knife. It was then pickled in a solution of chloride of lime and ammonia, with a bit too much ammonia than should have been used. And there was very little meat left. The meat had been previously removed with a knife."

"What about the torso?"

"It is a human male, race undetermined, missing its head, both legs, and both arms, which were sawn off. The torso was begun to be pickled in a solution of chloride of lime and ammonia."

"Begun to be?"

"The process was apparently interrupted, as the pickling was not complete."

"A human torso is thicker than a human leg, is it not?"

"Indeed."

"Could they have been pickled together, then removed from the brine at the same time, the leg, because of its smaller size, pickling all the way through, while the torso remained as it was presented to you?"

"That's precisely my conclusion."

"And why is that, Doctor?"

"Well, the leg is definitely from that torso. The cuts on the bone match perfectly. And it stands to reason they would be pickled together."

"Why would they cut off the limbs and head?"

"Well, the head would be cut off to avoid identification, in my estimation. As for the limbs, well, my guess is they were cut off so they would all fit in the pickling barrel."

"Why would you guess that to be the case?"

"Since the torso wasn't pickled completely, it would seem the pickler was in a hurry. Having one barrel, he'd have to fit it all in at once."

"What would be the purpose of pickling the body in the first place?"

"To destroy the evidence, of course. Burning it would create a distinctive odor that would attract attention. Burying it might not have been possible or practical. It's been my experience that people tend to do things after a murder that in the cold light of day appear peculiar to the rest of us. But in the panic that frequently follows a crime of this sort, these bizarre acts seem not only rational and expedient, but are often the only things the perpetrators can think of. Pickling the body would allow the bones to be disposed of without risk of decomposition."

"To what do you attribute the chucking of the body into the river?"

"Again, panic. Perhaps something happened that made the perpetrator afraid of being discovered."

"Very well, Doctor. Now, given the leg and torso, can you estimate from them how tall the person would have been?"

"About five-foot-eight or so. It depends on the length of the neck and the dimensions of the head."

"Thank you. Now about the famous jar . . . I understand you examined the contents of it also?"

"Yes."

"And your conclusion?"

"The meat is of the same consistency, firmness, and color as the pickled portions of the torso, and the brine is the same in chemical composition as that left in the meat attached to the leg."

"In other words, the meat is human and was pickled in the same barrel as the rest of Poker Tom's body."

"Your Honor," pleaded Reddy, interrupting, "I have no choice but to object to this unfounded assumption. This is little more than educated guessing, which is unacceptable in a court of law. I was silent during the good doctor's speculatory diatribe on the reason why the body was pickled, even though I could have objected on the grounds that it was preposterous, but I can no longer—"

"I get the point, Pat," Fales interrupted. "But I trust you'll remedy that in your cross-examination. If your colleague was playing to a jury I'd've stopped him myself, but since it's just me, don't worry about it. I'm quite capable of separating fact from fiction." He turned to the doctor. "I know you've been coached by the prosecutor, but please restrict your answers to what you can say with surety, okay, Doc?"

"Certainly, Your Honor."

McQuaid took the nod from Fales and continued. "Doc Keebles, you mentioned the pickling medium to be two chemicals—chloride of lime and ammonia."

"That is correct. Two very common chemicals."

"Common enough to be found in, say, a general store?"

"Absolutely."

"I have no more questions, Your Honor," McQuaid said, confident he had made his point. He sat down with a wry grin while Reddy stood, smoothing his coat.

"Doctor Keebles," Reddy began softly, "I'll not go into the equipment you used to arrive at these auspicious conclusions, nor the methods you employed, although if this goes to trial you can be sure I will do so in great detail." He paused to let that sink in. "What I want to make clear here are the results of your scientific examination." He walked around the table and stood off to the side, leaning on a railing that surrounded the empty jury box.

"You stated that the fluids of the torso and in the jar were chemically the same, and both were a little heavy on the ammonia, is that correct?"

"Yes."

"If I were to mix a batch and use exactly the same ratio as the brine in that jar, would you be able to tell the difference between my concoction and the brine in that jar?"

"Uh . . . well, no, I suppose not."

"And these ingredients are common, available in any general store?"

"Yes."

"Could they also be found in most homes?"

"Well, yes, I suppose so."

"Do you have some in your home, Dr. Keebles? Not your physician's office, but your private home?"

"Well . . . yes, I believe I do."

Reddy was hard-pressed to quell a grin.

"Thank you." Reddy thought a moment while stroking his mutton-chop sideburn with his only arm, then moved over to the counsel table, taking his seat. That's what he always did when he felt in command of the situation—like a rattler letting his victim know the deadly strike was imminent.

"You believe the meat in the jar to be human, do you not, Dr. Keebles?"

"Yes."

"But are you positive it's human? With scientific certainty, I mean?"

He shook his head. "No, not one hundred per—"

"Thank you, Doctor, you've answered my question. And you believe the torso—and thus the leg as well—to be male, based, I assume, on their appearance and certain characteristics that are commonly male? Muscle structure and all that?"

"Yes. Of that there can be no doubt."

"And of what race is the body?"

"I can't be sure. The head is the most common postmortem determiner of race."

"What about the skin, Doctor? Surely that would tell you a great deal."

"Yes, if it hadn't—"

"If it hadn't been pickled—is that what you were about to say?"

"Yes."

"Then you can't determine the race of the body, can you, Doctor?"

"No, not presently."

"So you don't know if the body is that of Poker Tom or not, do you?"

The doctor shook his head slowly. "No, I do not."

"Your Honor," Pat Reddy said boldly, "I move for a dismissal.

The prosecution hasn't even shown that Poker Tom is deceased, much less murdered."

"No, Pat, I don't think I'll do that," Fales said. "We're gonna see this one through, then I'll make my decision."

"Very well, Your Honor. The defense rests."

"It's not your turn yet. The prosecution hasn't rested."

"Well, when they do, so do I."

"Without bringing any witnesses?"

"The prosecution, in our estimation, has failed to prove anything regarding my client, as I'll attest to in my argument. May I request a recess to prepare?"

Fales looked at McQuaid, who said, "The prosecution rests, Your Honor. A recess is fine with me."

Fales banged the gavel. "One hour, gentlemen. Be prompt."

CHAPTER

SEVENTEEN

MATT DRIFTED DOWNSTAIRS and out of the courtroom, figuring he'd check up on the Paiutes milling around outside while Taylor stayed behind with Pat Reddy, the two sitting on opposite sides of the prisoner. Reddy made a few notes but generally looked quite prepared to begin his argument.

Things did not look good for the prosecution, especially in light of Reddy's not even feeling he needed to put on a defense. The prosecutors were missing several important links between Ah Quong Tai and Poker Tom's murder. Even if they could prove the torso belonged to the missing Indian, they needed to more convincingly connect him with the Chinese store owner.

Matt didn't have much faith in the testimony of Russell Draper, even though he believed he was telling the truth, or at least the truth as best he saw it. Reddy had been able to discredit the witness pretty thoroughly. And there was another problem: John Taylor was just plain wrong about the blood on the floor.

There were too many gaps in their case. Where were the missing body parts? It stood to reason the arms and the other leg were somewhere downstream, having been dumped at the same time but not having gotten hung up on the bank. But what about the head? And for that matter, the knife and saw? If Matt could find those things, they'd get a trial—and a conviction—for sure. Even Pat Reddy couldn't wiggle out of that, and Matt would show

Sheriff Taylor up for certain. Even more important, a guilty man wouldn't go free.

But they'd looked for the knife and head and hadn't found them. Taylor had even torn up the boards in Quong Tai's store where they'd found the blood. Matt hated to think what would happen if the Chinaman were released—

The boards in Quong Tai's store.

Matt snapped his fingers and tore down the street to Quong's old store, the one he'd recently vacated, the one where the poker game involving the missing Paiute had been held. Not having a key to the front door, he went around back and forced open the rear door with a single kick. He went in and began to look around, hoping something useful would get his attention.

Nothing did, so he dropped onto the floor and started looking for any loose boards. He crawled over the whole place, prying, thumping, stomping, but was unable to pull anything up. He also didn't see any new, shiny nails or fresh hammer marks. He even went into the back room but was just as unsuccessful there.

Sitting on the floor with his back to the counter, Matt ran a hand absentmindedly along the well-used boards, crying out when a splinter pierced his finger. He pulled the hand up and stuck the offended digit into his mouth, then inspected the damage. But even as he plucked out the intruder and flicked it away, shaking his injured hand as if to fling off the pain, a thought struck him. A splinter on a floor as worn smooth as this one?

He looked down slowly, then rolled over and away from the counter. The floor bore fresh marks corresponding to the edges of the counter, showing it had been moved recently. And now that he took a good look at the floor, he noticed a rectangle of lighter wood about the same size as the counter right next to it.

That's where the counter used to be, before it was moved.

Matt jumped up, put his shoulder to the counter, and shoved. Slowly it began to move until he had displaced it a good two feet. He examined the floor and found what he had been searching for.

A bloodstain, streaked from the counter being pushed over it— this one very likely Poker Tom's. Taylor had the right idea, just the wrong location. He'd pried the boards in Quong Tai's new place.

Grabbing a discarded piece of scrap iron from the corner, Matt jammed it between the boards and pushed. He groaned with the effort, but it paid off, and the board lifted. He repositioned the makeshift pry bar and grunted again as he pushed. This time the board came free with a groan and a creak. Dropping the bar, the lawman grabbed the board with his hands and yanked it up, then took hold of the adjacent board and did the same. In no time he had exposed a hole large enough to crawl through.

Removing his gunbelt and hat, Matt grabbed a piece of splintered wood from the back room and lit it with a match. Old and dry, it flamed immediately. He dropped it into the hole and let himself down after it. The space was cramped, with less than four feet of room between the ground and the bottom of the floor; but he knew he was onto something and didn't let the restricted access slow him down. Holding the torch as high as he could, he crawled through the damp, cobwebbed, insect-infested area, searching for anything useful he could find.

Not more than five feet from the counter, he found a canvas bag with a drawstring, about the size of a large pumpkin. His heart fluttered, and he wanted to look inside but decided that would be better done up above where the light and ventilation were better. He tossed the sack gently ahead of him near the opening, then crawled to it and set the bag on the floor of the store, climbing out after it. Without any more hesitation, he pulled it open and looked inside.

Back in the courtroom everyone had reassembled, and the judge rapped his gavel several times to quiet the men. No one had noticed the absence of Sheriff Matt Page, except for John Taylor, and he wasn't talking.

"Are you ready for arguments?" Fales asked, knowing the attorneys had better be ready or suffer the consequences.

"Yes," both attorneys responded simultaneously. McQuaid stood.

"The prosecution has the burden of proof," Fales said needlessly. "You may proceed first, Mr. McQuaid."

"Thank you, Your Honor. You have heard much testimony today. You heard Captain John tell how Poker Tom is missing and how a dismembered torso his wife believes to be Tom's was found in the Walker River, having been pickled. You've heard the testimony of Mr. Russell Draper that Poker Tom was last seen in a card game with Ah Quong Tai, from whom Poker Tom won over fifty dollars. You've also heard Mr. Draper testify that Ah Quong Tai threatened to kill Poker Tom because of it, then afterward bragged about doing so.

"After that we heard from Acting Sheriff Matt Page . . ." McQuaid swept his arm to where Matt should have been sitting and was a little taken aback to see the chair empty. But he went on, undaunted. "We heard him testify that Ah Quong Tai had this jar of pickled meat in his store, and how he found on the riverbank a leg belonging to the torso that had been located by Poker Tom's people. And we heard from Doctor Keebles how the brine used to pickle this meat, the leg, and the torso were chemically the same, all of them equally heavy on the ammonia. Your Honor, we have motive, opportunity, and a confession. The prosecution requests Ah Quong Tai be held to answer in Superior Court for the murder of Poker Tom."

As he settled into his chair, a murmur of agreement rippled through the gallery. But Pat Reddy was unfazed. He twiddled his singular thumb until the noise died, then stood.

"Very convincing, Your Honor, except for a few small details. No proof was offered that Poker Tom is actually dead. Someone is, to be sure. But is it Poker Tom? Only God knows at this moment in time, and He is not available to take the witness stand. But let's assume for the time being that the body is indeed that of Poker Tom. It is a reasonable assumption, we'll admit. What does this do to bolster the prosecution's case against Ah Quong Tai? Absolutely nothing. This hearing was set to decide if there was enough evidence to hold Ah Quong Tai to answer to the charge of murder, and sufficient proof has not been presented. There were no witnesses to the act. No instruments as described by the doctor were located in the possession of Ah Quong Tai. The sole witness with anything of value to the prosecution is a known roustabout and gambler whose statement could be purchased by anyone of even small means."

John McQuaid rose to protest this insinuation, but Reddy continued with his hand raised.

"I do not mean to imply that my honorable opponent or anyone else has done so in this case. Quite the contrary. I believe that Mr. Draper was telling the truth as best he knew how. The point is, however, that had the testimony Mr. Draper gave been offered by anyone else, including myself, it would be just as useless and inadmissible, Judge Fales, and therefore cannot be considered by yourself before rendering a verdict."

"Preposterous!" objected McQuaid.

"Can you support this?" Fales asked.

"Certainly," Reddy said. "Any confession, given in the absence of any evidence to support the veracity of the confession, is inadmissible. It's the Fifth Amendment right against self-incrimination. The prosecution must have something tangible to support the confession, and there is nothing. Not one single, solitary thing. Your Honor has no choice but to completely disregard the testimony of Mr. Draper. If Ah Quong Tai himself admitted the offense to the sheriff without giving any details, he could not be compelled to repeat it in a court of law without corroborating evidence. Mr. McQuaid knows that as well as you and I do, Your Honor. That is learned in the first year of law school."

McQuaid's face turned crimson. Reddy was, of course, absolutely correct. The prosecutor made no comment.

"Anything else?" Fales asked Reddy.

"There is one other matter . . . the alleged blood on the floor of Ah Quong Tai's store. If memory serves me correctly, didn't Quong Tai just move into that building *this week*? If I am correct about that—and I am, let there be no doubt—that could not be Poker Tom's blood, nor could it have been left by my client. He did not occupy that store the night of the card game. That bloodstain happens to have been left by a couple of notorious felons who had no better sense than to mix it up with one Matt Page several years ago when they were foiled by Page—before he was a deputy—during an attempted robbery."

A murmur rippled through the room, forcing Fales to wield his mallet.

"That about do it?" Fales asked when they'd quieted.

Reddy thought a moment, then simply said, "Yes" and sat down.

Fales was pensive. He studied his notes for quite some time before looking up and staring around at every face in the courtroom. Finally he took a deep breath.

"The court finds that Poker Tom may have died at the hand of another, and the body in question is very likely his. But there is insufficient evidence to warrant binding Quong Tai over for trial at this time. If more evidence is located, I will call another hearing to consider it at that time. Double jeopardy does not apply since this is not an actual trial, but just a hearing to determine the value of evidence collected and its relationship to the culpability of the defendant, of which I find little to none. I hereby order the prisoner released." He smacked the gavel one time and stood.

A myriad of emotions coursed through the courtroom. McQuaid was disappointed and mad, Reddy mildly pleased with himself, John Taylor chagrined and fearful. The spectators were impressed with Reddy, and Captain John was confused.

"What this mean?" he asked someone.

"Ah Quong Tai is free," he was told.

"Free?"

"As a bird."

"He kill Poker Tom," Captain John protested.

"Probably," the spectator agreed. "But McQuaid can't prove it, so they have to let him go."

Captain John considered this for a moment, then turned and hurried from the room. Judge Fales noticed the Indian's hasty departure and spun around to look out the window. Captain John emerged from the building and spoke a few words to his men, then waved his arm, and suddenly the braves, so quiet and still throughout the morning, broke into a frenzy of angry activity. This did not look good.

Even Ah Quong Tai was not happy about his release. He grabbed Sheriff Taylor by the sleeve, panic creasing his face.

"You must not let me go!"

"What?"

"They'll kill me. You must give me protection."

"He's got a point," Reddy said, trying to shove his papers into his briefcase with his only hand.

"You mean them Indians?" Taylor said.

"They believe he killed Poker Tom," Reddy said. "Frankly, so do I. But I had a job to do."

"I know," McQuaid said, moving over next to him. "Were the roles reversed, I'd have done the same thing."

"He's guilty, but we've got to release him," Taylor concluded.

"It's not our problem to protect his yellow hide from now on. Besides, I've got a town to think about." He moved over to the window. "Look down there."

The attorneys complied. The street was crawling with agitated Paiutes, the reserves from the edge of town also having been brought in.

"If we try to harbor this man, they'll go wild on us—probably burn the town to the ground and kill as many white people as they can, just for spite. Look at the white folk scurryin' for their homes and shops. They're arming themselves—you know that as well as I do. We'll have a bloodbath if we try to protect the Chinaman. I don't like the looks of this, not at all."

"A moral dilemma, to be sure," Pat Reddy said, rubbing his chin. "I think I'll sit here and catch up on some paperwork." He dumped the contents of his briefcase on the table and sat back down.

"Don't take no thought for me," Taylor said. "One Chinaman in exchange for a whole town—don't take no college mathematics to figure this one out. C'mon, little buddy—like it or not, you're a free man. You got your day in court, and you won. It's a happy day." He grabbed the Chinaman by the seat of the pants and a shoulder and hustled him out of the room, down the stairs, and into the street, giving him a little shove before retreating back into the safety of the building and slamming the door.

The Indians were on him like flies on rancid meat, whooping and hollering. In no time they had tied Ah Quong Tai's feet and were dragging him down Main Street behind a horse. The Chinaman screamed for help, but no one was listening.

CHAPTER

EIGHTEEN

MATT PEERED INTO the dark sack, then held the torch above it. As the light moved and the darkness fled, a stark-white, upside-down bowl came into view. Matt reached in, plucked the object out, and found himself staring face-to-face with a human skull. It had a grainy feel to it, and Matt smelled the familiar odor of brine on the bone. He set it carefully down with a shaking hand. Looking into the sack again, he was rewarded for his efforts a second time, and a third.

Also in the sack was a slender, stained stiletto and a cabinetry saw with a fine-toothed blade, used for delicate, close-tolerance work. He'd found what he needed.

Matt put the evidence quickly back into the sack. As he hurried toward the door, a cry went up on the street, a blood-curdling *whoop* that could only mean one thing. Matt threw the door open in time to see Indians on horseback race past him, following a lead horse dragging a screaming Ah Quong Tai, bound by a rope around his feet.

Matt watched from the boardwalk in dismay, knowing the time to prevent this very act had passed. Quong Tai's fate was sealed, and no power on earth could stop it. The lawman looked down at the sack, his emotions boiling, his soul grieving. What did this evidence matter now?

As he stood watching in disbelief, running footsteps

approached him from behind, and someone grabbed his arm and held on tightly.

"Oh, Matt, it's so horrible," Sarah said in between breaths.

"You don't know the half of it," Matt said solemnly.

"What are you going to do?"

"Nothing."

"Nothing?" Sarah looked up at him, shocked. She had never before heard him decline to do what was right, no matter what the danger.

"Sarah, there are over fifty armed Indians who vowed not to leave without justice being done to Ah Quong Tai, no matter how they get it done. And since the white man's court let him go . . ." His voice faded. He didn't want to tell her what he suspected had occurred: Ah Quong Tai had been turned over to the Paiutes by her father. He would have been the only man in the courtroom who could have done it. Being the elected sheriff, everyone would've deferred to him.

"What do you think they'll do to him?"

"I don't want to think about it."

Sarah glanced down and saw the sack hanging from Matt's hand. "What's in there?"

"Huh?"

"In the potato sack."

"Oh." Matt looked down at it as though he'd never seen it before. "Nothing important." He said no more, and Sarah knew better than to ask.

"I'd better go see . . ." Matt started to say as he stepped off the porch, but he didn't finish because he didn't know quite how to put it. *See to Quong Tai's remains*, he was thinking.

He left Sarah on the porch and walked across the street, ignoring John Taylor who stood in the upstairs window of the courtroom with Fales, Reddy, and McQuaid, all of them watching the Indians swarming in a field at the edge of town, not far from Matt and Sarah's small whitewashed house.

Once inside his office, Matt locked the sack in the desk, then ventured back onto the street, climbing onto Shadow's back and riding slowly in the direction the Indians had gone. He could hear them and knew approximately where they were. Before he'd gotten halfway there he heard the hoofbeats of their horses as they headed back into town, still whooping and hollering and whistling. He stopped to watch them pass, and Captain John reined up a few yards away. The two men regarded each other without words for a few moments. Then Captain John turned his horse and rode on with the rest of his band, on through town, across the bridge, and down the dusty road until they were gone, the dust had settled, and it was over.

Over for them perhaps, and seemingly over for the citizens of Bridgeport, but it wasn't over for Matt Page. He continued through town in the direction they'd taken Ah Quong Tai, and when he arrived at the killing field it was easy to see where they'd done their deed. His scalp, the queue still attached, hung from the fencepost at the corner of the field where George Day grazed his cows every spring and summer. Shadow shied, so Matt rode around the field and left his horse tied to the fence down the way, then walked back to the pasture and entered it carefully.

Quong Tai's savaged, knife-slashed body was in the center of the field. Matt stared at it, nearly choking in the presence of such a grisly sight. He couldn't leave it here. Too many curious children would want to come and take a look, and they'd be forever changed because of it. Besides, the route to the revival tent took folks directly by here, and that wouldn't do at all. Some souvenir hunters might even add some of the grisly artifacts to their odd collections.

Matt returned to Shadow for his leather trail gloves and began collecting the errant pieces that had become detached, laying them next to the body. He had been at it for a few nauseating minutes when he sensed someone entering the field behind him. Turning, he saw an Indian dressed in buckskin pants and a heavy wool coat striding toward him. Not Captain John, not even one of his braves, but a local Paiute tracker, his good friend Charlie Jack.

"Matt not look good," Charlie Jack observed.

"You know what happened here?" Matt asked.

"I know. Captain John tell me on road. He say Poker Tom dead, Quong Tai dead, pretty good."

"Is that what he thinks? Eye for an eye?"

Charlie Jack nodded. "Quong Tai guilty, yes?"

Matt dropped his head. "Yeah, I'd say so. But he wasn't found guilty in court, which is the only thing that matters in this country."

"For white men. For Indian, justice matter more than having

committee make decision. Sometimes committee wrong, or judge say sheriff make mistake, so guilty man go free. White man have crazy laws." Charlie Jack drew imaginary rings around his right ear with his index finger.

"Do you think what they did was right?"

Charlie Jack shrugged. "Not for me to say. Charlie Jack not killed. Not member of my tribe killed. Not my business."

"If it was a member of your tribe, would you have participated?"

"Matt want Charlie to say no. Maybe yes, maybe no. Depend."

"On what?"

"On whether it Tuesday or not. Charlie Jack take Tuesday off." For the first time Matt was not amused by the Indian.

"You're playing with me."

Charlie shook his head. "Matt want answer to question where there is no answer. I don't know what I do. When happen, I will know. Come, let us bury Quong Tai so his spirit not be confused."

"You know I don't believe that stuff," Matt said, putting his gloves back on.

"Yes, but it sound good." Charlie Jack unbuttoned his coat and helped Matt put Quong Tai's remains into the large potato sack Matt had brought with him. The scalpless head had been completely severed, Quong Tai's face still bearing a look of terror. Matt put it in last because he figured the head should be on top. He tied the sack to his saddle, having a little trouble as Shadow tried to move away from him. He finally overcame the beast and rode with Charlie to the cemetery, where Matt paid several dollars to the undertaker to have a worker dig a hole in the far corner of the property. There they laid Ah Quong Tai to rest, head up.

Only as they were riding back into town did Matt realize he'd left the scalp on the fencepost. He thought about it, then left it there and rode on, hoping his father-in-law would get a good look at it on his way to the revival that night.

This was not to be, however, as Matt discovered before he arrived back at his office. Taylor would see it all right, but it would not have the desired effect. Instead, it would serve as a symbol of the way John Taylor had saved Bridgeport from a band of wild Paiutes, savage renegades. That the Paiutes weren't actually renegades, nor particularly savage was lost on most people in town. These braves were mostly peaceful Indians who had their own deep-seated idea of justice and acted upon it, then left the way they came in and went back to their everyday lives. The threat they posed while they were here was all that mattered to the people of Bridgeport, and for them those few hours defined the Paiutes. It would be some time before they forgot that day.

And for now the hero was John Taylor. It was he who had decided not to risk an attack by the Indians. It was he who had decided it was better to sacrifice one insignificant yellow heathen rather than untold numbers of white folk and their homes and stores. It was John Taylor who, though still recovering from a nearly fatal shot in the back, single-handedly saved Bridgeport from sure destruction.

At least, that was the talk all over town. At that moment Matt realized that his bid to be the next sheriff would be more difficult now, seeing the sudden rise in John Taylor's popularity. Everywhere Matt went that morning he heard someone talking about their champion, John Taylor. Toasts in his honor were made in the saloons; women in the pharmacy were admiring the tall, veteran law officer. Though dreading it, Matt finally had no choice but to go home.

Matt hung his hat and coat on the rack and untied the knot in his neckerchief, wiping his face with it. Sarah came out from the kitchen.

"I'll get you a hot bath," she offered.

"No time. I'll just clean up in the bowl." He went through the kitchen to the back of the house and removed his shirt, wiped the road dust from his face, arms, and chest, then dunked his head and shook it as he drew it out, splattering water all over the rear porch. He dried himself and combed his hair back, then slipped on a clean shirt. Sarah watched him the whole time.

"You ready to go?" Matt asked as he buttoned his collarless shirt. He left his tie on the hook.

"You're going to the revival?" Sarah wondered. "Aren't you tired?"

"Of course I'm tired. But it's called a revival, isn't it?"

Though he hid his feelings as he walked hand-in-hand with Sarah to the tent, it took all Matt's strength to put one foot in front of the other. The last thing he wanted to do was sit in the middle of a crowd of people who thought being an accessory to murder was a good thing. Wasn't that what had happened? Didn't Taylor give Quong Tai to the Indians knowing they were going to murder him?

But the Chinaman *was* guilty, Matt told himself. He had found the proof himself, though no one knew about it except him. He hadn't even told Sarah. John Taylor certainly hadn't known there was proof of Quong Tai's guilt when he turned the Chinaman over to Captain John's band. Yes, he might have saved the town and some lives. Without question, the Indians would have gone on the warpath, and people would've been hurt. But it was still wrong, wasn't it?

Matt sat in the tent and put his head in his hands, covering his ears. He wasn't sure anymore. After all, the court had ordered Quong Tai released. Taylor was just following orders. Could Matt say with any certainty that he would have done any differently? Would he have stood against the town, the judge, the Indians, all for the sake of one man who was indeed guilty?

Jenny Miller at the organ relieved Matt of the responsibility of having to answer that question as the congregation rose to sing.

Matt paid no attention to the songbook, not even bothering to join the rest of the congregation. When Benson began his sermon, Matt heard nothing but the shrieks of Quong Tai.

Then something Reverend Benson said registered with the lawman.

"My friends, are you suffering today? Do you have problems? Is there a want of money? Do you get all the medical attention you need? What about food? Is there plenty? Or do you have to scrape and scrap for every meal? Maybe you're having problems with a loved one. They've died or left you. Take comfort, friend—Christ is with you. The Good Book says you will suffer, make no mistake about it. Right here in the pages of the Bible, God says you will suffer for being a Christian. 'Think it not strange, beloved, concerning the fiery trial you are having.' It happens to all of us. But rejoice! Do not be ashamed. Remember, your body is the temple of the Holy Ghost. Do you think He wants to reside in a temple that is infirm? That is incomplete or crippled? Do you think the Holy Ghost wants a damaged, impaired temple? Of course not!

That's why He has promised to respond to your faith by healing you. It's God's nature to want to heal you."

And just like that, Benson lost Matt's attention again. Faith healing. Matt had heard this before, and he didn't want any part of it. He wished he had stayed home after all, but it was too late. Benson droned on, naming all the common maladies that were sure to be present in the congregation, most of them the kind that could be found only in the minds of those afflicted.

Then Benson pointed out to a different section of the congregation and called for a man with a bad back, asking if he wanted to be healed. When a man hesitantly stood, Benson acted as though he'd known about him all along and urged him forward.

"Do you believe God still performs miracles?" he asked the man as he mounted the platform, wringing his hat between his hands and looking back over his friends in the congregation. Benson continued, "Tell me, friend, just when did He stop? Did He help the children of Israel cross the Red Sea on dry land? Did He cause clean, cool, clear, sweet drinking water to come streaming out of a rock, enough to quench the thirst and cleanse the bodies and launder the clothing of a million or more people? Did He guide that smooth, small stone from David's slingshot straight into the forehead of a nine-foot giant and bring him collapsing to the earth like a great felled tree?" His voice continued to rise in the same way an orchestra builds to a crescendo, his arms and face becoming more and more animated.

Benson stared down at the crowd, scanning their faces with a wide-eyed defiant look that challenged someone to tell him when miracles ceased. No one moved for fear he would notice and turn all his ire on him or her and him or her alone. When it was more than evident no one would accept the challenge, his face relaxed into a smile, and he stood erect.

"The truth is, my friends, God hasn't stopped. His miracles continue today through his servants, humble men such as myself who are willing to be used by Him for His glory. His power, channeled through me, can heal your infirmities. God has granted to me a great privilege. He told me many years ago that He wants to use me as a channel of his power. But it is not me, oh no. Think not that Josiah W. Benson has any power of his own. Nay, it is not I, but God working through me. Let me put my hands on you, and you shall feel the power of God come through me into your body. The healing power of God. Yes, that's it."

Matt watched with suspicious interest as the man with the alleged bad back let Benson put one hand on his spine and the other on his chest.

"In the name of Jesus, be healed!" As he said this, he pushed the man slightly, who reeled backwards, stunned. His face lit up, and he looked out at the crowd, his smile immense as he bent over double on the platform to show everyone that his back was healed.

Another man moved cautiously forward, complaining of having lost the ability to smell. Benson grabbed him by the face, placing his thumbs alongside the man's nose, and repeated the invocation. The man's head snapped back, and he lost his balance. But when he recovered, he took a big sniff, and his eyes widened.

"I kin smell!" he shouted. He danced a jig and at Benson's direction moved off to the side to make room for others who were beginning to come forward.

This activity continued for another half-hour, several more people with various ailments letting Benson "heal" them. But this kind of thing was new to Bridgeport, and despite the apparent successes, there were still skeptics. Soon Benson sensed he was finished for the evening. Making a comment about the quenching of the Spirit, he quickly thanked God for the power of the Holy Ghost He'd sent down that evening and asked the festive recipients of divine power to return to their seats. But he didn't dismiss the congregation, and when Jenny got up to play the organ, he begged her to wait.

"I wanted to tell you all," Benson said. "I wanted to tell you all just what a magnificent job your sheriff did today." Matt began to look around, wondering what he had done that was so magnificent that a traveling preacher should make mention of it. But the mystery was soon revealed.

"I owe my personal safety to Sheriff John Taylor, and I want to thank him in front of you all. As a traveler, just passing through your fair city, I could have been caught up in a most unfortunate scene, but quick thinking on the part of Sheriff Taylor saved us all. The Indians were ready to rise up, of that there is no doubt. Instead, they are gone, and the town is safe. Sheriff, from the bottom of my heart, thank you for being a superlative peacekeeper."

Matt heard nothing else, the blood pounding in his ears. In a few moments they were dismissed, and Matt hurried out of the tent, dragging Sarah straight home without a word to her or anyone else.

"Matt, what's this all about?" she asked once they were safely inside their house.

"That's not what happened today, Sarah. What Benson said, that's not what happened."

"What do you mean? The Indians are gone, aren't they? Weren't they going to attack the town if they didn't get justice?"

"Yes, I suppose. But your . . ." Matt cut himself off. "I'm sorry, Sarah. I'm letting my emotions run away with me again. Forget it."

"Oh, Matt, I'm so sorry things aren't going well for you." She hugged him, but his response was weak.

"I'm tired, Sarah. I'm going to bed."

"All right, Matt. All right."

But as he lay in the dark, he could not sleep. With Sarah's steady breathing keeping time, he watched the shadows from the flickering light on the post outside as they danced on the ceiling. He wondered what he'd be doing for a living when the election was over.

CHAPTER

NINETEEN

A PURPLE AND ORANGE SUNSET painted its colors on the white-washed buildings of Bodie as Jeff sat on his horse on the hill above the cemetery, soaking up the view, the sun at his back. His position afforded him a sight of the entire valley—the zebra-striped snow that still clung tenaciously to the ground on the hills surrounding the gold camp; the blue smoke rising from countless chimneys; the hustle and bustle of well-wrapped folk on Main Street; the high clouds bathed in reflected color from the setting sun. The contrast of the hues with the darkening eastern sky behind Bodie Bluff and High Peak was incredible, and Jeff was glad nothing was happening in town to keep him from him enjoying it.

Soon, however, the sun disappeared behind him, and the colors faded into shadow. With a glance of respect toward the cemetery he rode slowly back to town, back to work, back to the ordinary humdrum of daily life in a wild and lawless gold mining camp.

As he rode toward the livery to put away his horse for the night, Thomas Wellman hailed him from a block away, waving and running as fast as his stubby legs could carry him. He wore the only thing Jeff had ever seen him wear, but since it was always clean Jeff figured he must have more than one suit just like it. His hat was stiff, placed on his head at a jaunty angle, and he looked for all the world like a banker. It was the boots that gave him away. Miner's boots, knee-high and thick-soled, though he had begun to wear his pants over them to hide their origins. It was probably his miner's sense that kept him wearing the boots even though he no longer worked in the mines themselves but in the front office of the Queen Anne, Bodie's second largest concern.

Scraping for a living as a prospector first, then as a hard-rock miner before moving up in the company, Wellman was keenly aware of the value of a dollar. Nothing was thrown out if there was any life left in it at all. When his boots fell off his feet of their own accord, he'd toss them and get proper shoes. Until then, they'd do just fine, thank you.

Jeff stopped and waited for the mining supervisor to catch up to him, resting his hands across the pommel of his saddle. Wellman arrived red-faced and breathless.

"Whew!" he said, removing his hat to mop his brow. "Can't believe I'm this hot when it's this cold."

"What can I do for you?" Jeff urged.

"Well, we need your help," Wellman said. "The mine owners, I'm saying. We got a big shipment of bullion going out on the Carson City stage, and we need someone to ride along with it."

"What's that got to do with me?" Jeff asked. "That's a private concern. I work for the county."

"Yes, yes, of course. I understand that. Normally at least two, maybe three Wells Fargo agents would ride out with the stage. But it just so happens there is an inbound stage the same day carrying a great deal of cash, and all the local agents will be on it. All you need to do—hopefully you and your brother both—is ride on the outbound until it meets the inbound near the transfer station, then take the inbound back to Bodie. The Wells Fargo agents will take over on the outbound all the way to Carson City."

"Hmm. Doesn't sound like much of a problem. The way I hear it, the trouble spot is a couple miles this side of the transfer station where the canyon narrows. Once through there, it's usually clear sailing."

"You'd only be gone a few hours."

"I suppose it wouldn't hurt . . ."

"You'd actually be protecting the citizens and concerns of Bodie, which is your sworn duty," Wellman said. He smiled. "And I'm sure the mine owners will be glad to make it worth your while."

"Well, if we're doin' our sworn duty, then what the county

already pays is all we're obliged to take, but thanks all the same. When does the stage leave?"

"In about ten minutes."

"What? Well, in that case I'd better get Josh."

"Taken care of," Wellman said. "I sent someone to get him. The stage is getting ready as we speak. If you'd like, I'll see to it your horse gets properly taken care of." He took hold of the horse's bridle, then looked up the street. "See, here he comes now."

Indeed, Josh was hurrying down the street at a trot, still buttoning his coat. He waved at Jeff, who returned the greeting weakly.

Jeff glanced up the street at his brother, then looked back at Wellman with a raised eyebrow.

"What if we'd said no?" he asked the miner.

Wellman grinned. "I didn't expect you would. Leastwise I knew I could count on Josh."

Jeff grunted. "Okay, Mr. Wellman, I guess you've got yourself a deal. Maybe when we get back you can buy us both some dinner since we're gonna be missin' ours."

"My pleasure. A fair price to ask for such short notice. Good luck."

Jeff dismounted and joined his brother, and they walked to the American Hotel across the street where the stage stood at the ready. There were a handful of other passengers milling about, waiting to board. No one of a suspicious nature. Just a couple of businessmen, one of them with his stout wife, and a Wells Fargo bookkeeper—a timid-appearing bespectacled man wearing a bowler and woolen greatcoat and fine leather gloves, his cheeks and nose already red from the cold.

"Hope you're ready to start shiverin'," Josh told him as he looked inside the coach. "It don't get no warmer."

"Thanks for the comfort," the man said.

"No problem. Josh Bodine here. That's my brother Jeff. I'll be up top; he'll be inside with you. Where's the cargo?"

"In the boot, securely lashed to the coach."

"Think it's safe there?"

"Only place for it. Too heavy to be on top."

"Yeah, I s'pose that's true enough. Okay then, we all ready?"

Josh climbed up to sit beside the driver as Jeff settled into the coach, smiling at the young woman across from him. He hadn't seen her standing with the others; apparently she'd been inside already when he arrived. He quickly and discreetly sized her up, just as he had the other passengers. She didn't look like a prostitute, nor a stage robber, but it didn't hurt to be careful. It wasn't unheard of for a woman to be used by a gang to create a diversion. Satisfied she was no threat, he looked away, then chanced a second glance at her for personal reasons. As he admired her pretty face with the small nose and clear green eyes, she suddenly turned her head and caught him looking, and both of them reddened.

"Uh, hello," Jeff said, touching the underside of his hat brim, suddenly self-conscious. He didn't recall the last time he'd looked in a mirror, and it had been two days since he'd had time to shave. *I must look frightful. Better put her at ease.*

"I'm Jeff Bodine, deputy sheriff here in Bodie along with my little brother Josh. That's him up top. You leavin' town?"

"Pleased to meet you, Deputy. My name's Johanna Raymond. Actually I've just arrived here. I'm going back to Aurora for a few days to finalize the sale of my property there."

"You can call me Jeff, ma'am."

"Jeff it is then, but you must call me Johanna." She smiled. "I'm opening a laundry, next to the American Hotel."

"Gonna compete with the Chinese, are you?" asked a plump gentleman seated next to her who'd been watching the two of them.

"I'm going to try," she returned with a sincere smile. "Not everyone trusts the Chinese. They do so tend to overdo the starch." She looked back at Jeff. "If you two are deputies in Bodie, why are you taking the outbound stage?"

Jeff grinned. "Thought you might need some protection along the way."

Johanna blushed and dropped her head slightly, but not enough to hide her smile. "That's kind of you but doubtful."

Jeff shrugged. "Just a little business, actually. We won't be goin' all the way, just to the transfer station."

"Well, it's good to have you along."

"Thank you, ma'am—or is it miss?"

"I'm a widow," she admitted a little sadly. He didn't press her, but she explained anyway. "My husband died last year. I've been trying to make it on my own, and doing pretty fair, I'd say."

"I'm sorry about your tragedy," Jeff said. "I know how it feels. I lost my pa last year."

She nodded. "He was a good man. My husband, I mean . . . though I'm sure your pa was a good man, too. Henry was a miner. Spent too many years underground . . . died of silicosis. It was terrible near the end. He's better off now, in heaven with Jesus."

"You were . . . hmm, *are* Christian folk?"

"Not Christian folk, as you put it, Jeff. Just about everyone is that. I'm a Christian. I see that puzzles you. Let me explain."

Just then the driver whistled and shook the reins, and the coach lurched into motion, disrupting everyone on or in it. When it settled into its rhythm—jerky as it was—she continued, telling Jeff about her personal relationship with Christ as opposed to a general relationship with people based on biblical morals.

He listened intently, honestly trying to understand. That she was pretty, with a lilting, sweet voice, made the task easier. Their pa had always read the Bible to him and Josh—as their mother had done before she died. But Jeff never really understood it to be more than a collection of interesting and sometimes confusing stories about an ancient and faraway band of people, their mystical God, and the creation of everything—familiar tales he always thought were just made-up fables to entertain children or to scare them into not misbehavin'. The Bible was full of good advice, too; he knew that from when his father read from the book of Proverbs.

But something to pattern your life after, to build your future on? He'd always thought God would accept you into heaven if the good you did outweighed the bad. Now here she was trying to tell him that a Christian wasn't someone who went to church twice a year and read the Bible on occasion and tried not to eat too much at potlucks, but rather someone who turned his life over to Christ. What on earth did that mean?

Oh well, at least she was pleasant to look at while she chatted away happily about it all. He especially enjoyed the way her lips curled when she said her o's.

As the other stage traveled from Carson City toward Bodie, darkness settled onto the plains, and mirrors near the coach lights sent shafts of yellow light ahead of the horses to guide them along the trail. The driver kept up a constant barrage of shouting and reins snapping to keep the beasts motivated, while the passengers huddled together for warmth.

Suddenly a shadowy figure leaped into the road ahead of the coach, shouting for the driver to halt and raising a Henry rifle to make sure the command was taken seriously. Without hesitation the driver complied and pulled back on the reins, stopping the stage so abruptly, the passengers fell upon one another. Immediately a second dark figure appeared from the side of the road, and the two highwaymen approached the coach, their faces hidden behind black cloths tied in back, their hats pulled low.

"Let's all come out now," the man with the Henry rifle ordered the passengers, "with hands held high. No tricks. Don't go for no weapons, and you won't get hurt. We won't harm you unless you play loose with us." He motioned with the muzzle of his gun. The door opened slowly, and one by one the passengers disembarked, the men obliging the robbers by keeping their hands in the air, the women a little reluctant about making themselves vulnerable by coming out into the open. The robbers were willing to ignore their hesitancy, as long as they made no furtive moves. One woman clutched at the collar of her coat and held it tightly closed, not taking her eyes off the highwayman's own. He, however, disregarded her completely.

With the passengers all assembled and under the control of the Henry, the other robber shouted instructions to the driver and his companion, both of whom were still armed but had wisely not tempted fate by reaching for their weapons.

"You, next to the driver! Toss down that box."

The man riding shotgun complied with all due caution so his movements wouldn't be misinterpreted, turning in his seat and grabbing the strongbox with both hands. He pulled it down onto his lap, then hoisted it over the side and let it go. It landed in the dirt with a thud and rolled onto its side, though its weight prevented it from going farther. The robber stepped over to it cautiously and grabbed a handle while keeping his shotgun trained on the men on top of the stage, then dragged the box about twenty feet to the rear of the coach. He put the butt of his scattergun to the lock several times until it finally gave way, then hastily removed the broken lock, discarded it, and threw open the top.

Hearing him, the passengers tried to surmise what he was doing and prepared any moment for the command to turn over their valuables. One brave soul ventured a comment to the Henry-wielding highwayman.

"Just take our things and be done with it. You said no hurt would come to us, but the longer this takes, the more likely harm will occur."

"Why don't you shut up?" suggested another man, obviously well-off as evidenced by his resplendent accoutrements and the gold watch chain hanging from the pocket of his brocade vest.

The robber chuckled. "You needn't be concerned," he told both men. "We will soon be away from here, and your things will remain with you. We don't want them. They are identified too easily. We prefer cash that looks the same in Aurora and New York."

A collective sigh emanated from the relieved victims.

At the back of the stage, the contents of the box had been removed and now made the pockets of the other robber bulge. He whistled for his friend and could be heard running down the road and into the sagebrush. Mr. Henry Rifle thanked his victims, then backed off, keeping them at bay until he was swallowed by the darkness. He, too, could be heard in his retreat. Those with discerning ears heard yet another set of running steps, but no one saw the third man.

As soon as all was quiet, the men lowered their arms, and the woman clutching her collar fainted and collapsed onto the road. Her companion, a small nervous man in his Sunday duds, fussed over her and patted her cheek until she revived. Some of the others helped her into the coach as the driver urged them to hurry.

The Wells Fargo agent who'd handed down the box jumped down to confer with his partner, one of the passengers who'd been riding inside the coach. They spoke in hushed tones while the others gamely reentered the stage to continue their trip, hoping for safety from this point on.

"Was it him, do you think?" the first agent asked.

"Can't be sure. The man with the Henry wasn't our man, that I know. And the other didn't have the voice."

"I agree. He must've been off in the darkness. I heard a third man out there somewhere, which is why I didn't go for my gun. I had the drop on the Henry a couple times, but we were outgunned, and some of the passengers would've been hurt, no doubt."

"Yes, that's a fact. I maintained my surrender for the same reason. Which box did you give them?"

"The smallest of the three. The other two were in the boot. They never even looked there." He smiled wryly. "They only got ten percent of what we're carrying. We got off light enough. Let's get on our way before they figure that out and come back for a second try. We can go after them when it gets light."

The other man nodded and got back inside the coach while his partner climbed on top. When the all-clear signal was given, the driver prodded his horses into motion, the coach sailing down the dimly lit trail as if to make up for lost time.

An hour passed with Jeff Bodine hardly taking his eyes off Johanna Raymond's pretty face for even a second. Not only had he almost forgotten why he was on the stage, he hadn't the slightest idea if the coach was even going in the proper direction. It was only as he happened to glance out the window that something shook him out of his trance—a weathered, broken sign telling would-be trespassers to keep out, below which was the painted signature of William Bodine.

This was the road, now largely overgrown, that led to what used to be the Bodines' land—and their claim. Their mine and mill, founded by their father, had been sold to Jacob Page. It soon became evident he only bought it as a favor to the Bodines because he never settled in, instead selling it to one of Bodie's major mining concerns.

The Bodines had done okay by Page, having gotten a fair price for the land. He in turn got his money back plus a little profit from the mining company. That outfit's owners were the ones who "ate them rocks," as they described their loss. A week after they took over and began to work the mine in earnest, the modest vein petered out. They cut their losses and quickly stripped the mill of anything worth salvaging, tore down the house for its lumber, sold the furnishings, and abandoned the property. Jeff wanted to reclaim it, not to work the mine but because his father was buried at the top of the hill. But Josh had talked him out of it. In a good-willed gesture, an acre surrounding the hilltop and an easement to reach it were granted to the Bodines by the mining company—for free. It was rumored that Thomas Wellman had something to do with that, but no one knew for sure.

But since Jeff's duties in Bodie hadn't allowed him the luxury of two days off in a row, he hadn't been to the grave lately. In fact, this was his first sighting of the property since he'd left it six months back, and for a moment the pain of his bereavement was renewed in his spirit, like when a nearly healed wound is reopened by scratching.

"Excuse me, Mr. Bodine, are you okay?"

"Huh?" Jeff twirled his head around to see Johanna leaning forward in her seat, her face full of concern for him. And he suddenly noticed her hand lightly touching his knee. She drew it away gently as his attention came back to her.

"Oh, yes, Miss Raymond—I mean, Johanna. Pardon me . . . I'm fine. I was just thinkin' about something . . . No matter, I'm back now. You were sayin'?"

"I was just asking about you. Do you go to church?"

"Uh, not today I didn't." That was more than a slight exaggeration. He never went at all. He didn't even recall ever being in one, though his pa used to tell stories about church, so they must have gone when he was a little boy, before his family moved out west.

"Well, you really should go," Johanna was saying. "I assume Bodie has one. Of all places, Bodie should have a church."

"Well, yeah, of sorts. Not a church buildin', though. They use the Miners' Union Hall for the purpose. Protestants at 11 on Sunday mornin', Catholics at 1. Everybody else has to fend for themselves. The Chinese have their own place, but that don't really count."

"Well," she said, "it would be nice to see you there Sunday. I should be back in town by then. I hope so at least."

"If the stage don't get robbed and we all get murdered."

The voice came from outside, and Jeff jerked his head around to look out the window. There was his brother's face, upside-down as he hung over the side, spying on them.

There were groans from some of the passengers, not at Josh's face but his words.

"What're you doin', Josh? Tryin' to get ever'one all riled up?"

"Just havin' a little fun. Sorry, folks, didn't mean to scare the pants off of you. Oh, uh, excuse me, ma'am, I didn't mean you. It's just an expression." Josh's little laugh turned into a cough.

"Shut up, Josh, and get back up there where you belong. Or fall off, that would be even bet—"

He was cut short by a cry from the driver and a sudden slowing of the wagon. Josh disappeared, and Jeff craned to look out the window. The westbound stage was approaching, and as it slid to a stop near them the driver called out, "We was robbed!"

The shout brought gasps from some of the passengers on the eastbound stage, worried expressions from others, and nary a glance from one or two of the more sophisticated stage travelers.

"What's the fuss?" one man asked. "Happens all the time. The horses know where to stop, the stage gets waylaid so often along this stretch of road."

Jeff jumped out of the stage and joined Josh, who'd clambered down before they'd even come to rest. The Wells Fargo man told them the tale as the two drivers exchanged information. Some passengers took the opportunity to get out and stretch their legs, their breath fogging in front of their faces in the cold evening air. They huddled together and listened to the folks from the coach that had been robbed tell their tales. A couple passengers from the Bodine brothers' coach decided their trip to Aurora or points beyond wasn't as important as they thought and hitched a ride back to Bodie on the westbound. Not Johanna Raymond, however, much to Jeff's delight.

But there would be little time to enjoy her company. He took a seat next to the window this time, his attention now divided. He'd need to be alert to the road, keeping his eyes open for the robbers, for it was not outside the realm of possibility for them to strike twice in one night and so make their trek into the cold worthwhile.

Not once did he or his brother realize they'd just missed their ride back home. No other stage would pass that way until the next morning.

Josh took his place on the seat next to the driver, his eyes intent on the trail ahead of them as the coach lurched into motion behind the skillfully handled horses of driver Hank Monk. Oblivious to the cold, wet air, Josh reached down and gently rubbed the walnut grips of his pistol, feeling the icy curves of the metal frame.

"I hope they're still about," he told Hank.

"Why?" Hank asked, chewing on the end of his unlit cigar. With one hand handling all the reins, he deftly plucked a match from his pocket and struck it on the wood beneath his seat, then lit the stogie and tossed the match aside after shaking it out.

"Because," Josh said, staring down the road. "Just because."

"Well, son, you just might get your wish. It's one a them nights, it is. A dollar to a crumb cake we see them varmints before the moon is full above us."

Josh looked up. The cloud cover was so thick, he couldn't see the moon.

"Trust me, it's up there," the driver said. "Stands to reason they'll waylay us in the same spot. It's a good one for it—nowhere to run. I'll let you know when we're close."

Josh gripped his gun tightly.

CHAPTER

TWENTY

Ho! What's that?"

Josh leaned forward and pointed as the driver pulled back on the reins, slowing the coach gently. They peered ahead into the darkness at an object in the road—a box of some kind. Josh coughed into his fist, suppressing the sudden excitement and fear he felt.

"This is near where it happened," Hank Monk told the lawman.

"The holdup?"

"Yep." Monk spit a great wad of tobacco juice to the side, then wiped his chin with an already stained sleeve. Several hours of watching and listening to this—and getting spray on him when Monk didn't turn his head far enough and committed the cardinal sin of spitting into the wind—had all but cured Josh of any further interest in tobacco products.

"That's gotta be the strongbox," Josh proclaimed.

"Looks like."

"What's wrong?" Jeff shouted from below, sticking his head out of the coach. "Why'd we stop? We bein' robbed?"

"No," Josh assured him as he climbed down. "Looks like we found the strongbox."

"The empty strongbox, I'll wager," commented a knowledgeable passenger.

Josh knelt down and raised the lid, noting the damage to the latch. "Empty!" he shouted back toward the coach.

"Like it took brains to figure that out," the knowledgeable man said dryly.

Josh lugged the box back to the stage and handed it up to Monk. "I'm gonna see if I can find out where they went. Only take a second."

"Hurry it up. I don't like sittin' still when we could be puttin' some highway behind us." The driver spat again.

Josh waved and trotted up the road. He located what he believed to be the shoe prints he was looking for and began to follow them, crouching close to the dirt and doing his best to see in the dim—and getting dimmer with each step—light from the coach's lamps. In a short time he came to a barely visible, little-used side road—just a wagon trail with brush down the center where the wheels didn't roll. He stopped to consider whether he should follow the trail or not, then decided against it. It was too dark, and there were passengers on the stage who needed to get to their destination. The station wasn't too far away, and he and Jeff could report in there and let the Wells Fargo agents go after the robbers. After all, this was their problem.

But before he could act on his plan, a voice called out from the blackness ahead of him.

"You're tryin' to sneak up on us!" Before Josh could clear leather, the accusation was punctuated by a single gunshot, barely missing Josh's head and forcing him to duck and retreat. As he turned, he saw the coach's lead horse begin to sway. Its head dropped suddenly, his front legs folded, and he collapsed into a heap, creating fear and confusion in the other horses as the dead weight of the animal pulled on the rigging that tied them all together.

Monk kept a steady, experienced hand on the reins and kept the horses from bolting, which would have been a complete disaster with one of them dead on the ground and still connected. Josh darted back to the coach, and Monk gave a shout and tossed Josh's rifle down to him. Josh caught it and called for his brother, who was already on his way out of the stage.

"Everyone stay inside and keep your heads down!" Jeff ordered over his shoulder. He gave Johanna a fleeting last look, then ran to the rear of the coach, where Josh was already waiting. Josh, preferring his six-gun, tossed the rifle to his brother, who levered a round into the chamber.

Josh peeked around the corner of the stage just as the robber who'd fired the fatal shot to the horse presented himself in the yellow light of the lanterns. The highwayman raised his rifle toward Hank, but Josh swiftly cocked and fired without aiming, and the bullet struck home even as the man squeezed the trigger. He yelped, his shot went wide, and he clamped a hand to his shoulder as he beat a hasty retreat into the shrubbery and darkness at the side of the road.

"Robbery!" someone inside the coach shouted. "They're gonna kill us!"

"Not if we can help it!" Josh said, affirming his optimism by firing several rounds blindly where he thought the man might have gone. A twig snapped on the other side of the coach, and Jeff wheeled around, shooting toward the sound. A muzzle flash erupted from the brush alongside the road, and a hard, sharp, burning pain seared Jeff's side. He half-collapsed, half-dove into the dirt, not even having time to say he was hit. Josh answered the robber's fire by emptying his gun into the darkness. He holstered the spent weapon and grabbed Jeff's rifle, chambered a round and fired as fast as he could, chambered another and blasted, then turned and repeated the actions along the opposite side of the road.

Taking cover, he waited a moment and listened. All was quiet. He had no idea what the driver was doing, and he didn't know if the passengers were all right. It was his brother he was worried about. Jeff was tough, but he'd gone down awfully fast.

"I musta scared them off," Josh mumbled to himself. He cautiously dropped to his knee and peered under the coach to check his brother's condition. Jeff was prone, his face wincing in pain, but he was alive.

"Is it bad?" Josh asked.

But before Jeff could answer, there was a scream from Johanna Raymond. Josh jerked his head around to see the silhouette of a bulky man standing in the stage's light, his Henry rifle at his shoulder as he sighted in on the lawman. Josh was in full light now, and Hank, crouching on the floorboard beneath the driver's seat, reached out and twisted the lamp away, directing the beam at the robber. The light hit him full on the face just as a volley erupted from inside the coach, kicking up dirt at the man's feet, inspiring him to jump back and withdraw from sight. It had been no more than a second, but Josh had gotten a clear view of the man's face, just after the bandit had gotten a clear view of Josh's.

In a moment several horses could be heard, their snorts and pounding hooves and the whistles and shouts of their riders drifting through the night air as the three outlaws took flight.

Josh wasted no time checking the seriousness of Jeff's wound. By now Jeff was composed and able to talk.

"It ain't so bad, I don't think," he told his younger brother.

"No, it's a nuisance more 'n anything else. A nice crease on your side—just muscle and skin. A few more inches one way and he'd a missed. A few more the other and I'd be puttin' you to bed with a pick and shovel."

Jeff struggled to sit up, and Johanna Raymond came out of the coach, still holding the small Colt's Lightning she'd used a moment before to run off the robbers. Jeff saw it, and surprise took over his face.

Johanna was oblivious to his reaction as she crouched next to him.

"You okay, Jeff?"

"Yeah. Just a scratch."

"Here, let me tend to it." She handed Josh the gun with two fingers like it was something repulsive and ripped a long strip from the bottom of her petticoat, wrapping it around Jeff's midsection. Under it, directly over the wound, she placed a clean, folded handkerchief she'd withdrawn from her bodice, then tied the strip off, keeping the handkerchief in place. Blood quickly soaked through it.

"He'll need stitches," she said.

"Let's get him inside," said Hank Monk, coming from the front of the coach where he'd been seeing to his team. "We're down to three horses, but it's mostly level from here to the station, so I think we'll be okay. I'll need some help adjusting the harnesses and such."

"I'll do it," volunteered one of the other passengers, an older man in a business suit. "I hitched up my share of nags in my day." He peeled off his coat and draped it over the wheel as he joined Hank at the team.

"This yours?" Josh asked Johanna, holding up the silver Colt's Lightning self-cocking pistol.

"Oh, my heavens, no," she said as some of the other passengers helped Jeff to his feet. "It was my husband's. I was going to sell it in Aurora. A man there expressed an interest in it. To tell you the truth, I didn't even think about it when I shot. I just closed my eyes and pointed it out the window. I probably shot halfway up the hill. At least I hope I didn't hurt anyone."

"I hope you did, if it's all the same to you, ma'am."

Josh and another man helped Jeff climb into the coach, then Josh scampered up next to Hank. The dead horse was too heavy to move—Hank would come back the next day with a team to drag it off the road. But they managed to drive around it after cutting away whatever harness they couldn't remove.

Hank drove the stage carefully, more concerned about his injured passenger than about making up lost time, and it was an hour before they arrived at the station. The back half of the small wood-frame structure was the residence for the stationmaster and his wife. A few yards out back was a barn and corral for extra horses. As the stage came to a bumpy stop, old Ennis Peabody wandered out holding a lantern aloft and gazing at the oddly configured team.

"Say there, Hank, you, uh, lose something on the way? Maybe cut it too close to the hills a time or two?"

"Naw, you know better 'n that," Hank told him, throwing down the reins. "Robbers shot him dead." He jumped down and gave his back a stretch.

"What fer? Wouldn't you stop?"

"I stopped. They was shootin' at the deputy and missed."

"Tell the deputy not to stand in front of the horses next time. Them are valuable animals."

"We got an injured man," Josh told Peabody, ignoring the old man's remarks.

"He needs some stitchin'," Hank added. "Think your wife can handle it?"

"Sure. Bring him on in. While she's at it, she can darn your socks."

Two long-coated men with scruffy faces and wearing hats the color of buttermilk ambled around the corner from the rear of the building, leading their horses. They regarded Josh as one would something distasteful, looking him up and down, then at each other.

"So you got robbed?" one of them said with the hint of a grin leaking out from under his bushy mustache.

"You two Wells Fargo?"

They nodded.

"We got attempted," Josh corrected with a sneer. "But they didn't get nothin', and we plugged one of 'em. A mite better by my cypherin' than your men on the westbound did earlier."

They overlooked his sarcasm. Not much else they could do, considering he was right.

"We'll take over from here," one of them said.

"Sure, now that it's over. Thanks. Thanks a lot." Josh turned back to his brother and helped him into the station, not that he needed much assistance since his wound was just a graze. But having Johanna Raymond on his other arm made him act a little like it was worse than it was. They took him to Peabody's well-lit parlor, where Mrs. Peabody had Jeff lie back on the small divan. She got out her doctoring kit—living out where they did, she'd learned long ago to keep some medical supplies on hand—and soaked a cloth with whiskey to deaden Jeff's side.

"We got some hungry folks," Josh said. "Can I rustle them up something?"

"It's on the stove, ready to eat," Mrs. Peabody told him. "Help yourself. I'll see to you folks when I'm done here."

"We can manage." While Johanna stayed with Jeff, Josh went to the kitchen to see about the food, finding a huge cauldron of steaming chili on top of the stove and a large batch of cornbread in the oven. Using potholders, Josh carefully took the bread and chili to the passengers, who'd assembled inside and were chattering excitedly, now that the danger was over and they'd survived.

While Hank and Peabody hitched up a fresh team and replaced the damaged harness, the passengers sat around a plank table enjoying the grub. The table occupied the center of a large waiting room at the front of the house, built just for such a purpose. A large fire blazed in the natural stone fireplace. As they ate, the terror of the trail having subsided as their bodies—inside and out— were warmed by the fire and the food, they exchanged views on the robbers' identities and how marvelous Hank Monk was to drive a team of three. In the parlor Mrs. Peabody put five quick stitches into Jeff's side and applied a fresh bandage, then trotted off to get the apple pie she'd baked earlier. Jeff joined the others.

Johanna offered to bring him some food, but he assured her,

"Thank you kindly, Johanna, but I can sit with everyone else." To prove it, he made his way unaided to the table. A man who'd finished eating let Jeff take his place, and a bowl of chili was ladled and passed down to him. A hunk of cornbread followed, and soon Jeff and Johanna were leaning back, their hunger satisfied.

In an hour Hank was ready to roll. "Okay, folks, let's load up. I'll have you in Aurora in two hours or my name ain't Henry Morton."

"Your name already ain't Henry Morton," noted Ennis Peabody. "It's Hank Monk."

"Oh," said Hank. "Well, in that case I'll make it in an hour and a half."

His humor relaxed the passengers further, and they boarded the stage without prodding, anxious for this journey to be over, none the worse for the wear, all things considered. Johanna patted Jeff on the shoulder.

"I hope everything turns out okay."

"I'm sure it will. We'll get those men, don't you worry about that none."

They fell into an awkward but brief silence. Jeff broke it.

"Listen, about that little gun of yours . . . You, uh . . . I'd like to buy it from you, if you don't mind. It'd save you from havin' to fuss with it."

"All right," she said slowly, "if you're sure you want to. You're not just doing it . . . I mean, you really want it?"

"Yeah, sure. It'd make a good second gun. But I—I don't have the money on me right now. Maybe when you get back we can get together—"

"You keep it then—"

Josh listened to them, shaking his head. He knew how Jeff felt about guns, and here he was buying one. And a Colt's Lightning at that. They were plentiful in Bodie, and for a fair price. Jeff could have purchased one anytime he wished. Josh smiled as he left the two of them alone to iron out the details of their "transaction."

He sauntered over to the Wells Fargo agents, who were settling into their saddles. They planned to escort the stage into Aurora rather than ride on it, something Josh wished he'd thought of. But then again, he hadn't expected that he and Jeff would miss their transportation back to Bodie. Maybe Peabody had a couple horses he could loan them so they could return home tonight. Josh had a shift to work, and Jeff would be better off on a horse than in a hard old bumpy coach any day.

Hank yee-hawed and shook the reins, and the Bodines watched as the wagon and the two horsemen rode out of sight. Johanna waved through the coach window until she disappeared in the night.

"Well, let's get back to Bodie," Jeff said.

"On what?"

"On them two horses." He pointed to the side of the house where Ennis Peabody appeared, leading two old but sturdy mounts. Josh gave his brother a questioning stare, amazed that his brother was a step ahead of him for once.

"I made the arrangements with Mrs. Peabody," Jeff explained. "We'll tie them to the back of tomorrow's outbound stage. Come on." He grabbed Jeff by the sleeve. "How 'bout one more bowl of chili before we leave?"

Josh grinned as his older brother went inside. Maybe he'd turn out okay after all.

CHAPTER

TWENTY · ONE

THE FOLLOWING EVENING, Jacob page took a place at the edge of the crowd, climbing onto a stack of hay bales with some other men, miners he knew from his and another company. Money was changing hands throughout the crowd, and tally cards were being filled out. Two or three Chinamen wandered into the corral, avoiding a Paiute in white man's clothes who stood next to a post, and made their way to a gambler who gladly took their bets.

Jacob scanned the crowd for Billy. He saw the Catholic and Methodist ministers, members of the fourth estate—recorders of Bodie's current events—several of Bodie's lawyers and church elders, as well as businessmen, gamblers, miners, engineers, brewers, and layabouts. But no Billy.

The wrestlers entered the ring to thunderous applause and retired to their respective corners. They peeled off their robes and flung them to their seconds, then turned to face the spectators, rippling their chest muscles and biceps. Some bets were changed; others increased.

Ben Jowett, the challenger, stood in the corner with his back to the center of the ring, holding the ropes. He wore tight trousers, thin leather shoes with soft soles, and a black undershirt that revealed absolutely no fat on his upper body. He had close-cropped hair and no mustache. Jowett did several snappy deep-knee bends, then stretched his legs by lifting them one at a time onto the rope that encircled the ring—a good three feet off the ground, keeping his knee straight and drawing *oohs* and *aahs* from his impressed fans.

The champion, Rod McGinnis, wore no shirt at all and had shaved off whatever chest hair he had, making a smooth, no-grip surface. He bent at the waist and touched his toes, then straightened up and watched his opponent stretch, keeping a devil-may-care look of confidence on his handsome face the whole while. He was a pleasure for the women to look upon, there was no doubt about that.

The referee stepped over the ropes, and the wrestlers met him at the center of the ring. He reviewed the rules quickly—there weren't many—and in moments the match was on. The crowd rose to a crescendo of cheering as the two grapplers finally squared off, the former convention and graciousness a distant memory. This was serious business; though friends any other time, at this moment they were bitter enemies.

Jowett and McGinnis circled each other slowly, with arms outstretched, their eyes locked, each of them hoping the other would break contact and give him the upper hand. But neither did. Then at the same moment they pounced, arms grabbing arms, grappling for superior position. McGinnis dropped low and tried to swing Jowett over his hip, but the challenger anticipated the move and countered with a leap, landing on his feet. The dance was repeated again and again, without either man gaining an advantage. The men were so evenly matched that the first period, fast and furious as it was, failed to produce a fall.

While the band played and the wrestlers were rubbed down by their seconds, men and women moved about idly, stretching their legs and discussing the wrestlers' strategies. In short order the music stopped, the spectators returned hastily to their seats, the bell sounded, and the combatants again squared off in the center of the ring.

Two more evenly matched wrestlers had never faced each other in Bodie, perhaps anywhere in the West. They equaled each other in speed, agility, strength, and endurance. Neither made a mistake or caused the other to falter. The slapping of flesh, the cheering of the crowd, the grunts and growls of the wrestlers, and the resounding music of the brass band during rest periods continued unabated for over an hour.

Jacob Page, feeling a hunger pang as the match wore on, jumped down from his perch even though it was not a rest period. He pushed his way through the crowd to the chow wagon Harvey Boone had set up outside the corral where the ring was situated. Page bought a box lunch and headed back to his seat, then decided he couldn't wait any longer and made way for a low pile of hay at the outside edge of the property, away from the crowd, to sample the fried chicken. He figured neither of the wrestlers would get the advantage anytime soon, so he doubted he'd miss anything.

As he bit into a drumstick he thought he heard someone talking softly on the opposite side of the bales, but he wasn't sure due to the crowd noise around the ring. He looked over his shoulder across the hay and spied two men he didn't know huddled together, apparently uninterested in the sporting event in progress. Curious, he leaned closer to eavesdrop while trying to remain inconspicuous and was rewarded for his efforts as he heard an insidious plot unfold.

When they were finished and went their own ways, Jacob waited until he was certain the coast was clear, then jumped down from his perch and hurried from the corral, eating his food on the run. He made a beeline for the jail, hoping Josh would be there. Jeff was still recuperating in his room, assuring everyone he was fine, though the ride home had been taxing. Josh and others had convinced him one more day of rest wouldn't hurt, and Jeff agreed without too much cajoling.

Jacob scurried through the jailhouse door, and Josh looked up, startled, from his chair at the desk. He wasn't doing much, just idly rubbing an oil cloth down the barrel of his gun. At the intrusion he quickly snapped the hammer back, but when he recognized Jacob he relaxed, releasing the hammer and slipping the pistol into its holster.

"I know who robbed the stage!" Jacob bellowed.

"Shhh!" Josh urged. "Shut the door. Now, what's all this shoutin', Mr. Page?"

Jacob kicked the door closed and hurried over to the desk. "I was at the wrestlin' match—"

"Oh, yeah, the wrestling match," Josh groaned. "I forgot all about it. Who won?"

"Huh? Uh . . . I don't know, Josh. I left early. Are ya lis'nin'? I know who robbed the stage. Two of 'em, at least."

"The stage? You know who . . . How do you know that, Mr. Page?"

"I bin tryin' to tell you. I was at the wrestlin' match, an' I heerd two men talkin', an' they was talkin' 'bout havin' done the robbery."

"What'd they say?"

"One of 'em said they was headed to Yosemite to meet the one what got the money, but first they had to take care of that confounded depitty what got a good look at him."

Josh screwed up his face as he thought about the comment. Then his face slowly relaxed, his eyebrows raising, as he realized exactly whom the men had been talking about.

"Hey, they mean me!"

"Now yer catchin' on, Josh."

"Do you know these men?"

"Nope, can't say as I do. I heerd one man call the other Jack once, and then by his last name, Myers, and that time he got shushed for doin' so."

"Myers, huh? Don't know any Myers."

"He seemed to be the one in charge. He's the one who was doin' most of the talkin' whilst the other fella jes' listened. Oh, and the other man was favorin' his arm, I noticed that."

"What else did they say?"

"Myers said he was gonna take care of you for keeps." Jacob pointed his index finger at Josh and simulated the noise a gun makes.

"They're gonna kill me? When? Did they say?"

"Tonight, when you're alone somewhere. They're gonna meet at the Comstock at midnight."

Josh stood up and put his hat on. "We'll see about that. Come on."

As the clock on the mantel in front of the mirror showed five minutes before twelve, Deputy Josh Bodine waited at the end of the Comstock's highly polished bar nearest the door. Jacob Page drummed his fingers on the counter. Josh drank coffee from a ceramic mug, and as he sipped his brew he studied the reflection of the door in the mirror behind the bar.

"Yer nervous as a cat," Jacob said.

Josh took another sip.

"C'mon, you got the upper hand," Jacob went on. "You'll surprise him. He's not expectin' to see you here."

"If he suspects I know about his plan, he'll kill me on sight," Josh said quietly. "He's not going to give me a chance to talk to him, much less take him into custody. I don't want anyone getting hurt—including me."

"Then mebbe we should confront him outside."

"No, he'd see us as he walks up and suspect something. His partner will be with him, and we'd have a killing tonight for sure."

"Josh, that's exac'ly what he's plannin' to—"

The batwings parted suddenly, and Josh spun around. Myers walked in, laughing with his companion about something that had been said before they entered. Though he was facing Josh, he hadn't seen him. But his cohort, following directly behind, saw the deputy over Myers's shoulder. The long-haired outlaw said something to Myers, whose smile disappeared as he fixed his gaze on the lawman. Josh's hand was already tightening on the grip of his gun, and as Myers's hand began to emerge from inside his coat, Josh pulled his revolver. He cocked it as it cleared the holster, then pointed it at Myers in one smooth, lightning-fast motion. Without hesitation Josh fired, then cocked it and fired a second time as everyone in the Comstock dove for cover.

Myers staggered from the impact of the bullets, and with a look of shock freezing his face he backed into his compatriot. The long-haired man immediately retreated through the batwings, abandoning Myers, and fled up the street.

Myers clutched his left hand to his chest, blood flowing between his fingers as he drew his revolver with his right hand. The flopping batwings parted by his partner hit him in the back as he fired, the bullet tearing harmlessly into the ceiling, and he fell back through the doors and landed hard on the boardwalk, his gun jarred loose by the impact and skidding a few feet away from him.

"No—!" he gurgled, then was silent. Several patrons of the Comstock bravely left their positions and raced outside to see about the fallen man. But he was dead by the time they got to his side, his eyes staring skyward in surprise. One of the men ran off up the street.

Josh stood motionless at the bar, still pointing his smoking gun at the empty doorway. Jacob Page, taking refuge on the floor, his ears ringing from the blasts, looked up at his friend with a mixture of surprise and fear. But his face quickly relaxed, and he pushed himself up, then pried the gun from Josh's locked fingers. Bodine continued to stare at the door, his mind a torrent of fear, his chest heaving.

The onlooker who ran off was halfway to the jail when he realized the law was the one who'd done the shooting. He changed course for Jeff's room at the Empire Boarding House, pounding on the door until an irritated Jeff Bodine answered. Breathlessly, the witness told the lawman only that there'd been a killing at the Comstock and that Josh was involved. Jeff grabbed his hat, yanked on his boots, and went running, arriving at the saloon in short order. After taking a quick look at the obviously dead Myers, he stormed inside.

There stood Josh, still staring at the batwings through which his adversary had disappeared. Jeff started to ask him who had done it, but the look on Josh's face and the gun Jacob Page held by the barrel told the story. Jacob handed Jeff the revolver without comment, and Josh finally shook himself out of his stupor and looked at his brother.

"What happened, Josh?" Jeff asked.

"I shot him." Josh's voice was weak.

Jeff looked at Jacob. "Is that true?"

"Yeah, but he had good reason."

"Not that we could see," said a witness, the gambler James McCarthy, recently released after being fined by Judge Peterson for the whacking he had given Louise DuBarr. He grinned wryly.

"What do you mean?" Jeff asked.

"That man never had a chance," McCarthy lied. "He didn't know what hit him."

Jeff scanned the crowd for another witness. "Is that how you saw it?" he asked a man.

"Well . . . all I know is what I seen," the man said. "Your brother was standing at the bar, and as soon as this feller walks in, your brother blasts him two, maybe three times. Myers here tried to get one shot off afterward but fell over dead and only plugged the ceiling on his way down. That's all there is to it."

Jeff looked at the other men in the saloon. Most of them only shrugged, though a few nodded in agreement.

Jeff locked eyes with his brother, tears welling up in both lawmen's eyes.

"I don't have a choice, Josh—I gotta take you in."

"McCarthy's lyin', you know that. He's tryin' to pay me back for that shiner."

"You shot that man, didn't you?"

"Yeah, but he was gunnin' for me."

"Even so, under the circumstances—with all these witnesses and all—I gotta take you in."

"I know," Josh consented quietly. "I know."

Jeff hesitated, his eyes burning as he fought back his emotions. Josh sensed it, and he grabbed the handcuffs from his brother's hand and put them on himself, then headed out the door, forcing Jeff to go along.

Together, in silence, they stepped around Myers—Jeff directing two men to see to the body—then crossed the vast expanse of town as folks silently watched one Deputy Bodine take the other Deputy Bodine to jail.

Jacob Page couldn't bear to watch this tragedy unfold without doing something. He followed the brothers at a distance, letting them have their privacy. But as soon as they entered the jail, he did likewise. Jeff was already seated behind the desk, removing the cuffs from Josh. He stopped when the door opened, but when he saw it was Jacob, he continued what he was doing. Josh thanked him and took a seat next to the wall, rubbing his wrists.

"Kinda tight," he muttered, a weak grin twitching the corner of his mouth.

"That's your own fault," Jeff told him. "Shut the door, would you please, Mr. Page? I don't want anyone lookin' in here right now."

"Certainly," Jacob said as he kicked it with his boot. He went directly to the desk and leaned on it with his one arm. "He's innocent, you know. It was self-defense."

"Yeah, he explained it to me on the way over here. But because of the way things happened, I had to take him in—you know that. From what those other witnesses said, it looked like Josh ambushed him."

"But we know he didn't. I heard Myers plannin' an attack on

him. He was out to kill Josh 'cause he could identify Myers as one of the stage robbers. And that means it weren't only self-defense—Myers was a candidate for arrest, and Josh knew he'd resist."

"He went for his gun when he saw me," Josh said weakly. "When his eyes met mine, his hand went inside his coat. I didn't draw until then."

"Jacob?" Jeff looked at the elder Page for verification.

"Well, it happened so fast . . . You know yer brother's fast," Jacob said uncertainly. "He coulda done that. He's proved it here before."

"Don't remind me," Josh said with a groan. He leaned over in the chair, his elbows on his knees and his head in his hands. "How many times can one man get falsely accused in a lifetime?"

"There ain't no limit," Jeff told him. "I always told you that livin' by the gun would bring you to this."

"Just what I need—another 'I told you so' from my older brother."

"Can't help it, Josh. I did tell you."

"Boys, now ain't the best time to be runnin' each other down like this," Jacob scolded. "We need to put our heads together—think this through."

"We're gonna have to take it to Judge Peterson for an opinion," Jeff said. "It would look awful bad if I decide my brother is innocent. I want this to be without question."

"I agree," Jacob said. He turned his gaze toward Josh. "The last thing we need is the specter of doubt hangin' over you."

"The what?"

"Specter. Like a ghost, an apparition. You know, folks not bein' sure but figurin' you're guilty. Yeah, I heard the plot against you. But I can't be everywhere all them other so-called 'witnesses' are to speak out agin' their gossip. They'll add to their stories—make 'em more colorful. We need to get 'em into court so yer attorney kin pin 'em down and straighten out their heads—and so my testimony kin be heerd by all. That way when Peterson drops the charges, no one will question it. No more doubt."

Josh nodded his head slowly, beginning to understand Jacob's plan.

"That means I'll need an attorney."

Jeff's eyes widened. "Pat Reddy. He's never lost a case."

"He's in Bridgeport," Jacob said.

"I want Pete Jensen. He defended me last time. I want him."

"I know him," Jacob said. "I'll retain him tonight."

"I don't have much money," Josh said slowly. "See if he'll take my horse." He smiled wryly, remembering how he had paid Jensen the last time.

"Keep your horse," Jacob said. "I'll work it out with him. This is such an obvious case, I'll bet he'll take it in an eye wink."

Jacob told the Bodines to keep their hope strong, knowing the truth would do its work, then nodded a good-bye and left them alone.

"Well," Jeff finally said after a long and strained silence, "I guess you'd best get into your cell."

No job in a mine was safe. The powder monkeys spent their shifts with pockets full of gunpowder, stuffing it into long, thin holes drilled into the face of a crosscut or drift. Muckers shoveled blasted rock off the steel muck plate on the floor and into ore cars. Not only was this back-breaking labor, but entry into the mines shortly after blasting carried with it the risk of asphyxiation from lethal nitro fumes. The other enemy was silicosis, lung disease caused by breathing rock dust. The only so-called cure was death.

Even the mills were dangerous. The 800-pound falling stamps could easily crush a man's hand into pulp. And the poisoning from working with the quicksilver that leached gold from silt took longer than silicosis to kill but was just as deadly.

Underground, a man would occasionally get run over by an ore car, and more than once a man had taken a step back to get out of the way only to fall into an empty shaft. The hoist buckets raising and lowering men sometimes tipped or stopped suddenly, dumping men helplessly into black space, or became disconnected at the hoist or broke a cable, sending bucket and contents to a final crash at the bottom.

The closer one worked to the top the better, and Jacob Page, by virtue of being the superintendent, had the right to stay in the office if he chose, avoiding the dangerous underground. But that wasn't Jacob's way. He enjoyed mining firsthand and loved to do whatever task was needed, with the exception of those that required two good arms.

On any given day Jacob could be found somewhere besides the

comfort of the office, and the morning after Josh's arrest was no exception. A man whose wife had given birth had requested a day off to stay home with his family, and Jacob had consented, saying he'd work the new father's shift. About ten o'clock that morning, he and the experienced Elrod Ryan stood at the mouth of the shaft beside the hoist, dumping the bucket every time a load of ore came up.

Their shift had started four hours before. There was no longer any snow around the mouth of the shaft, since it was February and the end of a mild winter. But it was still cold, and some seepage from the pump bringing water from the bottom of the shaft had turned quickly into ice, making footing treacherous. The sun had not yet reached the area, since it stood in the shade of the bluff.

When the hoist engineer brought up the bucket, Elrod shut the wooden trapdoor that covered the shaft to prevent any loose ore from falling on the men below. He and Jacob dumped the bucket, Jacob doing the best he could with one arm. Elrod, bearing much of the burden but without any complaint, unhooked the trip rope and raised the trapdoor so the bucket could be lowered again. But this time the rope became tangled around the cable.

"Dagnab it! Steady the bucket, Jacob. I've got to untwist that blame rope."

"Okay, I've got it," Page assured his friend. "You watch yerseff, Elrod."

Elrod grunted. He'd performed this task more times than he could count. The rope was barely beyond his reach, and he leaned over to snag it. Unfortunately, there was a small, nearly invisible patch of ice right next to the hole. His body shifted as he leaned to grasp the rope, and when he put his weight on his front foot, the sole of his boot slipped. He sucked in his breath and for a second or two tried vainly to grab the rope, but it eluded him, and he grasped only a handful of air instead. Unable to regain his footing or shift his weight back, he knew he was about to fall. He called out to Jacob, who saw what was happening and was trying to reach out to him. But gravity, now in control, sucked Elrod into the shaft.

Even as he started to fall, Elrod knew his life was over. The shaft was 450 feet deep. He had no second chance, no hope, no time to say good-bye to his family. But in that moment of realiza-

tion before panic takes over, he knew that the men at the bottom
of the shaft were in danger, his plummeting body no less a hazard
to them than a 200-pound sack of nails.

With his last full breath, as the walls of the shaft began to blur
and the light above grew smaller, he shouted, "Look out below—
clear the way!"

Those were his last words.

As Elrod had reached for the rope, Jacob had reached for Elrod.
At least he bent a shoulder toward him. Had it been the shoulder
with an arm, Jacob might have been able to pull him to safety. But
Jacob was holding on to the edge of the trapdoor, leaving him
nothing with which to grab the other man.

It all happened so fast. One second Elrod was reaching for the
rope; the next he was shouting a warning with his last breath to
the men beneath him. Jacob could still see Elrod's body hurtling
downward when he cried out. Transfixed by the sight and by the
selflessness of the warning, Jacob momentarily forgot himself.
Before he knew it, one of his feet wasn't touching solid ground, and
he knew he was going over the edge too.

The men at the bottom of the shaft heard Elrod's shout and
moved quickly into an adjoining compartment, out of harm's way.
They could hear him strike timbers as he fell, but he said nothing
more. When he finally landed, the force crushed his entire body,
though he was probably dead before he hit.

But his cry at the start of his death plunge had saved the men
below from being crushed. They stood in silence in the dim light
at the bottom of the shaft, stunned, helpless, grateful.

A cry above them startled them, and they looked up into the
dark shaft at the small point of light.

"Is another one comin'?" someone asked. They all listened.

"No, I don't hear anyone fallin'."

"Someone else cried out," another miner insisted.

"They didn't fall. We'd a heerd it."

"We need the bucket down here," the first man said. "To pack
Elrod's body out." He reached for the bell to alert the hoist operator.

"Don't touch it!" shouted a ruddy-faced old miner with years
of experience. "Someone else fell. They just didn't fall all the way."

"You think they stopped fallin' partway down?" came the
snide reply.

"Course not. He landed on somethin'."

"We need to get up there."

"But we can't. The only way out is in that bucket. And we dare not ask it to be moved. It might kill the second man who fell."

Frustrated, the men sat down to ponder the problem, each of them staring at the broken body of Elrod Ryan as the steam whistle above ground began to blow incessantly.

CHAPTER

TWENTY·TWO

AT THE MOUTH OF THE SHAFT, hoist operator Claude Evers had watched Elrod move toward the tangled rope, then turned and lit a cigar while he waited for his cable to be cleared so he could send the bucket back down. When he shook out the match and tossed it down he glanced back, expecting to see Elrod and Jacob standing off to the side, their arms folded, waiting for him.

But he saw neither man. Having heard nothing but the noise of the steam engine in his ear, he glanced about, wondering where they'd gone. Only when he didn't find them anywhere in sight did he realize what had happened. He locked down the hoist and jumped out of the shack, moving carefully to the mouth of the shaft on his belly to peer over the edge. Elrod was nowhere to be seen, but the one-armed miner was faintly visible, hanging upside-down, his legs tangled in the cable and rope. His arm hung down as his body swung gently. He was unconscious.

Without a second glance, Claude ran back to the shack and pulled on the steam whistle, sending frantic, shrill cries for help that could be heard throughout the area. In no time men were converging on the scene, and Claude quickly described what he had seen. Before he was finished, one man tied a rope around his waist and the other end to a heavy steel rod on the engine and made his way to the shaft. He saw what Claude had seen, noticing no change in Jacob's situation from the way the hoist operator had described it. He shouted to the hastily assembled rescue team but stayed where he was to monitor the fallen miner while a plan was formulated.

But a new arrival to the scene had a plan of her own.

Rosa Page ran through the circle of men, lifting her skirt a bit so she wouldn't stumble. They tried to stop her, but she would not be thwarted. When she'd heard the whistle, she looked out from the restaurant and saw the throng converging around the mouth of the shaft where her husband had been working. She paused for a second, squinting her eyes to try to pick out his characteristic silhouette but couldn't. In an eye blink she threw down her apron and ran out the door.

"Somebody tie me off!" she shouted, looking at the men and motioning at the stout rope coiled on the side of the building. "Let me down—I'll bring him up!"

"Whoa, Mrs. Page," Claude told her. "You don't know what you're doing."

"I know I lost my daughter to a mine, and I'm not going to lose my husband!"

"Course not," said a strong but gentle voice behind her. Uncle Billy O'Hara strode toward her, taking her by the elbow. "These men can take care of it. Someone light will have to be put over and can tie Jacob off, then we'll hoist him on up." He glanced around.

"Carter! You're best fit for the job, and you've got plenty of nerve. Tie yourself off, and do it good. We don't want another man takin' a fall."

James Carter, the husband of Rosa's waitress Molly, obeyed immediately, tossing away his hat and cinching the rope around his waist, then under his shoulders to keep himself upright. The end was tied off, and the man who had been on his belly by the shaft crawled back away from it and untied his rope, handing the other end to Carter.

"I'm ready," Carter announced. He took a breath and moved to the shaft, while the rest of the men formed a phalanx and grabbed the rope, holding it taut but letting out enough slack for Carter to move ahead.

It was an odd sight as Carter sat down at the edge of the shaft and gave the men one last look that said, *Hold on tight*. He nodded and slid himself over the edge.

Calling up instructions to the men as he was let down, he was soon next to the inverted Jacob Page and in no time had secured the rope around him.

"Is he alive?" Rosa called down.

Carter took a second to check, then shouted back, "Yes! He's breathing."

A weak cheer rose up but died quickly as the realization quickly set in that he wasn't out of danger yet.

"Holler when you're ready!" Billy shouted down to him.

"He's tied off and untangled. Bring us both up at the same speed so I can keep an eye on him!"

Billy shouted his affirmation, then instructed the men to move next to the hoist cable while keeping the rope taut. He tied Carter's rope, as well as Page's, to the cable in several places while the men maintained their grasp, then signaled Claude to start the hoist.

Evers saluted and climbed into the seat. With a deep breath he engaged the cable and slowly began to increase throttle. Billy shouted down to alert Carter to what was happening. As the cable and ropes began to move in unison, the men backed up, keeping their grip despite some of them not wearing gloves.

In a few very long minutes, Carter's head appeared over the edge. He stared up at the men with wide eyes, his face pale, his mouth set in a grim line. Once Jacob and Carter were hoisted above the mouth of the shaft, several onlookers cautiously closed the doors underneath them, then grabbed Page as Billy motioned Evers to lower the cable. He did so, and in a few moments Jacob Page was lifted carefully onto a stretcher. Rosa stood to the side, tears streaming down her once hard, bitter face. Her hands wiped them away as quickly as they came, and when Jacob was ready to be moved she gently stroked his face.

"Don't leave me, you old goat," she said softly. "We've just begun this life—you can't leave me now."

The stretcher bearers started off, and Rosa kept pace, talking to Jacob all the way to Doctor Blackwood's office, not once taking her eyes off his expressionless face.

Once James Carter was helped out of his harness and took his first step on solid ground, he collapsed. The strong arm of Billy O'Hara helped him into a chair brought out of the hoist shack. The doors over the shaft were reopened, the ropes untangled, and the bucket let down for Elrod's body to be sent up.

The next day the community gave Elrod a hero's funeral, paid for by the Miners' Union. James Carter and the other rescuers had a special party thrown in their honor at the Miners' Union Hall that same evening.

Jacob Page, lying unconscious and near death in Doctor Blackwood's office, missed them both.

Jeff pulled a chair up next to his brother's cell and sat on the edge of it, his elbows on his knees, rubbing his hands together.

Josh moved his head far enough to see who it was, then looked back at the ceiling.

"What's up, brother? Good news, I hope."

"I spoke to Judge Peterson."

"He's in town?"

"A chance visit. Passing through on his way to go fishin'. He gave me a few minutes. I told him what's happened, told him what Mr. Page heard, asked if I could let you out on your own recognizance."

"And?"

"And he said no. Not on a capital crime. Theft or something, yes. But killin' a man in cold blood . . . He said something about the public trust, you bein' a deputy and all."

Josh sat up. "That's why I killed him. It was my job." He paused. "Kind of, I mean. Besides, it wasn't in cold blood."

"I told him so. He said that's fine, but until there's testimony under oath, there's nuthin' he can do. I think there's politics involved, Josh, you bein' not only a deputy and my brother, but with an election comin' up and Matt runnin' for sheriff against his father-in-law, John Taylor. Taylor's a personal friend of Peterson."

"And Matt appointed us."

"Exactly."

"So I have to rot in here until he gets around to a trial." Josh stood up and leaned against the bars. "Look, I won't leave the building. Just don't keep this door locked. During the day at least. You can lock it at night."

Jeff's brows knit together. "I don't know, Josh. I don't want to cross the judge." He scuffed his boots on the floor. "Aw, I suppose that would be okay, as long as you promise not to go outside."

"Don't worry—as long as you keep me in food and handkerchiefs, I won't even look at the door."

"The good news is, we won't have to wait long for your day in court. Peterson'll be back in two days. We won't have to wait for a week or two like we thought."

Josh was about to reply—probably to complain about two days being two days too many, but the opening of the door interrupted him. A familiar black voice called to them.

"Back here, Uncle Billy," Jeff answered.

O'Hara lumbered through the office and into the hallway that ran in front of the cells.

"How're you boys doin'?" he asked softly, muffling a cough.

"Better 'n you, I'd say," Josh told him. "You been to the doctor 'bout that cold?"

Billy shrugged. "Not much he can do, he says. It just has to run its course."

"You have a fever?" Jeff asked, noticing the sweat on the man's face. "Or did you just dip your head in a horse trough?"

"Ah'm okay." He put them off with a flip of his large hand. "Enough about me. Ah've got some bad news. Jacob Page slipped and fell down a shaft tryin' to save another man who done the same."

"Is he . . . ?"

"Dead? No, Josh, he ain't."

"That's a relief."

"But he ain't conscious. He could die yet."

The Bodines were silent, feeling especially sorry for Jacob and Rosa and Matt, but also for themselves because this meant Josh had lost his only favorable witness. Even so, neither brother would complain. Compared with the seriousness of Jacob's condition, Josh's situation seemed more like a mere inconvenience.

"What now?" Jeff asked finally.

"We can pray," Billy said. "It's about all we got right now."

"Don't seem like much," murmured Josh. "I wanna *do* somethin'."

"Doin' somethin' got you in here," Jeff reminded him.

"Josh," Billy began in a fatherly tone, "trustin' God *is* doin' somethin'. Sometimes it's the only thing you can do, when things are beyond your abilities. If we could always handle everythin' ourselves, what would we need God for?"

"Good question," Josh said sarcastically. "What *do* we need God for if He lets things like this happen?"

"I ain't big on bein' religious," Jeff interjected, "but I know enough to know that you made your choices, Josh. God didn't get you in this pickle. Now don't get your hackles up, I ain't sayin' you made a wrong choice. It ain't the one I'd've made, that's true enough, but that don't make it wrong. My point is, *you* made it. Not me, not God, not anyone but you."

"I like to think Myers made it," Josh said quietly, stifling a cough.

"Perhaps," Billy agreed. "And that's what we'll need to convince the judge. But without Jacob Page, all we got is God. Besides, what I think we oughta be prayin' is for God to deliver Jacob Page from the hands of death—for his own sake, not just 'cause he could help you, Josh. Thinkin' about others and puttin' them ahead of ourselves—that's what God wants."

"You pray, Billy," Jeff said. "We'll listen."

He bowed his head, and Billy did the same as he began to pray in earnest. Josh watched and listened for a few moments, then slowly lowered his head and closed his eyes. When Billy was finished, Josh tacked on an extra amen, and the others looked at him with pleased surprise.

After a time Jeff broke the reverent silence. "Can Matt Page help, do you think? He's been sent for, ain't he?"

"Not yet," Billy said. "Been too much happenin'. I gotta get word to him, that's for sure."

"Ain't Bodie got a telegraph?" Josh asked.

"Nope. Telegraph wires are usually strung beside railroad tracks—makes 'em easier to maintain. Ain't hardly no reason to string wire out here, much less build a railroad. Not yet anyways."

"Then someone has to ride to Bridgeport," Jeff decided.

"I'll go," Josh offered.

"That's funny," Jeff told him.

"Neither of you can go," Billy said. "Josh, you're in jail. Jeff, you're the only law left in Bodie. Was a time we could do without a deputy for a day or two, but not anymore. Too many people here."

"And you don't look well enough to make the trip," Jeff observed. "Are you, Billy?"

Before the black man could answer, the door creaked open, and
Noah Porter wandered in, looking lost.

"Oh, there you are," he said upon seeing Billy. "I bin lookin'
high to low for ya."

"What do y'all want, Noah?"

"Nuthin'. Not me anyway. Rosa sent me to fetch ya—"

"Is it Jacob?"

"Is what Jacob?"

"Did he come around? Or did he . . . ?"

"Go to glory?" Noah suggested indelicately. "Naw, there's no
change in him. Miss Rosa . . . I mean, Mrs. Page wants someone
to go to Bridgeport and tell Matt."

"We was jus' discussin' that," Billy told him.

"There ain't no one to go," Josh said.

Jeff's face lit up. "Say, how 'bout you, Noah? Why don't you go?"

"Huh?" said Noah.

"Huh?" echoed Billy and Josh simultaneously.

"You ain't doin' nuthin', are you?" Jeff asked.

"He ain't never doin' nuthin'," Josh pointed out. "Dependin'
on him to get Matt to come here, huh? You might as well just shoot
me in the head."

"You sure you want me to go?" Noah asked. "It never occurred
to me . . . I don't own a horse or nuthin'."

"We'll provide you with one. You can take Josh's."

"Hey!"

"You ain't usin' it," Jeff reminded his brother. "He'll only be
gone a couple days. He'll be back before you get out."

Josh sulked on the bed but had no further response.

"That's it then," Billy concluded.

"Actually," Noah said slowly, "now that I think on it, I'd just
as soon not come back. Not for a while anyway. I'm kinda tired
of the cold here in Bodie, especially since I blowed my shack to
smithereens. I'd like to relocate to Bridgeport, if'n you don't mind.
Start over, if you know what I mean. I can send the horse back with
Sheriff Page."

"That's fine," Billy said. "Come on, Noah, you need to get your
things together. Time's a wastin'." He turned to Josh. "From the
sound of it, you're catchin' a cold of your own. You'd best take
care of it now before it gets any worse."

"Tell my guard to keep the fire stoked and bring me tea with lemon and honey," Josh said with a smile.

Billy forced a grin as he and Noah tromped out together, closing the door behind them. Jeff unlocked Josh's cell.

"Make it yourself," he said. "There's enough wood by the stove for a couple days. Keep the door bolted when I'm gone. And remember, don't leave the building. If someone comes in, hightail it back into the cell, understand?"

"Yeah," Josh replied. "You know I'm as good as dead now, don't you? I don't have a chance."

"Someone had to go. Noah may tell tall tales, but that don't mean he can't deliver a message."

"We'll see," Josh said. "We'll see. I hope your faith hasn't been mislaid, that's all I can say."

CHAPTER

TWENTY·THREE

NOAH PORTER BOUNCED across the bridge at the south end of Bridgeport, his hat brim flopping comically as he complained out loud to his borrowed horse. The animal shook his head and blew hard, as if complaining back at his rider, then came to a grateful stop in front of the first watering hole—of the human variety—that Noah saw. He lifted a leg over slowly and dropped onto the dirt street.

"Hoss, I'm as thirsty as a camel that's been lost in the desert for a month," he told the animal while tying it to the hitching rail. "I'll see Sheriff Page in a bit. A few minutes ain't gonna make no difference." He climbed the steps gingerly, favoring his backside, and pushed his way through the floppy doors, letting them fan the breeze behind him. It was quiet inside, though that didn't surprise Noah, it being around noon on a weekday.

The saloon was empty except for three cowboys in the corner, quietly drinking warm beer and playing a closed game of penny-ante poker. Noah ordered his whiskey and drank it in a single gulp, then poured himself a second and scanned the room while he sipped.

"Where'd ever'body go?" he asked the bartender.

"We got a revival goin' this week," Dave Hays told him. Dave leaned on the bar, not bothering to wipe the glasses with a towel to keep busy. There'd been so few customers lately, everything had been polished three or four times. The bar, and the mirror behind it, were spotless. In fact, the place looked like he'd just opened the doors for the first time five minutes before.

"So?" Noah asked. "Since when did a revival put the kibosh on a good thirst-o-rama?"

"Since Reverend Benson got all the wives to nag their husbands extra hard. All the men are doin' what their wives say and stayin' home."

"Everybody in this town married?" Noah wondered.

"No, but between me and the other bars in this town, the single men who aren't workin' have divided us up, and about all I get outa the deal is them three cowpokes from the Anderson spread."

"Why ain't they workin'?"

"I didn't ask, friend. Ain't none of my business. Yours neither, I wouldn't imagine."

"Uh . . . I don't really want to know," Noah said, waving the cowboys off as though they were paying attention. He dropped a coin on the bar, put his hat back on, and got up to leave. "Say," he asked, remembering why he'd come, "you know where I can find the sheriff?"

"Which one?"

"What do you mean, which one? How many you got here?"

"Well, two in a way. One is elected but ain't feeling too good these days, and the other is only a deputy serving out the sheriff's term. It's kind of confusing."

"I want the one named Matt Page."

"He'd be the one actually working, and you'll probably find him at his office across the street, buried under a mound of paperwork."

"Thanks, friend," Noah said with a gap-toothed smile. "I'll be back later for some more, I'd wager. Save me a spot at the rail."

"Take your pick," Dave said dryly, "but don't wait too long. When these fellas leave, I just might close up."

Noah waved and lumbered through the batwings. Mumbling to the horse as he hobbled past, he crossed the wide expanse of Main Street, his head constantly turning as he took in the sights, pausing only when his eye caught a man dressed all in black, leaning against a post and staring up the street. Something clicked in Noah's brain, and he hesitated, then shook his head and continued on his way.

He entered the sheriff's office without knocking, finding Matt at his desk just as Dave had said, though he wasn't buried under a mound of papers. Matt was reading a Visalia Stock Saddlery Company mail-order catalog, his feet on the desk, his hat hanging from the toe of his boot. He peeked over the top of the catalog toward the visitor.

"Hi," Noah said with a little wave.

Matt scrunched up his face. "Hello. Is there somethin' I can do for you, friend?"

"Yeah. It's me, Depu—uh, Sheriff . . . Noah."

"Noah?" Matt took his feet down slowly, plucking his hat off his toe and dropping it on the desk. He stood and extended his hand. "Noah, my goodness, I hardly recognized you. Come on in."

"Didn't reco'nize me? Do I look diff'rent?"

"Well, not exactly different. I just didn't expect to see you without Bodie bein' all around you, you know what I mean?"

Noah puzzled over that one for a moment, then said, "No, I don't. Not a whit. But never you mind—it don't matter none. Kin I sit?" He pulled a chair up without waiting for an answer.

"Be my guest, Noah. So what brings you to Bridgeport?" Matt paused, then added, "And please don't say your horse."

"Nope. Josh Bodine's horse."

"Okay, I earned that. Why are you here?"

"Bad news, Sheriff—"

"Please, Noah, you can call me Matt."

"Sure, Matt. Anyway, I've got some bad news. Your pa had an accident—"

"Accident? Is he—"

"Dead? No, he ain't dead. But he's real bad off."

"What happened?"

"Fell down a shaft trying to save Elrod Ryan and—"

"What hap—"

"If you'd gimme a chance, Sheriff, I'd tell you." Noah raised his voice.

"Sorry," Matt said, holding his hand up. "I'm just a little anxious to know how my pa is, and you do have a tendency to ramble sometimes, you know."

"Says you. Anyway, Elrod slipped on some ice next to the shaft, and your pa tried to grab him, and they both fell in. Elrod fell all the way, but your pa got his feet tangled in the cable. He bonked his head on some timbers and is out cold, but Doc says he has a chance. They sent me to tell you about it."

Matt dropped his head and squeezed his eyes shut, rubbing them with his thumb and fingers. "Tell me everything, Noah. Is he gonna die?"

"Like I tol' ya, Matt, Doc says he might be okay."

"I hope and pray you're right." The acting sheriff gazed out the window, fear creasing his forehead. "I appreciate you ridin' all the way out here to tell me, though I'm a little surprised they sent you." He added quickly, "Not that I don't think they should have, it's just that . . ."

"That's okay, Sheriff, I understand. Surprised me a little, too. But that's what Billy wanted. He isn't feelin' too good himself lately. And Josh is—oh my, I almost forgot! Josh is in a peck of trouble! They wanted me to tell you about that too."

"What happened?" Matt asked for the third time, hoping Noah would be able to get it all out without any more prodding.

"He shot a man. A stage robber."

"That sounds serious, but why would he be in trouble?"

"Because he ambushed him."

"How does one ambush a stage robber?"

"It wasn't during the robbery, Sheriff. It was a couple days later in a saloon. The robbers got away, but Josh got a good look at one of them, and then your pa overheard two of 'em talkin' at a wrestlin' match—."

"You're doin' it again, Noah. You're ramblin'."

"No, I ain't. Not this time. You just don't understand yet."

"Okay, I'll try to be patient, but please get to the point. You can fill in the details later."

Noah pounded on the desk. "Stop interruptin' and I might!" Matt held up his hands in surrender but kept quiet. "That's better," Noah said. "Anyway, they was at the wrestlin' match, and your pa overheard 'em sayin' they was gonna kill Josh because he could reco'nize the one man. So when they came into the saloon, Josh shot him in advance in self-defense. Then your pa fell down the shaft and—"

"Now Josh has no defense," Matt finished. "Without my pa's statement, they can't even prove the man's a stage robber, much less that he was plottin' against Josh. It just looks like cold-blooded murder."

"You got it all wrapped up in a walnut shell."

"But I wasn't there, so what can I do? I can't testify about what my pa overheard."

"But Josh is innocent, accordin' to Josh at least. You gotta do something. I'd hate to think I rode all the way out here for nuth—"

"It wasn't for nuthin', Noah. You brought me news of my pa's accident. Besides, maybe the man Josh shot is wanted for somethin'. If he's a stage robber, he might already be a wanted man. You know what the dead man looks like?"

"Yeah, the whole town filed by his corpse in front of the undertaker's. Your pa says his name is Jack Myers, but a lot of folk thinks he's really Milton Sharp, the notorious stage robber. They'd heard he was in these parts."

"Check those posters, Noah. Even if he ain't Milton Sharp, he might be wanted. If he's in there, maybe that'll get Josh off without havin' to prove the man was plannin' on killin' him." He pointed toward the posters hanging on the nail. As Noah moved over to them, Matt mumbled to himself, "Maybe they'll finally come in handy for somethin' besides coverin' that bullet hole in the wall."

"What's that?" Noah asked.

"Nuthin'. Go on ahead."

"Okay." Noah yanked them off the wall. "And maybe that other man'll be in here too."

Matt was already deep in thought about his father. "Eh? What's that?"

"That other man. The one I saw outside." He nodded toward the street. "I seen him before. Can't place where exactly, but I know I've seen him."

"So you saw him before. That don't make him a wanted man."

"In his case it does. I've got a feelin' I seen him before when somethin' bad happened."

"Oh. Well, look all you want, Noah. Let me know if you find anything."

Matt shook his head, wondering why they'd chosen Noah to deliver these important messages, then turned his thoughts to his pa. He wanted to go to Bodie to see his father, but there was so

much to do here, so much to occupy Matt's thoughts and, potentially, his actions. Wanting to go but feeling like he should stay was
frustrating. To leave now would cause a great uproar and would
surely cost him the election. But his pa—

"There's nuthin' I can do for him," he mumbled.

"What's that?" Noah asked, not taking his eyes off the pictures
he flipped through.

"Huh? Oh, nuthin', Noah. Just thinkin' out loud."

"Hmm. Nope, not here." He put the stack down. "Neither one
of 'em."

"Neither one? What're you talkin' about? Is there another
man?"

"I keep tellin' ya, Matt, I reco'nize that man out there."

"What man?"

Noah went to the window and pointed. "That one."

Matt looked out. Reverend Benson stood on the boardwalk
across the street, talking and laughing with a group of ladies.

"That's the travelin' preacher," Matt said. "You probably saw
him at a meetin' someplace."

"Not me. Never been to one."

Matt shrugged. "Maybe you're mistaken then."

Noah looked hard at the man, squinting to improve his vision.

"No, I seen him before. No mistake about that. Only I can't
place him." As he turned from the window, he noticed the framed
pictures on the wall across the room, and he began staring at them.
Matt noticed the old man's actions and followed his gaze.

"Don't even think it," Matt said. "He ain't one of the presi-
dents. Those men are all dead, I think, except for U.S. Grant there,
on the end. Course, you know Grant personally, don't ya, Noah,
having loaned him a pen to give Jeff Davis at Appomattox to sign
the surrender with. And Grant's in Washington anyway, not
preachin' out here in California."

"Consarnit, Matt, I know I say a lot—"

"Sometimes you beat all, Noah, you know that? Like how you
were there during the Great Chicago Fire, not two years ago, even
though you were in Bodie at the time. And the Alamo and—"

"I'm tellin' you, I know who he is. He may claim to be a
preacher, but he ain't really. I ought to know—I held his horse."

"You held his horse? What are you talkin' about, Noah?"

"Listen!" Noah turned and leaned on the desk. "I'm tryin' to tell you, I was workin' there, and he asked me to hold his horse. How was I to know what he was up to? I knew him, you see, and didn't think . . . Well, anyway, pretty soon he comes out, jumps on the horse, and rides off." He paused for a moment, seeing Matt's puzzled expression. "Aw, what's the use. You wouldn't believe me if I told you."

"Hmm," Matt mused. "It was an interestin' tale, though hardly cause for all this excitement. So you didn't find any pictures of the dead man in the wanted posters?"

"Huh? Oh . . . no, I didn't." Noah glanced over at them. "And there weren't no pictures of Milton Shar—say, what's this? There's more posters over there on the floor."

"Where?" Matt leaned over and saw the posters he'd meant to discard the other day, still lying on the floor where he'd thrown them, partially hidden under the cabinet. "Oh, those. Leave 'em. Those fellas are all dead or in prison."

Noah ignored him, his pack-rat tendencies too strong, and scooped them up, blowing the dust off them. He shuffled through the papers, making guttural noises occasionally, then stopped and went back through a couple pictures again, staring at one in particular.

"You got a pencil?" he asked the lawman.

"Yeah, right here. Why?"

"Lemme see it."

"Help yourself." Matt pushed the pencil to the corner of the desk. Noah grabbed it, licked the tip, then set the poster on the cabinet and began scribbling. Matt watched him, his feet on the desk, supporting himself with an elbow on the arm of his wood and leather spring chair. His face was expressionless.

"Yep," Noah concluded, holding up his artwork to admire it. "He's deader 'n a can of corned beef all right."

"That's what I told you," Matt reminded him.

"Yeah, but this man weren't dead two days ago. It's definitely the man your pa called Myers."

"What are you talkin' about, Noah?" Matt removed his feet from the desktop and with seemingly great effort leaned over to glance at the doctored wanted poster.

"Noah, that's Charlie Jones, and that wanted poster's at least two years old. Besides, I know what happened to him. He's one of them convicts. You remember, the ones who escaped from the Nevada State Pen a couple years ago."

"Yeah, I remember. And I also remember he weren't never found," Noah said in a challenging tone.

"That's true. But he was last seen on his way to Death Valley, and he ain't been seen since."

"Until a couple days ago," Noah corrected. "And I seen him. People have gone to Death Valley and lived to tell about it," he pointed out. "Why, I myself spent a whole summer there, without shelter—well, maybe not a whole summer. More like a mon—a week, I think it was . . . Okay, don't look at me like that. I went there one day, then came right back out. But that don't change facts. This here man with a beard like the one I drawed was killed in Bodie two days ago."

"Okay, say you're right. So what?"

"This is the man Josh shot, that's so what." Noah slapped the poster on the table. "This is one of the stage robbers. Look here, Sheriff, right on this poster—he was doin' life for murder! That's him. I'll bet you a week's wages on it."

"You don't have a job, Noah. What wages?"

"That's beside the point. This is him, I'm tellin' you."

"But why would he change his name?"

"Like you never heerd of wanted criminals changin' their name to avoid arrest."

Matt's face flushed. Noah had him there. He stood slowly to stare at the poster.

"Look, Noah, I gotta tell you I have my doubts. But if you're right, you need to get this poster back to Bodie. If this is the dead man, he was a wanted killer, not to mention an escaped convict. Josh would be completely in his rights shootin' him for that alone. Don't matter that he didn't actually know it at the time. He actually shot in self-defense—he just can't prove it. This we *can* prove, and the truth will protect him. Noah, take this poster back to Bodie."

"Me? I ain't supposed to go back. I'm stayin' here a while. It was part of the deal."

"Someone has to go, Noah."

"Yep, that's true. You. Billy said you'd do it, and that you'd take Josh's horse back with you."

"I . . . I just can't go, Noah."

"But your pa . . ."

"Ain't nuthin' I can do for him, Noah, 'cept pray. And I can do that here. Besides, I've trouble here you wouldn't believe." *And an election coming up*, he thought. "I can't leave now. Look, get yourself a room at the hotel and leave your things there. Ride to Bodie with the poster, stay the night, then come back. Two days—that's all it'll take. I'll pay for your room while you're gone. When you return, I'll give you a bonus and see to it you get a job or something. Or at least a place to stay and three squares a day until something comes along."

"Three squares of what?"

"Meals, Noah—food."

Noah thought for a minute, a scowl distorting his face. Then it relaxed, and he said, "Okay, Sheriff. I'll do it for you and your pa. You two've always been good to me."

"Thanks, Noah. I mean that. And tell Rosa I'll be there as soon as I can, okay?"

Matt checked his pocket watch, the one Sarah'd given him for Christmas a few months before, then sighed. "On second thought, it is gettin' kind of late. No need for you to leave today. You'd be pushin' dark before you made it to the Bodie cutoff. Go get a room and some rest. Tell the hotel clerk I'll take care of the bill later. And get that horse put up. Here." He flipped a couple coins onto the desk, and Noah snatched them before they stopped teetering.

"Okay, Sheriff, okay. You drive a hard bargain." He wandered out with his poster, folding it and tucking it into his shirt pocket.

Matt ran a hand slowly down his face as he leaned back in his chair, stretching his legs out under the desk. Poker Tom's murder, Quong Tai's lynching, the suspicious Reverend Benson, Josh in jail, maybe for good this time, and now his pa hurt bad, maybe dying . . . *What else could go wrong?*

He bent over, folded his arms on the desk, then rested his head on them, his shoulders quivering as the fact that his pa might be at death's door took its toll. All the rest of it, though weighing heavily upon him, was just problems that had to be worked through or gotten used to. His pa dying though . . . that was different. That was personal. He'd lost him once before, and then

Matt's ma died. That fear, the sense of loss, the loneliness, all the confused emotions he'd felt when he was a kid, came creeping back from the depths of his insides, catching in his throat. It wasn't just a state of mind, a remembrance, that coursed through him like a wide river spurts down a narrow canyon. Adding to it all, and maybe the worst of it, was the guilt he felt for sending Noah back to Bodie rather than making the trip himself.

He was glad he was alone as the river crested its banks.

Noah grumbled to himself as he lumbered across the street. It had been a long time since he'd ridden a horse for any distance longer than the length of Bodie's Main Street, and he barely remembered that trip anyway, having "borrowed" the horse following a short relationship with a large bottle. He was mighty sore from his efforts of the morning and not altogether happy about the prospect of making the ride two more times before being allowed to heal. But it did feel good to know he was needed, that something important depended upon him and him alone. For the first time in a long while, Noah was anxious to prove himself.

Figuring one small drink before dinner to deaden the soreness in his britches wouldn't do any harm, Noah took the horse to the livery with an eye on the Comstock Saloon.

"Be right back," he told the establishment as he walked past.

With the money Matt gave him, Noah rented livery service that included a stall, some oats, hay, water, and a rubdown, then fingered the rest of the money that was burning a hole in his pocket.

He pushed through the weathered, creaking doors and stepped back into the sunshine, his wrinkled eyes squinting to ward off the sun. A freight wagon rattled past, the teamster shouting at Noah as the old man jumped out of the way, regaling the driver with his own colorful thoughts and best wishes.

Noah was still shaking his fist at the man as he entered the hotel. The clerk regarded him with a jaundiced eye.

"The saloon is next door," he said dryly.

"I know," Noah said. "And the quicker you gimme a room, the quicker I'll be there with my foot on the rail."

"That will be cash in advance, I presume." The clerk made no move to offer Noah the register.

"Sheriff Matt Page is payin' for this. I'm on county business. Now gimme a key."

"I'm afraid I'm going to need more than—"

"Here, this will cover it."

Someone had come up behind Noah and put a couple eagles on the counter.

Noah was astounded that someone would offer the ten-dollar coins on his behalf. "No, that ain't necess—" he started to say as he turned, stopping involuntarily as he looked into the face of Reverend Benson. He stared a moment, then forced himself to turn away as he coughed into his sleeve. "As I was sayin'," he began slowly, his voice cracking, "that ain't necessary. The sheriff is payin' 'cause I'm on county business."

"It's no problem, I assure you. Let's not bother the sheriff right now. I'm sure he has plenty to do. If he wants to, he can pay me back when he has a chance. You'll tell him, won't you?" Benson asked the clerk. The man nodded. "That's it then," Benson continued, then said to Noah, "Perhaps I'll see you at the revival tonight?"

"Perhaps," Noah said. Upon receiving his key he hurried up the stairs, leaving Benson in the lobby, and locked himself in his room.

"And perhaps monkeys'll fly to the moon," he said quietly, flopping onto the bed.

CHAPTER

TWENTY·FOUR

MATT AND SARAH sat in their parlor, Sarah darning Matt's socks and Matt staring into the fire, sipping hot coffee.

"I think you should go," Sarah said. "He might need you."

"They need me here, and there's nuthin' I can do for him right now."

"Maybe not, but you should still be there. I know I complain when you go traipsing around after outlaws, even though I know it's part of your job. But this is different. This is your father. I don't mind if you go."

"That's not why I ain't goin'. There are some things happenin' here that need my attention—"

"Not that silly election, I hope."

"No, not the election, Sarah. Look, if Pa was conscious and slippin' away to eternity, I'd be there in a heartbeat, you know that. But the way Noah described it, he's out like a light and wouldn't know if I was there or not. If he . . . if he dies, my being there won't change that. And if—I mean, *when* he comes out of it, I can ride there to see him. If I go now, I'll just be sittin' around and gettin' in the way. Kinda like your pa is around here."

"Just the same, Matt, I think—"

A bloodcurdling cry from some distance across town interrupted her, and they both sat still, listening, waiting for something to confirm what they thought they'd heard. It came again.

"Fire!" Several voices this time.

"Did you hear that?" Sarah asked.

"I think so." Matt strained to see through the curtains without getting up.

"Shouldn't you go check?"

Matt gave her a questioning look.

"You sure? I'm finally spending an evening at home with you and now you're trying to get rid of me?"

Sarah blushed. "No, of course not, Matt. But a fire . . ."

Matt was already up and moving to the window. Parting the curtains, he could see a column of smoke rising on the far side of town, reflecting the amber glow of the flames beneath. He was unable to see what was burning, but it didn't matter. They couldn't let even an outhouse burn if it jeopardized the rest of the town.

Without even grabbing his hat, Matt gave Sarah an apologetic look as he squeezed her arm on his way out the door. Sarah watched him run off into the darkness, praying silently for his safe return. Then she had a second thought, threw her shawl around her shoulders, and followed.

All available men were either on their way or already present when Matt arrived. The building was fully involved, the dry wood burning hot and fast. Black-orange smoke rolled and billowed through the windows and roof, the flames crackling and the wood popping as it weakened and broke, cascading downward in a splintering shower of sparks and debris. Since the conflagration was too intense for anyone to approach, the bucket brigade wasn't making any real attempt to save the structure, which was beyond hope. Instead, they concentrated on confining the blaze to the one building.

Fortunately for the citizens, the burning building wasn't adjacent to any others, sitting alone at the edge of town with a good twenty feet of empty dirt between it and the nearest structure, the new schoolhouse. As their parents fought the blaze, children stood across the street out of harm's way, watching the intense, brilliant flames in awe and hoping the blaze would leap the gulf and consume the schoolhouse too.

Everyone was there, so many in fact that a second bucket line was formed. Shopkeepers, city and county officials, gamblers, accountants—everyone pitched in when fire threatened the town. Some of the drinking professionals loitered with glasses in hand, just spectating . . . until someone pointed out to them how close their watering hole was to the fire. They quickly put two and two together, downed their glasses, and headed for the brigade to help.

Even Reverend Benson had taken a place in the line. Matt figured he'd be able to work this into his sermon the next evening, probably with some reference to the fires of hell being seven times hotter than the blaze they'd all felt so intensely on their foreheads while the store burned.

It was then Matt realized what was burning. Ah Quong Tai's old store, the one he had vacated.

Intuitively, Matt knew the fire wasn't accidental. Since the building was empty, there was nothing to start a fire, unless some wandering cowboy had decided to take shelter for the night and thought a campfire in the middle of the floor would be nice. But that didn't seem likely. Most cowboys, as simple as many of them were, had better horse sense than that.

It was just too coincidental that something like this would happen on the heels of Quong Tai's execution.

Matt made his way into the bucket line and went through the motions, but his thoughts were occupied with who might have started the fire and why. He scanned the orange faces reflecting the glow of the flames, trying to read the thoughts of the people of Bridgeport, looking for just one flicker of satisfaction that would let Matt know where to begin his investigation. But all he saw was fatigue and fear. The Indians were the most likely to be blamed, for obvious reasons. But why would they ride all the way back to Bridgeport to torch Quong Tai's store? And his old one at that? It would have been easier just to set it ablaze on their way out of town after the murder. At least that would have made sense, in a perverted sort of way.

Matt tried to imagine the Paiutes sitting around their campfire and Captain John suddenly slapping himself on the forehead and saying, "We forgot to burn down the Chinaman's store!" All the Indians would groan, then draw lots, the loser having to ride all the way back to set the fire.

The idea amused Matt, but it didn't make any sense. Even if they did have an afterthought and sent a brave back to do the deed, why do it under the cover of darkness? If it didn't bother them to hack a man into little pieces in front of everyone, surely they wouldn't be secretive about burning down a vacant building. Matt could draw no conclusions about who the culprit might be, though he pretty much ruled out the Paiutes.

The water sloshing out of the hastily exchanged buckets soon soaked Matt's pants and boots. In fact, probably as much water soaked into the ground as made it to the burn site. Even so, within an hour the fire was out, having consumed the building, leaving a soggy, charred tangle of smoldering lumber and ashes. Not a stick was left standing, though thankfully the rest of the town had been saved. All but a few of the curious citizens wandered tiredly back to their homes and beds or to their bottles and card tables, though too worn out to celebrate.

Matt stared at the mess in solitude, trying to figure out where the blaze had originated. The destruction was so complete, it was impossible to tell. He picked his way across the ruins, careful not to step on live embers or anything that looked incapable of carrying his weight, his soaked boots insulating him against the continuing heat. Wondering why he was doing this, he attributed it to the curiosity that goes with a badge.

A flash of white caught his eye, or actually a small area that wasn't black. He stared at the irregular patch, then squatted for a closer look. He slowly put his index finger on the object, discovering it to be hard. The shape was different than what he'd first thought, as only part of the object was exposed. He brushed debris away and then recoiled as a form took shape beneath him, a shape totally out of place, being rounded, not straight and angular like the remains of the wood that had framed the building. He recognized the light-colored material to be exposed bone surrounded by burned tissue.

It was a human body in repose—on its left side, arms raised, one leg crossed awkwardly over the other. Charred leather—belt and boots—and some metal buttons were about all that was left of the victim's attire. Being moist, however, the flesh had resisted burning longer than the clothing, though none of the features could still be recognized.

"Matt?"

He'd been so absorbed in his find, his wife's plaintive call startled him, and he jerked his head around.

"Huh? Oh, Sarah. Sorry, I . . . uh . . ."

"Aren't you coming home?" she asked, almost begging. "It's getting cold. It's all over, honey. The fire's out."

Matt answered slowly. "Yeah, but . . ." He stopped himself from looking down at the body. "You go on, Sarah. I'll be along shortly."

"What is it, Matt?" She sensed something in his voice but was unable to even imagine what could be happening. "Is there something you need to—" She cut her sentence short with a sharp intake of air. She'd seen it. Her hand went up to her mouth. "Oh, Lord . . ." she whispered, and she meant it as a prayer.

"Please, Sarah, this isn't something for you to see."

"Who is it?"

"I don't know," Matt said. "I need to try and figure that out, okay? Please go home. I don't know how long I'll be. You might as well go on to bed when you're ready."

Sarah looked purposefully away from the burned body and into Matt's eyes, seeing in them the pain, the suffering, the agony her husband dealt with routinely, and her respect for him deepened. He wasn't merely the big-hearted, brave, handsome young man she'd married. He was a lawman—someone who dealt in human misery, putting his life on the line for people who probably didn't care most of the time. Suddenly she became acutely aware of what she believed to be selfishness on her part for wanting him to spend more time with her.

"Okay, Matt. I love you." She barely choked it out, then hurried away before she started to cry in front of him. She scurried back to the safety of their little house and the comfort of reading the Bible beside the warm fire, leaving her husband alone with the victim.

Matt watched her go, wishing, almost praying that he hadn't found this. But as Sarah vanished from his sight, Matt turned, and there it was, still lying grotesquely in the burned, smoking rubble. Matt rubbed the back of his neck and ran a hand through his hair, now feeling the cold night air. The clammy sweat from his labors made his shirt cling to his skin, threatening him with illness. He backed away from the burned rubble and hurried to Dr. Keebles's house.

It took about an hour for the two of them to collect the body and haul it to Keebles's office. They had plenty of onlookers, especially once word spread and the saloons emptied, but no helpers. No one wanted to touch the horrid thing. Keebles had brought two pairs of treated canvas gloves and a large sheet, and they carefully placed all the pieces on it—the body had not remained intact when they tried to pick it up—then tied the sheet and carried it away.

Keebles had the presence of mind to draw a crude sketch of how the body was positioned before they moved it, which he traced so he could give a copy to the lawman, who confirmed its accuracy.

Once the remains were safely at Doc Keebles's place Matt returned his gloves, washed at the doctor's sink, and bid him good night.

"I'm going back to bed too," the doctor told him. "Come around first thing in the morning; we'll see to him then."

Matt thanked the doctor, left, and was soon slipping through his back door, boots in hand.

"I'm in here," Sarah called softly from the parlor where a small fire still blazed.

"What are you doing up?" Matt asked.

"I couldn't sleep."

"I'm sorry, I should—"

"I love you, Matt," Sarah said, standing up and putting her hand gently over his lips. "I hope and pray your pa will be all right."

"Yes," Matt said quietly as Sarah stroked his stubble-covered chin. "So do I."

She reached up with her lips to cover his, and soon all conversation was forgotten.

Matt dragged himself out of bed at the usual time and prepared for another day, though he'd noticed it was getting harder to do that with any sense of anticipation. Today it seemed almost a drudgery, and as he sat in the gray kitchen he considered just taking off his boots and going back to bed. He'd nearly fought off the temptation when Sarah came into the room in her dressing gown, a delicate but warm pale blue affair he had gotten her for a birthday present not too long ago. She also wore a smile and had brushed her hair so it fell around her shoulders in shimmering curls. In the light of approaching dawn, she was a vision.

Now it would really be hard to leave.

"Let me fix you some breakfast, honey," she offered. "You always leave without any." She stroked his hair.

"I don't like to start my day feeling full," he explained. "And I don't like to eat in a hurry. Besides, this morning I've got to go to Doc Keebles's, and I don't know how I'll react to that business."

"When should I bring it by then?"

"Nine o'clock or so. If I'm not there, you can wait if you want. I won't be long."

"Okay, dear." She kissed him on top of the head, then held him tightly. Matt closed his eyes and enjoyed the closeness, then reluctantly peeled himself away.

"Good-bye, Sarah. See you later."

"You still smell of smoke," she mentioned.

"I'll change later," he promised.

He smiled at her as he plunked his dirty hat on his bed-mussed hair and moved through the door into the dusty streets of Bridgeport.

When Matt arrived at the physician's office, the doctor was already up and working. He stood next to the table occupied by the burn victim, a puzzled expression on his face.

"Well, Doc," Matt said as he looked at the remains and marveled at the power of the fire, "what do you think?"

"I don't know. Has anyone been reported missing yet?"

"No . . . not to me."

"You'd think the next of kin would've said something already. There were plenty of people there last night. Surely the whole town knows by now."

"Yeah. Emil Potts was one of 'em. He'll tell Maude, and she'll make sure it gets spread pronto."

"So for now we'll have to assume it's nobody we know. The question remains, why was he—"

"He? You've established it's a man?"

"Not yet, but I suspect it. The boots are curled up from the burning. Can't really tell their size, but they look like men's shoes. I'd hate to think a woman burned to death in that old building. It'll be easy to tell for sure once I begin the autopsy. Even if this was just a pile of bones, I could tell."

"How's that, Doc?" Matt was genuinely curious.

"Easy. Women have babies, men don't. Their pelvic bones are wider."

"Of course." Matt looked the victim up and down. "Makes sense."

"Anyway," Keebles continued, "if it was a stranger just passing through, perhaps he took shelter in the old empty building and built a fire for warmth, then something went wrong. Perhaps he'd been drinking and passed out."

"Do the boots rule out an Indian?"

"No, they're pretty plain. Some of those folk wear them. I'll give him as good an autopsy as I can and let you know what I find."

"Okay, Doc." Matt took another look at the man and turned to leave, then looked back, his face puzzled. "Why wasn't he burned up more?"

"Why do you ask? Isn't he dead enough for you?"

"What I mean is, the buildin' was completely consumed. How come he wasn't?"

"The body is mostly water, Matt. That building was dry wood. It burned so fast that the fire ran out of fuel before the body was consumed, lucky for us."

"Lucky for us?"

"Sure. Look here." He pulled back burned flesh around the mouth to reveal the man's teeth. "Fillings. And a gold tooth. If he's local, the dentist should know who it is. Someone ought to recognize these teeth."

Matt grimaced. "Thanks, Doc," he muttered sarcastically.

Keebles smiled. "Listen, you don't have to hang around here. This is pretty unpleasant business. I'll let you know what I've found when I'm through."

"Thanks," Matt said, sincerely this time. "Listen, can I have Sarah rustle you up some breakfast?"

"No, thank you. Mrs. Keebles already handled that task, rather admirably if I may say so. Hotcakes and bacon." He smiled and patted his stomach.

Matt gave him a half-smile, half-grimace, wondering how he could eat just before a grisly autopsy, then figured he'd done it so many times he'd gotten used to it.

"Well, okay, Doc. I'll see you when you come by with some news then. Good luck."

"Right, Sheriff."

At least Doc Keebles knows who's sheriff in Bridgeport, Matt thought as he vacated the premises and headed across the street to his office.

Like the eye of a hurricane, the day passed uneventfully. Matt was fidgety about what the doctor was doing but didn't want to bother him, so he waited for the doctor to seek him out. He was worried about his father too but couldn't justify going to Bodie. He was needed here; his father was unconscious anyway. There was nothing he could do there but get in the way. As soon as he heard about his pa waking up, he'd be on his way. Until then . . .

Fortunately, no other problems arose that day. It was almost as if the exciting events of the past few days and weeks had tired everyone out so much they were too done in to stir up trouble. Even Reverend Benson, preparing for the final night of his revival service, had made himself scarce.

Benson. The thought of him made Matt wonder just who Noah thought the preacher was. He had sure seemed excited about him, but Noah was good for that. He'd been everywhere and done everything and knew just about every famous person who'd ever lived during the last seventy years—or so Noah claimed. Of course, no one believed any of it. He was just a kind old geezer who amused himself and everyone else with his tall tales but who couldn't be taken seriously. In fact, Matt wondered why he'd been chosen to deliver such an important message, but then again he'd done okay, so Matt had no reason not to send him back.

Benson's revival seemingly had been successful so far, if that kind of thing could be measured. Many in town had been commenting about the services and the healings some folks had reported and several professions of faith, and about Reverend Benson in particular. How dynamic his preaching had been, how God empowered him as he touched folks in Jesus' name and they were delivered from problems that had plagued them for years.

Like Norma Washington and her gout, and the lower back pain that had kept Clyde Sampson from holding a job since last Christmas. Matt had decided to wait and see if the gout flared up again, and when work was offered to Clyde if he took it. It was one thing to claim to be healed; it was quite another for time to prove it. Matt knew that Norma's gout came and went and that she was quite impressionable about certain things, having a tendency to bend whichever way the wind blew. And she did so like to be the center of attention.

And Clyde . . . Some folk thought there was nothing wrong with Clyde's back in the first place. For someone who could hardly lift his own weight out of a chair, Clyde had the habit of getting into frequent drunken brawls when the need arose, and he won his share of them. He claimed the alcohol numbed his back muscles, but Matt thought the only thing numb about Clyde was higher up in his anatomy. And Doc Keebles himself was Clyde's biggest detractor.

"I'm his doctor, and he's faking it," Keebles once said to a group of men when the subject came up.

"And he's a quack," Clyde responded when he heard about it.

And that's where the issue came to rest, especially since Keebles had been trying to embalm himself at the Red Dog Saloon the three hours before he made the comment.

But there were other claims of minor healing from more respectable quarters, so Matt couldn't dismiss the phenomenon altogether. Still, his doubt lingered, naggingly so. Having nothing better to do while waiting for Keebles to finish poking and probing his way through the victim's body, the sheriff went to Reverend Stone to talk it all over.

The knocking on the door was light but urgent, and Jonathan Edwards Stone rose from his upholstered chair, his one concession to extravagance. He was tall and slender, balding on top but with luxurious curly hair over the ears and down to his collar, black but graying at the temples. His face was gaunt but did not have that undernourished look to it. Heavily arched eyebrows shaded sharp blue eyes that twinkled when he spoke. His voice was quiet and scholarly, and he was a man not unlike his namesake. Naming him for the father of the Great Awakening, Stone's mother couldn't have chosen better. Asked whether she thought his name had influenced his decisions in life, she would always nod and say, "Perhaps." Even on her deathbed, the year he began his first church in Vermont, she told him always to remember his "heritage," as she called it, and to stay true to God.

Stone himself knew the name had no particular power. John Wesley Hardin, named by his Methodist minister father for the British preacher who'd founded his father's denomination, certainly drew no inspiration from his namesake, becoming instead a murderous outlaw. So, though proud of the name, Stone did not wave it like a flag but bore it in humility.

"Yes, yes, I'm coming," he told the unseen visitor who was still knocking. He opened the door, and there stood a familiar figure, that of the sheriff, Matt Page. Somewhat rumpled, the strong, young man looked tired—no, not just tired. Concerned. Worried even.

"Come in, Matt." Stone widened the door, and Matt forced a smile as he entered. They immediately took seats in the parlor, Stone offering Matt his upholstered chair, which the lawman took, raising a small cloud of road dust as he plunked down into it. This was not the first time Matt had been a visitor here, and it probably wouldn't be the last. Stone appreciated not only Matt's company but his dedication. Finding a lawman in the American West who was not only not a gunfighter but a devout Christian as well was rare indeed, and Stone had made a secret determination to do his part to make sure Page stayed that way.

"What can I do for you?" Stone asked when they were settled in and he'd poured a mug of coffee for his visitor.

"I need to talk to someone," Matt said, "and I think you're about the only one who'll listen to me. Besides, I need some good, heavenly advice."

"Well, that's quite a tall order, but I'll do my best."

"What do you think of Reverend Benson?"

Stone wasn't quite prepared for that question, and it took him a moment to recover.

"That's quite a broad inquiry," he said diplomatically. "Could you be more specific?"

"Is he a man of God? I mean, *truly* a man of God?"

Stone sipped his hot brew as a means of giving himself time to think without appearing to be hesitant. He looked hard at the Bible on the table next to his chair.

"Well, let me put it this way, Matt, I have no direct evidence to the contrary."

"But what about his preachin'?" Matt protested. "Doesn't it . . . bother you?"

"Bother me? It never bothers me when a man preaches the Word of God."

"What if he's teachin' something that ain't altogether right?"

"Then he isn't giving out the Word of God."

"Pastor, I hate to say this, but you're dancin' lightly around the fringe of the fire."

Stone chuckled. "I'm rather transparent, aren't I, Matt?"

"No. I just get the feelin' you're not gonna show your cards until you have to, that's all."

"Yes, I suppose that's true. Before I say anything, let me ask you this—why are you asking these questions? Is something wrong?"

"I don't know, Pastor. Not that I can put my finger on. But I've got this feelin' . . . It's been naggin' at me since the day he first drove through town. And now that I've been to his revival meetin's . . . well, the feelin' hasn't gone away—it's gotten worse."

"Is that the lawman in you, do you think?"

"I don't know."

"It could be the Holy Spirit."

"Huh?"

"The Holy Spirit gives certain people the ability to discern things, to have intuitive understandings about people and situations, to give them insight others don't have into the true nature of folk. Maybe God has given that to you."

"But how can I know? And what do I do about it?"

"That's hard to answer, Matt. What is it about Reverend Benson that bothers you?"

"Is Benson's preachin' okay? I mean, I'm not a Bible scholar or nothin'. If he threw somethin' in there that wasn't right, I might not recognize it. So might not a lot of other folk. I wouldn't want him leadin' folks astray."

"Nor would I. But this is a free country, and I'll not raise my voice against a man just because his style is different than mine. If I had a reason to believe he is a false teacher, I'd say so. So far, I really don't have a reason to."

"So he's okay?"

Stone shook his head. "I don't know for sure, Matt. I don't go along with his style of preaching. He's a little flamboyant for my liking. Of course, some would call me boring to listen to. But Jonathan Edwards, for whom my dear mother named me— Edwards's greatest sermon, the one called 'Sinners in the Hands of an Angry God'—he didn't preach it, not in the way we think of the term. He read it from his notes in an intentional monotone, lest the congregation be overcome by his presentation rather than the message itself. But just because Edwards felt that way doesn't mean Benson's style is ungodly."

"It's not just his style I'm thinkin' of. What about the things he says?"

Stone was pensive, sipping his coffee as he stared over Matt's shoulder, his mind focused on his thoughts rather than what his eyes had locked onto. "What about them?"

"Are they true?"

"Mostly. What I mean is, within the context wherein they are found in God's Word, the words Benson speaks are all true. I believe he has oversimplified a few things perhaps, and maybe he's said a few things in ways God didn't intend—"

"So he's a liar."

"Not necessarily. He might just be misled himself. He could be absolutely sincere."

"Sincerely wrong?"

Stone smiled. "Perhaps."

Matt leaned forward, his elbows on his knees. "Then the folks goin' forward to be saved—are they really saved?"

"God knows, Matt."

"Pastor," Matt said in an exasperated huff, sitting back in the chair, "if Benson is a fake, those people are in danger of hell."

Stone cleared his throat. "Matt, let me tell you something." He set his coffee cup down. "It is God who does the saving, not man. Can someone be saved by hearing God's Word even from someone who is not a Christian himself? I suspect that has happened more than once in the history of mankind. Besides, these people will be attending church here when Benson leaves, and with God's help we can make sure they understand how to have forgiveness and new life in Christ. Remember, Matt. God has never lost a person yet that he intended to save."

"Then what about the healings?"

"God still performs miracles, Matt."

"You're shufflin' your feet again, Pastor."

He chuckled again. "See what I mean? You're very discerning. You're in the right profession, Matt. Let me put it this way—I know God has not given me the blessing of being a conduit for miraculous healing. That doesn't mean he hasn't given it to Reverend Benson. I rejoice in a miracle of God regardless of whom He uses to bring it about, just as I rejoice in the true salvation of a person even if it occurs under the ministry of a charlatan. God's truth is so strong, it sometimes seeps through the cracks of a false teacher's sermons. I can't say whether the miracles are real or not. I do think some people are easily deceived and might not even know they've been hornswoggled. They might even want to believe something so strongly that they make it happen themselves. Maybe it won't last, but in their minds it's real. People believe what they want to believe."

"But don't you think Reverend Benson's doin' some damage?"

"I have a feeling about that, Matt, but since I can't see into his heart, I'll keep my feeling to myself. Perhaps if Benson had come to Bridgeport to stay, to establish a church, I might be more inclined to scrutinize him a little closer. As it stands. . . ." He shrugged and smiled. "Don't get me wrong, Matt. I'm not saying you shouldn't have come to me with your concerns. I'm glad you did. But God is in control, remember that. I'm suggesting that you use your discernment wisely. Be certain before you do anything. The devil is wily, Matt. Even if you're right, he can make things bad for you if you stick your neck out too far. To paraphrase a wise old saying, Benson, too, shall pass."

CHAPTER

TWENTY·FIVE

WALKING BACK from Stone's parsonage, feeling less than satisfied and perhaps even more confused, Matt passed Doc Keebles's place. Unable to wait any longer, he let himself in through the front door. The outer room was empty, and he called out, but there was no answer. He grasped the knob of the examination room door, hesitated, then opened the door slowly. The body, still spread out on the table, was fairly well picked apart—the head even seemed to be missing. But the doctor wasn't in. Matt gazed in wonder at the remains on the table, then backed out of the room and left the office, making his way around back to the doctor's private residence.

He knocked lightly on the door, which was soon answered by Mrs. Keebles, a jolly, solidly built woman with a round, ever-smiling face framed by stark white hair done up on her head but coming out of the pins at the sides and on her forehead. She swept the errant locks away as she regarded Matt with raised eyebrows.

"Yes, Sheriff? What can I do for you? Looking for the doctor?"

"Uh, yes, I am as a matter of fact. He's doin' . . . somethin' for me."

"The autopsy on the burn victim? Yes, I know. He's almost finished, but he got called away out to Ben James's place. The old man fell and couldn't get up, it seems. He was on the floor a couple days, no food or water, until his neighbor checked in on him.

Kidney failure will result, unless I miss my guess. They dry right up without water. Terrible thing."

"Do you know when Doc'll be back?"

"No, can't say that I do."

Matt was frustrated. "Well, did he tell you anything about the burn victim?"

"No, not particularly."

"Oh. Thank—"

"The skull's been cleaned off, I know that. He said to let you have it until he returns. Shall I wrap it for you?"

"Cleaned off?"

"Yes, of course. We removed the burned flesh and all. It's not as gruesome as it sounds. Our faces and scalps aren't really attached, except at the ears and mouth. Only when we can't tell who we're looking at do we need to expose the skull. Like burn victims or people who've been dead a long time and are in advanced decomposition. What doesn't scrape or pull off I boil off in a pot. Oh my, I see by your face that upsets you. It sounds horrible, I admit, but it really has to be done. Autopsies are terrible, there's no doubt about it. But they're necessary." She smiled, not because the image her words provoked was pleasant, but because she enjoyed imparting the mysteries of her husband's profession to others. "So, do you want it then?"

"Want it?" Matt said hesitantly. "Want what?"

"The burn victim's skull, of course. It's all nice and clean."

"Oh, sure. That'll be fine."

The last thing he wanted to do was appear as though he didn't know what he was doing.

"Come on in, then, have a seat." She stepped back from the door and let him in. "Care for a cookie while you wait? They're fresh."

The idea of eating something cooked in the same kitchen where Mrs. Keebles had boiled a human skull nauseated Matt, and he turned her down.

"Don't worry," she assured him as though reading his mind. "I did the boiling out back over an open fire. We have a fence around it, so no one can tell what we're doing."

"No thanks, just the same," Matt declined. Why risk it?

"I'll be right back then." She left Matt to himself, returning in less than three minutes bearing a covered wood box. "I packed it in sawdust to protect it. Thomas said he didn't know if this would help you, but it's all there is to go by. He said you'd understand. I certainly don't." She laughed at her ignorance.

Matt didn't understand what the doctor meant either but kept that fact to himself. "Well, thank you," he said hesitantly.

"I'll have him look you up the moment he returns," she said.

"That would be good," Matt told her, his meaning going well beyond his words.

He excused himself and took his prize back to the jail, setting the box on his desk and staring at it. After getting up his nerve, he lifted the lid and stared down at the top of a clean, white skull, then lifted it out. Matt began to chuckle at himself for his nervous acceptance of the skull and laughed a good long time. But when the clock on the wall bonged, he remembered the revival and put away the skull almost reluctantly, sliding the box under his desk. It was time to get ready for the final service.

"Now don't you go nowhere," Matt said, shaking his finger at the box. He stuck his hat on as he stepped outside and locked the office door behind him.

The citizens of Bridgeport were out in force for the last meeting. Many who hadn't darkened the doorway of a church in their entire lives were there, and hardly a single family was left unrepresented. Matt figured it had to be because of the Indian affair and now the fire—not that folks were ready to thank God for anything so much as they wanted to pass on and receive gossip.

The singing was begun with great fervor, the tent sides nearly flapping from the wind created by the loud, holy voices of the Bridgeport Angelic Choir and Potluck Society, as Matt had named the congregation in his mind. When Benson mounted the platform to deliver the revival's final sermon, a hush settled in over the crowd like morning fog on a still lake, just as it had during each of the previous meetings.

"Brethren, 'be not deceived; God is not mocked: for whatsoever a man soweth, that shall he also reap.' These words from the Apostle Paul to the Galatians reverberate today in Bridgeport. We have all witnessed great tragedies this week. First the discovery of the murder of the poor Indian, Tom. Then the cruel but just death of his killer, the Chinaman. And now another life has been taken, just when we thought it was over."

Matt was all ears.

"A man burned to death in the fire that destroyed Quong Tai's store."

His old store, Matt thought. *Quong Tai's store is just fine, thank you, and being purchased and occupied by Mr. David Hays at this very moment.*

Benson was oblivious to Matt's thoughts and didn't slow down.

"In a final attempt at retribution, one of the Indian band snuck back here under cover of darkness and in their perverted sense of justice burned the store to the ground."

Matt was incensed. How did Benson pretend to know that? And why was he making such prominent mention of it during his sermon?

"But," Benson went on, beginning to move about the platform like he did every night, "he has paid for his crime. God in His wisdom has seen fit to let the man's own act of injustice be the means whereby he paid the penalty, for it was the Indian brave who died in that fire."

Matt's mind reeled. "Now I know he's a phony," he whispered to Sarah, who shushed him.

"God is a just God, a righteous judge, and no one can escape His judgments. I spoke yesterday of the power of God to heal you, and we witnessed that power in a remarkable way, a miraculous way. We saw God reach down—" Benson reached almost to his shoes. "—and touch some of us, taking away the sin that beset us and healing our infirmities. But there is more to victorious living than physical health. We must live not for ourselves but to serve God. Serving God involves every aspect of our lives—all of it. It even reaches into our pockets. If we withhold from God what is rightfully His, we are robbing Him.

"Can He forgive you for that? Yes, of course He can. But will there be a consequence nonetheless? I believe it is clear there will be. I cite two examples. Turn with me to Malachi, in the Old Testament."

As Benson read Malachi 3:10 about bringing tithes into the storehouse and in turn getting a blessing too large to be contained, Matt understood why Benson had spoken about the fire. It was to make a point, to lead into his sermon on giving money to God—which meant giving money to Benson. Give or be judged—that was apparently today's message.

This was almost more than Matt could take. He set his jaw and dropped his gaze to avoid looking at the prancing Benson as the preacher, in all his theatrics, told of the hellfire and damnation to come. Many would later say how real and frightening he made it all sound, literally scaring two men into coming forward during the invitation. But Matt wasn't listening, his thoughts on something other than Benson's words—Benson himself.

Who was this man? Why had he come to Bridgeport? Was he truly an itinerant minister doing God's work and occasionally taking up the cause of others of his own choosing, or was there more to the man than met the eye? That he'd made a good living off the people of Bridgeport Matt had no doubt. The offering plates had been full every night. But had people truly been saved or healed under his ministry? Were that week's professions of faith real or just emotional responses to scare tactics?

And why did he get involved in local issues—praising John Taylor's actions regarding Quong Tai, for example? For that matter, how had he managed to show up at the fire? And what made him think an Indian had started it and was killed by it?

Matt wanted answers.

"So you see in very strong and clear language," Benson was saying, "God considers His children's withholding the tithe to be robbery, plain and simple. There are rewards for bringing all the tithes into the storehouse, friends, very real rewards. But there are also consequences for withholding from God. We read in Acts chapter 5 about Ananias and Sapphira, a husband and wife who cheated God and were struck dead by the living God for their sin.

"Will that happen to you this day, ladies and gentlemen? Will that happen to you? I pray that is not the case. Mrs. Miller, will you please come and play and give the folks the chance to be honest with God and not commit robbery before Him? Will you give them the chance to open the windows of heaven so a blessing may be poured out upon them? Play, Mrs. Miller, play! Stand, people, and sing your praises to God as you file out past the offering baskets. Pay no attention to your neighbor—this is between you and the Lord."

Of course, Matt knew everyone would do just exactly what

Benson had asked them not to do. They'd file out, watching what everyone else was doing as they passed the collection plates stationed at every exit and knowing that everyone was watching them.

As soon as he was clear of the crowd, rather than mingling with folks at the social at the town hall, he muttered an excuse to Sarah and fled for the solitude of his office. He sat at his desk in the dark, pondering everything and finally shutting his eyes and praying out loud.

"Dear God," he began, then took a breath. "Lord, this here's Matt. Matt Page, Sheriff of Bridgeport. I need Your help again. At least this time I'm not bein' shot at, and You can take Your time a little if You're of a mind. I've got me a real problem here and don't know what to do. Not just this Benson fellow, though I sure wish you gave out lists of the folks we could trust. Anyway, I got this other thing—with the Indians and now the fire and all. I've got a dead guy over at Doc Keebles's, and I don't even know who he is, much less what happened or why he was in that burnin' building. And with my pa hurt and maybe dyin', and Sarah unhappy, and the election comin' up . . . well, I don't even know what to ask for. You've got a better grip on this whole mess, I imagine, so please just do what You do best, and if You feel like it, let me in on it somehow. Thanks, God. Amen."

Matt looked up blankly, stretching his eyes as he sat back in his chair, and suddenly the words Dr. Keebles had uttered during his testimony a couple days back came to his mind.

Matt sat up straight. What was it Doc had said exactly? Something about the head being the best determiner of race? Now what did that mean? If you had a person's head, of course you could tell what race they were; all you had to do was look at his face. That couldn't be what he meant. In Poker Tom's case they only had the skull, no face attached, thanks to Quong Tai's knife skill. The county physician couldn't have been talking about the whole head—he must have meant the skull.

Matt took the skull of the arson victim from the wooden box and set it on his desk. It stared back at him in silence, telling him nothing. He picked it up and turned it over in his hand, looking at it from all angles. How could he tell a man's race by this? It was just a skull. It could have belonged to man or woman, Indian or white or Chinese—

Matt's eyes narrowed as he suddenly wondered about something. Did a Chinaman's skull look different from an Indian's? Or a Negro's? Or for that matter a white man's? Maybe a comparison would answer his questions. He put the burn victim's skull back in the box and grabbed his hat, making sure to put out the light and lock the door behind him, then stole up a back street to the rear of the hall where the social was in full swing.

As expected, he found several youngsters lurking in the alley, trying to muster up enough courage to do something that would undoubtedly get them in trouble. They started to run when they spied him, but he grabbed one boy by the collar and held his hand over the squirming kid's mouth.

"Relax," he told him, "you're not gonna be punished. I need your help."

The boy stopped struggling and looked up at the sheriff with questioning eyes. Matt released his grip on the boy's face.

"You're the law," the boy said. "What do you mean you need my help?"

Matt knelt down as he fished a dime from his pocket. He held it up in plain view.

"You know Mrs. Keebles?"

"Doc Keebles's wife? Sure."

"Go tell her Doc Keebles is home and wants to see her. Don't tell her it was me that sent you, and don't let anyone know about this. Go straight in, deliver the message, and go straight out again, you hear?"

The lad nodded and reached for the dime, but Matt drew it away from him.

"When you come out and I know she got the message."

"Don't put it away," the boy said over his shoulder as he turned toward the hall. "I'll be right back."

True to his word, the lad returned in a few minutes, his pockets full of sandwiches and cookies pilfered from the long table where the food was laid out. But shortly Matt saw Mrs. Keebles pass by the opposite end of the alley as she left through the front doors. He thanked the kid and flipped him the coin, then hurried to beat Mrs. Keebles to her house.

He was on the porch when she passed through their small gate. "Mrs. Keebles," he said, alerting her to his presence so he wouldn't frighten her.

"Matt, what brings—"

"Doc isn't home yet. I sent that message."

"You? Why did—"

"I need your help, and I didn't want anyone to know. It's not a pleasant idea I have."

"Well, come in then. Let's not stand out here where the whole world can see us."

Matt glanced around at the deserted street, then followed her inside without comment. She lit the lamp but kept the flame low.

"What's the big secret, Sheriff?"

"I need another skull . . . cleaned off."

"Why? Who?"

"The Chinaman, Quong Tai. I can't explain it, really. It'll take too long. It's part of my investigation into the identity of the man burned in the fire."

"You think they might be related in some way? I mean their deaths, not the people themselves."

"Maybe, but I really think seeing their skulls might convince me they're not related, which is just as important. I'm sorry to drag you out of the social like that, but you can understand . . . I needed your help with this. I haven't, you know, boiled too many—"

"I understand," Mrs. Keebles said, raising a hand. She smiled compassionately. "Does it have to be Quong Tai? I mean, hasn't he already been buried?"

Matt thought on that. "No, I suppose it doesn't. He's just the only Chinaman I know who's recently died. Besides, the Indians already did half the work."

She shook her head. "Terrible business, that. Quite unlike the Paiute to resort to such behavior after all these years. They must've really wanted to make an impression."

"They did that all right."

"Indeed. Well, if it's any old Chinaman you want, perhaps I can save you the trouble of digging up old Quong Tai. Come with me." She led Matt through her husband's examination room and into a rather large closet—or perhaps it was just a very tiny room, Matt couldn't tell which—lined with shelves stuffed from ceiling to floor with boxes and books. She lit the lamp and turned it up, then studied the room for a moment.

"There," she said finally. "That trunk over there on the bottom . . . bring it out, would you?"

Matt obliged and set the trunk on the examination table. Mrs. Keebles opened it, and Matt peeked in, seeing eight or ten skulls of various sizes and hues, some white, some amber, at least one a dark shade of brown. She pulled a few out and looked them over, reading small tags attached underneath.

"Here we go," she said. "Chinese male, age thirty. Will this do?" She handed it to Matt.

He turned it over and read from the tag, then nodded. "I suppose. I, uh . . . Thanks. It'll be fine. I'll bring it back when I'm done."

"Okay, Sheriff. Here, let me get a sack for that. Wouldn't do to have you walking through town carrying that out in the open." She grabbed a cloth pouch from the shelf and held it while Matt carefully dropped the skull inside. "I'm glad I could help. Maybe one of these days you'll have time to tell me what you're doing."

Matt forced a grin. "If I ever figure it out myself, I'll be glad to, Mrs. Keebles. Uh, you'll keep this . . ."

"Entirely confidential. Of course." She winked.

Matt ran back to his office to avoid being spotted and having to explain himself, then locked himself in. For a while he sat in the dark, his breathing fast and deep, and waited for someone to come by. But no one did, and he felt confident he wouldn't be disturbed.

He did not light the lamp, utilizing only the pale glow from the post lamp outside, and put the newest skull, the Chinaman, on the desk. Next to him he set the burn victim, then dug into a drawer and pulled out the potato sack containing Poker Tom's skull he'd found under the floor of the general store and placed it at the end of the grisly lineup. He crouched down and faced them, his heart thumping against his ribs.

Matt stared at the three skulls, going down the line from one to the next and back again, wondering at first what the doctor had meant. But the more he looked, the more he began to realize that the skulls were indeed different. On one the eye sockets were round; on another they were almost square. On one the cheek bones were more prominent than on the other two. One had a more sloping forehead. The burn victim even had a curious fracture on the back of his head.

Matt picked up the skulls and turned them over, noticing the teeth on Poker Tom's skull. He felt his own teeth with his tongue, noting their irregular chewing surfaces and the vacancy where he'd had a cracked tooth pulled the year before. The Indian had flat teeth, and all of them were still in place. He had no fillings and no cavities in which to put them. Of course, no Indian would go to a dentist, but apparently there was little need. Perhaps the Paiute's distinctive diet kept his teeth from rotting and ground them down flat. Grinding grain on rocks must add grit.

The Chinaman's teeth were like his own and the burn victim's, with pronounced points on the corners of the molars. The oriental diet consisted mostly of soft rice, something that wouldn't wear the teeth down. Significantly, the burn victim had fillings. So he was definitely not an Indian. Benson was completely wrong about that. Matt banged a fist down on the table.

"I knew it," he exclaimed out loud. But could the man be Chinese? No. The burn victim's skull was larger and had very small, low cheekbones, and the eye sockets were of a different shape. Also, the Chinaman had no protruding bone at the point that would equate to the bridge of the nose, whereas the burn victim had a distinct protrusion, signifying a large nose. He definitely wasn't Chinese either.

"Who are you?" Matt asked him. "Why were you in that building? And why did Benson make such a big deal about you being an Indian? Not just to enhance his sermon, I'll wager."

He mulled this over while he stared at the upper teeth of the burn victim. Something was familiar about them. He began to realize . . . he'd seen those teeth before. They were rather large, very yellow front teeth—incisors, he thought they were called. He reminded himself they wouldn't appear so large in life because the gums would have covered a good portion of the teeth. The incisors were surrounded by ragged, stained, gold-filled canines and molars. He tried to imagine those teeth with different faces surrounding them, some of them quite comical, until the whole scenario spinning through his mind suddenly clicked into place.

Why would Benson falsely accuse an Indian? Ignorance? No. Benson wasn't an unschooled man, and there would be no benefit to his speculating about the victim's identity for no reason. It had to be because *he knew it wasn't an Indian who died in the blaze*. And the only way he could have known that was because he knew who the person was, which would mean Benson had to have had something to do with his being there. That would explain Benson's being in town to help with the bucket brigade. He'd started the fire! Matt fingered the fracture on the back of the skull. Benson had hit the man on the head and dragged him into the building, which explained why the deceased was lying the way he was—arms over his head and all. Matt reached into his pocket for the sketch Keebles had made. It fit his theory perfectly.

Matt Page was sure of it—Benson had torched the building to get rid of the body, then blamed the Indians. He'd used the Quong Tai affair to cover a murder, a murder committed because . . . Matt was at the end of a box canyon. What reason did Benson have to kill someone? What did the dead man see—what did the man know about the itinerant preacher? What did the preacher have to hide?

The answer came to Matt in a rush. As he stared at the skull, the words returned to him clearly. *I held his horse.* Those were the old coot's words as he tried to tell the sheriff he knew Benson from somewhere. But Matt wouldn't listen. The face of Noah Porter formed in his mind—a perfect fit around the teeth on the skull before him.

Matt was floored by the realization that the dead man could be Noah. Just yesterday he had spoken to him, and today he held the man's skull. Matt set it down but continued gazing at it, then shut his eyes tight and imagined Noah. There was no doubt about it. Matt's hands began to shake with grief and shock. He leaned back, rubbing his chin.

Just who did Noah think Benson was anyway? Noah claimed to recognize him and ended up dead. Did Benson have something to do with it because Noah remembered him from somewhere else? Had Noah tried to confront him? And was Benson trying his best to make sure Noah's body wouldn't be recognized? Benson didn't necessarily know if Noah had told anyone, but he must have assumed he had, or that he would. So Benson had to get rid of him, but in such a way that no one would know it was Noah. And what better opportunity than to burn him in Quong Tai's old store and blame the Indians?

Then another realization gripped the lawman. If this was Noah's skull, that meant the old geezer hadn't gone back to Bodie to deliver proof of Josh's innocence. And that meant Josh was still in trouble.

What should Matt do first? Confront Benson or race to Bodie to help Josh? What did he have to confront Benson with anyway? Matt hadn't paid Noah any mind, hadn't let him speak, didn't know who Noah thought Benson was.

"If only Noah wasn't so good at telling whoppers, maybe folks would listen to him more," Matt muttered. Then he recollected that Noah had taken the wanted poster of Charlie Jones. Where was that? Did it burn with him? If so, how would he be able to help Josh?

The two problems both needed to be dealt with that very minute.

"Oh, God," Matt whispered. He prayed a while, then slowly opened his eyes and gazed at Noah's skull, waiting for an answer from above.

Perhaps the answer to all these questions was in Noah's room, amongst his things, Matt decided. He said he'd brought everything with him when he left Bodie, intending to stay in Bridgeport for a spell. Matt could only hope the wanted poster was in his room too, though he feared it was in Noah's shirt when he burned. All Matt could do was look. If it wasn't there, he'd just have to ride to Bodie and hope the judge would believe him.

What about Benson? Maybe Matt could try to find him on the way back and confront him with his theories. With any luck, Benson would confess—if not to his identity, at least to starting the fire.

If not, well . . . Matt would just have to cross that bridge when he came to it.

Matt packed away the skulls hastily and trotted across the street to the hotel, getting the key from the suspicious and reluctant desk clerk. Taking the staircase three steps at a time, he let himself into Noah's room with a shaking hand.

CHAPTER

TWENTY · SIX

THERE WASN'T MUCH to be found. In a bureau drawer Matt located a few articles of clothing and some personal items Noah probably would have taken with him had he gone to Bodie, even for just one night. In the other drawer was a small metal box. Matt placed it on the bed, sitting next to it and gazing thoughtfully at the lid. Slowly he clicked open the latch. Peering inside at a pile of old papers, he spotted the wanted poster on top, neatly folded, and immediately put it into his shirt pocket.

He pulled out the rest of the contents with a single grasp and spread them out on the bed. They included a few personal documents and a newspaper clipping or two, including one from Bodie's first newspaper about Josh's trial for bank robbery, a trial in which Noah was a key witness.

The next piece made Matt's heart skip a beat. It was a program from a theater. Ford's Theater, to be precise. The play: *Our American Cousin*. The date: April 14, 1865.

Matt, not knowing what to make of what he'd found, suddenly remembered Noah's interest in the pictures on his wall, including one of Abraham Lincoln. What had he said? "I held his horse." He'd held Lincoln's horse? No, that couldn't—

The truth hit Matt like a rifle shot. Not Lincoln's horse—the horse of his assassin. Could it be that for once in his life Noah had actually been where he said he was? Ford's Theater, where

President Lincoln was shot by John Wilkes Booth? Booth, Benson—John Wilkes Booth, Josiah W. Benson—both men J.W.B.

Fear gripped Matt. Was it possible . . . Could this man, this itinerant preacher, be John Wilkes Booth? Wasn't Booth dead? His body had been identified by . . . Matt hesitated, recollecting stories he'd heard about plots and counterplots, about Secretary of War Edwin Stanton being suspected of arranging the murder of Lincoln and the attempted murders of others in order to ascend to the presidency. If that were true, the death of Booth could have been staged, or someone could have been killed in that barn in his place. After all, the burned body was unrecognizable, "identified" by a doctor who'd been paid off, according to some. The similarity between that scene and the one last night in Bridgeport did not go unnoticed by Matt, and a shiver ran up his spine. It was a very theatrical scenario.

Theatrical. Booth was an actor, wasn't he? And what was a fiery preacher with a flair for showmanship but an actor with a message from God? A true message from a false prophet—could that be? Hadn't Reverend Stone said as much? Booth certainly had the talent for such an enterprise. And Benson's age was just about right.

Matt, not liking the direction his thoughts were taking, thought of Booth's face from pictures he'd seen and compared it to Benson's in his mind, then overlapped them. There was very little difference—no more than ten years might make. Booth was a young man when he killed Lincoln, and Benson, though his hair and beard were touched with gray, was no more than in his mid-thirties. But why become a preacher? To make enough money to finance a call to arms again in the South? That hardly seemed likely. Maybe he was just making a living in a way that would utilize his particular talents, yet not cause folks to think of him as an actor. And maybe he really had been saved and was preaching God's Word with sincerity; only when his true identity was near to being exposed did he panic and commit another murder, this time to protect himself.

But this was all speculation. He had no proof. And he still had Josh to worry about. Like it or not, Matt had to get to Bodie soon. But first, on his way out rather than on his return, he'd confront the preacher, see if he could find a way to prove any of this. If not,

Booth would remain dead. It's possible this was all a wild fantasy, and Matt hoped that was the case. He shuddered to think that Secretary Stanton might have been involved in an assassination plot against Lincoln. That would not be good for the country. And who would believe Matt anyway? People are reluctant to accept the facts about such situations, even when the evidence is staring them in the face, and especially when it's just the wild ideas of a rural county sheriff—a temporary sheriff at that.

Matt put away Noah's things, then had a second thought and took some of the items with him. As he passed the wary clerk, he explained, "I'm taking some of Noah's possessions—official business. I owe you for the room."

The clerk informed him, "It's been taken care of. I was told to tell you that if you wanted to repay the man who covered the bill, you should see Reverend Benson."

"Benson paid the bill?"

"He was here when Noah checked in. The old man had some wild story about you paying for his . . . Well, I guess it wasn't so wild after all." He grinned sheepishly.

Matt glared at him, then softened as a question formed in his mind. "Did they leave together?"

"I'm quite sure I don't know. The old man went upstairs, and Reverend Benson stayed down here. I went in the back room for a moment, and when I came out . . . Well, I never saw either one of them again."

"Thanks," Matt said halfheartedly. The clerk's statement added to the mystery. Matt nodded to him and left the hotel. He went first to his office, locking Noah's stuff in the small safe he used to secure prisoner's property and recovered valuables. Matt had a thought and chuckled out loud. He wondered if Doc Keebles knew how much one could learn by staring at a man's naked skull.

The lawman took a walk to the edge of town. The revival was officially over, and men from the church were hard at work taking the tent down. Benson was nowhere to be seen. Perhaps he'd been invited for dessert at someone's house, or he might have been so tired from his prancing and shouting and other antics that he just decided to ride on back to his camp, count his money, and bed down for the night, intending to return for his tent in the morning.

That possibility was confirmed by one of the workmen Matt

questioned. Satisfied, Matt went home to get a night's sleep in preparation for the morrow. He wanted to be well-rested when he confronted Benson. He'd missed the social, not that he cared, and Sarah was probably already safely at home and asleep.

He'd have to tell Sarah he was going to Bodie to see his pa and to try to help Josh Bodine. And that was all he'd tell her, and that he'd be back the following day or the next. If he told her what else he was doing—and why—she'd have him handcuffed and thrown into one of those sanatoriums. It was too unbelievable.

So unbelievable, in fact, that some hours later by the cold light of dawn Matt wondered, as he lay in bed and stared at the ceiling, if he hadn't given his imagination too much free rein. But when he reviewed it all again, he decided it was at least worth checking.

It wouldn't be easy leaving Sarah again, even for a few days. But this time she'd understand. After all, his father was perhaps at death's door. Matt prayed that wasn't the case, that when he got there he'd find his pa up and around. Hadn't Noah said no bones were broken, that it was just a bump to the head that had sent Jacob to bed?

In the morning when he got up, he told Sarah he was leaving for a few days. She hugged him and said she understood and that her prayers would go with him. She began packing some food for him while he went to get Shadow.

As Matt led his horse from the livery, he looked long and hard at the tent, the organ, and the other things belonging to Benson, finding them carefully folded and stacked and still awaiting their owner's arrival. *Good*, Matt concluded. *With any luck I can catch him lingering at his camp*. Matt led Shadow back to his house and loaded up, gave Sarah a long hug and a longer kiss, then caressed her cheek, smiled, and assured her everything would be all right. He mounted Shadow, gave his wife one last look punctuated with a wink, and rode through town.

He was careful to leave town across the bridge, as though he was headed directly to Bodie. But a couple miles outside Bridgeport, when he was sure no one would be able to see him, he turned Shadow off the trail and cut across the open range toward the mountains, back to the trail that led to Bloody Canyon.

The morning was pleasant, though chilly, and both he and Shadow blew steam with every exhale. He turned the sheepskin

collar up on his leather coat and buttoned the collar of his flannel
shirt against the breeze. The mountains were as magnificent as he
had ever seen them, the snow on the peaks glistening in the new
sun. The clouds forming behind them were dark and full of mois-
ture. It would most likely snow up there, maybe as early as that
night or the next day. Whether it would snow down here in the valley, Matt couldn't tell, though it certainly was cold enough to do
so. Winter was over, but this area was known for snowstorms at
unexpected times.

Either way, Matt was prepared. Sarah had seen to that. He was
carrying his slicker in addition to the heavy coat he wore, and out
of habit he'd packed his bedroll and everything he'd need for an
extended trip, even though he didn't plan on being on the trail
more than a day between towns. She'd also packed him plenty of
jerked beef and smoked ham, and even a little sack of flour for bis-
cuits if he felt like it.

Shadow enjoyed the run across the meadow, ignoring the cattle that grazed here and there, the grass feeling good under his
hooves after so much time on rocky roads and trails. With the
majestic mountains ahead of him, Matt also relished the trip, and
for an hour or so Matt lost himself in the grandeur of it all, more
than once praising God for what He had created.

Coming to the overgrown trail into Bloody Canyon brought
reality pounding down on him again, however, and he pulled
Shadow up. Squinting up and down the track, he decided the cot-
tonwood grove Benson had camped in was between him and
Bridgeport, so he wheeled the horse to the right. Figuring it
couldn't be more than two or three miles back, he maintained a
steady gait. Shadow was up for it, hardly even laboring after the
ride he'd made so far.

True enough, Matt reached the grove in a few minutes and
reined Shadow in. There was no smoke rising above the treetops,
but that didn't surprise Matt. In the still of the morning he listened,
but there were no sounds coming from the trees. With a sharp
sucking of his cheek, Matt urged Shadow forward and walked the
horse to the grove.

The closer he got, the more uneasy he began to feel. There was
no sign of the wagon from this distance, not like there had been
the other day. Even when he was close enough that a good portion

of it should have been visible, he saw nothing but trees. Matt wondered if the woods obstructed his view because he was approaching from a different angle.

His speculation became more doubtful as he continued to advance until finally he was within the trees. He came to a small clearing and knew he was not going to find Benson here. The preacher's fire ring was now just a burned spot circled with stones. Matt slid down from Shadow and checked the ashes, finding them cold and damp. The many footprints were all the same, all made by Benson's fine leather work shoes. Matt inspected the place where the wagon had sat and followed the tracks and horse droppings out of the clearing. He retreated and pulled himself back onto his mount, then followed the tracks to the road, where they turned south, toward Bloody Canyon.

He hadn't paid any attention to them as he rode in, concentrating as he was on the grove, but now they were clear. Checking carefully for several hundred yards in both directions to make sure he didn't miss anything, Matt confirmed that Benson hadn't gone to Bridgeport at all. His tent and the old organ and the other things must still be there waiting for him.

Benson had fled!

What else could it all mean? Why else would an itinerant preacher leave the things he'd need to continue his ministry? Something had frightened him off. But what?

Matt put the question to Shadow, who didn't know. The lawman sat there in the saddle, shoulders hunched, staring up the trail toward Bloody Canyon. The man had a good head start, several hours at least, as dead as his fire was. How long would it take Matt to catch up to him, if that were possible at all? Half a day, maybe a whole one. Even two. If Benson was indeed running, he'd be smart to abandon the wagon and just ride the horse, assuming he had a saddle.

Of course he did, the sheriff thought. He was in town every night, and Matt never saw the wagon. Benson's horse was a Morgan, after all, and could pull a wagon as easily as it could carry a human. But then, why did he take the wagon at all now?

Matt peered up the trail. To throw potential pursuers off, that's why, Matt concluded. If folk found the wagon abandoned here, their suspicions would be raised. Otherwise they'd never pay it any mind. But wouldn't the tent remaining in Bridgeport do the same thing? Matt shook his head. It didn't make sense. Nonetheless, he decided to ride up the trail awhile, to see if anything ahead would give him an idea how far Benson had gotten in his flight.

Not an hour later, as he approached the canyon walls, he got his answer. The wagon tracks turned off the road, and not too far away stood the wagon. There was no Benson and no horse, but plenty of footprints to tell Matt he was at least partly correct— Benson had saddled the horse and ridden off. Curiosity being what it is, Matt went to the door of the wagon to peek inside. It was locked, but at this point he felt no compunction against breaking it off with a large stone. In moments he was peering inside.

Apparently Benson had gathered only what he could carry easily and forsook everything else. The lawman saw blankets, clothing, food—all stacked up with plenty of space left for the things Benson had stored in Bridgeport. Matt rummaged through drawers hoping Benson had kept some proof of his true identity—if he was indeed someone other than Josiah Benson—though the lawman didn't really expect to find anything. Whoever Benson was, he wasn't stupid. As anticipated, the drawers yielded nothing.

One thing Matt did find bothered him, though he couldn't put his finger on why it did so. The big, black Bible Benson pounded on frequently during his sermons sat on a shelf in the wagon. Matt took it down reverently and opened it to the front page, then read the inscription: *To J.W.B. from S.* The names those initials represented could be guessed at but not proven, Matt knew. The first set could be Benson's or Booth's. But who was S.? Edwin Stanton? Secretary of State Seward? Besides Benson himself, who could tell? Without proof of who S. was, the inscription meant nothing.

As evidence, the Bible was worthless, so Matt left it where it lay.

Buried under a pile of personal rubbish was a trunk covered with ornate, inlaid designs and having an arched top. Its lock was broken, and Matt lifted the lid slowly. The interior was filled with costumes of all sorts—clowns, military uniforms, you name it, including some ladies' garments. And shoes to match. Matt found one large boot wrapped in a long, black coat. It had no mate. That was curious, to be sure, but it proved nothing. With a shrug he let the lid slam shut, no closer to a solution than he'd been before.

But at least Matt knew Benson was indeed running, though he

could only surmise what that meant. Whether flight would be sufficient cause to bring him back to stand trial for murder and arson, Matt doubted. Benson could create a dozen excuses for his actions. Furthermore, the lawman knew it would take days to catch him because he had a significant head start and because the far end of Bloody Canyon opened into a large valley called Yosemite. Beyond that, a man trying to hide would have plenty of places to do so.

Besides, Matt's father still lay in Bodie. Whether he was already dead, hovering near death, or recovering, Matt didn't know. But chasing after a ghost that he had no real evidence against wasn't going to accomplish anything and would do nothing to help his father either. Disappointed at losing Benson, Matt left the wagon and mounted Shadow, gave the scene one last look, then headed down the trail and across the range to the Bridgeport-Bodie road.

Arriving there, he turned without slowing and headed toward Bodie, but hadn't gotten far when he caught sight of a rider behind him, keeping pace. Not wanting to turn full in the saddle to take an obvious look, Matt kept riding until the road took a bend at the Bodie turnoff and disappeared into a narrow canyon. Rounding the cliff so he was out of the other rider's sight, Matt quickly reined in Shadow and jumped off, leading the horse to the side of the canyon and behind a rock outcropping. He scampered to the top, drawing his Colt as he ducked behind cover and pointing the business end in the direction of the other rider.

But the man didn't show. Either he'd stopped or turned back or . . .

"What Matt hiding from?" The voice was above and behind him, and Matt rolled over, swinging his gun toward the sound. But even as he did so, he recognized the voice. There, looking down on him from the cliff above, was his old friend Charlie Jack, as usual dressed in the clothes of the white man—a heavy coat and a faded black felt hat that drooped over his face. The casual observer looking at him from a distance would never guess he was Paiute.

Matt lowered the gun with a relieved sigh, his face twisted in chagrin. "You coulda got yourself shot," he chided the Paiute.

"Charlie Jack think you get shot first."

Matt laughed. "Yeah, you had the drop on me, all right. But you couldn't of shot me first. You don't carry a gun."

"Matt make good point."

"How'd you get up there anyway?"

"Horse."

"No . . . I mean I didn't know there was a trail up there."

"There is way to get everywhere. Some just more difficult."

"Story of my life," Matt muttered. He climbed down from the rock. "So what are you doing up there? Are you following me?"

Charlie just shrugged. "I hear Matt's father sick, maybe dying. I go with you to see great friend. You not ask me go."

"I'm sorry, Charlie. I had a lot on my mind."

Suddenly Charlie disappeared from the ridge above. Used to his Indian friend's ways, Matt climbed on his mount and rode back out to the road. Soon the Indian was riding abreast of him.

"Who man from wagon?" Charlie Jack asked.

"Huh? You mean in Bloody Canyon?" Charlie nodded once. "Well, I think that's the man who started the fire and killed the man who was inside. Did you know a man was burned in that building?"

"I hear when I come back from Captain John."

"I figured you'd go see him. What'd he have to say?"

"I tell him he should trust you, he make many unhappy. He say he no care, it over. He no talk any more about it."

"So you were with him when the fire broke out in Bridgeport."

Charlie nodded. "Captain John and his band all there. They no start fire."

"That's what I thought. The man who died was ol' Noah, from Bodie. You know him. He likes to tell tall tales."

"He big liar," said Charlie Jack matter-of-factly.

Matt couldn't help but laugh. "Yeah, that's him. Well, he told a bundle of whoppers, but he just might have been right this time."

"Man in wagon?"

"Yeah. Reverend Josiah W. Benson. Noah seemed to think he was John Wilkes Booth."

"Who Booth?"

"He shot our president some years back—Abraham Lincoln."

"He kill white man's Great Father?"

"Yep. They say Booth was captured and killed in a barn that burned down, but there were a lot of rumors that it wasn't really so. You know, they made it look like he's dead when really he ain't, because someone else was really the mastermind behind the whole assassination. Nobody believes those theories, though. Every time someone important gets killed, people bring up conspiracy theories like that. I'll be glad when this whole country gets educated— maybe they'll stop that nonsense."

"Noah believe nonsense. Now Noah dead."

Matt shrugged. "Yeah, that's what bothers me. Problem is, I don't have any proof—of who Benson is or if he started the fire. Even if I could find him, what would I do with him? It's been a long time since the assassination. Nobody'd believe me. If Noah was alive, nobody would believe him."

Charlie nodded. "Maybe better you not find."

Matt shook his head. "Boy, that's a scary thought. It goes against my grain even to think it, but you could be right. Come on, let's get to Bodie." Matt pressed his knees together and jerked in the saddle, and Shadow jolted into a gallop. Charlie Jack on his sorrel was right behind.

CHAPTER

TWENTY·SEVEN

JUDGE PETERSON SAT with the prosecuting attorney, Horace Givens, in the small room that served as his chambers when he was in town, preparing to go into the adjacent courtroom and begin the trial. He had a large chaw stuffed into his lower lip, and Givens watched him miss the corner spittoon several times.

"You know, Judge, you got the cleanest cuspidor in Bodie."

Peterson ignored him and sighted in on a roach crawling up the wall behind the lawyer. He let loose with a big wad, scoring a direct hit on the insect's back with a disgusting splat. The roach fell off the wall and landed on his back, his legs kicking as he struggled to right himself. Givens watched until the roach finally turned itself over. As a reward for its efforts, the lawyer stomped it.

Givens turned to Peterson with one eyebrow raised in puzzlement.

"Moving target," said the justice matter-of-factly. "I gotta have me a moving target."

"Well, this defendant isn't moving," Givens said, rising and grabbing his papers. "He's a sitting duck."

"We'll see about that, Horace," Peterson said. "I've learned never to number newborn domesticated egg-laying birds before they've broken free of their birth capsule and seen the light of day for the first time."

Givens laughed. "I'll say one thing for you, Judge, you didn't let your education go to waste."

Peterson stood and expelled his chaw into the spittoon, to his own surprise, before putting on his coat. "You got a fair jury impaneled?"

"Yep. Twelve Bodie men who don't read the papers, most of them because they can't. That's about as fair as it gets around these parts."

"Good enough. Let's get this thing taken care of. I don't want to spend two days on something you describe as clear-cut and obvious."

Horace followed the judge out into the courtroom. Peterson took his place behind the bench, then told everyone to sit down.

"Is everyone here?" he asked Jeff Bodine, serving as bailiff.

"Almost, Your Honor. Both attorneys and the defendant are present, as are all the witnesses save one. He's . . . unconscious. Mine accident."

"Too bad. Is his return to consciousness imminent?"

Jeff thought that one through a moment, then shook his head. "No way to know."

"Well then, we'll have to muddle through without him. Let's get started." Peterson turned to the jury. "All right, men, you've been chosen to sit in judgment over the defendant, Deputy Sheriff Josh Bodine." He pointed to the defendant just in case someone on the jury was too stupid to have picked him out. "He is charged with murder in the second degree on the person of Jack Myers, punishable by up to life in prison. Your task here is to listen to the evidence and the testimony of the witnesses, and upon conclusion of the presentation of all such evidence and testimony you will be responsible to decide whether or not Deputy Bodine is guilty of the things with which he is charged. If you find beyond a reasonable doubt that he is guilty, you will bring a verdict of guilty. If you decide there *is* a reasonable doubt that he is guilty, you will bring in a verdict of not guilty. It must be unanimous, gentlemen. If you can't all come to an agreement, the court will declare it a hung jury and we'll start over."

A hand went up in the second row. "You gonna hang all of us or just the ones what don't agree?"

The spectators laughed, and Peterson banged his gavel. "Don't worry, friend. That's just an expression." He turned to the courtroom and spoke to the gallery. "I don't want any outbursts today or I'll clear the room. This shouldn't take more than a couple hours, so keep it down."

He looked at both attorneys. "You fellows ready?"

Both men nodded, but Pete Jensen added, "I move for a mistrial, Your Honor."

"On what grounds? We haven't started yet."

"On the grounds my client was denied due process. He wasn't given a preliminary hearing to decide if there is sufficient evidence to warrant a trial, nor was there a grand jury hearing."

"Interesting points, but the motion is denied. Judicial expediency takes precedence over a time-consuming, expensive, and largely unnecessary formality. I'm familiar with the facts of this case, and had there been a preliminary hearing I would've bound him over for trial."

"Why isn't the case being transferred to the county seat as is usual in these kind of cases?" Jensen asked.

"This is murder in the second degree. Since the defendant is a law officer and the deceased was a crook, the prosecution isn't seeking a first-degree charge, and therefore it can be tried here, which it will be. Right now." He rapped the gavel twice on the table. "Gentlemen, you may proceed with your opening statements."

Matt rode the frothing Shadow as hard as he dared, Charlie Jack keeping pace. He'd wasted too much time trekking after the elusive Benson. Besides, he needed Josh if they were going to go after those stage robbers. Just himself and Jeff Bodine, as good a man as Jeff was, wouldn't be enough when facing desperate, bloodthirsty outlaws.

There was a stirring of his emotions as he crested the final hill and Bodie came into view, spreading out over the valley much broader and denser than he recalled. He pulled the horse up to take a good look. He couldn't help it.

Charlie Jack came to a halt beside him. "Why you stop?"

"Look at that, would you, Charlie?"

"I already look. What?"

"Bodie. Ain't she somethin'?"

Charlie Jack leaned forward and squinted his eyes, then sat back up and shrugged, saying nothing.

"I can't explain it," Matt said. "It's just a pretty sight. Let's go."

He gave the reins a flip, and Shadow immediately stepped forward, Charlie taking one more befuddled look at Bodie, then following on his sorrel, not understanding Matt's appreciation for the ugly little gold camp. They traversed the last mile at a quick pace, the two of them not attracting any attention as they merged into the Main Street traffic.

Anxious for news about his father, Matt rode directly to Doc Blackwood's, hoping Jacob wouldn't still be there. He stopped short of the place and let Shadow linger by a water trough, giving two bits to a young street urchin to lead the horse over to the doctor's office in a few minutes before he drank too much and got a bellyache.

Matt went into the downstairs office, but it was empty. He peeked into the examination room. The bed had no one in it. Hope mingled with fear gripped him as Doc Blackwood walked in.

"He's gone home," the doctor said. When he saw Matt's face sadden, he quickly added, "To his house, I mean, to his house. Came to last night. He's still groggy, but we packed him off at Rosa's insistence. She said he'd mend better there than here. Can't say as I blame her."

Matt thanked him and left the office. He told the waiting lad to bring the horse to Jacob's house when he was done tending to him.

With Charlie Jack standing right behind him, Matt knocked, and Rosa opened the door, her eyes red and swollen from lack of sleep. She broke into a pained smile. "Matt, you've come. I'm so glad. Come in, please."

"Rosa, you look like you need some rest," Matt said, giving her a squeeze around the shoulders. "How's Pa?"

"He's about the same. Doc says he's out of danger, though he's still sleeping all the time. But we can't know for sure if he's going to be all right. His mind, I mean. Could be today, could be a month before we can tell whether there's brain damage. But Doc's hopeful. I've been praying till I can't pray no more."

"The Holy Spirit takes over then," Matt said. "You need to take care of yourself. Who's minding the store?"

"Molly's got it handled, the dear woman." Rosa smiled. "If you can believe this, she's even got Flora Bascomb helping her."

"Flora Bascomb! I guess God does still work miracles."

"Oh, yes. I just pray He works one on your pa. I'm gonna miss that man if God takes him." Her eyes began to well up.

"Aw, He won't. If you were God, would you want him hangin' around heaven?"

Rosa thought about it. "Yeah."

"I wouldn't. Can you imagine what kinda trouble he'd be with two arms?"

Rosa almost laughed through her tears. "I never thought of that. It'll be nice to get a big bear hug from that pa of yours."

"One day," Matt said.

"Yeah, one day." Just then a scuffing on the porch made Rosa look out, and she saw Charlie Jack. She didn't recoil like she had the first time the Indian walked into the Quicksilver.

"Charlie Jack, you too? Please, come in out of the weather. Oh, Jacob would be so glad—"

"Will be glad," Charlie corrected, stepping in and removing his hat. "When he recover."

"Yes, Charlie, yes. Thank you." Rosa fell silent for a moment, then a look of concern creased her face. "Oh my, Matt, I almost forgot . . . I assume you didn't just come to see your pa but to help Josh Bodine."

"Yeah, that's right."

"Well you'd better get a move on."

"Okay, but what's the hurry? He's okay in jail, ain't he?"

"He's not in jail."

"They let him out?"

"Not exactly. He's in court. Judge Peterson decided to go ahead and try him on manslaughter charges. They started this morning."

"What? I'd better get over there pronto. Peterson has been known to finish a trial before lunch." Matt gave her another squeeze, told her and Charlie Jack he'd be back soon, and ran out the door, jumping onto the back of his watered and waiting horse. He waved to the kid who'd tended him and put his heels to Shadow's flanks.

The prosecution laid out its case carefully and swiftly, calling several witnesses including the recalcitrant James McCarthy. They had seen Josh in the saloon, standing at the bar drinking only coffee, the implication being that he had some other purpose for being there. Then, when Jack Myers walked in, Josh spun, drew his pistol, and fired from close range into the unsuspecting Myers's midsection, causing a fatal wound. Josh hadn't spoken a word, and Myers had been given no chance to go for his weapon, not to mention being given a chance to surrender. It was obvious, to the prosecution at least, that Josh's purpose in being there was to kill Myers, which he proceeded to do with great dispatch. The act was not in the line of duty, and Myers posed no threat to Deputy Bodine, so the witnesses said.

The prosecution rested, and it was now the defense's turn. Unfortunately, their only witness lay unconscious in his bed from a blow to the head in a mine shaft fall that might as well have been a blow to Josh's head. Jensen was at a loss. He had no one to call to the stand except Josh. What Jacob Page had to say would be disallowed as hearsay if anyone but Page took the stand and said it.

"You're going to have to get up there," he told his client.

Josh shrugged. "I want to. I have to tell my side of this sometime."

"Okay." Jensen stood. "The defense calls Deputy Josh Bodine."

This was a bold move—albeit Jensen's only possible move—and prosecutor Givens sat up straight in anticipation, a spark in his eye. The opportunity to cross-examine the suspect in front of a jury was every prosecutor's dream. Ninety-nine times out of a hundred, when a defendant took the stand, they drove the final nails into their own coffin.

Josh, unaware of the statistics, strode gamely to the witness stand and was sworn in, then settled into the chair. Jensen moved to the lectern next to the counsel table—placed there only so lawyers would have something to lean on—and leaned across it. He was giving himself more time to think but trying to make it look like nothing more than lawyer's dramatics.

He needn't have bothered. Before he could phrase his first question, the door flew open with a resounding bang, and a black horse with rider clomped into the room, the horseman ducking to miss the lintel. Everyone in the courtroom turned to stare at the brash intruder, especially Judge Peterson.

"Hold on, Your Honor," Sheriff Matt Page ordered.

"See here, Sheriff, what's the meaning of this?" Peterson asked indignantly, banging to quiet the murmuring crowd. "In case you weren't aware, there's a trial going on here."

"That's what I understand," Matt said, looking around the room. "Kinda soon for a jury trial, don't you think?"

"That's what *I* thought," said Jensen.

"I needn't explain the fine points of the law or justify my actions to you, Sheriff. Now if you'll please remove that horse so we can get on with this—"

"If you'll give me five minutes, Your Honor, we can all go home. Whose turn is it? Which lawyer, I mean?"

"Mine," Jensen said. "For the defense. I was just about to start questioning Josh."

"Excuse him and put me on." Matt climbed down from Shadow and handed the reins to the nearest member of the audience, then walked up to the witness chair, stopping momentarily to whisper some cues to Jensen. He helped the perplexed Josh up and showed him the wanted poster Noah had scribbled on, then let Judge Peterson and Pete Jensen see it as well. They both nodded their heads as prosecutor Givens craned his neck for a peek. Matt let Judge Peterson swear him in and took the chair. With minimal prompting from Jensen, Matt began his tale.

"That's good enough for me," Peterson declared when Matt was finished. "If the deceased was an escaped convict and murderer, I wouldn't care if Deputy Bodine shot him in the back, which this court is prepared to declare he didn't, but was only firing in self-defense at a man with murderous intent that he had previously declared began to draw on him. Under these circumstances, I'll take Jacob Page's statement on faith because I know the man. However, should he recover and tell a different story, I might be inclined to reopen this case. Does the prosecutor have any objections?" He leaned forward and gave Givens a squint-eyed stare.

"Uh, no . . . of course not. No objections," Horace Givens said meekly.

"In that case . . ." The judge rapped the gavel hard enough to damage it. "Case dismissed, and the bar is open!"

The three lawmen strolled from the courtroom without talking, Matt leading his horse. Josh was just glad to be free again. Jeff didn't know what to think, except that they had some robbers to get after. He said as much to Matt.

"We ain't got much to go on," Matt told him.

"We know where they were headed."

"Right. Yosemite Valley. That's a big place. But that was before Josh shot Myers. That might've changed things."

"Yeah," said Josh. "Now two of 'em get to split the cash instead of three. But if one of 'em is waitin' in Yosemite, then he don't know Myers is dead and will wait until the other man gets to him with the news. And he's got a full day's head start."

"Yeah, maybe so. But it'll wait a few minutes more," Matt told him. "I'm gonna go see my pa."

"You gonna stay there till he wakes up or . . ."

"Dies? No. If he's still unconscious, I won't be long. But I wanted to stop in and say hi to Uncle Billy too. I haven't seen him in a long time either. Frankly, I couldn't care less about the Wells Fargo cache. They can go hunt it down themselves if they want. The only reason I'm botherin' at all is because those robbers shot Jeff." He kicked at the dirt in disgust. "Don't crooks stay local anymore? Why do they have to ride to the uttermost parts and force me away from home so much?" He wasn't asking anyone in particular and didn't expect an answer. And he got none, just blank looks from the Bodines.

"Uh, about Billy . . ." Jeff started to say.

"What about Billy?" Matt asked.

"He, uh, he ain't been feelin' too well lately, and he, uh, up and—"

"Died?" Matt finished. "Billy's gone?" Matt was overwhelmed with so great a sense of loss that his legs began to quiver, and he reached up to grip the pommel.

"No, no," Jeff said quickly, seeing Matt's face blanch. "No, he ain't dead. He's moved in with your pa, so Rosa can tend to both of them at the same time. I just wanted to warn you ahead of time so you weren't surprised is all. Jaspers, I didn't mean to scare you."

Matt began to laugh from relief, and the Bodines looked at each other, wondering what was wrong with him. Except for the fact that the sky had been clouded over for nigh unto a week now, they would've thought he'd gotten too much sun.

"I'm really sorry," Jeff said again. "You okay?"

"I'm fine, Jeff. No harm done," Matt assured him. "I'm just tired, I guess. I shouldn't have let my mind go off on its own like that. Listen, I'll be back soon, and we'll see if we can find them robbers." He shook his head as he led Shadow up the street, then called back over his shoulder, "You boys get ready for the hunt. I'll see you at my pa's in an hour."

Jeff waved his acknowledgment, and he and Josh went the other way, leaving their horses tied to the rail.

Matt knocked softly on the door, which opened as soon as he touched it. Rosa smiled at him and motioned him in.

"He's awake," she said, closing the door again.

Matt's eyes widened. "Is he . . . okay? You know, all there and everything?"

"As much as before," Rosa told him with a smirk. "Yes, he seems fine, though he doesn't remember what happened. To him, it's the morning of the accident. I don't know if he recollects much of the past couple weeks at all; he got knocked pretty hard. Did things go all right in court?"

"Josh got off okay. We found another way to do it. Can I go in and see Pa now?"

"Of course. He's a little groggy, but don't let that worry you. He'll come around, I'm sure. Uncle Billy's here too. He's sick real bad. Doc Blackwood left him here a few days ago. Figured I wouldn't mind since I was already nursing one patient. He was right, of course."

"What's wrong with Billy? He's bad sick, you say?"

"'Fraid so." Rosa was grim. "This isn't the influenza, like we thought at first. I fear Billy just might be on death's door. Best not disturb him, Matt."

"Okay, Rosa, thanks." He sighed. All this was starting to seem a bit overwhelming. Matt tossed his hat on a convenient chair and eased into the room where his father lay, keeping his footsteps as quiet as he could. As he neared the bed, Jacob Page turned his head and gazed up at his son.

"Where you bin?" he asked with a cracking voice. "Ow, that hurts."

"Your throat's dry," Matt said. "Ain't been usin' it for a couple days."

Jacob gave him a look that said, *Yeah? No foolin'?*

"Here, take some water." Matt ignored his father's silent sarcasm and helped Jacob sit up and sip some water. It pained him to see his pa so helpless.

"Thank you, son," Jacob croaked. "That's better."

"I'm glad you're back with us," Matt said. "Rosa tell you what happened?"

Jacob nodded. "Too bad about Elrod. Blame fool stunt on my part, thinkin' I could catch him." He took some more water. "If I'da caught hold, he'da yanked me right down with him."

"Sometimes we just have to try, even if it's foolish."

"You oughta know," Jacob said, his smile fleeting as his throat again protested the earlier neglect.

"Good thing you're sick, Pa. I'll let that one pass this time."

"I'm your pa—I can say that when I ain't sick."

Matt smiled. Yeah, his pa was going to be fine.

"Listen, Pa, I gotta get goin'. Me and the boys—the Bodines, I mean—gotta try and catch the stage robbers. You remember them, don't you?"

"Stage robbers? Sure, them guys at the wrestlin' ma—Uh oh . . . Josh . . . I gotta get—"

"You stay put," Matt said, grabbing his father gently by the shoulders as the elder Page struggled to get out of bed. "Josh is fine. We took care of it. Remember I said me and the Bodines were headed after the robbers? That means both brothers."

Jacob relaxed. "Oh, yeah. Heh heh. Sorry, my brain ain't workin' quite right yet."

"That's okay, Pa. You get some rest, you hear?" Matt backed toward the door. "See you later, Pa."

"Be careful, son."

Matt nodded and closed the door behind him. He headed to the next door, which he figured would house Billy since that was the only other room in the house with a bed in it. He wondered as he opened it where Rosa slept, then remembered the quilts piled up on the divan in the parlor. Hardly long enough for her, poor thing.

Billy didn't stir when Matt opened the door. He was asleep, his breathing heavy and loud, and Matt decided not to bother him. Probably the first good sleep he'd gotten in days. Sorry he couldn't speak to him, Matt retreated and shut the door quietly. Rosa was waiting for him in the parlor.

"What happened to Charlie Jack?" Matt asked her.

"Your Indian friend? He hung around awhile, then went in there with your pa—I peeked through the door and saw him rubbing some poultice on his forehead."

"So that's what that smudge was. I wondered."

"Then he went to see Billy, stayed for a spell, and quietly left. I haven't seen him since."

"Hmm. Well, I've learned not to be too concerned about Charlie Jack and his mysterious ways. He has a habit of showing up at all the right times." Matt smiled at Rosa. "You know, you're good for both Pa and Billy," he told her.

She blushed. "No more 'n anyone else. They just need care. Don't matter from who."

"Still, I'm glad it's you."

"Thanks, hon. I'm happy it's me too. You be back soon?"

"Hope so. Don't know how long it'll take, or even if we'll have any success. May be over before it starts. You take care of yourself, you hear? Wouldn't do to have three sick people in this house."

"I have to stay well," she said. "No more beds." She laughed, but it was hollow.

"Get some sleep," Matt ordered. He nodded and replaced his hat, then paused and gave Rosa a hug and a kiss on the cheek before letting himself out.

The Bodines rode up just as Matt came onto the porch .

"How's your pa and Billy?" Jeff asked.

"Gettin' on. Pa's awake."

"Just in the nick of time," Josh muttered sarcastically.

"Shut up, little brother. It's high time you were more grateful for things."

"I'm glad about his pa, don't get me wrong. It just woulda been nice if he'd woke up sooner, that's all. So I wouldn't of had to spend time in my own pokey."

"Don't be too hard on him," Matt told Jeff. "He's been through a lot."

"Mostly of his own doin'."

"Yep, that's true. And that makes it even harder, knowing some of it could have been avoided, eh, Josh?"

Josh Bodine only scowled. "You ready finally?" he asked, drumming his hands on the pommel of his saddle.

"You still think we got a chance?" Matt asked. If there was a way he could reasonably get out of traipsing after these men, he wouldn't mind finding it. In Yosemite, they'd be needles in a haystack.

"That one hombre don't know anybody heard him and Myers, remember?" Jeff said. "Anyway, I'll bet he lit out right after the killin', not wantin' to wait around and see if Josh would shoot him next." He grinned at his brother, who snarled his lip in return. "And without his leader, who knows if he'd even be able to think up another plan. Myers and him seem like the type to do what they planned to do, then think about alternatives later. Why else would they have hung around Bodie after doin' their crime?"

"These men are full of themselves, like Jesse James and the Youngers," Matt said. "Not too smart. They got real big ideas about themselves and how they can't be apprehended. They think we ain't smart enough to catch them."

"Myers don't think that no more," Josh said.

"Don't press your luck too many times," Jeff warned his brother. "Anyway, Matt, I think we have a shot at catchin' the remainin' two. I'd like to at least say we took a crack at it."

"I see your point," Matt admitted with a sigh, "and it might be worth a try. But while we're away no one'll be left here or in Bridgeport to take care of business. What'll happen to this town with both of you gone?"

"I reckon not much," Jeff said. "Look yonder."

Matt and Josh peered up the street in the direction Jeff had nodded and saw a contingent of armed men headed toward them on foot. Miners, all of them. Jeff smiled.

"What's this?" Matt wondered aloud.

"I hope it's not a lynch mob," Josh murmured weakly, unconsciously rubbing his throat.

Thomas Wellman, supervisor at the Queen Anne and a longtime acquaintance of Matt's, was in the lead. He hailed Matt with a wave and a shout, and Matt waved back feebly, still perplexed.

"Here we are," pronounced Wellman when the group had reached the lawmen. "Just like you asked, Jeff."

"Here you are what?" Matt asked.

"Why, we're your replacements, of course."

"Replacements?" queried Josh.

"Sure. While you authorized agents of the county are off recovering our payroll from those road agents, we'll be here in Bodie, taking turns keeping the peace. We'd go with you, but none of us have any experience with that kind of thing. But we can walk around town and break up fights, sure enough."

Josh faced his brother. "When did you—"

"While you were making small talk with that young gal in Harvey's store, I hailed Mr. Wellman as he came out of the tobacconist's."

"Are you volunteering?" Matt asked Wellman slowly. "Mono County can't pay—"

"It's our civic duty," Wellman assured the sheriff. "Right, men?" There was general nodding and murmurs of agreement. "Well, what are you waiting for? Get going."

The Bodines looked at each other while Matt just shrugged.

"Okay," Matt said. "Everyone raise their right hand. The other right, Mr. Smith. Now repeat after me: 'I swear to uphold the laws of the state of California to the best of my ability, so help me God.'"

They repeated the oath, more or less, and then Matt said, "By the power vested in me, you're all temporary deputy sheriffs for Mono County, assigned to patrol in Bodie. Thank you, gentlemen."

They congratulated each other and wandered off as Matt gave Wellman a few instructions and told him they'd be back in a few days.

"Good luck," Wellman said.

"I appreciate the sentiment," Matt told him, climbing onto Shadow's strong back, "but 'go with God' is more to the point. Luck has nothing to do with it."

Wellman smiled. "That's what I meant," he said with a wave. "Oh, here you go, Josh. For the trip." He tossed a sack to the deputy, who looked inside to find a fresh pouch of tobacco and some cigarette papers.

"Thanks, Mr. Wellman," Josh told him, "but no thanks." He tossed it back. "It's high time I stop kiddin' myself. That ain't for me."

Wellman nodded. The lawmen put heels to flanks and rode toward the mountains and the magnificence of California's Yosemite Valley. Matt looked for Charlie Jack as they left town, but there was no sign of him anywhere. Undaunted, Matt put the Indian out of his mind and squeezed his legs together while sharply sucking the inside of his cheek. Shadow broke into an easy lope.

CHAPTER

TWENTY·EIGHT

FOR FOUR HOURS the only sounds the search party heard were the pounding of their horses' hooves and their foggy breath blowing through their nostrils, the creaking of the leather saddles under the riders' weight, and the flapping of their canvas slickers. And of course the groaning and complaining of Josh Bodine as his companions refused to stop to cook a hot lunch.

"We need to get further up the trail," Jeff Bodine explained to his brother. "It's not our fault you didn't get enough to eat before we left. If you hadn't spent so much time talkin' to that gal . . . You shoulda been feedin' your face instead."

"I wasn't just gabbin' or flirtin'—I got some jerky then," Josh protested, pulling his horse up sharply. He reached back into his saddlebag and pulled out a hunk of stiff beef, then heeled the unfamiliar horse—his own mount still languishing in the Bridgeport livery where Noah had left it—and raced to catch up, since Matt and his brother hadn't slowed down for him. Pulling off hunks of jerked beef as you ride your horse at a dead run isn't the easiest task in the world, but Josh managed capably, hunger driving him to execute the feat without mishap.

The mountains loomed high above them when they finally stopped for the day to make camp. They'd ridden in a half-day what men usually rode in a day and a half, and they were plenty tired, especially since they hadn't started the day fresh. Their horses were spent too, and the men removed the saddles and blankets and picketed the animals under the relative protection of a fanning oak. After rubbing them down and tending to their food and water, Jeff pitched a lean-to, and Josh gathered wood and built the fire while Matt opened a tin of salt pork and beans.

"Men, I'm exhausted," Matt admitted as they sat around the fire watching the flames battle the darkness. Jeff followed the smoke as it drifted upward into an overcast sky.

"What do you think?" he asked. "Rain?"

"Tomorrow afternoon," Matt said, "it'll rain here. Where we're headed, it'll probably snow."

"Snow in Yosemite Valley this time of year?" Josh asked. He sneezed and shivered, then picked up a stick to play in the fire.

"No, not in the valley. But we gotta get over the Tioga Pass first. We should hit the sack, boys. I don't want to be caught in the Tioga in the middle of a late season snow. We'll need to get an early start."

"How early?" asked Josh suspiciously.

"More like late tonight than early tomorrow," his brother informed him, showing Matt a smirk.

"If you go to sleep now, you'll get plenty," Matt said.

"I ain't tired now," Josh protested. He wiped his running nose on his sleeve.

"Ain't you ever gonna grow up?" Jeff asked.

"Shut up," Josh rejoined, unable to think of something more witty.

"Tell you what," Matt suggested, "I'll read a little from the Good Book, kinda quiet us down, make it easier to get to sleep."

"You brought your Bible?" Jeff asked.

"Yeah, of course. I always have it." He reached inside his shirt pocket and pulled out the small book, flipping it open. "That okay?"

"Sure," Jeff said.

"Since when was you interested in Bible readin'?" Josh asked his brother.

"Since now."

"You mean since you took that ride on the stage with what's-her-name."

"Ain't so, and that ain't none of your business neither."

"What are you two arguin' about?" Matt asked.

"He met some gal on the stage the other day—she's new in

town, openin' a laundry—and she turns out to be religious, so suddenly he's real interested in God."

Matt laughed. "Well, maybe that's so, and maybe it ain't."

"It ain't," Jeff said dryly.

"Don't matter to me none. Just so long as the interest in God
is real—for His sake, not just for hers."

"It's real, and I don't mind sayin' so," Jeff said. "I ain't ready
to be a preacher or nuthin', don't get me wrong. But she said some
mighty interestin' things, so I thought maybe I'd look into it."

"And if you get interested in church, maybe she'll let you take
her to the social," Josh accused.

"Okay, you two, this will get us nowhere. I don't care why Jeff
wants to get interested in the Bible, just so he does. That goes for
you too, Josh. So can I read or not?"

Neither Bodine protested. They were used to their father reading to them from the Good Book nightly. So Matt settled on a passage and began to read as the Bodine brothers squirmed around
and got comfortable under their blankets.

"How about Psalm 84? 'Blessed is the man whose strength is
in thee,'" Matt read, "'in whose heart are the ways of them. Who
passing through the valley of Baca make it a well.'"

"Where's the Valley of Baca?" asked Jeff sleepily.

"Ain't a place," Matt said. "Reverend Stone, our pastor in
Bridgeport, says it means 'weeping.' You know, passing through a
valley of hard times. Men blessed by God not only pass through
the valley—they make it a well that gives water for themselves and
others." He continued reading. "'The rain also filleth the pools.
They go from strength to strength.'"

Matt ran his finger down the page, skipping a couple verses.
"'For a day in thy courts is better than a thousand. I had rather be
a doorkeeper in the house of my God, than to dwell in the tents of
wickedness.'"

"You shoulda read that one a couple years before you left
home," Jeff told his brother.

"I knew you couldn't go a week without bringin' that up," Josh
complained. "I think a bad day workin' in Bodie is better 'n a good
day listenin' to you, big brother. Read the Twenty-third Psalm,
Matt. That always shuts my brother up."

Matt obliged, turning slowly and thoughtfully to the familiar passage, the pleasant noises of the night providing a suitable setting for the comforting verses. As he read the well-known psalm of comfort and assurance, the feuding brothers seemed to calm down.

"Well," Matt said quietly as he finished and closed the book, "that certainly—" He stopped short when he noticed that both Bodines had fallen asleep. Jeff's breathing was heavy and regular, Josh's a little troubled, wheezy-like but deep. Matt pocketed the Bible and grabbed his own blanket, stuck a couple of large logs in the fire, and settled down for the night.

Sleep was elusive for Matt, though. Too many things were running through his mind. Knowing his anxieties were too much for him, he prayed that God would completely heal his father and Uncle Billy, bring the Bodines and himself home from this manhunt soon and in good health, and set things right at home in Bridgeport. He left the details of that up to God since he wasn't sure what "right" was anymore, especially when it came to John Taylor.

Matt still hadn't decided whether or not Taylor was right in giving Quong Tai over to the Paiutes. But he'd saved the town in doing so, hadn't he? It appeared that way, but would they ever really know? He was reminded about a lesson Reverend Stone had given a couple months back, about the harlot Rahab. She hid the Hebrew spies, then lied about it, and God blessed her. She was even listed in the book of Hebrews in the New Testament as a heroine of faith. Did that mean God approved or excused her lie?

Reverend Stone concluded that it didn't; he said lying is wrong regardless of the circumstances. Rahab was blessed for a different reason, he stated; God rewarded her faith that drove her to protect His servants even at the risk of death. Matt wasn't sure he quite understood all that. Taylor wasn't doing God's will, was he?

The question went unanswered as uninterrupted sleep finally overtook Matt, though he awakened well before dawn, still bothered by his thoughts. He stoked the fire and spent the rest of the night looking into it, longing for a peaceful evening at home without all these difficult decisions.

The Bodines woke up because the smell of breakfast penetrated their minds, not because of any noise Matt made preparing it. They all ate quickly and heartily, then broke camp and saddled their steeds. They were soon on the hunt once again, the trail rising

above them into the gray mist of dawn as they finally reached the
foot of the Tioga Pass.

The road up the Tioga was narrow and treacherous, a challenge to
man and beast even on a good day. And this day was shaping up as
something considerably less than good. Unable to run the horses up
the steep incline, their ascent of the pass was slow and frustrating.
Though they had gotten an early start, the gathering storm had laid in
thick, dark clouds that settled over them. No one doubted that it would
snow at the upper elevations before dark. Their best hope would be to
crest the pass and make for the valley before that happened.

But then what? Too many people used this road to leave an outlaw trail to follow. Not so many you'd run into them if you shut
your eyes, but enough that following a trail several days old without some identifying clue such as a characteristic gait or a damaged
or thrown shoe would be nigh impossible.

Most of the travelers who used this byway were Paiutes from
the various local tribes and those of Yosemite Valley, moving back
and forth with goods to trade with each other. The Mono Kuzedika
Paiutes would swap gull eggs, pine nuts, and baskets for beaver
pelts and venison from the Yosemite Miwoks. The Indians also used
the pass to access their hunting grounds or, in the case of the
Miwoks, to get to Mono Lake for the annual koochabee harvest.

For a brief moment Matt hoped they'd meet some Indians
going the opposite way who'd seen the men they sought. But the
likelihood of that happening—or that they'd speak English or tell
him what he wanted to know without asking for payment of some
kind—quickly faded into the vastness of the narrow canyon winding several hundred feet below them.

Turning his sheepskin collar up against the chill swirling around
them, Matt stole a glance back at his deputies. Jeff's face was largely
expressionless, but his wide eyes drank in the magnificent scenery all
around him—the sheer cliffs on both sides of the trail (climbing on
the right, dropping precipitously on the left); the blue-gray mirrored
lakes in the valley below; the enormous granite monoliths reaching
up farther than the trees, their tops enveloped in the blackening
clouds that were tumbling forward at an alarming speed.

Josh hadn't made a sound since they broke camp. Matt's breakfast of pork, fry bread, and black, double-strong coffee, coupled
with the biting cold, was apparently sufficient to keep the younger

Bodine quiet and secluded inside his coat. Only the bridge of his nose was visible between the top of his collar and the brim of his pulled-down hat.

Matt gave a slight pull on his reins, and Shadow halted immediately. Jeff's mare saw this and stopped in her tracks without prompting, forcing Jeff to urge her forward with words driven home by well-placed heels, pulling up next to Matt. They both waited for Josh, who neither sped up nor slowed down, and probably didn't notice they'd stopped until he was abreast of them.

"What'd we stop for?" he asked.

"You're the one always complainin' when we don't," Jeff reminded his brother.

"Let's feed and water the horses while we can," Matt said. "I figure it's pretty close to noon."

"How can you tell?" Josh looked up into the sky, which gave no hint as to the location of the sun.

Matt shrugged. "I can just tell. And it looks like that cloud'll be on us in a half-hour, if not less. And that ain't sunshine filtering down from it."

"We almost make the crest?" Jeff wondered.

"This is it," Matt said. "We might reach the valley by dark if we keep going once the horses have been tended to. Let's stop jawin' and get to it."

A bit later they rode on, the sky darkening by the minute, the air growing increasingly cold and damp. Their breath and that of their horses appeared to freeze in front of their faces. For an hour they descended. Matt hoped they'd reach the valley before the storm broke.

They didn't. At first just a few errant flakes drifted down. With their heads bent to keep out the cold, they almost didn't see them. But soon the snow began to fall with a vengeance, and it continued to increase until they could see no more than fifty feet ahead of them. But the immediate trail was still visible, and Matt wasn't worried. He hoped that by the time the snow was deep enough to make following the road difficult, they'd be out of the storm. It would be raining in the valley, but that was far better than snow.

Josh moaned about being cold, and Jeff muttered something about the whole trip being not only more than he bargained for, but that the prize—the capture of the robbers and the recovery of the money—just wasn't worth the effort.

"You swore an oath," Matt reminded them, remembering how intense they were about going after the highwaymen when he didn't want to.

"Remind me to talk to you about that when we get back," Jeff said.

Matt ignored the remark and turned his face back into the biting wind that was blowing the falling snow toward them, making visibility even more difficult. With each minute that passed, the snowflakes grew larger and closer together. The trees to either side of them—thickening now that they had descended past the tree line—were no more than hazy gray shadows. The road before them was quickly being swallowed by the storm. They and their horses were so dusted with snow, the only color visible to them was the redness of their faces.

Josh shivered as he continued to bring up the rear, and Jeff soon started to fall back, his horse sensing that its rider was no longer pressing him forward. The wound he'd suffered at the hands of the robber, though not serious in comparison with those received by others, was beginning to tingle from prolonged exposure to the cold, and Jeff felt like an icicle had been thrust through him.

"You okay, Jeff?" his younger brother inquired.

"Huh?" Jeff barely moved his head in response to his brother's question.

"You don't look so hot."

"I ain't hot—I'm freezin'."

"Yeah, I'm chilled to the bone myself. It feels like the stuff running out of my nose is just hanging there, frozen solid."

"It is."

"Thought so."

"Matt says we're close, so we've got to keep goin'. We've got no choice, the way I see it. It's all downhill from here. If we turn back, we'll be in snow a lot longer than if we just forge on ahead."

Jeff grunted.

"What is it?" Josh asked. "Your bullet wound?"

Jeff nodded.

"Well, grit yer teeth, brother. Once we warm up, you'll be fine."

Josh moved next to Jeff's horse and whipped its rump—not hard, just enough to remind it to keep pace with Shadow—and kept his nag next to it for the sake of both horses.

Matt could no longer guess the hour, much less how long they'd been on the road or how far they had to go. Though he hadn't said anything to the others, he was no longer even sure they were headed in the right direction. Snowblind, men called it when wind-blown snow made it impossible to keep one's bearings. As flurries stung his face and forced him to keep his head down, Matt longed for the simple things in life—a fireplace and blankets and hot cof-fee and his wife at his side . . .

Hopeless—that's how he felt. This wasn't the first time he'd ever felt that way, to be sure, but this was certainly the worst. And this time it wasn't just him. He had two men depending on him—his deputies. And three horses—dumb animals he'd guided into a death trap.

A cry ahead snapped Matt out of his despondency. He craned his neck and squinted his eyes to see into the blizzard, at first dis-cerning nothing. But then a shadow began to materialize, growing as it darkened. Finally he could make out the shape of a man on horseback. He was riding tall, seemingly not affected by the storm. Instinctively, Shadow stopped, head hanging low, as the other rider approached.

Matt hoped it was a friend, or at least not an enemy. Nevertheless, he stretched his gloved but freezing hand toward his gun, not remembering it was buried under his clothing and largely inaccessible with his body as lethargic from the cold as it was.

He needn't have bothered. The rider came into view, and Matt recognized the stoic face of his favorite Indian, Charlie Jack.

"Come," he told the lawman. "Cave near. Fire already burn."

The ubiquitous Indian turned his sorrel and whistled low, and Shadow followed without urging from Matt. Matt looked back and saw that Jeff and Josh had seen the Indian and were also coming. He relaxed as much as the intense cold and blowing snow would allow.

The three lawmen huddled around the blazing fire at the mouth of the shallow cave, their frozen hands all but in the flames. They had ridden no more than a half mile farther before Charlie Jack brought them into this place of refuge. They dined on rabbit, not bothering to ask him where he found it, and pine nuts from their saddle bags, quenching their thirst with mouthfuls of coffee made from rock-ground beans boiled in freshly fallen snow. No longer a threat, they were finally able to utilize and even enjoy the snow.

His injury now dry and warming, Jeff's pain subsided, and he returned to his normal self. He silently recalled his last trip on horseback in search of robbers, when he could barely stay in the saddle and the thought of being in a shootout almost sent him running. A smile came to him, which he hid from his brother and Matt. Charlie Jack saw it but sensed it was some private matter that amused the young man and so let it pass unacknowledged.

Josh was quieter than usual, more self-reflective than he'd been in the past. His youth was slipping away from him, replaced by savvy and understanding. The passage was not complete, however, and once they had all eaten and were returning to normal, he stepped out for a moment and returned with a snowball behind his back, which he promptly dispatched toward his brother's head, scoring a direct hit and prompting an out-and-out war in which Matt and Charlie Jack joined.

The fighting was soon over, and the men once again huddled around the fire—all of them acting a bit sheepish. Josh had a serious coughing spell. When he had quieted, Matt finally got around to asking the questions that so obviously needed answering.

"Charlie, how did you find us? And for that matter, what are you doing here?"

"I hear Josh say robbers go to Yosemite. You very busy, with father and Uncle Billy sick, so I go ahead to find them. When cold rain begin, I know it snow at high place, and you slow to follow, so Charlie Jack think you caught in storm. I find cave and build big fire, then ride to find you. I know Matt's horse not get lost. Shadow good horse, much sense." Charlie Jack pointed to his own head.

"We was plenty lucky," Josh observed with a great sniff.

"Not luck," the Indian dissented. "Charlie Jack pray to Matt's God, ask Him help poor Indian find friend. He answer prayer, here you are."

"Well, I've got to tell you, Charlie, it never ceases to amaze me how you always seem to be at just the right place at just the right time," Matt mused.

"Yeah," agreed Jeff. "It's a miracle."

Charlie shook his head. "Not miracle. Just Charlie."

"He's right," Matt said. "It happens too often to be a miracle."

Charlie nodded humbly, then shrugged. "It just what Charlie

Jack do," he explained. "I know land, I know ways of nature, I know ways of men."

"That about sums it all up," Jeff said.

"Yeah," agreed Josh, "but do you know the ways of the robbers?"

The Paiute just grinned and played in the fire with a stick.

"Tomorrow at dawn," he said and stretched out with his feet by the fire, pulling his colorful woven blanket over him and closing his eyes. In minutes he was asleep.

Josh glanced questioningly at Jeff, who just said, "He knows where they are."

Jeff too settled down for the night, leaving Matt and Josh sitting by the fire. They were both silent, each deep in his own private thoughts. But Matt had sensed something was troubling the younger man and asked him about it.

"I feel bad about Myers," Josh admitted quietly. "Or rather Charlie Jones. Whatever his name is. I know that sounds crazy, him being a wanted killer and all. But when I look back on it, I feel like I shot him in cold blood. In God's eyes I murdered him, even if the law let me go."

"I can see how you feel that way," Matt said. "But he was gonna kill you. He'd already tried once. Yeah, it looked and felt like you did it in cold blood. But you didn't. He was a killer on the loose, a convicted man who tried to shoot you and who professed he would kill you on sight."

"That don't make it feel any better," Josh said.

"Nothing I say can give you peace about this," Matt said. "And maybe nothing ever will, no matter how much time goes by. But it wasn't wrong in God's eyes, and He won't hold you accountable for it. Other things you've done, yes—you need His forgiveness there. But not with this."

Josh didn't answer but shut his eyes, and Matt wondered if he was praying. He couldn't tell. But whatever Josh was doing, he was soon asleep.

Matt stayed awake, listening to the breathing of their horses as the animals huddled close to each other deeper in the cave. He dreamed of the day when he would only have to eat food cooked over a campfire and sleep outside under the stars or in temporary shelters when he wanted to instead of when he had no choice.

CHAPTER

TWENTY·NINE

T HE MORNING BROKE CALM, with no snow falling, although plenty—at least a foot or two—covered the ground. The sky was clearing, and it appeared that the storm was over. One day earlier or later and they would have missed it. But here they were, and there was no point complaining about what might have been.

Charlie Jack was ready to go by the time the others were just finishing their coffee, but he sat patiently by the fire, warming his hands, watching the white men go through their routines. It took a while, but all three of them eventually were saddled and ready. Matt reluctantly spread the fire logs and dumped a few handfuls of snow onto the hot coals.

Josh looked at the smoking, melting snow longingly, then turned with a sniff and followed the departing Charlie Jack. Jeff and Matt came after, all three of them—if their faces told the truth—unhappy about hitting the trail again.

Charlie Jack kept a steady, though not neckbreaking, pace, knowing that the sooner they were out of the snow, the better off they'd be. During the first hour on the trail Matt passed the Bodines and kept within talking distance of the Indian, while Josh dropped back behind his brother. Jeff turned in his saddle and saw his brother's head droop.

"Josh, pick up the pace or you're gonna get left behind."

Josh waved him off but didn't answer, drawing his arm across his lower face again. His sleeve was shiny with frozen snot.

Riding without stopping for two full hours, they almost didn't notice the decrease in the snow on the trail until the first patches of wet ground peeked through, the dark earth a marked contrast to the purity of the snow. Charlie Jack held up, conferred with Matt, then continued ahead for a few more minutes until they were in a clearing with more bare earth than snow. He slid off his sorrel and bid the others do the same. They followed suit without even questioning the Indian, then gathered close to him.

"Valley near, through big trees, down trail. We ride that way, cross small river, then stop in trees at base of big rock with flat face."

"Aren't you going the rest of the way?" Jeff asked.

"Yes. I go as far as big rock."

"He's just letting you know so you won't keep wondering how far it is," Matt told the Bodines.

Josh nodded. "I don't even care," he said. "I just wish I was home in bed."

"It's almost over. We're a couple hours away from them, according to Charlie Jack. He spoke to some of the Miwoks, who told him our boys are holed up in a small hunter's cabin at the far end of the valley. They traded with the Paiutes and have enough supplies for a few weeks."

"What are they up to?" Jeff wondered. "Why haven't they fled for parts unknown?"

"For one, the brains of the outfit is dead. Josh saw to that. For another, they don't know we know where they went, so I imagine they're waitin' for things to calm down. If they show up in town—any town in this half of the state—they're afraid they'll be spotted. For all they know, we have their exact identities. Or maybe they're just bidin' their time, tryin' to figure out what to do."

"So they're just layin' low," Jeff said thoughtfully. "That don't strike me as bein' too smart."

"Ain't much dumber than us ridin' here through the snow lookin' for 'em," Josh muttered.

"They ain't clever men, I'll wager," Matt said. "Myers had all the brains. They were just handy with the pistol. That's usually the way it works." He paused to let that sink in. "The important thing is, they're here, and once we arrest them, we can go home. You'll be home tomorrow night, day after at the most."

"Maybe, but we'll have to ride there, and I ain't lookin' forward to that none," Josh said quietly.

"Maybe you won't have to," Jeff said sarcastically, trying to light a fire under his brother. "Maybe you'll ride home draped over your saddle. Never can tell."

"Wouldn't mind that so much," Josh said, uncharacteristically letting the taunt go by without rising to the challenge.

"Well, let's get on with it," Matt urged with a sigh. "We've still got some ground to cover. When we hit the valley floor we'll have something to eat, then ride the rest of the way and plan our assault."

"Can't wait," Josh muttered as he mounted his horse and took to the trail.

They rode through grove after grove of pines and redwoods, trees larger than either of the Bodines had ever seen. Though the air wasn't substantially warmer, it certainly wasn't as cold as it had been the day before, and the men seemed to perk up—all except Josh. Matt was becoming concerned and dropped back next to him.

"Are you sick or something?" Matt asked.

"I'll be okay," Josh assured him.

"That ain't what I asked. Your face is a little red. You have a fever?"

Josh shook his head slowly. "Don't think so. I just got a little cold, that's all." As if to contradict himself, he coughed harshly from deep inside and spit out the phlegm he'd raised.

"You can wait here for us if you'd like . . . build a fire and keep warm, get some sleep."

"No, I won't be doin' that. Jeff would never let me hear the end of it."

"Probably not," Matt agreed. "Well, let me know if you change your mind."

"That ain't likely to happen."

Matt nodded and put heels to Shadow's flanks, riding to catch up to Charlie Jack again.

Hours of winding down the trail through the thick trees eventually brought them to the valley floor, which opened up before them magnificently. The golden grass contrasted sharply with the majestic granite monoliths rising above the distant trees. The rivers and far-off waterfalls were stunning. Even Josh stopped to admire their rugged beauty, silently wishing he could move here, away from the treeless grassy valley in which they'd built that brown, featureless town they called Bodie. Here was a place where a man could enjoy just going out in the morning and taking a breath. Chopping wood, building a homestead . . . Shoot, even doing the laundry over a tub would be enjoyable in a place like this. No wonder the Paiutes made themselves at home here.

Charlie Jack dismounted and let his sorrel wander free. She didn't go far since there were grass and water just a few steps away. The Paiute began collecting sticks. Figuring he was going to build a fire, the others slid from their horses and helped gather firewood. Soon they had a roaring blaze and were roasting a rabbit Charlie had killed with one throw of his knife.

"Won't they see the smoke?" Jeff asked presently.

"Doubtful," Matt told him. "They're several miles away, there are a lot of trees between us and them, and the valley is a crescent and we're at opposite ends. Besides, Yosemite is full of Paiutes. I'm sure they've seen smoke before."

"They pay Miwoks to tell when stranger approach," Charlie Jack said. He smiled. "Charlie Jack not stranger. They no talk."

"One of us needs to scout out the area so we can come up with a battle plan," Jeff concluded.

"I imagine Charlie already did," Josh said matter-of-factly, gnawing on a piece of rabbit and washing it down with hot boiled coffee. Matt noticed his color had improved. Maybe now that he was out of the severe cold he'd get better.

"Where men are, difficult to sneak up on," the Indian said. "In middle of meadow. Best one of you ride up, knock on door."

"You gotta be kidding," Jeff said. "They'll gun us down before we have a chance to say hello."

"Hold on," Matt said, "I think he's got the right idea. If we have one of the Miwoks tell him there's a lone rider approachin' and one of us rides up to 'em like we're lost or somethin', they'd never suspect. Then whoever's inside can keep 'em occupied while the other two of us sneak up. At some signal the man inside can get the drop on them while the other two bust in. I think it'll work."

"I think it's suicide," Josh volunteered. "I'll go."

"You? You don't look well enough for that," Jeff said. "Fact is, I'm gettin' a mite concerned about you."

"You needn't worry about me, big brother. I can take care of myself. Have before, will continue."

"Yeah, you take care of yourself real good. Look at all the trouble you've gotten yourself into—"

"Let's not go into that again, Jeff. I ain't in the mood for it."

"Besides," Matt noted, "they've seen Josh. They might recognize him."

"Jeff too," Charlie Jack said. "Jeff on same stagecoach."

"I guess it's me," Matt said.

"But what if they're locals?" Jeff asked. "From Bodie, I mean. They might remember you from before."

"Might," Matt admitted. "But just look at me. Do I look the same?"

"As what?" Josh asked.

"As the way I looked six months ago. I don't. It has to be me. There's no way around it."

"Why don't we just call 'em out?" Josh asked.

"What if they won't come?"

"We start shootin' or wait 'em out."

"Wait 'em out?" Jeff barked. "They've got food and shelter. We've got nuthin'!"

"I don't like the idea of forcin' them into a shootout," Matt said. "I was kinda thinkin' we could get the drop on them, make them surrender peaceable. What do you think, Charlie?" He turned toward the Indian but saw only an empty rock. They looked all around but didn't see or hear anything.

"Where'd he go?" Jeff asked.

"Don't worry," Matt said, "he'll be back. He's up to something."

"Right," said Josh as he went back to his meal. They finished eating and sat around the fire, nervously fingering their hats or playing with their weapons. Josh scooted down until he was nearly prone, his head on a log, and pulled his hat down over his eyes.

He shook visibly, and in a short while his breathing became steady but labored.

"He's asleep," Matt said quietly.

"He don't sound good," Jeff noted, compassion for his brother evident in his voice.

"We'll do what's gotta be done and go home, soon as Charlie gets back."

No sooner had he said this than Charlie Jack stepped silently up to the fire and extended his hands over it. He was silent, as usual, so Matt asked him what was happening.

"Miwok friend go to cabin, trade news for flour. He need flour, we need men to know you come alone."

"I'd better get ready," Matt said, standing.

"No. Two hours. They say you far-off, weary traveler in need of place to stay. No food, cold. Very stupid white man travel this time of year from west. They say they tell him way to cabin."

"Sounds pretty good, except for the stupid part."

Jeff grinned. "I don't know. I think we're all pretty stupid to have come here."

"I tried to talk you out of it," Matt said.

"Well, that's water under the bridge. We're here. Maybe I'll get some sleep too. Somebody wake me when it's time."

"Okay." Matt leaned back too, but he couldn't sleep. He wasn't thinking so much about the upcoming charade but about Sarah. Jeff's "water under the bridge" comment sent his mind reeling back to town—and to his wife. More than ever, he wished he was home for keeps. How in the world had he ever thought this kind of life was glamorous?

He bent his head and began to pray.

The cabin was small, log fitted upon log. A natural rock chimney, set into one wall, was burning hot, a pot of coffee set next to it to keep it warm. The roof leaked in spots and needed fixing. The windows had cheap glass—small panes, thick (so they wouldn't break on the trail) and barely clear, with irregularities in them that distorted the view. But they were only meant to let in light, not allow those inside to see the world. It was the door that allowed folk to view the splendor of Yosemite firsthand. The cabin hadn't been built to live in, but just to eat and sleep in, and for shelter from storms.

The men sitting at the table playing cards were not the ones who'd built the cabin. They were squatters, occupying what wasn't theirs. Not that it mattered. The owners, if they could be called that, were long since dead or had moved on. No one knew who they were, not even the Miwok Paiutes who made the Yosemite Valley their home.

The men chewed on jerky and drank from a single bottle of whiskey as they played, several stacks of twenty-dollar bills in front of them. But they might as well have been playing with matchsticks or pine cones since it wasn't for keeps. They decided early on to play poker only as a way of passing the time. Otherwise it would be too easy for the loser to get angry and the winner to get suspicious, and then neither of them would get any sleep.

So they whiled away the time playing no-stakes poker with large bills, their face value meaningless, with all money going back into the pot at the end of the day. They would divide the money for good the day they rode out of this lonely valley and split up, one headed for San Francisco, with its wharf and gambling halls and bordellos, the other for a sleepy little town on the south coast called Los Angeles. His half-brother had a rancho there, and he hoped to meet some wild Mexican women he had heard about and eat beans and tortillas until they came out his ears.

"I tell you, Carl, I'm getting real anxious to head on out of here." He dealt them each five cards, then set the deck facedown in the middle of the table.

"It's only been a few days, Mort. We have to wait, like Jack told us when he planned this job. That's how he survived all those years—patiently waiting. People forget about you after a while, and then you can move about freely, go someplace where they don't know you, spend money like you don't have much so no one gets suspicious. Myers was right about that."

"Yeah, I know." Mort spread his cards and closed one eye. "That fella ought to be here pretty soon. What're we gonna do with him?"

"We need to hide this cash, that's for sure."

"Why don't we just kill him?"

"Kill him? In cold blood?"

"What's it to you?"

"Robbing a stage, that's one thing. Protecting myself, that's one thing too. But killing a man just 'cause he's cold and hungry? I don't know. Someone might miss him."

"And where they gonna look? This is a big country. Only a fool would ride out here this time of year."

"Or someone on the run from the law."

"Yeah," Mort said thoughtfully. "Maybe he's an outlaw like us. We'll get him talkin'. If he committed a robbery, just like us, maybe he's got some cash on him. We'll take it from him, and if he resists . . ." Mort smiled wickedly.

"And if he killed someone, well, we'd be doing society a favor by getting rid of him. No one would come looking for us . . . unless it was to thank us."

"What if there's a reward for him?"

"Forget it, Mort," Carl said, pushing his chair back and standing up. "How we gonna collect?"

"Oh, yeah." Mort scraped the money together and under Carl's watchful eye stuffed it back into their pillowcases. Carl wandered over to the fire and poured himself a cup of brew, then strolled to the door and opened it.

"Whoops, here he comes," he told his partner. "Those Injuns were right. He looks plumb whupped."

Carl gave the visitor a wave, and the stranger returned it weakly. His black horse was slow but steady and in a short while approached the cabin door. The rider half-slid, half-fell off the animal, and Carl set his coffee down to go help him.

"They were telling the truth," Matt said as Carl helped him inside.

"Who?" Carl asked.

"The Indians. I didn't believe there was a cabin here, but I had to come find out."

"Well, we're here all right. Just a couple of hunters. Good thing for you too. What's your handle?"

"Huh?" Matt slumped into a chair, and Mort set a mug of coffee and a plate of cold beans before him.

"Your name," Mort said.

The sheriff was surprised by the question. He hadn't even thought about them asking him his name.

"Oh. My name's Jacob—Jacob . . . Taylor."

"Well, Mr. Taylor, what brings you to our little corner of the world? I mean, there ain't nowhere to go but back the way you come."

Matt sipped the coffee and ate the beans, distasteful as they were, especially since he wasn't hungry. But he had to play the part.

"Well," he said with his mouth full, struggling to choke the beans down with the lukewarm, bitter coffee, "I wasn't really headed here. I'm goin' up Lundy way, to visit some friends. The Indians told me the Tioga was snowed in. I asked if there was someplace I could hole up, even for the night, and they told me about your cabin. I hope you don't mind."

"No, course not," Carl lied.

"Lundy, you say," mused Mort. "I know some people in Lundy. I wonder if they could be your friends. It's a pretty small place."

Matt shook his head. "Doubt it. They just moved there a few weeks ago. Went to work in the sawmill. Say, these beans are pretty good. You fix 'em yourselves?"

"Could say that," Mort said. "I opened the tin."

He and Carl laughed, and Matt hooted along with them.

"Man, I got me a chill," Matt said as the laughter waned. "You mind if I go stand at the fire a spell?"

"No, be our guest." Mort motioned to the fire, and Matt wasted no time going over to it, standing with his back to the men while he rubbed his upper arms, then opened his coat to let the warmth in.

With a motion of his head Mort directed Carl to the other side of the one-room log shanty. When they were both there Mort said, "What do you think?"

"Seems harmless enough. We can tolerate him for a night, I think."

"Don't he look familiar to you?"

Carl glanced over at the shivering man. "No, he don't. Why?"

"Well, the Mono County sheriff's name is Taylor."

"So? Ain't he an old man? This fella's not yet thirty. Maybe not even twenty-five."

"Maybe it's Taylor's son."

"That don't make sense," Carl said. "You got worry on the brain. This guy look like a lawman to you?"

"No, but what difference does that make?"

"Okay, none. But he came here alone. If he was tracking us, you think he'd do that?"

"Maybe he's got someone here with him."

"The Injun said he was alone."

"And you trust an Injun?"

Further conversation on the matter would have to come later since the stranger had turned from the fire and moved off to the side.

"That feels better," he said. "Thanks for the food and for the coffee too. I won't bother you boys no longer. I think I can make do on my own."

But Mort wasn't anxious to let him go so fast. At least not until he was sure their guest wasn't the law.

"No sense rushing right back out into the cold, stranger—not when you're welcome to stay here a spell. You play cards?"

Matt glanced nervously at the fire. "Uh, yeah, sure. Well, not really. I don't gamble much." *Not as much as I'm gambling right now, at least.*

"Well, come on, sit a spell. We'll teach you." He held out a chair for Matt. "Don't worry, we don't play for money. We just play to make the time go by. Carl, get the—"

Mort was interrupted by a sudden hissing from the fireplace just as Matt turned away from the fire and dove for cover. Immediately there was a *whoosh* and a *bang* as a ball of flame shot up the chimney, followed by a larger ball that exploded out into the room, singing the hairs of the two robbers as they recoiled from the flames and dove onto the floor. During the confusion Matt drew his Peacemaker, shouting that he was the sheriff and they were under arrest. In the same breath he ordered them to throw down their guns.

Carl, seeing Matt draw out of the corner of his eye, disregarded the sheriff's orders and yanked out his pistol. But as he swung his gun toward Matt and cocked it, the door burst open, followed by the hurtling body of Josh Bodine. Carl jerked his pistol toward the new intruder, firing an errant round that missed everyone.

Matt wasn't so careless, however, and fired, striking Carl square in the chest. Jeff came through the door in a crouch and kept a steady aim on Mort. But the robber wasn't putting up a fight. Not with the lawmen, at least. He lay on the floor, gasping for breath. The fireplace explosion had brought a finger of fire down his throat. He suffered for a few moments in agony, then cried out and died.

Carl dropped his gun as soon as he was hit and spread out on the floor, his life escaping from him through a bubbling chest wound. He gazed questioningly at Matt with eyes already beginning to glaze. Then his line of vision moved to Josh, not missing the badge displayed prominently on his shirt. The young deputy kicked the pistol out of the outlaw's reach. Carl had recognized the face, and Josh recognized Carl too.

Understanding, Carl said nothing as he breathed his last. His body settled onto the floor, and his heart ceased beating.

CHAPTER

THIRTY

WELL, THAT TRICK OF YOURS worked pretty good," Jeff remarked, surveying the carnage.

"Too good," Matt said, picking himself up off the floor. "I guess I put too much powder in it."

Jeff studied the face of the robbers, first one, then the other. Matt watched him.

"You know them two?"

"They look familiar. I think I saw them come to town on the stage a few days ago. Thought they looked like trouble."

"Not anymore," Josh said as he pulled out a chair and sat down. "Let's bury them, find the money, and go home. I'm not feeling too good."

"I'm all for that," Matt agreed. He took another look at the men and bent his head to ask forgiveness. He hated killing, even when there was no other way. And this time he'd killed two men in a matter of seconds, one of them by accident. The explosion was supposed to have been a diversion only.

Jeff moved over to him and put an arm around his shoulder.

"It's like you told us, Sheriff. Sometimes there just is no other way, and the Lord don't blame you for it. It was Him who give you the right to exercise the authority to keep law and order."

Matt nodded. "Let's get this done."

He went outside to scout a place to bury the bodies, returning in a few minutes. Jeff had dragged the dead outlaws outside while Josh searched for the money, finding the pillowcases only when he had about given up and lay down on one of the beds. The crackling of the bills where feathers should have been ended his search.

They found a rusty shovel out back of the cabin, and Jeff and Matt took turns digging. They removed any papers the men had and dumped the bodies into the holes, then covered them up and tamped the earth down over them. Matt prayed over them—not for their salvation since it was a mite too late for that, but for his own peace of mind. Jeff stood with hat in hand, listening. Then they both turned and walked away.

"Where's Josh?" Matt asked.

"Avoidin' work."

They returned to the cabin to find the younger Bodine still on the bed, the two pillowcases on the floor beside him. He appeared to be asleep, one arm dangling over the side of the bed, the other over his face. His breathing was labored and shallow.

"Come on, Josh, the hard part's done," Jeff said. "Charlie's waitin' for us at the other end of the valley. We need to get a move on."

Josh didn't answer. The doorway darkened, and a shiver ran up Matt's spine. He turned, not knowing what he would see, but it was only Charlie Jack. Matt expelled a sigh.

"I hear boom," the Paiute said simply, then came over to the bed and looked at Josh.

"Josh hurt?"

"No, he wasn't," Matt answered.

The Indian put an ear to the younger Bodine's chest, then regarded Jeff with a solemn glance. "He not good."

"What do you mean?" Jeff asked.

"He has big pain in lung."

"Big pain?" Matt repeated. "You mean, like pneumonia?"

Charlie Jack nodded. "He cannot be moved." With that, the Indian pulled the blanket up to Josh's chin. The sick man wearily moved his eyes toward his brother.

"Sorry," Josh said weakly. "I tried to tell you I was sick."

"I'm the one who's sorry," Jeff said, compassion evident in his voice. "You'll be okay. You're tough."

"Yeah. Just give me a day to rest up." He forced a chuckle. "And you always said I'd die by the gun."

The end came swiftly. He'd been much sicker than any of them realized, including Josh himself. He held on until the middle of that night, able to listen as Matt told him of God's love for him and how He sent His Son Jesus to die on a cross for the sins of all mankind. Matt also told Josh that his decision had to be a genuine desire to serve Christ, not just a panicky desire to avoid hell.

Josh said he understood, and Matt prayed with him. Soon after, following an intense, quiet exchange with his brother, God took Josh into eternity.

Matt didn't know if Josh was really saved that night. Only God knew for certain. But Matt had done all he could; he had told his friend the truth. The rest was in God's hands.

They stayed the night, neither Matt nor Jeff getting any sleep. Charlie slept on the floor in the corner on a pile of saddle blankets, leaving the white men to themselves. Matt did his best to comfort the elder Bodine, with words and prayer and Scripture. But Jeff was not easily consoled. At the same time, he was a realist, and he knew life would go on despite the death of his father and now his brother. He also understood, too late perhaps, how close he and Josh really were.

By morning's first light they were ready to go. Matt asked Jeff if they shouldn't go ahead and bury Josh here, but Jeff was emphatic.

"Not where we buried two criminals, two men whom I believe are responsible for Josh's death."

"How do you figure that?" Matt wondered.

"They robbed the stage, and Josh died while chasin' them."

"I suppose," Matt remarked quietly, though he knew God was in control and that Josh died when God saw fit. But he knew this wasn't the time to explain such things to Jeff, and he certainly wasn't going to quibble over where Jeff Bodine laid his brother's body to rest.

"I'll take him home," Jeff said. "I know you want to get back to Bridgeport, back to that wife of yours. I can get home okay."

"Charlie Jack help," the Indian offered. He grasped Jeff by the arm. "Josh great friend of Charlie Jack. My honor to join on last ride."

Jeff choked back the tears. "You'd be welcome, Charlie, if it won't take you out of your way."

"It is my way."

"Thanks. Uh, Matt, can you help me wrap him up?"

Matt nodded, and they began the solemn task of wrapping Josh in sheets and blankets. Matt couldn't help but think of Christ being wrapped for burial after His crucifixion, and he wondered how the Savior slipped out of the grave clothes without disturbing them.

The task complete, they draped the body over Josh's horse, tying him on securely. Matt offered Jeff his hand, unable to speak, and Jeff took it, pulling Matt into a final embrace before silently climbing onto his horse. He took the reins of Josh's mount and lightly tapped his animal's flanks, then began the longest ride of his life.

Matt watched Jeff as Charlie Jack pulled himself onto his sorrel.

"You remember way?" Charlie asked the grieving lawman.

"Yeah, Charlie, I do. Thanks."

"Matt be careful. Bloody Canyon quick journey to Bridgeport, though not easy ride. You make town tonight if you listen to Charlie Jack."

Matt nodded. "Thanks, Charlie. Will I see you soon?"

"I think maybe." He turned and urged the sorrel away, riding at a lope to catch up to Jeff.

Matt watched them until they disappeared, then solemnly stepped into the stirrup and pulled himself onto Shadow's back. He breathed a heavy sigh of emotional release and headed home.

The day was a marked improvement over the previous one. There were no clouds above him or on the horizon, and though the air was cold and every breath visible, Matt rode toward home expecting that once he arrived, things would be different. He was sure Shadow sensed it too because the horse ran smooth and steady, with the muscles of his neck and shoulders twitching, showing he was either frightened or excited.

As they moved through the entrance to Bloody Canyon, the foliage so prevalent in Yosemite and the surrounding area began to recede, and the trail—smoothly packed dirt before—now grew rocky and rough. As the miles fell behind them, the stones increased in number and severity until the trail was almost entirely sharp-edged stones and no dirt. The whole canyon wasn't like this, but enough of it that horse travel was treacherous.

Shadow began to balk, and Matt finally stopped and slid off. Checking Shadow's hooves, he found the tender area inside the circle of steel reddening and tender. Bloody Canyon. Not a place for horses. No wonder the Miwoks avoided it. They could little afford to lose the animals they possessed, but they had an abundance of time, so they chose to travel the long, relatively easy Tioga Pass.

Matt began to lead Shadow, not wanting to cause further cuts to his hooves. Carrying only his own weight, Shadow could traverse the rocks with the least damage, though now it would take Matt considerably longer to get home.

But hadn't Charlie Jack said he could make it home that night? And the Indian was well aware of the rocks, for he had warned Matt about them. Strange. Matt pressed on, so anxious to be home that he refused to take time to eat more than the two pieces of jerky he had left. The going was not easy for him either, even in his gum-soled boots. Several times he lost his footing and fell, breaking his fall with his hands, which played havoc with the skin on his palms until he remembered the gloves in his saddlebags.

Two hours after entering the canyon Shadow hesitated, then pulled back on the reins, refusing to let Matt lead him farther. Matt chastised him, but still the animal resisted.

"All right, boy, I guess you need a rest whether I like it or not. I'll get you some—"

As he scanned ahead of him for shade for refuge, Matt saw a dark object on the trail, something he immediately recognized and that churned his stomach—a dead horse. Bloody Canyon had taken its toll again.

Leaving Shadow tied to a dead, fallen tree, Matt went ahead to see if the horse's rider was injured or killed in the fall. As he approached the animal, smelling its decomposition and waving at the flies that swarmed over it, he saw a bullet hole in the middle of its forehead. He glanced at the animal's feet. As expected, the hooves were bloody. The rider had tried to ride all the way through Bloody Canyon, and his persistence had cost him.

But where was he? Matt hadn't passed him, so he must have turned around and headed back to town—back to Bridgeport.

That meant he had been coming from Bridgeport on a black horse, and judging by the state of the horse it had been several days. He knew of only one man who fit that scenario.

Matt scanned the immediate area. Where had he gone? Had something happened to him? He checked the rocks for evidence of a fall—blood, torn clothing, anything—but found nothing. Obviously the man had survived long enough to put the horse out of its misery, then wandered off. But could he have walked all the way back to Bridgeport?

Two days would be long enough to get back, especially if someone picked him up on the road near town. There was nothing Matt could do but press on. No point standing out here wondering about it.

Matt returned to Shadow and coaxed him to continue, leading him past the fallen horse as quickly as he could. Shadow didn't want to pass, but Matt let him know who was boss and was able to get him by the offensive body. A couple more hours, he figured, and he'd be out of the canyon and could mount up and ride home, probably arriving just after nightfall.

A moan from the big rocks along the canyon wall drew his attention, and he stopped to listen. It came again—a low, mournful wail. Matt told Shadow to stay put, which Shadow was more than willing to do, and went toward the sound to investigate.

The man was lying just off the trail, looking like he hadn't eaten for days; he was dirty, unkempt, and possibly injured. Matt rushed to his side, unslinging his canteen from his shoulder, and helped Josiah Benson take a sip. The preacher drank the water so greedily that it flooded down his cheeks. Matt tipped the canteen down, stemming the flow.

"Whoa, slow down there, Reverend." Matt helped him sit up, and Benson drank until his thirst was slaked, then looked into the face of his deliverer.

"Ah, the young sheriff. You have my undying gratitude, I assure you." He half-choked the words.

"What happened?"

"Horse went lame and threw me. Happened very fast. I didn't even realize the road had changed. Never saw these sharp stones. I cracked my head on a rock when I landed. When I came around, the poor animal was suffering, so I shot it. But an old injury aggra-

vated by the cold weather kept me from walking too far, so I figured my best chance was to wait for a passing traveler. I thought
I was finished. It's an act of God, you happening by."

"You could've froze to death out here," Matt said. "What did
you do to keep warm?"

"Prayed, my boy, long and hard. These rocks, for all the cold
in the air, retained the sun's rays for quite some time, and I was able
to stay warm enough. By day I collected a bit of brush to burn at
night. I am a mite hungry, of that you can be sure. I don't believe
I would have lasted another day."

Just my luck, lamented Matt, immediately chastising himself
for the thought. Then he realized the position he was in. He had
been considering the possibility of hunting Benson down like the
murderer Matt thought him to be, and here God had dumped him
right in his lap!

"I have to get you back to Bridgeport," Matt said, not stating
why he needed to do so. "You could use some doctoring. Come
on, let me help you to my horse. I've got some food there you can
eat."

"God bless you, Sheriff." He let Matt help him up, then leaned
against him as they walked to Shadow, waiting patiently a few feet
away. As they moved, Matt noticed Benson was favoring his left
leg.

"Hurt yourself?" the lawman asked.

"Aggravated an old injury, as I stated. Nothing to worry
about."

Matt helped Benson into the saddle. "We'll take it slow," he
said. "As you found out, this canyon is hard on horses."

"Yes, so I discovered."

They began the slow, torturous trek through the rest of the
canyon. Matt, keeping a sharp eye on Benson while trying not to
look suspicious, kept the conversation going.

"So, what made you leave your wagon?"

"Eh?"

"I mean, I noticed you don't have it with you. Why is that? You
might have fared better with the wagon. At least you would have
had shelter and clothes and maybe some food."

"That's very true. I wish I'd known in advance how treacherous this canyon is."

"So why'd you leave it behind?"

"Well, after the revival—after each and every revival, for that matter—I try to get away, to go someplace alone and secluded to commune with God and renew my strength for the next town."

"Excuse me, Reverend, but couldn't you drive the wagon and still be alone with God?"

Benson cleared his throat. "Let me just say that how I conduct my affairs is no business of yours." His tone had changed abruptly, but Matt wasn't ready for a confrontation.

"Beg pardon, Reverend, I'm just naturally curious. I didn't mean to pry."

Benson forced a smile. "That's all right, son, I suppose I was a little quick to jump at you. It's just that I'm feeling mighty poorly."

"Let's get some grub," Matt said. "There's a place over there where we can rest a spell." He led Shadow off the beaten path and helped Benson down, then built a small fire and heated some beans and ham—all he had left by way of food—and let the preacher have the rest of the water in his canteen. They split the beans, and Matt continued to converse with Benson, searching for an opportunity to bring it around to the fire.

"Tell me, Reverend, if you don't mind, what made you go into the ministry? You know, tent meetings and such."

"The same thing that makes any man begin doing the Lord's work, son. God called me into it."

"How'd He do that? I've heard men say that before, but I've never heard God's voice myself."

"Oh, it's clear when God calls a man. His voice is as clear and sweet as if He was standing right there beside you."

"And the healin'—when did you realize you had the power to heal folk?"

"I don't have the power, Sheriff. Only God has that power. He just uses me because I'm willing to let myself be used."

Not unlike the people you prey on, Matt thought. "I wonder, Reverend, are you being used of God, or does your ability come from somewhere else?"

Benson gave him a long, hard look. "It's a sin to judge, my friend. The Good Book tells us that plainly."

"I'm not judging, not in the courtroom sense where I find you guilty and pass sentence. The Good Book also plainly tells us to judge preachers in regard to the truthfulness of their message. We are to be discerning Christians—to weed out false teachers. The Bible says we are to be wise."

"I'll not even grace that with a response. I know I'm doing the Lord's work—I'm not obligated to prove anything to you." His voice suddenly rose. "Just where did you acquire the authority to question me anyway? You're a young lawman in a two-bit town, not some theologian from a great Christian university."

Matt remained calm. "You said some things the night after the fire—about how it was done by an Indian come back to remove everything associated with the murderer Ah Quong Tai."

"Yes, that is so."

"The victim wasn't an Indian, Reverend."

"I beg your pardon?"

"I said, the dead body in the fire was not that of an Indian."

"Of course it was."

"Nope. I had Doc Keebles check it out. It was a white man. No question about it."

"Hmm. That's interesting."

"Yep, it sure is. And what's more, it was a *particular* white man."

"What do you mean?"

"It was an old codger by the name of Noah Porter." Benson's face remained blank. "The name may not mean anything to you. He said some wild things about you though."

"People often do. It seems to follow a healing ministry such as mine. Folks always talk about us—some good, some bad. It's a cross I have to bear."

"No, it wasn't nuthin' about your ministry. Noah Porter never heard of Reverend Benson." When Matt spoke the name as though it belonged to someone else, someone who wasn't seated next to him, Benson's face altered slightly. Not so much that Matt could describe it, but there was a change. Perhaps it was just his eyes; maybe they twinkled and opened a hair's width. Whatever, something about his face told Matt that Benson was definitely interested in what he had to say.

"Yeah," Matt continued, trying to act as if he didn't believe Noah before he even revealed to Benson what Noah had said, "he said somethin' crazy. Course, he was known for that."

"What did he say?"

Matt's taking his time was having the desired effect, obviously making Benson anxious for the answer.

"Well . . . he said . . . you're not gonna believe this . . . he said you're John Wilkes Booth." Matt began to laugh but noticed the color drain from Benson's face. Then Benson started to laugh along with him.

"Yes, that is as funny as it could be."

"Yep. Old Noah. What an imagination." The lawman slapped his knee as his laughter subsided. "You know, you do kinda look like Booth. I mean like pictures I've seen of him. Only older." Matt stopped and got a serious look on his face. "Say, of course you'd look older. Those pictures of Booth were six, seven, maybe even ten years old. Plus you've grown that beard." He snapped his fingers. "What a strange coincidence. Now that I think on it, your initials are the same as Booth's—J.W.B."

"That is strange," Benson said quietly, "but I no longer see the humor in it."

"No, I don't imagine you do. You, uh . . . you wouldn't . . . Naw, you couldn't be Booth. He's dead, and it was verified. Wasn't he shot in some barn that was on fire? His body would've burned, maybe so bad as to be unidentifiable."

"Yes," Benson said through clenched teeth, "I've read that's how it happened."

Matt shook his head. "You've got to admit, it's a pretty strange coincidence. Now, I'm not sayin' this is true, you understand, I'm just thinkin' out loud . . . What if you really were Booth? Wouldn't that be somethin'?"

"Not to me."

"No, I suppose not. Make life kind of difficult, I suppose, always wonderin' if some small-town sheriff somewhere is gonna recognize you, or somebody who knew you before. People gunnin' for you. Make livin' tough, I would guess."

Benson nodded. "That it would. I never thought about the initials. Now that you mention it, that is quite a coincidence."

"And you're both from the South, unless your accent is fake."

"No, I can assure you this is how I have always spoken. Besides, if I was Booth, why would I want to leave my initials the same? I'd make up a completely new identity."

"Yep, so would I." Matt leaned down and drew in the dirt. "Unless I owned somethin' that meant a lot to me that had those initials printed on it. Then I couldn't change 'em."

"Like what?"

Matt slowly swung his head to look Benson square in the face. "Like a Bible. The one in your wagon."

CHAPTER

THIRTY · ONE

WITHOUT A SECOND'S hesitation Benson threw a handful of dirt in Matt's face, then dove at him, his 180-pound frame hitting Matt like a locomotive, knocking them both onto the rocky soil. As they grappled, Matt sought to fight Benson off and deliver blows of his own at the same time, also trying to keep his gun out of Benson's exploring hand.

They rolled as one, both men crying out from the wounds inflicted upon them by the sharp stones. They were too close for their blows to land with much force. Benson's swollen leg, though seemingly a hindrance to him when walking, did not seriously affect his ability to fight. As they struggled, Matt realized Benson wasn't as bad off as he had seemed, and he also realized Benson had been waiting for an opportune moment to dry-gulch whoever happened by and take his horse. Maybe he would have been happy just to steal the animal and leave Matt stranded, had the lawman not shown his hand, but now all bets were off, and Matt knew he was fighting for his life.

And he was not overcoming his foe.

With a mighty groan Matt drew his knee up as hard and as fast as he could, not caring where it landed. It struck Benson in the side, and Matt heard ribs crack. Benson let out a cry and rolled away. Despite his injury Benson did not give in, and from his prone position he kicked Matt hard in the knee.

Pain exploded in Matt's leg, then traveled up to his hip and down to his toes. Though he shouted in pain, he too did not give in, and he took the opportunity to roll out of Benson's reach while trying to draw his gun.

Benson was on his feet though and kicked Matt's hand, knocking the gun several feet away. It clattered on the rocks, and Matt did not know where it came to rest. As he reached for it, as though doing so would bring it back to him like steel to a magnet, he heard the unmistakable double-click of a six-gun being cocked about an inch from his ear. Matt froze, waiting for the explosion, but heard only the heavy breathing of his opponent. Matt slowly turned first his eyes and then his whole head toward Benson, who stood over him wide-eyed, the gun in his right-hand, his left held against his side.

"I'm genuinely sorry about this," Benson said in a hoarse whisper, their brief but intense flurry having taken his voice. "But you've left me no choice."

"You claim to be a man of God," Matt reminded him. "God heals people through you, yet now you're going to take a life?" Though he was being sarcastic, Matt hoped Benson wouldn't think so.

"'The Lord works in mysterious ways,'" Benson quoted, "'His wonders to perform.'"

"I guess. So tell me, since I'm about to die . . . are you John Wilkes Booth?"

Benson smiled strangely as his finger began to tighten on the trigger.

"That's a question for—"

His body suddenly jerked upright, his eyes flashing as his gun discharged. The bullet grazed Matt's head, burning a groove above his left ear. The flash of the powder scorched the side of Matt's face, and the noise shocked his eardrum, sending stabs of pain accompanied by a high-pitched ring into his brain. Benson did not fire again. His grip on his gun relaxed, and the weapon twirled around his finger and dropped to the ground. He doubled over in a crouch, clutching at a knife that now protruded from his fleshy upper arm. He struggled to his feet and began to back away as he grabbed the hilt of the knife, all the while staring at the frightening figure bearing down on him.

When the blade finally came free, he let the knife clatter to the stones and grabbed the arm tightly to stem the flow of blood, then turned full around, breaking into a limping run. He headed toward Shadow, but the skittish black horse shied away from him. Unable to control the beast, Benson took off haltingly up the trail, finally disappearing into the canyon.

Matt watched him in disbelief, his vision blurry as the pain in his head swelled, the pungent odor of scorched flesh and hair puzzling him. Then the dark figure who had saved him came to him— a hulk of a figure, looming and lumbering toward Matt like a great bear, squatting down on one knee and reaching toward Matt's wound. And yet, it couldn't be a bear; bears didn't throw knives . . . did they?

The intense pain threatened to overcome Matt until finally his vision blurred, his eyes crossed, and his world faded to black.

The cave was warm from the fire crackling in its mouth. Matt remained on his back as he awoke, wary of moving and the discomfort that might result. His bandaged head didn't feel painful, really, but on the brink. His knee was on fire and grossly purple from the swelling.

Matt began to wonder where he was, but deep inside he knew. It just took a moment of letting his head clear to realize the Wild Man was the only person who lived in this canyon. Matt didn't recall from his trip up here with Sarah the treacherous sharp stones on the trail, but he figured that must be a bit farther up the canyon than the Wild Man's cave. Matt had no idea how far from the Wild Man's cave they were when Matt had encountered Benson. But he was indeed grateful the hermit had happened along.

Happened along. Matt knew better. God had sent the Wild Man to him.

His host was nowhere to be seen, nor could Matt hear him. Probably out collecting wood or catching game for a meal, Matt reasoned. No doubt he'd return soon. Matt was hungry and thirsty but was satisfied to wait. Unknown to him, a meal had already been prepared for him and set out where he'd find it when he got up. The same food he and Sarah had brought the man a week before.

Slowly Matt moved his head from side to side, trying to determine the extent of his injuries. There was no thunder, no flickering stars, no headache. His vision was fine, and he took stock of the curious nature of the man's abode. The cave was deeper than Matt could see, and the Wild Man had built a shelter around the mouth of the cave—sort of a porch where he could sit and enjoy the scenery without getting wet when it rained or burnt to a crisp by the summer sun. The place was stocked with many items one would find in any general store. Quite comfortable by anyone's standards.

Finally he noticed the food that had been left for him and forced himself to sit up, then discovered he had a headache after all. It had just been dormant until he raised himself up. He stayed upright and in a few minutes felt well enough to pull on his boots and stand up, favoring the knee and using a crude cane his host had whittled for him. He pressed a hand over his injury, wincing at the sharp, tingling pain that caused, then did the same to the wound in his head. He could feel the swelling through the bandages, but the wound didn't feel open, and there was no seepage.

The Wild Man had doctored him pretty well. Matt felt like he could ride, even with the bad knee. He sure wasn't going to wait here for a week until his knee got better, and he couldn't ask the Wild Man to go to town and bring back a wagon. He'd just have to endure the pain while traveling.

His muddled mind finally got around to wondering what time it was and how long he'd been unconscious. He looked outside. The sky was bright, the sun shining, but it was a different hue than he remembered when he encountered Benson on the trail. Bluer perhaps. No, brighter. And the shadows seemed different, though he couldn't quite place why.

Matt stared wistfully out of the cave and up the canyon as he munched a slice of canned ham, wondering where the Wild Man was. He was anxious to head for town, and he knew only unconsciousness could keep him here. But he didn't want to leave without expressing his thanks. At the very least he wanted to shake the man's hand and call him by name.

"The fact is, though he helped me, he's not really the one who saved me," Matt muttered out loud, raising his eyes skyward. "Thank You, Lord . . . again."

Matt retreated into the cave to collect his gear, so he wouldn't have to tarry a minute longer than necessary once the Wild Man returned. His gunbelt was coiled and sitting on a crate, his hat on top of it. His heavy coat hung on a stake driven into a crack in the cave wall. Everything else he still wore.

As he reached for his hat and gunbelt, his eye caught sight of a dusty black book on a primitive shelf made of crates. Curious, he stepped over to it and blew the dust off the cover. It was an old Bible. No, not an old Bible, just a little-used Bible. In fact, it looked like it had hardly ever been opened. Matt carefully thumbed open the cover.

The light dimmed as someone—or something—filled the mouth of the cave.

"That's personal," the Wild Man said quietly, his voice low but tense.

Matt let the cover drop easily and pulled his hand away. "Sorry. Didn't mean to pry. I was just—"

"Curious?" The Wild Man dropped the load of firewood he carried onto the ground next to the fire ring.

"I, uh . . . N-normally I d-don't do this," Matt stammered. "I'm a Christian, and I was just interested in your Bible, that's all. M-mine's so small, it'd be nice to have a big one like this. You're lucky."

His host grunted as he set a couple logs on the dying fire. "How are your injuries?" he asked, beginning to busy himself with domestic chores and apparently dropping the subject of the Bible.

"Okay, I guess. Knee hurts the worst."

"Figured that would be the case."

"How long was I . . . you know . . . ?"

"Unconscious?"

Matt nodded, a sheepish grin on his face.

"Maybe a half-hour. The weather can change pretty quickly here, make it look like more time has passed, even like a different day, if you aren't paying attention."

"Am I hurt bad?"

"Naw, don't think so. The bullet could've slammed into your skull pretty good, but lucky for you it glanced off."

"Yeah, lucky me. I . . . uh, owe you my life, Mr. . . . ."

The Wild Man just stared at him, as though the lawman had

committed an unpardonable sin by wanting to know his name. Then his face relaxed.

"Ah, what difference does it make. Name's Tom Fitzsimmons."

"I'm Matt Page. Pleased to make your acquaintance." Matt was somewhat relieved. The Wild Man—now that he had a name—was suddenly just another human being, not the savage animal-man he'd been characterized as by the townsfolk, though Matt kept that thought to himself. "And I do mean pleased. You saved my life."

Fitzsimmons grunted.

"No, it's true. He was going to kill me. What happened to him anyway?" Matt hobbled over by the fire. "Did you kill him?"

"Would you arrest me if I had?"

"Of course not. You were defending me. That's not why I asked, you know. It's because of who that man is."

"Well, whoever he is, I didn't kill him. But he won't soon forget me . . . if he survives out there."

"What do you mean?"

"About which? 'He won't soon forget me' or 'if he survives'?"

"Both."

"His arm will bear the scar for the rest of his life. As to the other, he went up the canyon, toward Yosemite. He'll probably starve or freeze—he doesn't seem to have any provisions. Unless he can find some sympathetic Utes, he isn't likely to live much longer." Fitzsimmons finally sat by the fire, and Matt followed suit, not an easy task with a knee the size of Texas. When Matt settled in and the pain faded from his face, Fitzsimmons continued.

"So who is that man that he's so all-fired important?"

Matt opened his mouth to tell him but closed it slowly, then said, "He's a traveling preacher—one of them revivalists."

Fitzsimmons hooted. "And he's trying to kill you?"

"That ain't what he really is," Matt said. "He's a phony."

"I see. Hiding a notorious past that you apparently uncovered."

Matt nodded. "That's about it. Least it seems that way. But I can't prove it."

"So who is he really?"

"You wouldn't believe me."

Fitzsimmons shrugged. "I suppose it doesn't matter, does it? After all, he's gone."

"Shoot, I gotta tell someone, and you're the only human on earth I can count on to keep it to himself."

"What're you talking about?"

"That wasn't Reverend Josiah W. Benson, traveling preacher and faith healer."

"Who was he?"

"That man was John Wilkes Booth."

Fitzsimmons stared at him blankly. "Your head wound is worse than I thought."

"No, I'm serious. There's lots of—" A dissatisfied look on his face, Matt picked up a stick and tossed it into the fire. "Shoot, there ain't much evidence at all. Just circumstances. He was about to tell me the truth when you tossed your knife into him."

"Listen, you look like a fine young man, obviously dedicated to your work. But Booth has been dead for nigh unto seven, eight years now. For that to have been him, there would have to be a big government conspiracy to hide the fact that he was alive. I read in the newspapers—this was before I came out west—that doctors examined the body, with government officials standing right there. If that wasn't him, then not only did they conceal his avoidance of death, but they had someone killed in his place. Not to mention that those officials would have not only had to be part of the conspiracy to let Booth live in secret, they would've also had to be involved in the plan to kill Lincoln in the first place. Son, let me tell you something—John Wilkes Booth is one man you better leave dead. Whoever that man is, if he is Booth, you'd better hope he's never discovered. You could tear this country apart if an assassination conspiracy that high in the government is uncovered. Not to mention your life wouldn't be worth a plugged nickel."

"Huh? What do you mean?" It was obvious Matt's personal safety in this issue was something he'd never considered.

"Silence, man—to protect themselves, they'd need your silence. Voluntarily, under threat, or by death—whatever it took. You just leave Mr. Booth in the grave. Whatever that man did, whoever he claims to be, leave it at that, and deal with it however you care to. As far as I'm concerned, it probably doesn't matter. The odds of him surviving out there are slim anyway."

Matt furrowed his brow as he considered Fitzsimmons's statements. He knew the man was right. The lawman couldn't help but wonder, who was this so-called "wild man" who knew so much about politics and human nature? Why had he turned his back on the society of which he had obviously once been a part?

He took another look around the cave for some indication, any sign that would explain this mystery. When he looked back at Fitzsimmons, the man was watching him.

"You're wondering why I live like this."

Matt knew denying it would be futile. "The thought crossed my mind."

"I'm not comfortable around people. People tend to betray you, given the chance."

"What happened?"

"I'd rather not talk about it."

"You brought it up."

"You did, the way you were poking around."

"That didn't make you speak up. I think you *want* to tell me. You've probably wanted to tell someone for years."

Fitzsimmons looked away. "You're awful smart for such a young pup."

"Naw, just experienced. I've been around some in this job."

"Yeah, I suppose that's so. If you didn't pick up a little savvy here and there, you'd be dead."

Matt considered that and wished he'd pick up a little more. He'd been too close to death too many times.

"Look, you don't have to tell me. It's none of my business." He stood. "I have to get back."

"On that leg?"

"Only legs I got."

"You should stay here awhile, let the swelling go down."

"Thanks, Mr. Fitzsimmons—"

"Tom."

"Okay, Tom, thanks, but I've got people waitin' at home for me." A shadow seemed to cross Fitzsimmons's face. "Is that it? You have no one waitin' anywhere for you?"

Fitzsimmons sighed. "Only person I ever had was my sister, back east. A few years ago she died while I was out here trying to make a living for us both. Without her there was little point in me keeping on, trying to make a strike. I drifted into this canyon, stayed in this old cave one night, realized I liked being where there weren't any people, and I've been here ever since."

"You have to come into town to buy things now and then."

"A necessity. Unpleasant but necessary."

"And you have money. Where do you get it?"

"I earn it, all legal. Beyond that, ain't none of your business."

"And you have a horse, yet you walk into town. Why?"

Fitzsimmons smiled slightly, then suppressed it, but still didn't answer.

"For the same reason you wear a bear hide, I'll wager," Matt guessed. "To scare people off, to make them think you're crazy."

Fitzsimmons smiled again. "That wasn't my original intent. I killed the bear for his hide to keep warm, never thinking about how it looked. But it was a happy surprise to see the way people reacted."

"What do you have against people?"

Fitzsimmons sighed heavily. "My sister was sickly and got involved with a religious group, folk who believed in miracle healings like that Benson fellow I ran off. Shoot, if I'd known he was a preacher, I'd have aimed to kill. Look, don't get me wrong—I didn't care if my sister wanted to believe that stuff. She was happy. But she needed constant care, and I couldn't afford it. So I came out west to earn the money to get her some proper doctoring. Did some prospecting, sent all the money I didn't need back to her. I found out she gave all her money to them people to take care of her, and they never even had a doctor look at her."

"You sure it wasn't her idea?"

"Don't matter. She was sick—they had a responsibility. And they called themselves Christians." He spat into the fire.

"That don't make what they said true," Matt stated quietly. "Lots of folk say what ain't so when it comes to that. They really believe it, mind you, but they're deceived."

"Hmm."

"I take it that was her Bible?"

Fitzsimmons nodded. "The only thing of hers they sent me."

"I guess I understand . . . some. But I think you're blaming everyone for what just a few people did to you. I'd like to think we're not all like that. I, for one, believe in miracles, but I don't think they happen so often as some folk claim. I've seen things happen that no one could explain, but that don't make them miracles. Thing is, if miracles happened as often as folk say they do, they wouldn't be miracles. They'd be . . . ordinaries. I heard one lady claim it was a miracle when her grocery list was filled properly."

Matt paused and took a breath.

"You come to the church sometime, Tom. See if you don't like some of the folk there. You won't like them all, don't get me wrong. I don't like a few of them myself." Matt smiled sheepishly. "But for the most part they're good folk. Shoot, Tom, if you went to a convention of hermits who lived in caves, you'd meet a few you didn't like."

Fitzsimmons was forced to smile at this, but he turned his head and quickly suppressed it.

"We'll see," he answered quietly.

"Fair enough." Matt rose gingerly, using his cane for support. "Well, I'm off. Where might I find my horse?"

"Right outside. Saddled and ready to go."

"You knew I was leavin'."

"I just guessed it, is all. You look the type to have someone waiting at home."

"Yeah, that's so." He hobbled to the mouth of the cave, then turned. "Thank you, Tom. I owe you my life."

"You said that already, Matt."

"Yeah, I guess I did. Listen, I'm serious about that invite. After church you can come to my house, meet my wife, Sarah."

"Sarah?" Fitzsimmons's eyes seemed to water. "That was my sister's name."

Matt didn't quite know what to say, so he just looked away. Finally Fitzsimmons spoke. "I don't have anything proper to wear."

"That don't matter. You wouldn't be coming for our sake but for God's. And He accepts you just like you are. He don't leave you that way, in your heart, I mean, once He gets ahold of you, but that's how He starts."

"Like I said, we'll see."

"Good-bye then, and thanks again." Matt untied his horse and pulled himself into the saddle, using mostly just his arms, then stopped to look at Fitzsimmons one last time. "Why'd you tell me all this?"

Fitzsimmons returned the look for a moment before he answered. "I figured you were different. Not like all the others. I saw you that day, when you brought the food—you and . . . it must've been Sarah."

"I thought you might be watching."

"I was. I didn't know what to make of you. You're a rare man, my friend."

"I appreciate that, Tom, but it ain't so. There are lots of people like me, people who'd give you the shirt off their back."

Fitzsimmons didn't answer, and Matt didn't press him.

"Christianity—true Christianity—makes people care. There's even good folk who aren't particularly Christian but who'll treat you right. Your sister just got in with some strange folk. Don't judge the rest of the world by them."

With that Matt wheeled Shadow around, gave Fitzsimmons a wave, and headed home.

CHAPTER

THIRTY·TWO

T HE RETURN TRIP to Bodie was not an easy one for Jeff Bodine. Though no new snow fell, what was on the ground made travel treacherous. Charlie Jack was too capable a guide and tracker to let them get lost, but even his skill couldn't make the way any easier for the horses. Jeff hardly said a word, which suited the stoic Paiute just fine. They prepared and consumed their meals with a minimum of conversation, and their only night on the trail—spent below the snow level, much to Jeff's relief—passed with little more than a nod and a grunt.

Charlie Jack understood Jeff's pain, having felt it himself several times in his life. Bereavement was not new to Jeff either, having gone through it the year before when he lost his father. But this was different. No matter how much they had clashed in life, he and Josh were brothers, as close as two humans could be, and Jeff grieved for his often wayward younger sibling. He would miss the stubborn rebel.

When they made town the second morning of their journey and rode up Main Street, they drew stares from the townsfolk. The onlookers thought it odd that an Indian was riding with Jeff and wondered what had happened to Josh. But when they saw the body draped over Josh's horse, they understood. More than one spectator respectfully removed his hat as the horsemen slowly rode by.

Jeff caught sight of James McCarthy standing outside the

Rosedale with a drink in one hand and his other thumb hooked over his pants belt. The lawman caught McCarthy's eye and held it as he rode past, daring McCarthy to say something, to grin, or even to blink in an offensive manner. McCarthy read the glare, dropped his head, and retreated back into the saloon.

Jeff stopped in front of the undertaker's, dismounted, and untied Josh as the undertaker came outside to help. Charlie Jack rode on to check on his old friends Jacob Page and Billy O'Hara. He hoped they were both on the mend. Another death would cast a great cloud of grief over the Paiute. He liked so few men who weren't Indian . . .

As he was mounting the steps, Rosa opened the door, her face dour. One didn't have to be Charlie Jack to read what it meant.

The Paiute hesitated before going in. "You have bad news?"

"Some."

"Jacob?"

"No. He's improving. I suspect he'll be up and around in a few days. You know how he is, hates lying around the house."

"He lie plenty. Tell tall tale all the time."

Rosa couldn't help but smile. "I don't mean telling an untruth, I mean lying . . . being in bed."

Charlie Jack just nodded. The bad part about being an Indian in a white man's world was that no one expected an "uneducated" Paiute to engage in verbal wit.

"And Uncle Billy . . . How is Uncle Billy?"

"Not too good, Charlie. I'm worried. He might not make it if we don't do something for him. Trouble is, we've done everything we can think of. Doc isn't even sure what ails him."

"Charlie Jack fix," the Indian said as he moved past Rosa into the house. He disappeared down the hall, not even stopping to stick his head inside Jacob's room, and closed Billy's door behind him.

As Jeff drove the wagon away from the livery stable, he happened to glance at the American Hotel. He thought about going over to the new laundry next-door, then, shaking his head, decided against it and turned away. But he'd been seen, and Johanna Raymond stepped out onto the boardwalk, drying her hands on her apron and unsuccessfully trying to wipe a lock of hair from her face. She watched him, hoping he'd notice her and come over. Dignity and grace kept her from hailing him or trying to follow. Besides, she had work to do. Unaware of his new sorrow, she let him go and walked sadly back inside the steamy room.

"Johanna."

She stopped and stuck her head back out the door. Jeff sat in the wagon, emotionless eyes regarding her. She tried to smile at him, but his fallen face and the curious but telltale box in the back of the wagon kept her from it.

Jeff read the question in her concerned face.

"Josh," he said simply. "My brother. He had pneumonia. The ride to Yosemite chasing the robbers did him in. We didn't know . . ."

"Oh, Jeff, I'm so sorry."

"I know."

"I wish there was something I could say, something I could do."

"I appreciate that, but this is something I've got to do for myself. I'll be back, Miss Raymond."

"Johanna, Jeff. You never have to call me Miss Raymond."

"I'll be back, Johanna."

"Where will you take him?"

"Up the canyon, to bury him next to our pa."

"I understand. I'll be here when you get back. I'll be . . . I'll be praying for you, Jeff."

"I'd appreciate that, Johanna. More than you know." He dipped his head once and snapped the reins, and the horses jolted forward. The wagon turned once again and headed out of town. As she watched him in sorrowful silence, her hands twisted a towel she had been laundering, and her lips mouthed the prayer she'd promised. She continued praying until he was out of sight.

Jeff couldn't look her in the eye as he drove off. His throat was so constricted from choking back the tears that he could hardly breathe. Once he'd put Bodie behind him he relaxed, and his shoulders shook with powerful sobs.

As the sun disappeared behind the Sierra-Nevadas, Jeff stuck the shovel into the ground and wiped his brow with an already-stained sleeve, then admired the intense colors in the sky. He couldn't remember it ever looking so beautiful here, and yet it was as

unhappy a sunset as ever dusted the high plains of eastern
California. He stood watching until the sky was nearly dark, then,
with the shovel in one hand and his coat over the other arm, walked
slowly away, stopping only briefly to take one more look at the two
wooden crosses—one faded and worn, the other new and white.

His respects paid, Jeff Bodine donned his hat, hitched his pants,
and went home.

Bridgeport had never looked as good as it did this evening.
Squatting silently in the center of the broad valley, the red brick
and brown or white wood buildings beckoned Matt to hurry. He
could even see his little home on the edge of town, and as he closed
the gap he could make out individual people attending to their day-
by-day routines, headed this way and that . . . No, just *that* way.
They all seemed to be going in the same direction.

That's odd, I wonder what—

Then Matt remembered—he'd accepted a challenge to debate
Sheriff Taylor in the center of town on the steps of the hotel, and
it was past time. Matt shook his head. He just wasn't in the mood
for this. Perhaps he never would be. The trials of the past few days
had sapped the spunk clean out of him, and right now winning an
election was the furthest thing from his mind.

A bath and a hot meal and a change of clothes and a pillow
under his knee and his wife in his arms—that's all he wanted.

And yet, as he rode past the scattered buildings at the edge of
town, then onto Main Street, he found himself riding right on by
his place and following the crowd uptown. They had gathered at
the steps of the hotel where John Taylor, Irene standing by his side,
was addressing them. Matt gently pulled the reins back, and the
horse stopped without hesitation.

"And so," Taylor was saying, "if you reelect me to the position
I've held all these years, I promise to deliver unparalleled service
that my opponent is incap—"

Taylor's roving eye landed on the taciturn Matt Page, seated on
his horse at the fringe of the crowd, leaning forward casually with
his hands resting on the pommel of his well-worn saddle. Taylor
was surprised but recovered quickly.

"And speaking of my opponent, I guess he decided to show up
after all. Come on up, Deputy Page, and take your turn."

All eyes were on Matt as he sat for a moment, thinking and scanning the crowd, finally finding Sarah at the bottom of the stairs on the far side. She looked at her husband with a combination of love, admiration, and shock on her face, the latter no doubt prompted by his appearance.

Matt flashed her a grin and threw a leg over the back of his horse, landing on his good leg and taking down his cane. He handed the reins to a bystander, then threaded his way slowly through the parting crowd toward the hotel porch. As he mounted the steps he looked at Sarah's wide-eyed stare from the corner of his eye but didn't turn toward her. He then shot Taylor a vacant glance and turned to the crowd. Sarah continued to gaze at her husband in horror and relief, then pushed her way to the front of the crowd and up onto the steps, where she joined her mother. They clasped hands.

"I'm not much on speeches," Matt began self-consciously, "and my leg ain't feelin' so hot, so I'll make this short. First, I apologize for bein' late. Truth is, I plumb forgot about this debate Sheriff Taylor arranged. I was up in Yosemite with the deputies from Bodie chasin' a couple men who robbed the stage there a few days ago."

He paused as murmurs spread through the crowd, then continued, "I also met up with the man who . . . Well, it don't matter what he did, I took care of it. The point is, I was doin' the work of a lawman—and gettin' a mite banged up in the process—while John Taylor stayed in Bridgeport takin' care of things here. But I ain't complainin' or criticizin' him for it. That's the way it oughta be.

"You see, bein' sheriff ain't such a big deal to me anymore, not like I thought it'd be. It's a good job and all, but it ain't for me. Paperwork and all that kind of thing just ain't—well, I like bein' on the road, ridin' a horse, that kind of stuff. Sheriff Taylor here, he rides a desk better 'n I do. He's more cut out for bein' sheriff than me. So when it comes time to vote—if I'm not runnin' off after some criminal—I'm votin' for John Taylor for Mono County Sheriff. You will too because he'll be the only candidate on the ballot. I'm officially withdrawin' from the race."

Matt looked Taylor square in the eye. "Your turn, Sheriff."

A dumbfounded John Taylor moved forward while Matt hobbled aside, tossing a wink at his stunned wife. Sarah wasn't sure if her husband's decision was a good one or not. Did this mean he was going to be spending most of his time away from home as her father's deputy?

Sheriff Taylor cleared his throat and stammered something unintelligible, then coughed and collected himself and started over.

"Uh . . . folks, I don't quite know what to say. I was prepared to stand here and tell you how much better I'd be as sheriff than Matt. But I'm inclined maybe that ain't so. He'd be a dandy sheriff." Taylor looked back at Matt, who'd moved over to Sarah's side. She clung to his arm.

Someone in the middle of the crowd shouted, "But he woulda let them Injuns burn us down and kill us over the likes of some Chinee!" There was a smattering of agreement from the spectators. "You so much as said so yourself!"

"That ain't so!" Taylor shouted as his face reddened. He pointed at the man. "I said Deputy Page didn't want to give the Chinaman up to the Paiutes. Well, there's nuthin' wrong with that by itself. I didn't want to either, but I had no real choice. The important thing, though, is that when it happened, Matt wasn't there. He was out tryin' to dig up more evidence to hold the Chinaman accountable. Pat Reddy told me so. Ain't that so, Matt?"

Matt shrugged. "I suppose." He didn't add that if Taylor had just waited a few more minutes, Matt would have brought back what he'd found so it could be introduced as evidence. That no longer mattered. "But you people listen to me," Matt went on. "Who of you would've had the courage to do what Sheriff Taylor did that day and has done for years? He can make the hard decisions, and that's what this county needs. I say let's forget all this small stuff and think about all of us pitchin' together to make Bridgeport a safer place to live. And we can start by turnin' out on election day and makin' sure Sheriff Taylor keeps his office. If you don't like me, fine. I ain't tryin' to win no popularity contest—"

"And you ain't," cracked one of Bridgeport's layabouts.

"Shut up, Frank," Taylor ordered for all to hear, and the people standing around Pascoe took up the chorus. Taylor held his hands up for quiet.

"Well," said Matt when order was restored, "I'm done talkin'.

You all heard me, you know how I feel. The rest is up to you. Now if you'll excuse me, I need to get this leg up."

Matt looked down at Sarah, her mouth agape. "Come on, honey, let's go home." With that he hobbled off the porch with Sarah in tow and led her through the crowd, leaving Shadow with the man to whom he'd handed the reins.

But they hadn't gone far when they spied a familiar figure walking up the street, large and bulky in his bear coat. They stopped and watched him, and the dispersing crowd behind them began to buzz as they saw the Wild Man from Bloody Canyon head for the new general store, now owned by Dave Hays. If the Wild Man saw them at all, he didn't let on.

"That's him, isn't it?" Sarah asked. "The man we took food to out in the canyon."

"Yeah." A wry grin tickled the corners of Matt's mouth. Sarah saw it.

"You know something. What is it, Matt? What do you know?"

"Know? I don't know nuthin'."

"What's he doing in town?"

Matt shrugged. "Gettin' his supplies, I reckon. Come on, let's go home, leave the man in peace." Matt turned to the rest of Bridgeport's inquisitive citizens. "That goes for all of you. Leave the man be. How'd you like someone staring at every move you make?"

"I'd expect it," Frank Pascoe said, "if I lived in Bloody Canyon like a hermit and wore a bear on my back."

"You've got your own quirks," Sheriff Taylor told Frank, wading through the crowd. "If you want, I'll spell 'em out here and now for everyone. That goes for you too, Jim. And you, Mark. And you, Mrs. Halstead."

The pinch-faced, plump woman emitted a tiny shriek and spun quickly—so quickly her skirt twirled and kicked up dust—and made a hasty retreat to keep her secret sins from being exposed. Just about everyone else also took the hint, and the crowd dispersed. Even Matt and Sarah had left, leaving John Taylor standing in the middle of the street. Otherwise, only Reverend Stone remained, and not for the purpose of gawking. He hailed Taylor and made his way to him.

"Reverend," Taylor nodded. "Good mornin' to you."

"You're a fortunate man, John Taylor."

"How's that, Pastor?" Taylor bit the end off a new cigar and spit the piece into the dirt, then stuck the stogie in his mouth and lit it with a match struck on the bottom of his boot.

"You've got the best deputy this side of the Mississippi."

"Maybe." Taylor puffed the cigar thoughtfully and said no more. But he gave the pastor a wink and took a long look at his town. "I'll see you in church." He strolled toward his office, whistling, leaving the pastor standing there, just watching him go.

Sheriff Taylor suddenly noticed his back wasn't hurting quite as much as it had been.

CHAPTER

THIRTY·THREE

THE SMALL, WHITE CHURCH with the stained-glass windows was packed, evidence that the afterglow of the revival had not yet abated. The pews were so crowded that several men had to stand at the back of the sanctuary. Even so, largely due to the absence of the magnetic Josiah Benson, there were fewer in attendance than had attended any of the tent meetings.

This didn't seem to bother Jonathan Edwards Stone as he rose from his little chair off to the side and mounted the platform in his threadbare black robe, his ragged Bible clutched in his strong hand. He quickly scanned the faces of the faithful, noting to his delight several of the new converts from the revival. More notable were the absentees, those who had made professions of faith during Reverend Benson's meetings but hadn't made it to "regular" church. Stone made a mental note to seek those folk out during the week and counsel them about their revival experience.

He led the congregation in "Amazing Grace" but closed his hymnbook afterwards and put it away, surprising many of the people, who were used to four or five songs. Most of the men were relieved but tried hard not to show it lest they get an elbow in the ribs. Stone waited a moment for the rustling and adjusting to stop, then cleared his throat.

His voice was strong, though not booming, and all in attendance could hear every word. His delivery, as usual, was casual and

passive—some would say boring. He spent most of his time honing the content of his sermons, not the modulation of his voice. He
gripped both sides of the pulpit and gazed out at the crowd, his
eyes making contact with just about everyone.

"Good people of Bridgeport, we have had, to say the least, an
interesting three weeks." He smiled wryly, and there were a few
nods and murmurs of agreement in return. "Much has happened,
both good and bad. In some cases it's hard to tell which is which.
It's good the Indians didn't attack the town and burn it down,
killing innocent people. But it's bad that a man was taken out and
so cruelly murdered. We were also paid another visit last Sunday
afternoon by the man from Bloody Canyon.

"I have also heard many tell how their spirits were refreshed,
their passion for God renewed at Reverend Benson's revival meetings. That is indeed wonderful. But I feel led to caution you all to
hold fast to the faith with which you began your walk, and not to
be swayed by any emotions you might have experienced during the
meetings.

"I also feel led this morning to speak to you of God's grace. We
heard last week of the power of the Holy Spirit to heal, and we have
heard that there are consequences to disobedience. But there are
also consequences to following the wrong teachers. God's Word
tells us, in Second Timothy, chapter 3, 'This know also, that in the
last days perilous times shall come. For men shall be lovers of their
own selves, covetous, boasters, proud, blasphemers, disobedient to
parents, unthankful, unholy . . .'" Stone skipped a couple verses and
continued, "'From such turn away.' In Second Peter, chapter 2, we
read these words: 'But there were false prophets also among the
people, even as there shall be false teachers among you, who privily shall bring in damnable heresies, even denying the Lord that
bought them, and bring upon themselves swift destruction. And
many shall follow their pernicious ways; by reason of whom the
way of truth shall be evil spoken of. And through covetousness shall
they with feigned words make merchandise of you.'"

He scanned the congregation, looking for some reaction, then
went on. "'But they shall proceed no further: for their folly shall
be manifest unto all men, as theirs also was. But continue thou in
the things thou hast learned and hast been assured of, knowing of
whom thou hast learned them.'" He closed his Bible.

"Friends, it is important to remember that God's grace has provided us with an escape from the penalty of sin. Please open your Bibles to . . ."

There was a distraction at the back of the church, and all heads turned to see who'd come in late. There in the doorway stood a stranger, a large man with a clean-shaven face and wearing new duds. Embarrassed at the attention he was being paid, he removed his hat and stepped to the right to fade into the corner of the room. Reverend Stone cleared his throat to regain the attention of the congregation and pressed on.

"How many of you know for a certainty that if you were to die tonight you'd go to heaven? If the Lord Himself asked you why He should let you in, what would you tell Him?"

Stone paused to let them think on these questions, then went on, "Whatever your answer, if it involves any effort on your part—good works—you will not be allowed into heaven, because the right to enter is a free gift and is not awarded to us on the basis of merit. The Word is abundantly clear on that. It comes only by God's grace—His undeserved kindness.

"To whom is this gift offered? To sinners, my friends—those who need to be saved. And that includes each and every one of us. 'Oh, but I don't sin,' you say. Well, to that I say, balderdash!" One of the more prudish members of the congregation gasped but quickly fanned herself and tried to look nonchalant. "None of us is without sin. And what is sin? It's not just drunkenness and stealing and murder, though those most certainly are sins. Sin is anything—*anything*—that falls short of the glory of God. A bad thought, being lazy in your work, anger without cause, lying, even gluttony!

"The outlook is indeed bleak, my friends, but the good news is, God loves us and doesn't want to see us punished. And yet His justice demands punishment for our sins. How did God solve this immense dilemma? He paid the penalty Himself, in the person of His Son, our dear Lord Jesus Christ, who voluntarily left heaven and came to earth as a man to suffer, bleed, and die on the cross in our place. He paid the price so we don't have to.

"All of mankind can now rest easy—heaven is ours! Is that right, dear folks?" Stone waited with eyebrows raised. "No, of course not. What, then, is required? Faith, my friends, faith. Many

believe faith to be mere acceptance of a set of facts about Jesus
Christ. But faith is much more than that. Faith is trusting Jesus
Christ for our salvation. You see that chair over there?" He
pointed at the small wood chair at the edge of the platform, and
all heads turned. "That chair represents salvation. Now, how
many of you believe that chair is there? Don't be shy; go ahead,
raise your hands. Yes, all of us, except for a few in the back who
can't see it. Now, will that chair hold a person's weight and keep
him from falling onto the floor? Certainly. You saw me sit in it earlier. So then, we all believe in that chair's ability to do what it was
designed to do. But how many of us are putting our faith in that
chair right now? May I see hands please?

"That's right, none of you. No one is sitting in the chair. Your
faith in that chair is real only when you actually rest yourself upon
it. Putting your trust in something or someone goes beyond just
believing in it in an intellectual sort of way. I would like to invite
you this morning to put your entire trust upon the Lord Jesus
Christ as your Savior from sin, thus committing your life to God.

"What rewards are there for a life of faith, not just when we
die, but here on this earth? Joy in the Lord, comfort, strength to
make it through the trials we face, wisdom to know God's will and
being able to do it. But the first step is faith, that moment when
you come face to face with God, when you meet Jesus, the One
who died in your place . . . in your place . . . in your place." He
pointed his finger at folks in the crowd, then at himself. "And in
my place. That is what we must all deal with, my friends. Not miracles, not healings that may be genuine or may be questionable,
not revivals. The real issue is your relationship with a personal
God and His Son, Jesus Christ. Is there room in your hearts for
Him today? Does your future involve heaven or hell? You must
make the choice."

The preacher gently closed his Bible, and there was a hushed
stillness in the room as the Holy Spirit worked in the hearts of men
and women. No one moved or looked around; all kept their eyes
on Stone. One woman near the front began to weep quietly. Folks
started to fidget but still refrained from speaking.

Many preachers would have seized the opportunity to help the
Holy Spirit by making an altar call, appealing to the emotions and
fears of the people to prime the pump. But not Jonathan Edwards

Stone. Like his namesake, he just stood there, an imposing figure—
not in his stature but in the magnitude of his message—and waited.
The words of the sermon may have been his, but the message was
God's, and He would produce any saving faith.

Before long, the clean-shaven man in new clothes who had
come in late took a tentative step forward, then another, and soon
was walking slowly up the center aisle, twisting his hat in his
rough, callused, sun-stained hands. He paused next to Matt and
looked down at him, and Matt stared back.

Those eyes—Matt had seen those eyes before. Suddenly Matt
knew.

The man nodded, almost imperceptibly except to those in the
immediate vicinity, and his watering eyes smiled at Matt, though
his mouth remained tight and drawn. He looked toward the
preacher and, with a tear dropping onto his cheek, approached the
platform and bent down on one knee. Stone moved down to him
and put an arm on the man's shoulder, kneeling beside him as the
Holy Spirit began a good work.

Matt and Sarah left the church with the rest of the people and
walked slowly home, hand-in-hand. The sun was bright, the air
clean and crisp, a nip still playing at their ears. But they didn't
notice.

"Matt," Sarah said slowly, "who was that man? He looked at
you like he knew you."

Matt smiled. "Let's just say we know each other better today
than we did a couple of weeks ago."

"What's that supposed to mean?"

"It's hard to explain," Matt commented. "His name is Tom
Fitzsimmons, and he saved my life."

"Saved your life—"

"Yep. It's only fitting that now God is saving him. Come on,
let's go home. We need to get ready for supper at your folks'
place."

They assembled around the table, and after Matt said the blessing—at John Taylor's request—they got down to the business of
eating the bounty prepared by Irene Taylor and Sarah Page. There
was roast beef, mashed potatoes, corn on the cob, a steaming bowl

W. E. DAVIS

of greens, and freshly baked bread, to be followed by one of Sarah's peach pies.

As soon as they'd filled their plates and began indulging themselves, the conversation started . . . all of them at once.

"Did you hear about—"

"I've got something to tell you all—"

"We need to talk about what we're—"

"I've got a request to make—"

They all stopped just as abruptly as they'd started and looked around at each other, waiting for someone to take the lead.

"You're the head of the house, John," Irene said. "You first."

"Suits me. I was just gonna tell Matt we need to talk about the immediate future—what he's gonna do and where he's gonna go."

"Go? I'm goin' somewhere?"

"Only if you want. I need someone in Bodie to be the head of the new police force there."

"Please, Daddy, don't send us back to Bodie."

"Why not, Sarah? You liked it there okay."

"Not really. I went there because Matt was there, not because I liked it."

"Well, if he goes there again, you'll go with him."

"John, it's their choice, remember?" Irene reminded him.

Taylor grunted as he stuck a forkful of mashed potatoes in his mouth, some of them sticking to his mustache.

"What's wrong with Bodie?" Matt asked Sarah.

"Don't tell me you want to go?"

Matt shook his head. "No, I suppose not. Listen, Sheriff, I know someone who'd do just as good in that position."

"Wmm?" The potatoes made his speech incomprehensible.

"Jeff Bodine. He's handlin' things by himself now, you know, since his brother died."

"Yes, that was terrible news," Irene said sadly.

Taylor swallowed. "Do you really think he can manage it?"

"Yep, I do. He's got a knack for directin' others. He ran his pa's mine."

"Well, it's okay with me. But tell me something, Sarah—why were you so dead-set against it? What's wrong with Bodie?"

"I don't think it's a good place to have a child and try to bring him up. Too cold in the winter, too hot, too dry, no trees—"

"What do you mean, 'have a child'?" Matt asked, her words just then sinking in. Irene Taylor tried unsuccessfully to hide a smile. "Are you . . . ?"

Sarah nodded, beaming at her husband. "I'm going to have a baby, Matt."

"Th-that's . . . g-great!" Matt stammered. "Ain't that great, John?"

"Yeah," Taylor said snidely. "Just great. Sheriff Grandpa. Has a real ring to it, don't it?"

"Stop it, John. You know you're thrilled," Irene scolded while Matt and Sarah embraced.

Taylor tried to retain his usual gruff look but couldn't, breaking into a wide grin.

"Yeah, it's wonderful." He took a swallow of coffee. "Okay, I'll give Bodine a chance. But you'll have to help get him goin', Matt. Spend some time out there with him, show him the ropes, make sure he'll get on okay. You know the town best. Help him hire the right men. The County Council approved three officers. A couple weeks ought to do it. Sarah can stay here with her mother or go with you, I don't care."

"I'll go," Sarah said quickly, unwrapping herself from her husband. "I do have some friends I'd like to visit."

"That's settled then," Taylor concluded. "Now, that takes care of what I had to say. Who's next?"

"I said my piece," Sarah told him.

"Mine was just gossip," Irene said. "It didn't matter. Matt?"

Matt shrugged. "I just was gonna ask the sheriff if there was some way Sarah and I could . . . once I'm done in Bodie . . . if we could move to Coleville and I could open the office there again. I've been lookin' into the town, and I think it could use a full-time deputy. Bridgeport's fine, don't get me wrong. But the weather's more moderate in Coleville, it don't hardly snow there. And now, what with the baby comin' and all—"

"It just so happens," Taylor began, "I got a request from the Coleville Concerned Citizens Committee just the other day." He looked at Matt suspiciously. "They wanted a deputy assigned there. I wasn't thinkin' of you for the position, but since you asked . . . I don't suppose it would hurt."

"Sarah?" Matt said, making it sound like a question.

"Yes, Matt. Anywhere you want to go is okay with me . . . just so long as it isn't Bodie."

"Can't go right away, of course," Taylor reminded them. "There's too much to do here right now, what with the trip to Bodie and some other things I've got planned before you go. We're lookin' at the fall, if that's okay. If it ain't . . . well, that's just too bad."

"That's fine, Sheriff," Matt said, gazing at his bride. "Just fine."

"Anyone for pie?" Irene asked. Three hands shot up.

CHAPTER

---◆---

THIRTY·FOUR

Sarah Page looked up at the ceiling, concentrating on the swirls in the plaster to keep her mind off the pain. But it was to no avail as another contraction seized her, blurring her vision and making her eyes shut. Sweat poured from her face as she forced them open and moaned in agony.

"Come on, girl," Rosa Page coached, standing at the foot of the bed. "It's coming. I can see its head."

Irene Taylor held Sarah's hand, who nearly crushed her mother's bones as another contraction gripped her.

"Bear down, honey," Rosa went on. "Push. You can do it. Help it out. Come on. That's good. It's coming."

Sarah cried out as the head emerged, then sucked in a breath and prepared for the next push, the next jolt of pain. Rosa cradled her hands under the baby's head.

"Oh, it's beautiful," she said. "Look here, Irene. Come on, let's see some more of it, Sarah, so we can find out what it is."

Sarah grunted a response, squeezed her eyes shut, and strained to expel the child.

Two men sat on the porch of the small, yellow clapboard house with white trim and lace curtains in the windows—John Taylor smoking his pipe, Jacob Page rocking slowly and staring vacantly across the street at nothing in particular. Though he'd recovered from his injuries, the blow to the head or the coma or perhaps both had done something to him, and he wasn't completely his old self. The difference wasn't noticeable, however, to anyone but those who knew him well. It showed mostly in his memory, like a chunk of information had been knocked loose. Sometimes he recalled things, sometimes he didn't.

No one minded, though. Least of all Rosa.

"Shoot, what do I care if he can't remember the past, just so long as he remembers who to come home to," she'd say.

Matt paced nervously across the porch, hands stuffed deep into his pockets.

"I wish we'd moved here sooner," he muttered, "so I could have the house in good shape before this happened. I thought she wasn't due for a few weeks."

"Don't have much control over things like that," Taylor told him, puffing blue smoke into the breezy air.

"Don't sweat it, son," Jacob said. "We'll give you a hand." He chuckled at his inadvertent joke. "Leastwise I will. John kin give you two hands. I assume yer back is all better now, eh, Sheriff?"

"That depends on what he thinks he's gonna have me doin'."

"You don't have to help," Matt said. "Either of you. It's my responsi—"

A cry from inside the house stopped him in the middle of the word—a baby's cry.

"You hear that?" he asked excitedly.

"We ain't deaf," Jacob reminded him. "Well, don't jes' stand there thinkin' 'bout it. Go on in and see yer baby! We'll be along shortly."

Matt wasted no more time and tore inside, nearly knocking over Rosa as she came out of the bedroom wiping her hands on a towel, her hair disheveled but her face covered with a satisfied smile.

"Sorry, Rosa," Matt apologized hastily.

"Go on, Matt. Don't worry about me."

"Thanks, Rosa," he said as he disappeared into the room, leaving the door open. Rosa chuckled and headed to the kitchen, meeting her husband and John Taylor, also drifting toward the bedroom.

"Not now," she said, grabbing them each by an arm and taking them with her. "Give them some peace. You've got time for a mug of coffee."

"How're they doin'?" Jacob asked.

"They're fine, just fine."

"Well, Mrs. Page," Taylor asked testily, "what is it?"

"It's a baby," she told them, pouring the steaming brew into three cups.

"Of what variety?"

Rosa just smiled, enjoying their frustration.

Sarah sat against the headboard, her face shiny from the sweat and her hair in more disarray than Matt had ever seen it. She held the still, small bundle to her breast, covered with a tiny blanket, as Matt came in. Irene Taylor smiled, patted her daughter's shoulder, and gave Matt a quick hug, then left the room, closing the door behind her.

Matt sat next to them on the bed and pulled the corner of the blanket back, then looked at Sarah questioningly.

"He's a boy," she said, her voice slightly hoarse.

Matt beamed. "You okay?"

"I'm fine. He's fine too. Perfect."

"He's so quiet."

"He's busy. Enjoy it. They aren't always so quiet."

"So I understand." He leaned over to kiss his wife full and easy on the lips, and she returned the affection with great enthusiasm.

Matt staggered outside into the sunshine, the realization that he was a father overwhelming him more than he'd ever been overwhelmed. More than when he fought face to face with Benson, or several months back when the Younger brothers had ventured through the area. More than when he'd first been made a deputy and chased some escaped convicts. Even more than when Sarah had accepted his proposal.

He was a father! For the first time in his young life, Matt seriously doubted his ability to rise to the challenge. He wandered up the dusty street, hardly aware of where he was headed. He could only see himself trying to handle the immense duties of raising a child. He shook his head sharply to clear the images, but they stubbornly remained. He closed his eyes and prayed as he walked, asking God to give him wisdom and strength. But before he could say amen, he was interrupted by someone calling his name.

He turned his head to see Reverend Hinkle, the town's Protestant preacher and a man who'd helped Matt in the past, hustling toward him. Hinkle was a good man, much like Stone in many ways, their differences most notably being in their preaching styles. Though just as fundamental in doctrine and practical in approach, Hinkle was more flamboyant in delivery.

"Good morning, Matt," Hinkle said, hurrying to catch up to the young lawman.

"Reverend Hinkle, nice to see you again."

"Welcome to Coleville, Matt. In town to stay, I hear."

"Yep. Me and Sarah have decided to settle here."

"We're awfully glad about that, I must tell you."

"You, uh, wouldn't be a member of the Coleville Concerned Citizens Committee, would you?"

Hinkle laughed. "Not just a member, Matt. I *am* the Committee!"

Matt shook his head but couldn't help smiling.

"The missus tells me she heard through the grapevine your wife is expecting."

"Not anymore," Matt beamed. "She just had it—I mean him, not an hour ago. There are so many of our relatives here, I just had to take a walk."

"I understand," Hinkle said, though he didn't elaborate. "Well, we'll have to get together sometime, once Sarah's up and around again."

"We'd like that."

"I'll send Mrs. Hinkle over with some . . . well, with something. She'll figure out what to do. Women are good at that."

"They're good at a lot of things."

"Very true. Better, I daresay, than we are at most things. I'm glad God put us in charge or the women wouldn't have any need for us." He laughed heartily at his humor, then clapped Matt firmly on the shoulder.

"Tell me, Reverend," Matt said, "how are the DeCamps? And little Samuel. Doing well, I hope."

The preacher's face soured a touch. "Well, Fred never made a go of the mine. His little stamp mill is in ruins up the road. Farming just didn't work either. He decided to take his family to Oregon. They left a month ago. Samuel went with them, of course. The good news is, they were doing well as a family. That would never have happened without your help, son."

Matt shrugged. "I didn't do anything really. God was behind it all. We just have to do what's in front of us and trust God to take care of it, then put us where He wants us next."

"Very wisely spoken, Matt."

Again the lawman shrugged but said nothing.

"So, you planning on staying a lawman?"

"I've thought about that," Matt said. "Even considered taking off the badge and gun. But I don't know anything else except farming, and I don't have any land for that. I'm kinda stuck."

"Don't think of it like that," Hinkle said. "You just got through saying that God puts you where He wants you and you do what needs to be done. My guess is, He wants you to be a lawman."

"I'd like to do the Lord's work, I just—"

"Beg your pardon, but if you're where the Lord wants you, you *are* doing the Lord's work. You think He wants everyone to be a preacher or a missionary? Some folks He wants in regular jobs— owning businesses or digging ditches or even—though I hate to admit it—practicing law or writing for newspapers."

"Christian lawyers and journalists," Matt mused. "An idea I never would've thought of. You sure about that?"

"Lawyers and journalists being Christians?"

"No, I mean about me staying a lawman and still being able to do God's work."

"Oh. Certainly. Do you think God wants the Devil's people enforcing the laws of this country?"

"No, I suppose not."

"There, you see. Of course, it's tougher to be a lawman when you're a Christian because you're not inclined to beat the tar out of people so quickly and have to use your tongue instead. But I'm convinced that God honors those efforts at being fair and just."

"I hope you're right."

Hinkle smiled and nodded confidently, grasping Matt by the arm. "You're right where He wants you, Matt. Don't ask me to explain—I can't. I just know He gave you special talents to do this work. Maybe He'll change His mind later, but when He does, you'll know. When you don't want to do this any longer and you get a severe hankering to go somewhere or do something else, it's probably God putting those desires in your heart. And if Sarah agrees, or if it's her idea in the first place, you can be sure it's from God. Listen to the counsel of your wife, Matt. God speaks to women." He chuckled. "When they stop talking long enough to listen." He snickered again, then added, "Now don't go repeating that last bit—I was just kidding. I meant everything else though."

He pulled out his watch. "Oh my, I've got to go. A pastor's work is never done." He shook Matt's hand. "God bless, Matt."

"Good-bye, Reverend. See you Sunday."

Hinkle waved and trotted off. As Matt watched him go, he caught sight of something coming up the street—something from his recent past, and a shiver ran up his spine.

A black, fully enclosed wagon, just like Benson's.

He held his breath and stared at it as it approached. His hand reached slowly down to his side but found nothing there since he had left his gunbelt at home. He didn't need it anyway, for as the wagon drew close enough for Matt to read the proclamation on the side, he discovered it belonged to a traveling salesman dealing in elixirs and patent medicines. Matt was relieved and laughed at himself. He never would have thought he'd be glad to see a snake oil salesman come to town.

The butterflies in his stomach subsided and, finding himself near his new office, Matt headed for it. The key was rusty, as it had been the last time he'd opened it, though now it was worse. He forced the lock open and stepped inside.

The air was thick with dust, and Matt sneezed, then waved his hand in the air to get it circulating and moved inside, looking around and trying to visualize what it would look like when he was finished.

He moved past the scratched and dented old oak desk with its leather-covered swivel chair, running his fingers through the thick covering of dust. Behind it, empty and forlorn, stood a rifle case, the glass in one door broken. A hat rack stood like a bony wraith in the corner. He wandered through the doorway and into the cell hallway and stood outside one of the two cells. He didn't go inside, remembering the last time—when the door closed itself behind him, locking him in. That time someone was there to let him out.

Little Samuel DeCamp. Lost and lonely, unwanted by his father, his mother incapable of taking care of him. He was an admirable character in spite of the hardship he'd had to endure at such an early age. Matt hoped his own son would turn out all right.

The thought of his son drove him to prayer, and he bowed his head, gripping the bars of the cell as he poured out his heart to God, expressing his fears and his needs. He didn't hear the door open.

"It'll take some cleaning up," a voice behind him stated.

Startled, Matt wheeled around. "Uncle Billy! What're you doin' here?"

"Ah wouldn't miss the birth of my grandnephew for the world," Billy beamed, then laughed out loud. "And since Ah'm here, Ah figgered Ah might as well give you a hand fixin' up this dum—Ah mean, this place. Then maybe you can take me out to see your pa and Rosa's new place."

"What do you mean their new place? Are you tellin' me they're stayin'?"

"They didn't tell you?"

"No, I . . . I guess maybe they were waitin' for the right time."

"Well, bless my soul, Ah'm sorry you had to hear it from me first."

"Don't worry, Billy, I'll act surprised. But how can they come here? Rosa has the restaurant."

"You ain't gonna believe this—Molly Carter bought the restaurant . . . her and Flora. They're gonna run it together."

"Flora Bascomb? Flora Pruneface Bascomb? Maybe I do believe in miracles after all."

"Me too, and Ah was there when it happened."

Matt's smile suddenly disappeared. "You know, Billy, there's somethin' I don't understand."

"What's that?"

"When I saw you in Bodie you were dyin', or at least you looked like it. Now here you are, a little thinner maybe, but walkin' around like always. I hear from Rosa that your condition changed after Charlie Jack paid you a visit, but she didn't know what he did. No one would tell her." He looked Billy square in the eye. "Was it that horrible tea? Or one of his poultices? Don't tell me he shook some beads over you and chanted."

Billy laughed. "No, nuthin' like that. Ah was lyin' there dead to the world, everythin' gray, and he come in so quiet, Ah hardly knowed he was there till he started to speak. Ah strained to listen, to understand, so's Ah could answer him. Then Ah realized he weren't talkin' to me."

"Who then?"

"He was talkin' to God, Matt. Our God. Jesus by name. He was prayin' to the 'God-man who gave His life for the sins of men.' Those were his words. He was prayin' for·me, Matt, and for himself. Even in my delirium, Ah knew God was workin' in that Injun, and Ah knew it wasn't time for me to die."

"So you got well."

"Well, it wasn't quite that fast, but yes, Ah got well. Ah don't know if it was his prayer directly or God's plan all along, but the result is the same. And here Ah am."

"And Charlie?"

"He's still learnin', God bless him. It takes more 'n jus' a few words to overcome a lifetime of believin' what them folk do, but Ah know God is leadin' him in. He'll be saved, Matt, of that Ah have no doubt whatsoever."

"That's great, Billy. But where is he?" Matt glanced forlornly up the street, as if the mere mention of Charlie's name would cause him to materialize, just as it seemed to have happened so frequently the past couple years. But the Paiute did not ride into town this time. Matt sighed. "I hoped he'd be here for this."

"Oh, he'll be by, I reckon," Billy said. "You know Charlie. Wherever there's free food, sooner or later he'll be there."

EPILOGUE

JUNE 23, 1932

A BATTERED MODEL A FORD bounced and rumbled and clanked up the narrow dirt road, kicking up a cover of dust and rocks behind it. The driver, an elderly man with a thinning head of gray hair and clear eyes squinting into a bright, cloudless sky, gripped the steering wheel tightly with both hands, not in fear of the car or the roadway, but in a self-assured, determined effort to guide the vehicle to its destination.

The narrow, winding canyon he drove through had been cut by a small stream that still flowed next to the road. The stream was only a trickle now, and the wind that funneled itself through the cut on this summer day was warm and dry and offered no respite from the heat.

As the canyon walls fell away and widened, the road gained altitude steadily until the cliffs became hills and the hills became slopes. The panorama here was full circle—to the west and north, the Sierra-Nevada mountains, rugged and purple and still tipped with snow; to the south, the White Mountains; and to the east, a set of low, undulating hills that rose to 10,000 feet, then eventually disappeared into the plains and deserts of Nevada. But not before giving way to the treeless valley where the old gold camp of Bodie rested in solitude.

In solitude, yes, but not in silence. Although fifty years had passed since Bodie's heyday, gold was still being taken from her mines, and her people still eked out a living with stores, hotels, restaurants, and other services and commodities, just as they had done during the boom years of the early 1880s, though of course on a much smaller scale.

Bodie was as tenacious as its people and, unlike most gold towns, continued to hang on in spite of extreme adversity. The difference between Bodie and the hundreds of other gold camps before it was that there'd been no new strikes nearby to draw the people away. And times had changed sufficiently so that the people realized they didn't need to move just because the gold was petering out. Bodie was truly the last of the old-time mining camps.

J.S. Cain had been one of the early settlers who loved Bodie so much that even after the boom, when the town began to die and the population dwindled, he stayed. Cain saw his vision early on and began buying properties, including the Bodie Bank, and soon became the principal landowner. But Bodie's decline, though slowed by Cain's perseverance, was inevitable, and it would only be a matter of time before the town would lie vacant.

That time, however, had not yet come.

Bodie was now electrified, and cars motored up and down its streets, which were still dirt in the center but covered with prairie grass closer to the boardwalks due to a decline in the amount of foot traffic. The people, though much fewer in number than in the town's peak years, were as rugged and high-hoped and jubilant in spirit as ever.

It was toward this Bodie the old man drove. Although nearly out of fuel, he was unconcerned. He had enough to get him to town, and there was a pump now in front of Boone's store—still called that even though the Boones had left long ago. If the old man decided to leave, he could refuel there.

The Ford circled a hill, dipped into a shallow valley, then up the other side, and the old man coughed the road dust out of his lungs. They were bad enough without this. His heart was slowing too, he knew, but he pressed on.

At last it came into view. The cluster of wood buildings that had once filled the valley had decreased some in a half-century. Many had been taken down board by board and burned in fireplaces or were hauled off to be used in structures elsewhere. Some of the town had burned in 1892, precipitating a major exodus, and some of the buildings that survived remained empty and were now unfit for human use.

But the heart and spirit of Bodie went on, and several hundred residents, including Jim Cain—who now owned the only remaining mine and mill, the bank, and most of the rest of the town—called Bodie home and planned never to leave if they could possibly help it.

Wheeling his car down Green Street, the old man hung a left at Park and motored slowly up the residential street. He gazed with fond memories at the house that had once been Pat Reddy's. The people who were outdoors watched him with curiosity. Visitors didn't come to Bodie much anymore, despite its colorful past. It was too out-of-the-way, and the road to Bodie led nowhere else. Sure, it still wound its way to Aurora, Nevada; however, Aurora was nothing but a cemetery these days. Only the knowledgeable could tell a town had ever been there.

He braked to a grinding, squeaking halt in front of the last house, near the edge of the rise that overlooked what was once King Street and Chinatown, now an empty field. He exhaled sharply and wiped a handkerchief across the grit stuck to his forehead, then climbed slowly out of the car and made his way down to Main Street.

Standing in the middle of the street, he drank in the sights, sounds, and smells of the camp—past and present—and wished he was young again. The Standard Mill still pounded away, and men tipped their glasses in the saloons that peppered the street. There was less hustle and bustle than he remembered—much less. The pedestrians were scattered, one lone wagon moved slowly up the road toward him, and there were no Paiutes or Chinamen to be seen.

The town had a ghostly quality as a light, warm breeze kicked up enough dirt to raise a low cloud. This, added to the lack of people, gave the ancient town an eerie appearance. But the smell of pies cooking and the tinkling of a piano and the conversation of folks outside a nearby meat market all said Bodie was still alive, still hanging on. It was enough to make a grown man cry.

A little boy, not even three years old, came tearing around the corner of the Old Sawdust Saloon. Looking behind him as he

scampered, he ran smack into the old man's leg, sending himself
sprawling into the dirt. The old man bent over, picked the young-
ster up, and started to scold him about being more careful, but he
noticed fear in the boy's eyes. At the same time a new smell reached
his nostrils.

Smoke.

He glanced around until he saw it—a column of black smoke
rising from behind the saloon. Leaving the boy, he hurried up the
street as fast as his seasoned legs would carry him, eyes transfixed
on the black column. By now others had seen it also, and the cry
went up. *Fire!*

Quickly chaos and fear engulfed the populace. The dry wood
building was fully involved in no time, and the fire was starting to
spread. A second building caught a spark on its shingled roof, and
flames crackled into life instantly. A third structure was soon
threatened—all this within minutes of the start of the blaze.

The Bodie Fire Department volunteers mustered and brought
out their rigs and buckets and hoses, but catastrophe struck.
Through neglect brought on by complacency, the pipes were brittle and gravel-filled, and the water pressure created when the valve
was opened forced the debris ahead, blocking the hoses.
Underground pipes had broken or were stopped up. The hydrants
were useless.

Bucket brigades formed as the old man rushed up to help. He
pushed his way through the front door of the saloon, shouting,
looking for people trapped inside. There was no answer to his
calls, and the heat and flames forced him back. Smoke constricted
his throat, and he began to cough. Undaunted, he checked the next
two businesses, both of them now burning unabated, then
retreated to join the bucket brigade.

Much of Bodie was lost that day. The death knell sounded—to
some prematurely, to others not soon enough. Half the people
were put out of their homes because of the spread of the blaze, and
most of the business district burned to the ground. All that was left
of Jim Cain's Bodie Bank was the triple-thick brick vault, its contents undamaged.

As the cleanup continued into the evening, a grisly discovery was made—the body of an old man was found in the field behind the old jailhouse.

"Who is it?" a woman asked.

"Don't know," someone else answered. They crowded around him.

"How'd he die? Is he burned?"

"Naw, he smells of smoke, but so do we all."

"Probably his heart stopped."

"Of course his heart stopped or he wouldn't be dead."

"Is he the one that drove in this morning?"

"It is," said a woman. "I saw him. That's his car on Park that burned."

"What'll we do with him?"

"Let me in, folks," Mr. Cain said, gently pushing his way through the circle of gawkers. He knelt down beside the old man's body, made sure he was expired, then fished around in the man's trousers for a wallet.

He found nothing but a few dollars in his pockets.

"Someone check his car," he said, looking around. "He probably left it in there."

"It burned up."

"Maybe its not too bad."

A lad of seventeen ran off up the hill toward Park Street. They could hear him rummaging through the old car. He shouted, and in a minute he was racing back to them, clutching a steel box, the outside black and covered with soot, but the box otherwise apparently undamaged. He presented it to Mr. Cain as one would present a birthday present to his first girlfriend.

Cain opened it carefully, almost reverently, as the crowd unconsciously leaned toward him. There wasn't much inside. Just a few papers and newspaper clippings. Cain opened one of the clippings carefully since it was dark yellow and brittle with age.

"My, this is old," he said softly. He strained to read the crumbling article.

He could make out part of a date. —*ber 27, 1871*. He tried to read the story the old man had kept all these years.

"It's about the prison escape," Cain said.

"What prison escape?" a young man asked.

An elderly gentleman answered, "Nevada State Pen. The one that ended at Convict Lake."

Cain nodded. "I can't read much. It's too dark and worn." He folded the clipping carefully and set it aside.

"What else is there?"

Cain waved a hand. "Be patient. If I go tearing through all this, it'll disintegrate." He went through the contents piece by piece.

"Looks like a theater program," Cain said. "Can't read the theater name though. I can make out 'For,' but that's all. For-something Theater." He put it with the newspaper clipping.

He withdrew an envelope containing a letter. "The return address is the White House," Cain said, bringing a hush to the onlookers. He drew out the letter and unfolded it but was largely disappointed. "Can't hardly make anything out," he said, putting his nose almost on the paper. "Just a few words. '. . . bravery . . . San Juan Hi . . .' I guess that would be Hill . . . something about the Panama Canal . . . and a signature—Theod—Roos—. It's all smudged."

"Roosevelt," a man presumed.

"Likely," admitted Cain. "Can't think of any other president with a name like Theod Roos."

"Here, see if you can read this," said an impatient woman, digging into the box and handing Cain another newspaper article.

He took it with a perturbed glance at the woman and peeled the folds apart.

"It says, 'A contingent of Pinkertons yesterday effected the capture of the notorious something Bunch gang . . .' I can't read the name."

"The Wild Bunch," exclaimed the teenager who'd retrieved the box from the old man's car. "Butch Cassidy's gang. It would have to be them! Is there something in the bottom? It felt too heavy to just be papers."

"Let's see," mused Cain, pulling out the rest of the papers. In the bottom of the tin rested an old pistol—a Colt's Peacemaker, much worn, the walnut grips shiny and smooth, but without a speck of rust or dirt to be found. Next to it was a small black Bible, stained and weather-beaten, the pages mottled and torn, some of them completely separated from the binding. Cain opened the cover carefully, looking for the inscription.

"Who is he?" a man asked.

"Just says 'To my son.' No name."

"What do you suppose he's doing here?"

Cain shrugged. "Something tells me this man—whoever he is—came to Bodie to die. Perhaps he came *back* to Bodie to die, if you catch my drift. Though I don't believe he was quite prepared to die in just this manner. I think we should accommodate him, folks, that's what I think. If some of you'll give me a hand with him, I'd like to prepare him for his final resting-place in our cemetery."

"I wonder who he is," someone repeated quietly.

"God only knows," Cain said sadly as the body and the box were carried away. "God only knows. But perhaps we'll find out on Resurrection Day, and won't it be grand that we can be proud on that wonderful day that his body was resurrected from Bodie?"

AUTHOR'S NOTE

ALTHOUGH I TOOK some artistic license with dates, many of the people and some of the events depicted in these tales are actual. "Uncle" Billy O'Hara died in 1880 after serving Bodie's citizens for fifteen years. Harvey Boone's store still stands in Bodie today, as does the jail. The old man's car can be found where he left it. Ah Quong Tai was indeed murdered by Poker Tom's tribe, though his guilt in the death of Poker Tom was never proven (though widely assumed). John McQuaid, Pat Reddy, and Judges Fales and Peterson all practiced law in Mono County for many years. And Pat Reddy (who some say lost his arm in his youth trying to hold up a stage) never did lose in court. His house in Bodie still stands.

Bodie never did get a telegraph, though in 1881 a narrow-gauge railroad line was built around Mono Lake, terminating in Benton, about thirty miles east of Bishop. Bodie was electrified in the 1890s.

Bodie did indeed burn that day in 1932, but some of the people hung on for another decade before it was finally abandoned. Much of the town remains as they left it, and you can look inside J.S. Cain's bank vault, run your fingers over the rusted fender of the old car on Park Street, and look into the window of Boone's store. Bodie stands as a memorial to a glorious chapter from the story of the American West and is well worth a trip off the beaten path.